Gods &

Monsters

by V.R. Christensen

Captive Press Publishing
Eden, NC

Library of Congress Control Number: 2015906091

Acknowledgements

Many thinks for the tireless, patience and longsuffering of my friends, editors, and beta readers who, without their encouragement and sometimes brutal honesty, this book never would have seen publication. My especial heartfelt thanks to Jenny Baxter (who has endured much from me and has continued to be there when I needed her), M. Louisa Locke whose encouragement has been pivotal in my finishing the final rewrites, and Rachel Ross who has tirelessly read and reread everything I've written.

Immeasurable thanks must also go out to B. Lloyd for her constant and continued support, for her honesty and encouragement, and for the inspiring illustrations that have, once again, turned a book into a work of art.

Part one

August 1897

Chapter one

"WILL HE COME TONIGHT, DO you think?" Laynie asked of her sister's reflection in the mirror.

Beth's gaze shifted to meet hers momentarily before returning to her own. "Who?" she asked, though Laynie knew she understood her.

"Mr. Hartright, of course."

"I really do not know," Beth answered. "And to be quite frank, I don't care."

Laynie turned to her, but Beth would not look her in the eye. Instead, she kept her attention focused squarely on her appearance, working as quickly as she could to mend the damage that had been done to her hair by the gusting of the wind upon their arrival at the assembly rooms.

"Beth?" Laynie said at last and tentatively.

Beth ignored her.

"It's quite all right, you know, if you are feeling anxious. I know I would be. I'm sure he must come tonight and bring her. If you want, I could go out and see if he's come—"

"I'm quite all right, Laynie, dear," Beth interrupted her. "It's nothing to me if he comes or if he doesn't. There are plenty of other fish in the sea, and tonight I mean to prove it."

Laynie didn't believe her sister quite so indifferent as she professed to be but knew it best not to pester. She chose, instead, to change the topic. "I understand Mr. Vaughn is expected to come."

"Harold Vaughn?" Beth said, with a brief and doubtful glance. "I thought he was at University? Isn't he training to go into the church?"

"I believe he's come home from University. It's something to consider."

"I don't know why you think I should consider *him*. He was always so awkward—do you remember?" And Beth laughed at the thought of him. Laynie remembered him well enough.

Perhaps he had been a trifle awkward as a boy. He had always been extraordinarily tall for his age, and it did not help that he was very lean as well. The two things combined did not provide much to admire in his appearance. And it was true that he was reserved around strangers, as uncomfortable in a crowd as a cat in a room full of rocking chairs.

"*You* thought much of him once upon a time, if I recall," Beth reminded her teasingly.

"He was a good friend to us both and I expect he will be still. And there's no telling but that he's changed a great deal in the time he's been away."

Beth rolled her eyes, smoothed the last stray hair, and adjusted a curl. "Then perhaps," she said as she prepared to leave the ladies' refreshing room, "you ought to try him for yourself. A humble and socially withdrawn curate would be just the thing for *you*."

Laynie ignored this and followed her sister into the assembly room. Beth stopped upon entering and scanned the crowd while trying to appear indifferent to the company. A breeze blew through as the doors opened once more. Ashworth's Chapel Hall was a favorite place to hold country balls and little social gatherings such as these, as it had the advantage of a determined and consistent draft, which on any given night during the summer months was a welcome thing. Tonight would prove the exception. A gale was blowing without, and the rain was threatening any moment to come down in torrents.

Beth shivered in the draft and Laynie thought to offer her shawl, but Beth's attention was fixed on the doors that had now closed. Standing before them was Mr. Jonathan Hartright and his new bride, the former Miss Headley. Mr. Hartright seemed not to notice Beth, but his wife's gaze was fixed firmly upon her. She gave Beth an assessing look, which quickly turned cold and then immediately dismissive. She took a firmer hold of her husband's arm, as if her claim on him was not already sealed by the Bible verses which had two months ago been read over them, and led him into the crowd and out of sight of the sisters.

"It's all right, Beth. It's nothing."

"Of course it's nothing!" Beth snapped and forced a smile just in time to welcome the friends who were now coming to greet her.

"I hope you are not lamenting your losses, Miss Durham," said Miss Annabelle Sharp. She had become, since Caroline Headley's betrayal, Beth's closest friend.

"Certainly not," Beth assured her. "There are bigger fish than he, you may be assured of it."

"There is nothing to regret, if you ask me," Miss Harriet Fisher said in an attempt to reassure her. "I hear the rooms at Hartfield are ever so small, and there is not nearly as much money as he likes people to believe. I do not envy the brave face poor Caroline must maintain."

"Perhaps she loves him, after all," Laynie offered.

Miss Fisher scoffed and turned from her to look out upon the dance floor. A smile slowly crept upon her face as she turned back to speak confidentially to Beth. "Mr. Harold Vaughn is come home. Did you know?"

Beth rolled her eyes and released a breath. "I don't know why everyone seems to think I should have any interest in Mr. Vaughn's return. It is unkind of you to suggest, Harriet, that I can do no better for myself than an aspiring curate."

Harriet's smile was smug. She leaned close to Beth and whispered a few words into her ear. Whatever they were, they served their purpose. Beth's attention was now fully upon Mr. Vaughn.

"You were once good friends with him, I believe?" Miss Sharp asked of Beth.

"Yes, I was," Beth answered, and she did not add that of the two sisters, Laynie had been the closest.

"Then perhaps you had better strike while the iron is hot. He'll have no shortage of dancing partners tonight, nor admirers either."

Admirers of Harold Vaughn? Beth seemed to imply with a dismissive toss of her head. But she was considering; Laynie could see it.

"What do you say, Miss Sharp," Beth suggested, "to a walk around the assembly rooms?"

"If you wish it," she returned with a smile that was, in itself, a little greedy.

"We will walk in his direction," Beth continued, "and if he chooses to acknowledge us, we'll speak to him. How is that?"

It was Harriet's turn to roll her eyes, but Beth reprimanded her with a look. With another look, Laynie knew she was in the way and so retreated to the far end of the room, where tables had been set up for those who did not wish to dance or who required rest and refreshment.

She had not been sitting there long when she found she had company. A young man with auburn hair and decidedly ginger whiskers had approached her. An invitation to dance would be welcome. She was hardly a wallflower, but she often had to play one for the sake of her sister's equanimity.

"I was hoping," he said, standing there in flattering temerity as she waited for the invitation, "I was wondering if it would be possible, Miss Laynie, to…"

"Yes, Mr. Granger? It is a simple question. All you need to do is ask it. I'm sure to say yes, you know."

He offered a smile that was at once anxious and grateful. "Would you mind awfully if I sat?"

The request puzzled her. It was not what she had expected. "Of course not," she said and watched him do just that. And then she waited patiently for him to go on.

"I hope you won't consider me forward, nor impolite…"

"What can I do for you?" she answered patiently.

"You see, the thing is… I was hoping for the opportunity to speak with your sister. Alone, you see. Only…" He looked in the direction of Beth and her companion, seemingly inseparable, and engaged in the admirable exercise of walking. "Well, she is never alone. And I thought it time to enlist some help. Will you help me, Miss Laynie?"

"I suppose so," she said, and resisted the temptation to feel slighted. "What is it you would like me to do?"

"If you could perhaps contrive some time for us to meet, when I can be certain she is alone—and available—and where I will have her undivided attention…"

"You might come to the house any day you like, Mr. Granger."

"But your father…"

"You needn't fear him. He won't interfere."

"Should I speak to him first, do you think?"

Laynie considered this. It was the gentlemanly thing to do, only… "I think you would be wise to feel her out first. My father is eager to see us provided for, but he is inclined to put the pressure on rather thickly at times."

Mr. Granger seemed to consider this a helpmeet to his aim.

"I think it would be unkind to use my father's influence to manipulate her into giving you audience, Mr. Granger. Surely you would prefer your own merits to do that."

"Of course," he said. "Would Monday suit? Perhaps two o'clock?"

"Certainly, Mr. Granger," she said. "I'll be sure we are at home to receive you."

"Thank you, Miss Laynie." He arose, bowed, and was gone.

She was not long alone when, once again, she found she had been approached. This time by a large woman with a hat full of black feathers.

"My dear Miss Durham," she inquired, "why are you not dancing?"

"Lady Vaughn," Laynie said, surprised, and prepared to stand.

"No, don't get up. I'll sit, if you don't mind."

"Please," Laynie answered, and welcomed her to a chair beside her.

"You didn't answer my question," the woman reminded her.

"Well…" Laynie said, "I suppose it's because I haven't been asked."

"That was not Mr. Granger's intent, then?"

"No, ma'am. I'm afraid not. He only wanted my help in gaining an interview with my sister."

Lady Vaughn exhaled loudly. "Men can be so infuriatingly stupid," she said and then paused to study her a moment. "What a tragic loss was your mother's death. What has it been, ten years now?"

"Nearly that, yes, ma'am."

"You were old enough to remember her, and you are old enough now to miss the counsel she would offer you during this delicate time in your life. If only you had someone to guide you."

"I have an aunt in Gravesend," Laynie reminded her.

"Yes, yes, but how often do you see her? You would benefit by her influence though, I dare say. It would put you in the way of… But perhaps I am too forward. Forgive me."

"You are right, Lady Vaughn, to suggest our prospects are not good. But I never expected much. Beth, if she does not marry a man with property of his own, will inherit the house, but there is not much more for my father to leave us than that. We live comfortably, but when he is gone… Forgive me. I do not like to think of it."

"And who can blame you? You will be thrown into a life devoid of so many of the comforts you have been raised to enjoy—even to take for granted. It will be a bitter adjustment, I fear."

"Oh, I don't mean that, Lady Vaughn. I am prepared for my fate. At least I am working to prepare myself for it. I do not dread having to do so much for myself. It's my father's death I cannot bear to think upon."

Lady Vaughn smiled to herself, as if Laynie's words had pleased her. "Now, now, dear. Do not fret yourself. Your father has years ahead of him. I promise you."

"I hope you are right. I believe you must be, but he is not so mentally attuned as he used to be."

"Or perhaps you have grown up and are beginning to realize he is not quite as rich in wisdom as you had always thought him."

"Lady Vaughn," Laynie returned, a little shocked by the statement. She would certainly never own to such a thing, even if she *had* considered it.

Lady Vaughn, however, seemed to make much of her own joke and laughed, which inspired Laynie to laugh too—just a little—at her father's expense. She quickly repented of it, however. There were few things more important to him than his confidence in his own wisdom. A man's self-respect was nothing to laugh at.

Lady Vaughn's laughter ended in a cough, which she quickly stifled with a handkerchief and seemed to struggle with for a moment or two before recovering enough to speak. "Forgive me, my dear," she said more soberly, "that was unkind. You love your father and esteem him, as you properly should. And your spirit of self-reliance does you credit."

Laynie smiled gratefully.

"I propose a change of subject," Lady Vaughn suggested.

If it was up to Laynie to choose, she could think of nothing.

It seemed Lady Vaughn was already prepared with a new topic of her own. "My son is home," she said. "Have you spoken to him yet?"

"No, ma'am. I haven't had the privilege. I hope his studies have been going well. There is no trouble, no difficulty that has brought him home, I hope?"

"Yes, some difficulty," Lady Vaughn answered with a look of apparent suffering, which Laynie regretted; she prayed her old friend had not somehow gone awry. "Oh, not from dear Harry!" Lady Vaughn quickly qualified. "Never from him! He is a good and dutiful son and ever shall be, I trust. It's his elder brother who has caused us the trouble. And so Harold has come home to assume his brother's duties, and to keep me company. I cannot bear the house alone, you know. It's true I had high hopes that Harold would take orders, but it seems it was not to be, and it's no fault of his own. Still, I wonder if it is perhaps wrong for a mother to be too firm in her planning on behalf of her children. It is a sure road to disappointment, for fate and circumstance will have their own designs. He will make himself useful, no doubt, whatever he does—and whatever his circumstances." This last she added with a knowing wink, but the gesture was lost on Laynie.

"I'm sure you are right, Lady Vaughn. He is just the type of man who was always good and who always will strive to make himself useful to those he loves."

Lady Vaughn gave her a proud smile and took her hand once more, this time as it sat in her lap under the table. "You know, it has always been my wish," she said, "that he would find someone who truly appreciated him for who he is. Whatever her situation, she must, first and foremost, understand him and love him as I do, for his goodness, for his integrity and sincerity of character."

Laynie suddenly felt a little uncomfortable with this turn in the conversation. Surely Lady Vaughn did not mean to suggest *she* should marry her son. Though they had been friends since childhood, the possibility of loving him, of marrying him, seemed nearly as preposterous as marrying a sibling. In many respects, he had been like a brother to her.

Lady Vaughn's attention was still on her, but it wasn't the weight of her gaze alone she felt. She looked up to find her father watching approvingly on. He gave her a nod and a wink before turning a knowing look upon the unaware Mr. Vaughn. Harry was even taller than when she had last seen him, but he was not so lean. He appeared more man now than boy, though he was as tow-headed as ever. Neither did he seem so uncomfortable in a crowd. At least not in this crowd, for he appeared to be quite popular, amongst the ladies in particular. Though he was not extraordinarily handsome, there was yet something appealing about him. He was honest, trustworthy, and painfully polite. How had time improved him?

Laynie's attention shifted from Mr. Vaughn to her sister, who was just walking past him, arm in arm with Miss Annabelle Sharp, who was looking bored and a little put out. She was hardly the only one to appear annoyed. The dance floor was now being trespassed upon by no less than a dozen young women who, like Beth, were trying to attract Mr. Vaughn's attention as he stood in conversation with old school-mates and childhood friends. He took no notice of this parade of would-be admirers, so engrossed was he with his present company. And so the walking—and the trespassing—persisted, to the mounting annoyance of those trying to dance in formation.

"You have not spoken to him at all, you say, since he has come home?" Lady Vaughn said, recalling Laynie's attention.

"No, ma'am. Not yet. I did not know he had returned until I arrived tonight."

"I have been keeping him to myself, I'm afraid. He has spoken of you, however. Do not fear he has forgotten you."

"Oh, I had no fear of that, ma'am."

But Lady Vaughn was no longer listening. She put a hand in the air, waved a distinct figure with her glove, and Harry's attention was summoned. He looked, first to his mother, then to Laynie, smiled, and, ignoring the admirers who had flocked about him, approached.

Laynie stood, though whether out of respect, or fear, she could not be certain.

"Miss Alayna Durham," he said, upon arriving to stand before her. "What a pleasure. I had hoped I would see you here."

"How very good it is to see you, Mr. Vaughn."

"Have you no dancing partner?" he asked her and seemed surprised to find that it was so.

"No, none," she answered.

"That is a pity," he said, his brow furrowing.

"Not much of one, Mr. Vaughn. I have had the great pleasure of keeping your mother company."

Lady Vaughn gave an encouraging nod, and Harry posed his question. "Would you care to dance?"

"Well… the set is not quite finished yet." It was so like him to not have noticed.

"Shall we get some refreshment while we wait?"

"Yes, of course."

He led her to the refreshment table, where she chose some punch and nothing else. He took a glass for himself and turned to examine the dance floor. "What is going on over there, do you suppose?" he asked, nodding in the direction where several of the young ladies had stopped walking and now stood in an odd and haphazard manner, struggling to determine their next move.

"I really do not know," Laynie answered. She was not about to try to explain what she herself did not understand. Why this apparent desperation to gain one man's attention? Harry Vaughn had hardly been the sort of gentleman women fawned over before. He seemed a little more self-assured than when she had last seen him, but he was much more the same than changed. Was there something about him, some magnetizing, hypnotic quality she had not yet realized?

"How have you been, Miss Laynie?" he asked as if remembering his manners, or perhaps broaching the subject they might naturally have come upon had they been dancing, after all.

"Very well, thank you. You have come home to stay, I under-stand."

"Yes. I have."

"You are not disappointed, I hope, that your studies are at an end."

"A change in plans is always a little disorienting, but I would not go so far as to say it is disappointing."

"I'm glad of that. Father would like to see you. I hope you will not be a stranger."

"A stranger? To oldest and dearest friends? I think not."

"I'm glad of that. Beth will be glad to see you, I think." She was not certain it would be true. She was not certain it wasn't. With Beth it was always hard to tell. She had expressed her resolute indifference toward him, and yet she was presently going out of her way to seek him out. She was approaching them now. Laynie alerted him to the fact.

Harry's attention was arrested. If he had not changed in his time away, perhaps it bore some consideration that Beth had. She had always been the more gregarious of the two sisters, if not always the most reasonable. She had always been the prettier, but now she was the established beauty between them. Laynie, average in every way, could hardly compete. It was perhaps a good thing she had no desire to do it. Beth's fair hair set off an angel's complexion. The rosy hue of her cheeks and lips was quite natural, and she could raise the color in the former as if on command. She was blushing now, and Harold Vaughn was quite plainly entranced.

"Miss Beth," he said, then stammered a correction. "M-Miss Durham, I mean. Of course. Forgive me. Old habits, you know."

Beth giggled, then nodded at the refreshment table. "Would you be so kind, Mr. Vaughn? I'm quite parched."

"Of course!" he said, as if waking from a trance. "Yes, of course." He delivered the requested refreshment and apparently knew not what else to do or say.

"You are home, then? Do you mean to stay?" Beth asked him with a look that begged for the unnecessary reassurance.

"Oh, yes," he said. "That is, I've not quite finished my studies, but mother is alone now, and my brother, well…" he cleared his throat and glanced at Laynie as he struggled for the words to relate, in uncondemning terms, the trouble his brother had caused.

But Beth, it seemed, had other plans. "I don't want to hear about your brother, Mr. Vaughn," she said. "I want to hear about you. You have left University? Don't tell me you were sent down!" She affected a look of surprise. "You weren't, were you?"

"Oh certainly not, Miss Durham. No, of course not."

"And now you are home, what do you mean to do with yourself? I hope you will be a regular visitor at our humble home at the Bowery?"

"Yes, of course," he said. "If you will welcome me, I'll consider it an honor."

There was an awkward silence, and then Beth took Mr. Vaughn's arm. "I think you were just about to ask me to dance," she said in a confidential tone.

"Good heavens, yes!" he said. "Would you do me the honor, Miss Durham?"

"Yes, of course," she said, looking up at him through her lashes and holding to his arm all the tighter. Together they walked away toward the dance floor, leaving Laynie to sip at her punch and to watch after them. She did not resent the slight. Truly it was hardly a slight at all. If Beth found something to admire in Mr. Vaughn, that was a very good thing, perhaps for them all.

She watched them for a little while, as Beth led the conversation, as she smiled and flirted, and as Mr. Vaughn responded with increased confidence and enthusiasm. Before the set had ended they both seemed to be sincerely enjoying each other's company, and Laynie was pleased. At least she felt the pressure to consider him for herself fall away as her sister worked her charms on him, and with apparent success. She considered Lady Vaughn's words on the subject of her son and turned to share in the pleasure of the happiness her sister seemed eager to give him. Only the look on Lady Vaughn's face was not one of pleasure at all, but of pain. Was she so displeased by the thought? It seemed she was not the only one to observe the woman's altered state. Two gentlemen helped her to her feet, and the doctor, who had been in attendance, was very soon at her side. It seemed he understood the matter at once and ushered her out, stopping in the foyer only long enough to retrieve her things.

Laynie, honestly concerned, followed them outdoors. In the drive she stood and watched as the doctor placed the woman in her carriage and then as he entered to sit beside her. Laynie could not help but wonder at the severity of Lady Vaughn's ailment, and what Harry's unexpected return portended.

A gust of wind blew Laynie's hair out of its pins. A clap of thunder, and then the rain fell in torrents. She returned to the shelter of the assembly hall and nearly ran into her father as she did.

"Good heavens, child! Where have you been?" He looked her over disapprovingly. "You're nearly drowned. You'll never win Harold Vaughn this way!" And he appeared truly sorry to know it might be true.

"Father, please. I don't want—"

"You're a girl of nineteen. You don't know what you want!" And taking her by the elbow he led her to the carriage, where she was to wait while he got her things and while he retrieved Beth—who would not be pleased to have to quit the dance early because her sister had managed to get caught in a deluge—and then he drove them home, lamenting all the way on the difficulties of being a single father with two daughters who *would* prove impossible to find suitable husbands for.

"It's nothing to me if he comes or if he doesn't."

Chapter two

ETWEEN THE SISTERS THERE WAS little but silent tension as they traveled home. It was only upon reaching their bedroom that any conversation took place. It was conducted in raised voices that echoed through the walls and could be heard by anyone undetermined not to listen.

"What did you think you were doing, Laynie?"

"Lady Vaughn was ill. I was concerned. I forgot about the rain. It came down all at once and I wasn't thinking what—"

"Exactly! You never think! And while I am irritated—and I *am* irritated—that we had to leave the ball early, I'm more concerned about your treachery. What do you have to say for yourself?"

"Treachery, Beth? I don't understand you."

"What would you call it? You knew I had an interest in Harold Vaughn."

"You told me quite plainly you didn't. Don't you remember?"

"Yes, but then…" she stopped, and then proceeded on more cautiously, as if she were holding something back. "I have my reasons for considering him now I have taken the opportunity of reacquainting myself with him," she said and sat down upon Laynie's bed.

"And what did you find, Beth?"

"What do you mean?"

"Did you find that your objections are done away with? You called him awkward, socially withdrawn? Have you found that he has grown in charm and self-presence? What is it that has changed your mind?"

"I don't know," Beth answered dismissively.

"Yes you do. Tell me. What did Miss Fisher say to you that persuaded you to consider him differently than you were otherwise inclined to do? You had no interest in him at all until she spoke to you. What did she say?"

"Don't tell me you don't know. You spent an hour at his mother's side. You can't tell me the subject never came up, or that wasn't your own reason for cozying up to her."

"Truly, Beth, I don't know what you're talking about."

"Harold Vaughn is to inherit!"

Laynie joined her sister on the bed, and the two sat there silently for some time. Mr. Vaughn was to inherit? It was surprising news—wonderful news—only… "Beth?" Laynie asked at last and tentatively. "Do you really mean to tell me that the only reason you were persuaded to consider the merits of Mr. Vaughn is because he suddenly, and quite unexpectedly, stands to inherit a fortune, where before he did not?"

"You make me sound a mercenary, Laynie. And as far as it goes, I don't know that I am prepared to consider him, fortune or no fortune. But you know I cannot marry a poor man. I have to have something to live on."

"Yes, I know, Beth," Laynie answered, feeling a little disappointed in her sister.

"I have to marry my security. As do you, whether you like to admit it or not, so don't you dare think of condemning me. You'll be in the same boat sooner or later yourself."

"I'm not condemning you. I only hope that, when you marry, you will do it for love as well as security."

"Is that what you mean to do, then? Is that why you flew straight to his mother?"

"His mother came to me, Bethany. I don't know why. I'm sure I did nothing to encourage her."

Beth appeared not to have considered this.

"Do you care for him, Beth? Do you think you might learn to? If you do, then that's all that matters."

"You're not listening, Laynie," she said and stood to pace the room. "It's *not* all that matters, that's the thing! I may like him, he may like me, she may disapprove of the whole thing! Or worse, he may

15

find someone else he likes better after all, and how do I know that it won't be you!" Beth was left breathless with this and nearly in tears.

"Beth. You don't... You don't think I would...that I *could*...do to you what Caroline did...do you?"

"Of course not," Beth said and sat down on her own bed. "But how can I be certain of my own feelings when I know in my heart that a man is never certain of his own?"

"I don't think that is true. Mr. Vaughn is hardly Mr. Hartright, is he? He always seemed to me a bit of a flirt. I hardly think you could say the same about Harry Vaughn."

"No," Beth said and, considering him in that light, smiled mirthfully. It was almost admiringly. Almost, but not quite.

"If you really think you could love him, Mr. Vaughn I mean, you have nothing to worry about from me. He is a friend and nothing more. I could hardly think of loving someone whom I can remember eating dirt and chasing me with worms. Even if he was a child."

"Laynie!" Beth said and laughed.

"I am sorry for ruining your night," Laynie said.

Beth sighed. "There will be other assemblies, I suppose."

"And who's to say his disappointment in your having to quit the party early won't have increased the intrigue? Perhaps he'll have all the more reason to be thinking of you tonight than if you had remained the whole evening."

This suggestion seemed to offer Beth something to consider as she arose and prepared for bed.

"In the meantime, do tread carefully, won't you, Beth?"

"I'm always careful, Laynie," Beth answered.

"But with *his* heart as well as your own, dear. Will you promise?"

Beth didn't answer, but neither did she argue. It was good enough for Laynie. At least it would do for the moment.

* * *

With the resonant volley of voices now ended, Mr. Durham released a sigh. These girls were driving him to distraction! What's more, he was lonely. He had no intention of marrying again, but his daughters needed some guidance, and he had none to give. If Lady Vaughn would take an interest—and it seemed she might—then perhaps Laynie would soon be off his hands. It would be strange to have the youngest married first, and certainly Beth would not like that, but there was no mistaking the change of expression on Lady Vaughn's face as she had watched—and with apparent pleasure—her son speaking with Laynie. Her countenance became almost condemning as she observed the older sister push the other out of her way in her vying for Vaughn's atten-tion. Of course the young man would prefer Beth over her sister. Who wouldn't? But if his mother approved of Laynie, and there was a fortune to be gained by his obedience, well, it was quite easy to guess where it would end. Laynie, unremarkable as she was, was unlikely to have such an opportunity as this again. And if she—by the grace of God—should do so well for herself, then what might she help her sister to accomplish, who might have anyone she set her mind upon?

In the meantime, he needed some kind of reprieve. He needed some company that stimulated him to something more congenial than the madness of trying, and unsuccessfully, to find suitors for his daughters. He needed the companionship of likeminded gentlemen. Perhaps a few of his old friends from university might be willing to get together as they used to do. A trip to London would do him good. A trip to London might be just the thing!

Chapter three

"I'M OFF TO TOWN in the morning, my dears," Mr. Durham announced to his daughters the following evening.

The news left Laynie feeling a little anxious for her father. "It's been some time since you've been to Town, Papa. Are you sure you don't want some company?"

"Quite certain," he assured her. "At least I mean to get it once I am there, and to have as little as possible of it beforehand." He eased the barb of his jesting with a kiss delivered to the forehead of each of his daughters, and then he wished them goodnight. He turned again at the parlor door. "You'll behave yourselves while I'm away," he admonished them. "And if any gentlemen come to call, you'll treat them with the respect they deserve." Mr. Durham looked to Beth meaningfully.

"I don't know why you look at me, Papa."

"Don't you? Certainly you have enough eager admirers to provide for some advantageous opportunity while I'm away. Will you give an old man a little something to hope for? What do you say?"

Beth shook her head at him. "I say good night, Papa, and have a good time in Town tomorrow."

"And do be careful, won't you, Papa?" Laynie added. She did not like the idea of his going to London alone.

* * *

As far as Laynie was concerned a perfectly pleasant afternoon was one that did not necessarily include visitors. She knew, however, that the feeling was not shared by her sister, who, since the ball two nights ago, had been on pins and needles waiting for the doorbell to ring.

Fortune, it seemed, was to favor Beth, for the bell did ring. And yet the arrival of the visitor seemed to do more to exaggerate Beth's anxiety than to alleviate it. Upon hearing the bell, she flew from the sofa to the mirror, dropping her book in the process, determined to take advantage of the time allotted her between Mrs. Fowler's answering of the door and the announcement of their guest, to straighten the collar of her dress, to adjust the brooch that was pinned there, and to check her reflection in the mirror. Laynie watched with great interest as Beth, having finished her fussing, turned just as the door opened. She stood, prepared to greet the visitor—whomever he may be—and in a manner perfectly calm and composed.

"Mr. Harold Vaughn," the housekeeper announced.

"We'll be pleased to receive him, Mrs. Fowler, thank you," Beth answered, standing very erect. Her effort to seem unaffected by his arrival was impressive, but the glowing of her cheeks betrayed her anticipation.

Laynie, eager to assess the results of Beth's work at the ball and to learn for herself what impression her sister had made on him, watched Harry carefully as her sister received him.

"Good afternoon, Miss Laynie, Miss Durham," Mr. Vaughn said upon entering the room. His bow to Beth was a little deeper, lasted a little longer than that which he had offered Laynie. She took no offense. In fact she was happy to think Mr. Vaughn might have formed a preference for her sister. While Mr. Vaughn could certainly provide for her future security, she knew him far too well to imagine he could excite any strong emotion in her. Still, while there was any chance that Beth might learn to love him, she would watch them, the both of them, looking—hoping—for any sign of budding romance.

"Do have a seat, won't you, Mr. Vaughn?" Laynie begged him and gestured toward the nearest chair.

He took it.

"How are you today?" he asked of both sisters at once.

"Very well, indeed," Laynie answered.

"Yes, of course," Beth chimed in at last. "We are *very* well. Thank you."

"You quit the party early the other night," he said, more to Beth than to Laynie. "I hope there was no emergency."

"No… No emergency," she answered haltingly. "Not unless you count Laynie getting caught in a deluge an emergency." She was

19

clearly pleased to know that her absence had been noted and she was consequently warming to the conversation.

"It was my fault we left, Mr. Vaughn," Laynie explained. "To be quite honest it was your mother's sudden indisposition and my concern for her that drew me out of doors. I hope she was not unwell?"

"Only briefly," Mr. Vaughn answered. "She occasionally has spells. It's an ongoing complaint, but not a serious one."

"I do hope not. Will you send her my regards?"

"Yes, of course, Miss Laynie. And thank you."

"Do send mine as well," Beth added.

"Indeed I will, Miss Durham," he said, turning to her and allowing his gaze to linger. "I'm grateful."

"Not at all," Beth answered, her voice faltering once more under the weight of Harold Vaughn's admiration. "Is that why you've come home, then?" she asked him. "To care for her?"

"Partly," he said. "Mother is getting on, and she feels it imperative that there is a man at home. There are other reasons, of course, of which you may or may not have heard…"

That his father had, a year or so ago, moved out of Elverton to share a London flat with an actress was a scandal of which everyone knew and no one spoke. The present difficulties with his brother they had learned of only in the vaguest terms, but such subjects were hardly the stuff of parlor conversation. Neither did Mr. Vaughn seem eager to say more on the subject and instead chose another.

"I did not think I would like being home so much," he said, directing the statement more toward Beth than Laynie. "I've found an unexpected pleasure in reuniting with old friends."

Beth was almost effusive now, a very good sign indeed. She smiled and batted her lashes in her characteristically blushing manner. "We were ever so happy to learn you had come home to stay, Mr. Vaughn," she said, which of course was not quite the truth. Not at least at first. But if her feelings were changing on the matter it was all Laynie could wish for. "I do hope we will see you often. I shall be disappointed if we do not."

Mr. Vaughn was positively transfixed. Beth held his gaze only long enough to make her point and coyly looked away. In the silence that followed, Laynie said a little prayer of gratitude, while Mr.

Vaughn took the opportunity of looking about the room. Once upon a time he had been a regular visitor here. Alterations had been made in recent months—an attempt to keep things looking fresh. Her father thought it would serve to display his daughters' talents in housekeeping. Laynie had doubted—until now—that anyone would ever take notice.

"It's changed, I think," he said at last, "and somehow it seems just the same."

"Laynie undertook to redecorate about a year ago," Beth explained. "I think her tastes run after dear Mama's. It's a little dull and drab for my liking. Too many dark colors and not enough light and lace, if you ask me."

"I like it," Mr. Vaughn assured her. "I like it very much."

His compliment misfired. His expressed satisfaction with the room was praise—if indirectly—of Laynie's skill in decorating. Well intended though it was, it was just the sort of thing to spark Beth's jealous ire, and as she began to fidget nervously with the cuff of her sleeve, Laynie could only hope that her sweetness, for Mr. Vaughn's sake at the very least, would endure.

"I dare say, though," Mr. Vaughn continued, "the house does seem a little smaller than I remember it."

"That's only because you've grown so much since last you were here," Laynie said, laughing.

"As have you," he returned, and added jestingly, "though perhaps not so very much as I have."

"Oh, Laynie will never be tall," Beth said, as if they had at last landed upon a subject for which she could feel real enthusiasm. "She'll never be as tall as me, I'm sure of it."

"Then it's a good thing height was never one of my ambitions," Laynie returned. "And it's not as if I'm unusually short."

"No, not short," Beth conceded. "But not tall, either. You are perfectly average in every way. Oh don't look so dour, Laynie. I'm sure it's a good thing, after all. Just think, you'll never have to worry about standing out in a crowd."

The back-handed compliment was more painful than Laynie wished to let on. For Mr. Vaughn's sake alone did she hold her tongue, and in the meantime she prayed he would not be put off by Beth's tendency toward jealous spitefulness. It was not her sister's best trait, by far.

"Whether we've grown in stature over the last four or five years is hardly consequential," Mr. Vaughn said, interrupting the argument he had inadvertently started. "The fact is, we've all changed a great deal. We are, none of us, children anymore."

"Which changes things, doesn't it?" Beth very pointedly asked.

"It does, rather," he answered and looked at Laynie half-ashamed. The gesture reminded her of his mother's words, those that had encouraged her to think of him as something more than a friend. Beth saw the look, made her own interpretation of it and arose to stand at the window, where she looked out at the dull and misting sky. Laynie understood her. She had turned her back on present company as a form of silent protest to the attention Laynie was receiving.

"What is it that occupies your time these days, Miss Durham?" Mr. Vaughn asked, addressing Beth directly. Laynie was impressed that he had caught on to Beth's perturbation. Would he know how to overcome it? His attempts to express a pointed interest in the most mundane aspects of her life were certainly a good place to start. "Surely you have some prepossessing hobby?"

Beth answered very calmly, and yet with eyes that flashed her frustration, as she turned to face him squarely. "I wait, it seems, Mr. Vaughn. That is what I do."

"You wait?"

"Yes. I wait. That is my prepossessing hobby. A young woman of my age and situation, of my *station*, if you will," she added, as if trying to make some distinction Mr. Vaughn might particularly take note of, "has little else to do but wait. It is the chief purpose of her existence. To wait until she is called upon, to wait until her company is sought, never to seek it out on her own. I wait. That is what occupies my time."

Laynie cringed. She disliked contention, and she did not thank her sister for allowing her vanity to rule her emotions at a time like this. It was imperative that Beth impress him, but he was not the type to admire caprice.

"I..." Mr. Vaughn began, but he was clearly at a loss as to how to answer her. He gave Laynie a helpless look, which, as it turned out, was precisely the wrong thing to do.

Beth heaved an annoyed sigh and turned once more toward the window and her back upon the awkward tension of two childhood friends, who, reuniting as adults, no longer knew how to communicate. If only Laynie could think of some way to help them.

Beth turned to look at Laynie, her eyes wide, but she could not interpret her meaning. A moment later, the doorbell rang. Beth's look suddenly made sense. It was accusation, or confusion. Perhaps both. They had a visitor and there was little need to wonder who it was that had come. How had she forgotten?

"Are you expecting someone, Laynie?" Beth asked her.

Laynie listened in silent apprehension while Mrs. Fowler answered the door, as her footsteps were heard to approach, and then as the door opened on softly creaking hinges.

"Mr. Anthony Granger to see Miss Durham," the housekeeper announced, and looked to Beth and Laynie in turn, as if she were not quite sure which one, after all, was wanted. Of course she knew. At least Laynie knew, for the awkward scene that was about to ensue was entirely of her own making.

"Well," Beth said, her patience now quite spent, "show him in."

The door opened wider, and Mr. Granger entered. He looked uncomfortably about the room, his gaze resting a moment on Mr. Vaughn. Eventually he fixed a look upon Laynie that was half question, half accusation, and vaguely laced with disappointment.

"You know Mr. Vaughn, of course," Laynie said, feeling all the guilt consequent of the awkward situation. He had come, as she had assured him he might. Her sister was not alone, as she had assured him she would be. Quite the opposite, in fact. Oh, very much the opposite!

"Yes. Of course I do," Mr. Granger answered tersely. "Mr. Vaughn, good day to you."

A cloud of confusion, of imminent disappointment, hung over Harold Vaughn as he replied, "And to you, Mr. Granger."

"Forgive me for the intrusion," Mr. Granger said, addressing Beth directly. "I was given to understand that you would be free to receive me. I ask for ten minutes of your time, and no more."

Beth offered Laynie another accusing look, but there was nothing to be done. Beth was obligated to grant Mr. Granger his desire. With a stiff smile of forced patience, she answered him. "Of course, Mr. Granger. If you'll follow me." And she led him from the room—leaving Laynie and Mr. Vaughn to sit in a stupor of defeated silence.

"My mother quite enjoyed her conversation with you the other night," Mr. Vaughn said at last, but all the spirit seemed to have gone out of him.

"As did I, Mr. Vaughn, as I have said already. I do hope she is recovered and will remain in good health."

"She thinks very highly of you, you know," he continued, to Laynie's mounting discomfort.

"That is kind of you to say, Mr. Vaughn. Kinder of her to think of me so. The favor is more than returned."

His own equanimity seemed to be diminishing. He continued on nevertheless. "She was hoping I'd have the opportunity of finding myself alone with you."

"Oh, don't, Harry."

He looked for a moment stunned.

"We are such very good friends," Laynie said. "And I hope we always will be. But I can see that you have a preference for Beth."

He exhaled and sat back hard in his chair.

"Please don't despair, Mr. Vaughn. It's far too soon to despair."

"But Miss Laynie, I dare say, what is the point in my pursuing the matter?" And with a look he indicated the door through which Beth had just gone.

"She does have many admirers," Laynie confessed, which seemed as yet another blow to poor Mr. Vaughn. "But she will not accept Mr. Granger."

"That she has admirers does not surprise me. It does not give me much in the way of hope, but it does not surprise me. What pains me more is to see how much she has changed."

She *had* changed. It was true. "This past year has been one filled with bitter disappointment. She has learned to be distrustful and not without reason. I beg you will be patient with her."

He looked to the door once more and stood.

"Don't leave already, Mr. Vaughn."

"I really think I had better. If she refuses him, she'll hardly want company. And if she does not, then I shan't."

Laynie watched as he turned from the room, pulling the door shut as though pulling curtain upon all his hopes. She did not like to see anyone hurt, particularly so good a man as Harold Vaughn. She thought of him returning home. She thought of him telling his mother what had taken place and the counsel she would no doubt give him in consequence.

Laynie arose and followed after him. He had nearly reached the lane, his horse in hand, when she caught up with him.

"Mr. Vaughn," she called to him, out of breath.

He turned.

"One moment, if you will. We often walk in the afternoons. If you were to meet us… Perhaps Wednesday?"

"If you think it worth the trouble," he said, and despite his somber expression, he appeared to take a little hope.

"I do."

"Shall I meet you here?"

"No, not here, I think. Do you know Juniper Lane? It's a particularly scenic walk when the flowers are in bloom, as they are now. Perhaps you will find it…inspiring?"

"Yes, I know it." He considered the idea and smiled to himself. He was really almost handsome when he smiled, the sun shining through his very blonde hair. "Wednesday it is," he said, in spirits significantly lifted. "What time?"

"Shall we say two?"

"Two o'clock it is. Thank you, Miss Durham. You truly are a friend."

Laynie watched him go, feeling a little proud of herself for her peacemaking endeavors. She turned back toward the house, and upon nearing the door, the sound of raised voices could be heard within. She hung back and waited. Finding a tree, she shielded herself from view of the house, and waited for a very red-of-face and dejected Mr. Granger to make his escape, kicking dust and striking the flower heads with the end of his stick as he went.

When it was safe, she entered the house.

"And how was your walk with Mr. Vaughn?" Beth asked her in a voice too sweet to be sincerely congenial. "Made the most of your opportunity, did you?"

Laynie stopped and looked at her. In truth she did not always feel as patient with her sister as she liked to let on. This old game of hers—the jealousy and mean-spiritedness of her quest, of her near des-peration to find a husband—was growing old. "I don't know what you're talking about," Laynie answered. "The moment you left the room he made his excuses and was gone. I've been walking alone in the garden this half hour. The sun is at last out, you know?" She did not wait for a reply but mounted the stairs to her room, desperate for an hour or two to herself before her father would return home.

Chapter four

IN A LONDON PUBLIC HOUSE, Nathaniel Durham had found precisely what he'd been looking for. At least it would do for the moment. He had found old friends and listening ears, into which he had been pouring, this last three quarters of an hour, the sorrows and agonies of his dotage: namely his daughters and the obstinacy that was the right and privilege of every woman to refuse every man who might be willing to take her off her father's hands.

"You should count yourself fortunate, Nathaniel Durham," replied a certain of Mr. Durham's friends as he nodded his request for another drink, "that a man of your age has someone to keep him company. I've sons enough, but when do I ever see them? They've no time for me now they've wives and children of their own."

"What I wouldn't give for sons!" answered Mr. Durham. "Two of them, by Jove. Better yet sons-in-law, which I might have soon enough if my girls would only quit with their foolish games and adopt a bit of sense."

"When you're young the game is half the fun," said another of the party, "it's how they reel a fellow in. It's like the bait at the end of the line, you know. It isn't the real thing, but it looks a little like it, and it's certainly fun to chase."

"There's reeling enough, to be sure," Mr. Durham returned. "It's the netting I'm interested in. When they do have one in hand, they toss him back and try for another, just for the fun of it! Over and over again, it's always the same. They'll be at it when they're my age I have no doubt!"

His companions laughed at this, but Mr. Durham was a man of spent humor. He finished his drink and pushed the empty glass aside. "I hardly understand them. I can't have a rational conversation with

27

them. They spend all their time vexing each other when they're not driving me mad with their trivialities. I hate to lose them, truly I do, but time's getting on. My only hope for a little peace before I die is to have it all settled and done with at last."

"You oughtn't to complain, Nathaniel. When you're all alone, you'll regret your words."

"Ah! I don't mean anything by it. You know I don't. But a bit of peace and quiet's all a man of my age really wants—and some sensible companionship. Why I'd pay a man a good wage to come and read to me now and then, to challenge my intellect with some sensible conversation, provided he can think reasonably and is well read. An educated man, mind, and a clear-headed one."

"Your educated men, I think you'll find, don't often hire themselves out," said the first gentleman. "I'm not sure you could afford him if he did. It might solve two problems in one, though, if you mean what you say."

"How's that?" Mr. Durham asked.

"Well, if you were to bring someone in to read to you a couple nights a week, you could set him onto your girls the other nights, and before long you'd have a daughter married and a companion besides. And one you wouldn't have to pay, I'll wager."

"You miss the point, my friend," Nathaniel answered gravely. "A man can't think when there are such distractions. I want a clear head and no nonsense. The girls had best keep away. Ah! You're right, of course. Who in their right mind would want to come all the way out to Surrey two or three nights a week just to read with an old man? The girls would scare him off the first chance they got. What am I saying? It's a lost cause. It'd serve me better just to come into Town more often."

"You don't mind leaving your daughters alone?"

"Mind? I look forward to it! It's not as if they're all alone, after all. There's the housekeeper and cook to look after them. And if they do get into any scrapes while I'm gone, I can only pray they're the right kind."

Laughter joined this, but Mr. Durham found he had not much energy left to spare. He'd had enough to drink long ago, and his thoughts were growing clouded and muddled. It was an hour's train ride home. He had best be on his way. He took his leave of his friends and went outside, where he stood for a few minutes, taking in the night air and a moment to appreciate the stars. The door, which a moment ago had sealed off the noise from within, opened with the rattling of the bell. He was no longer alone.

Mr. Durham shook out his coat, fastened one button across his chest, and prepared to begin his walk to the station.

"Nice night," said the stranger who had just recently joined him.

"Yes, it is," Mr. Durham returned. "A lovely night."

"A good night for a walk."

"It certainly is."

"May I join you?" the gentleman asked.

"I'm only going as far as the station."

"Yes, I know," he answered. "I overheard you inside."

Mr. Durham took a moment to look the young man over. He was well-groomed and admirably built. Clearly he had come from good English stock. If he hadn't met him outside a public house on a London street, he might have mistaken him for someone of importance. "If it pleases you to join me," Mr. Durham answered at last, "you are welcome." And he led the way toward the station.

"Daniel Holbrook," the gentleman said by way of introduction.

"It's a pleasure to meet you, sir. Nathaniel Durham."

"A privilege," Mr. Holbrook said.

There was silence as they began their short journey. And then: "I hope you won't think me presumptuous," Mr. Holbrook began. He did not finish right away, but waited instead for some sign to go on.

Mr. Durham gave it.

"I was listening in on your conversation."

"Oh? Which part was that?" Mr. Durham answered with a laugh. "Are you in need of a wife, perhaps?" He examined the gentleman more closely. He was not so young as he had at first supposed him to be. Perhaps closer to thirty than twenty.

"No, sir," the young gentleman answered. The gravity with which he had offered his answer tempted Mr. Durham to lose interest. The temptation only lasted a moment. "It was what you said about hiring a reading companion. Were you in earnest?"

Mr. Durham stopped his walking and examined Mr. Holbrook even more closely. "Well, I don't know," he said. "I suppose that depends. What are your credentials?"

"Well," the gentleman began, "I was educated at Cambridge, where I read Classics and Literature. I've done some traveling as well. In fact I've been some years abroad now and have only recently returned home. I'm in need of some little employment to keep me busy while I look for something more regular."

"Are you, indeed?"

"If you were serious, that is."

Nathaniel Durham considered a moment before answering. Though he had aired his wish on more than one occasion, it had never seemed a real possibility. If he had not considered it in a serious light before, he did so now. And all the more for finding a gentleman before him who professed the desire to fill such a position. It seemed providential. He liked the look of him, too. He seemed a steady sort of chap, well-bred and yet apparently lacking in that sort of well-bred pride Nathaniel deplored so much. "I'm not sure I can pay you what you ought to have," he answered at last and honestly.

"I have modest expectations," Mr. Holbrook answered. "And, as I said, I hope to find something more by and by."

"Yes, of course," Mr. Durham answered as he considered the matter a little further.

"It won't get in the way, I dare say, were I to come of an evening. I mean if I were to find something to do with my days, I might still come after hours or on the weekend."

"Yes, of course," Mr. Durham said, though he was really thinking more than listening at this point. "You've been abroad, you say? Rome?"

"Most lately Florence, but of course I spent some time in Rome and Athens. The Alps as well."

"You are well studied in History?"

"Somewhat, yes."

"Philosophy? Theology?"

Mr. Holbrook smiled. "I believe I can keep up."

"Would you be open to a trial?" Mr. Durham suggested.

"Certainly, if you wish it."

"I live some distance out. Near Ashworth, in Surrey."

"So I gathered, sir."

"Well then. If you're willing to come to me on, let's say, Wednesday afternoon, we'll make an evening of it. You'll stay to dinner, and if all goes well, we'll discuss the particulars thereafter."

"I'm very grateful, sir."

Nathaniel Durham then took Mr. Holbrook's hand and wished him good evening.

Chapter five

IT WAS DARK WHEN LAYNIE returned downstairs. She had dozed a little while reading her book and had awoken with the sinking feeling of knowing her father had not yet returned home. She entered their favorite parlor, uncertain of the mood she would find Beth in.

Beth, sitting beneath the pale glow of one solitary lamp, put her needlework down as Laynie opened the door. She looked at her a moment before speaking. "You've missed dinner."

"I'm not hungry."

"They say love will do that to you." The words, as they left Beth's mouth, were untinged with spite. Still, Laynie chose to ignore them.

"I'm worried about Father," she said.

"He'll be home soon. Within the hour, I should think."

"What if he's missed his train?"

"Then he'll catch another." There was silence for a moment while Beth studied her, and Laynie tried to decide if it was safe to remain. "Do sit down, Laynie," Beth said at last, making room for her on the sofa.

Laynie took a seat beside her sister. Nothing, however, was said for some time.

Beth smoothed the stitches of her embroidery. "I'm sorry about earlier," she said at last. "I shouldn't have behaved the way I did."

"No, you shouldn't have," Laynie answered, glad to have her say. "It was very bad form, Beth. You practically chased him off."

"That was not entirely my doing, though, was it?" Beth answered, growing a little defensive, but plainly trying to maintain her placid demeanor. "You knew Mr. Granger was going to call. Admit it."

"I did. And I forgot. I'm terribly sorry about it."

"And he came the day, the very hour, Mr. Vaughn should be here? Do you mean to tell me that was coincidence?"

"Yes. I do," Laynie answered.

Beth looked at her a moment, then relented. "Oh, Laynie. What luck we have!"

"Are you truly disappointed?" Laynie asked and really wanted to know.

Beth turned the needle between her fingers and absentmindedly unthreaded it. "There are other fish in the sea, I suppose." She was silent again as she attempted to rethread it, and failing, plunged it into the fabric. "Oh, who am I deceiving?" she said, and it sounded as though there was a catch in her voice. "I keep telling myself that. But one of these days there won't be any fish left. What does it matter anyway? He was always sure to choose you."

"No, Beth. I think not. But you really must treat him gently. He's not the type to put up with your sporting."

"I'm sure it cannot matter now, Laynie." Beth looked up at her. There were tears in her eyes. Laynie thought to assure her once more, to tell her of the plans she had made to meet him for a walk in a few days' time. She was not certain, however, that that would be entirely wise. Beth might not appreciate her meddling. And a great deal could happen between now and then. If the weather should turn bad there would be no walk at all. Beth might, somehow, discover the charms of someone else... Perhaps Laynie *had* better tell her... But before she could quite make up her mind to do it, Laynie heard wheels in the drive.

Father was home.

Laynie arose to meet him in the foyer and Beth followed, checking the mirror first and dabbing the tears from her eyes.

He entered a moment later.

"Papa!" Laynie said and hugged him tightly.

Her father received the embrace and laughed. "Were you worried, silly thing? You see? I can manage myself as far as London and back."

"I know, Papa."

Her father looked to Beth, and then turned back to Laynie. "What is this? Quarreling again, are we?" Beth's still red eyes had given her away. Mr. Durham's look grew narrow. "Did you have any visitors?"

"Just Mr. Vaughn," Beth answered.

Mr. Durham turned his attention full upon his younger daughter. "Oh, ho! I like the sound of this! You were kind to him, Laynie?" he asked her. "You did not chase him off, I hope."

"Of course not, Papa," Laynie answered him and, observing her sister's gaze drop dejectedly to the floor, wished that she had told Beth of the arrangements she had made. Perhaps it might have done something to ease the sting of her father's uttered wishes in Laynie's behalf.

Laynie helped her father off with his coat and tried, very carefully, to make him understand how things stood. "I've told you, Papa. I can't think of him that way. I do think, however, that he—"

"Can't think of him what way, my dear?" he asked, turning to her. He finished the task of removing his coat for himself and hung it, rather violently, upon the hall tree. "You've known Harold Vaughn since you were children. You are now both grown. You can think of him any way you like." He made his way to the parlor, where Laynie and Beth followed him. "You couldn't ask for a steadier fellow, a better situation." He stood at the door and waited for them to enter. "What is it you want, Laynie?" he asked once they had joined him. "What is it you are waiting for? It's not as though you can have your pick of any young fellow you like, you know? You must be sensible!"

"I know, Papa," she answered, understanding very well what he meant. He seemed to think it would take an act of charity for a man to take her on. If her hopes were not sensible, at least she had the comfort of knowing that neither was love. It struck where it would, without rhyme or reason. Perhaps it was impractical. Perhaps it was downright foolish, but it was, whether her father approved of it or not, her determined aim to marry for nothing less than sincere admiration and affection.

Her father, plainly disappointed with his daughters' news, lowered himself heavily into a chair and took up his pipe, which he emptied and then stuffed again with an equal combination of tobacco and paternal frustration.

In the silence Laynie looked to Beth, who appeared more discouraged than ever to find that her father was so resolutely set on Laynie winning Mr. Vaughn. Laynie herself hardly understood the reason for it. He had overheard Lady Vaughn's expressed desires, and consequently he saw an opportunity where there would be little obstacle besides that of Laynie's own feeling. If he had fixated himself upon seeing the match formed and solemnized, had Harry's mother done the same?

And what of Mr. Granger? They had yet to tell their father of his arrival. Perhaps there was no point in doing it, after all. For her father to learn he had come and had been sent away would only cause trouble for Beth.

"How was your trip, Papa?" Laynie asked when at last he'd lit his pipe and had begun to relax a little. "Was your outing enjoyable?"

"Enjoyable indeed," Mr. Durham answered, brightening perceptibly. "In fact it quite exceeded my expectations. Do you know," he said, and sat up in his chair, "I think I have procured for myself something of a treasure."

"A treasure, Papa?" Beth asked with sincere interest. "What sort of treasure?"

"Now, now, I'm not sure I ought to tell you. You're likely to steal it from me if you can."

"Don't be cruel, Papa," Beth pleaded. "Do tell us what it is," and she sat down on the arm of his chair. He appeared to enjoy the attention. For all his complaints about Beth's coquetting, even he was not immune to it.

"Very well," he said and began to explain. "For years now I've been saying that I would one day like to hire a fellow to read with me and to challenge my wits now and again."

"You know you have us," Beth offered. "I'd be only too happy to read to you."

Nathaniel Durham gave his elder daughter a patient smile and patted her hand. "There is no need of that, Beth, but I thank you," he said to her and omitted, this time, his well-rehearsed speech on the deficiencies of the female mind and a woman's unsuitableness for such intellectual exercise as he wished to engage in. "You see," he explained at last, "I have done what I said I would always do. I have

35

hired a gentleman to come discuss the classics—and history and theology—two or three nights a week. It will do me good, I think. I've been rather languishing of late, and this is the very thing I need."

Beth appeared a little alarmed at the thought that their already dwindling resources might dwindle all the faster for her father's extravagance. "A gentleman...?"

"Now don't set your thoughts on it for a moment, Bethany," Mr. Durham said, misinterpreting her concern and the question she had not been allowed to finish, for evidences of exaggerated interest.

"I'm sure I never thought of it," Beth protested.

He cast a similarly warning look upon Laynie.

"Truly, Papa, aren't you being a little ridiculous?"

"With you two minxes about? I don't think so," and he laughed deprecatingly.

"He's too old for you," he said. It was a point that needed little explanation. "Besides, I believe he is quite happily married with a family of his own. So there'll be no need to worry and fret him with your coquetting about. He's here to attend me, you understand?"

"Of course, Papa," Laynie answered, frustrated at her father's determination to see both his daughters as coquettish teases. He considered Laynie her sister's equal in minxishness on the one hand, and yet wholly incapable of playing her rival on the other. It was not pleasant to be always so very misunderstood by him. Even Beth was peeved by his aspersions. She slid off the arm of the chair and with head held high in indignation, she made her way to the door.

"What did I say?" he asked of Laynie, and with a glance in her sister's direction.

"Nothing, Papa. It's been a long day, that's all."

He sighed and shook his head. "Kiss me," he said, "and off to bed with you."

They each obeyed and left the room for their own, where they did not speak, but prepared for bed in silence. Laynie considered once more telling Beth of the plans she had made but, in the end, thought better of it. A day or two of quiet reflection might serve Beth very well. Perhaps she would take some time to consider what she was missing in having so nearly tossed away the admiration of Harold Vaughn.

Chapter six

LAYNIE HEARD THE RINGING OF the bell and checked the clock on her bedroom mantel. It was a quarter past two. She closed her eyes in frustration. Of course the overly-eager Harold Vaughn would not wait in Juniper Lane but had come to see what had detained them. With her walking hat, and her sister's too, in hand, she rushed downstairs, anxious to greet him before Beth should find him and spoil everything.

"Don't let him in, Mrs. Fowler," she called as she descended the stairs. "I'm coming now, and I'll—"

But it was too late. The housekeeper opened the door, and on the other side of it was a gentleman every bit as tall as Harold Vaughn but perfectly proportioned to his great height. She came to a stop at the landing and simply stood there, confused and a little in awe.

"I've come on invitation from Mr. Durham," the gentleman said to the housekeeper, glancing at Laynie.

Laynie blinked but could not quite draw her gaze away from him.

"Of course, sir," said Mrs. Fowler, greeting him. "Mr. Durham said I was to expect a visitor for him today. Won't you come in?"

She opened the door wider, and Laynie slowly descended the last of the stairs to find that the foyer seemed suddenly very small now that it was filled with their visitor's frame. Or perhaps it was she who felt small in consequence of his very piercing gray eyes. She did wish he wouldn't look at her so. But then what choice had he when she was staring at him?

"Your name, sir?" Mrs. Fowler prompted him.

"Forgive me," he said and returned his attention to the house-keeper. He presented his card. "Daniel Holbrook. I am Mr. Durham's reading companion. At least I hope to be, if I pass muster."

Laynie was further astounded. "His reading…?"

"Companion, yes," he finished for her. "Have I come at a bad time?"

"Not at all, sir," Mrs. Fowler assured him. "I'll just let Mr. Durham know you're here."

And then it was just Laynie and the visitor alone. This was her father's hired companion? Well no wonder he thought it necessary to issue the warning. Good heavens, what would Beth make of him? She almost dreaded to know. Her father was not likely to have much peace with him in the house. Not if Beth must live here, too. And poor Harold Vaughn! Who was this man to come and ruin all her carefully laid plans?

"Were you going out?" he asked her, waking her from her thoughts and reminding her that the villain yet stood before her. He made room for her to pass.

"I was, yes," she said. "Excuse me. I must go and find my sister."

"I'm here," Beth said, appearing from the dining room. She had been outside, it seemed, and carried in her arms a large bouquet of flowers—peonies and irises. She was a vision, and Laynie felt a little sick. "Were you looking for me, Laynie, darling?" she asked with a voice sweet as honey and not looking at Laynie at all. "Hello," she said to the visitor. "I don't believe I've had the pleasure of making your acquaintance."

"Daniel Holbrook," he said and seemed to laugh just a little as he looked at Laynie.

Did he find them ridiculous? She looked to Beth, and the change in direction of her attention reminded her that she was not entirely innocent either, for she had, once again, been staring at him. Yes, they were certainly ridiculous!

"Bethany Durham," Beth said, "and this is my sister Alayna."

"I'm pleased to meet you," he said. "I've come to see your father."

"Has Mrs. Fowler gone for him? Are you waiting for him now?"

"Yes," he answered simply.

Laynie thought it necessary to offer some explanation. "Mr…" If only she could remember his name.

"Holbrook," he said, assisting her.

She nodded her thanks and continued. "This is our father's new reading companion, Beth. The one he told us of the other night?"

Beth turned to Laynie with a look plainly confused. She looked to him again and appeared, not unable to believe the news, but actually unwilling to do it.

"Excuse us, sir," Laynie said to him, trying to avoid a crisis. She took the flowers from Beth and laid them on the vestibule table for Mrs. Fowler to take care of when she returned. "My sister and I were just going out for a walk."

"No we weren't," Beth protested. "You never said anything about a walk."

"Well, we are." And she pulled Beth through the door, where they stopped on the front stoop to place and adjust their hats. Laynie glanced back to see her father's new companion watching the pair of them, a look of positive mirth in his eyes.

"Mr. Holbrook!" Mr. Durham said, appearing and greeting the fellow enthusiastically. "I'm so glad you could come."

Mr. Durham took the gentleman's hand as Mrs. Fowler shut the door upon the scene, leaving Beth and Laynie to stand before the front door, staring at the house, and then at each other.

"Well, what do you make of that?" Beth asked her.

But Laynie had no desire to discuss him, or the situation, or anything they had just witnessed. "Come, Beth," she said, "or we will be too late."

"Too late for what? Where are we going?"

"For a walk," Laynie answered impatiently and walked on almost too fast for her sister to keep up.

"You said that. But where? And why now?"

Laynie observed Beth take another look toward the house. "Because, Beth. I made plans today, and it would be rude to disappoint."

"To disappoint you? I don't understand."

"Not me, Beth." Laynie sighed in frustration. "We are walking Juniper Lane, with the hope of meeting Mr. Vaughn there."

"Mr. Vaughn?" And Beth stopped in the middle of the drive.

Laynie took her sleeve and pulled her along. "I understand he rides there on occasion, and that he means to ride there today. It's my hope we will run into him."

"You arranged this?"

Laynie hated to confess it in quite those terms, but it was the truth, after all. "Perhaps, I did," she said, with a sideways glance toward her sister. "I thought you deserved another chance to make things right."

Beth took one last look toward the house, just visible from the beech-lined avenue.

"Beth. Please."

Beth returned her attention to her sister. "You planned this before Mr. Holbrook came?"

"Yes, of course. And it cannot matter anyway, Beth. You heard father's admonition. We are not to think of him."

"Well it's hard not to, isn't it? Did you *see* him?"

"Oh, Beth, you really can be very trivial, you know."

"Trivial? I don't think you can call a man like that a subject of triviality. Did you see the size of him?"

"He's no taller than Mr. Vaughn, I'm quite certain."

"Only Mr. Vaughn is not built like *that*."

"Like what, Beth?" Laynie said, wholly exasperated and walking on.

"Like a Greek god, what do you think?"

"I think I would like to go for a walk, and I would like to take my sister, and I would like to give her an opportunity to recover her dignity with a man who might admire her very much if she would only behave and stop thinking of men she cannot have. Our father's *hired* companion, Beth? You say you must marry security. Tell me, will you, what manner of security you are to find with a man who hires himself out as a reading companion to country gentlemen of humble means?"

A look of disappointment crossed Beth's brow with this reminder.

"And he is married, after all." She herself had nearly forgotten and was grateful to remember this most important point. "What would Father say?"

Beth was silent for half a moment. "You are right," she said at last and hurried to catch up. "Is it going to cost Papa very much to keep him, do you think?" she asked and seemed truly irritated at the thought of it.

"If it keeps him happy it doesn't matter."

Beth seemed not to believe her and considered the visitor further. "He did seem rather dull and slow, don't you think? I mean he hardly spoke."

"Well then, he's a perfect companion to Papa, for Papa will do all the talking and all the thinking for them both, I dare say."

Beth laughed. "Yes, I think you may be right."

The conversation turned upon more mundane topics: the weather, the flowers that were in bloom, the birds, the next ball...until they reached Juniper Lane. Harry was not there, but they hadn't far to walk before he appeared. It seemed he, too, was running behind schedule.

"Mr. Vaughn!" Laynie said, pretending to be surprised. As she had informed Beth already of their plans the need for pretense was questionable. Still, Laynie was eager to impress upon her sister the likelihood that he mightn't have come at all.

"Good afternoon," he said to them both, bowing at the waist and removing his hat briefly in greeting. "Miss Laynie, Miss Durham." Again he offered that show of deference to Beth, which was a bow slightly lower and a look that was lingering.

Beth, blushing charmingly, was thankfully spared from being tongue-tied this morning. "Why, what are you doing here, Mr. Vaughn?" she asked, joining, it seemed, in the pretense of happenstance. His explanation was the same as Laynie had given.

"I was informed that you occasionally walk here, and I came to see if I might meet you. I hope I am not imposing."

Beth raised her eyebrows and lifted her chin. The gleam in her eye as she gave him a sideways glance suggested that he very well might be imposing, or, on the other hand, he might be very welcome, de-pending on how things progressed.

41

"How are my favorite sisters getting on today?" he asked them.

"Don't be silly, Mr. Vaughn," Beth answered with an impish grin. "We are not your sisters."

"Thank heaven for that!" he said and dismounted so that he might walk beside them rather than riding behind.

With two sisters, a gentleman, and a horse, it was difficult to know just who should walk where and with whom. The road was a narrow one, and as it was rarely used, the trees which lined it and which provided shade against the sun had grown so dense that there wasn't room on the path for everyone to walk side by side, particularly with Titan as Mr. Vaughn's companion. If he should be forced to walk behind, alone with his animal, then what would have been the point in arranging the walk at all?

Laynie hung back so that Mr. Vaughn could walk with Beth, but his horse repeatedly proved an impediment, as he seemed particularly intrigued by the flowers on Beth's bonnet and so kept reaching over Mr. Vaughn to nibble at them.

"Mr. Vaughn, I do wish you would control your animal," Beth protested when Titan had at last snatched hold of a silk flower.

"My apologies, Miss Durham," Mr. Vaughn said, but there was no immediate solution to the problem.

Or perhaps there was one... "Might I lead Titan for you?" Laynie asked. "There will be more room that way, and you know I love horses."

"Have you no longer horses of your own, Miss Laynie?" he asked over his shoulder.

"There is only Father's left. It's too expensive to keep them, and Papa doesn't like us gallivanting all over the country unchaperoned, as we were once used to doing."

"Well," Mr. Vaughn answered with a teasing smile, "I don't blame him for that."

"Do you fear, like he does, our getting hurt?" Beth asked him.

"No, I fear the excitement two young women such as yourselves, riding alone across the countryside, would stir up among the local gentry."

"Perhaps, after all, Father should reconsider," Beth said, "since he's so desperate to be rid of us."

"I don't think he wants us running at young men in quite so literal a sense, Beth," Laynie said and laughed.

"No," Harry returned. "Far better to keep you at home, where only carefully vetted suitors might apply."

Beth answered in the form of a dejected look in Laynie's direction. Mr. Vaughn observed it and appeared suddenly regretful. After all, if he had been vetted and granted approval to court one of Mr. Durham's daughters, that one was not Beth. Beth walked ahead, and Laynie, with a nod of her head, urged Mr. Vaughn to go after her. He handed over the reins and went in pursuit.

With Titan in hand Laynie followed, lagging behind until Beth and Mr. Vaughn were far enough ahead that their conversation could no longer be overheard. Laynie hoped very much that they would make the most of this opportunity. There would not be many like this one, particularly if and when their father learned of it. She observed Titan, who was walking along quite pleasantly, happy to nibble at Laynie's hat now that her sister's was out of reach. The flowers in her hat were not silk but dried and provided him a more palatable snack.

Laynie stopped a moment to admire him. He *was* a beautiful animal. As black as night, his coat glistened in the dappled sun as it shown through the trees. If there was anything Laynie missed in their growing extremity it was riding. She missed the liberty such exercise afforded her. It was the freedom to travel distances otherwise impossible, to fly across fields and meadows and have adventures and daily diversions of her own creating. It had always been a secret longing of hers to join the men on their fox hunts, leaping over rails and hedges and running mad-dash across the countryside.

Laynie and Titan walked on, and before long they came upon a part of the lane that bordered a meadow, where poppies and cornflowers bloomed in red and blue profusion. From here she could see the trees that surrounded her cottage home. She could even see, if she moved out into the meadow itself, the steeply pitched roof and a chimney or two. How difficult would it be to cross the meadow on horseback? The fence that divided the field in half was certainly short enough to jump. It had been some time since she had ridden, but she was certain it would all come back to her. And with her father occupied with his new companion, there was little chance of her being seen from the house. As for there being any danger, Titan was the safe, sensible sort. Surely she could get into little trouble on an animal such as him.

"What do you think, Titan?" she asked him.

He answered with a snort and a toss of his head.

It seemed it was decided, then. Laynie tucked her skirt and mounted.

* * *

Daniel Holbrook sat in Mr. Durham's well-stocked library and listened. He was somewhat anxious for the job, though no doubt there were others out there to be found if he only took the trouble to look for them. This one had presented itself to him in so propitious a manner, on the very eve he had decided he must begin looking for employment, that he was tempted to think it fate. He resisted the temptation, for the old man was likely to have his own eccentricities regarding the matter. As it turned out, they were not long to reveal themselves.

"I have not had a very exciting life," Mr. Durham was saying, as he gazed contemplatively out the bank of windows that lined one wall of his sanctuary. It looked out onto a grassy courtyard, on the other side of which was the main part of the oddly-angled house. "I have lived most of my adventures by proxy," he continued, "through books and reading and listening to the stories of others. It is my single regret in life. I loved and married early, had children—you have met my daughters, I think?"

Daniel nodded.

"And while I cannot regret any of that—and I do not, mind you—"

"Of course not," Daniel assured him.

"I do regret the experiences I've missed out on. It is partly for that that I read. And it is partly for that that I want someone to discuss with me what I've read. How long were you abroad?"

"Four years, sir."

"Four years, four years. Family troubles? Or perhaps your pilgrimage was owing to a woman."

Daniel did not answer this.

44

"It is a natural weakness of mine, to pry into the secrets and misadventures of other men's lives. Forgive me. I envy your experience. I have so precious little of my own."

"It's nothing, sir."

"You are married?"

"No, sir."

Mr. Durham minced his mouth to one side and gave him a sideways look. "Hmmm," he said. "Pity, that. I have told my girls you are. It was the only thing to do. They'd be driving you to distraction otherwise, and I want none of that here. But I suppose if there is no wife at home, there is no one to be upset if I keep you late of an evening or take up more time than she would like."

"No, sir. You have no need to worry on that account."

"Still...it is a difficulty. I can trust you, I hope, to steer clear of them."

"Yes, sir. I have no plans to marry. I am firmly committed to my bachelorhood."

"You are awfully young to confirm yourself a bachelor. You are five and twenty, did you say?"

"Eight and twenty, sir."

"How did they receive you?" Mr. Durham asked him next.

"Sir?"

"My girls. What was their manner of receiving you?"

Daniel was tempted to smile at the recollection but feared it would be misinterpreted. One of them, the younger he thought, had met him with an expression of alarm and then of mild suspicion. The other was all artifice and blushing smiles. Mr. Durham hadn't a thing to worry about. But how to answer the question?

"Let me guess," he said. "They rushed to the door to get a look at you, and then dragged each other away to lament together over your married state."

"I really have no idea," he said. "They were not unpleasant, only..."

"Desperate minxes?"

"You have to know I would never say such a thing."

"Even if you thought it?"

Mr. Durham waited for an answer, and when it didn't come he laughed. Daniel joined him, tentatively.

"Just steer clear of them," he said more seriously. "It is my one and only stipulation to my taking you on."

"You have my solemn promise, sir."

"Now," Mr. Durham said, standing, "shall I show you about the place?"

A two-story structure of whitewashed stone, the house was a collection of odd angles and asymmetry. It's gothic, traceried windows gave it an almost ecclesiastical quality, and yet it was quaint and inviting, too.

The tour of the outdoors began from dining room, where French doors led out onto a perfectly manicured lawn, in the center of which stood an extraordinary beech tree. Similar trees surrounded the entire property, but here stood the finest of them by far. Beyond the little yard lay a garden, profuse with sculptured boxwoods and flowering shrubs. In the very center stood a fountain, and against the periphery were other flowers: foxglove, hollyhocks, and the like. Directly opposite the yard near the eastward end of the house were situated the kitchen and kitchen garden, profuse with herbs and vegetables. Coming round to the far side of the kitchen garden lay a wildish area in which rambling vines, blackberry and raspberry, were allowed to grow at will along trellises designed for the purpose. Beyond this a large field of poppies spread out before them, interrupted at intervals by fences and the occasional hedgerow. Here the two men stopped to observe a horse and rider approaching through the fields at a considerable speed.

"Harold Vaughn," Mr. Durham said with a certain air of pride, "come to see my Laynie, I'll wager." His brow lowered. "And showing off, it appears. Come," he said and turned back toward the house.

Daniel, happy to follow, only hesitated long enough to observe the horse and its rider. They were running at break-neck speed and approaching a fence. Daniel watched with a certain amount of anxiety as the animal gathered its momentum as it approached the obstacle. There seemed something not quite right about it. The horse was an admirable animal, but the size and shape of the rider were completely off. In fact he was inclined to suspect it was a woman, though to jump side-saddle... Or was she riding astride? Certainly no one would be so foolish as to allow.... But it was none of his concern, truly, and he turned to follow his new employer indoors.

He stopped upon the threshold, a chill running through him, when a scream rent the air.

She didn't want his help.

Chapter seven

LAYNIE LAY ON THE GROUND, the clouds and the sun spinning like birds overhead. The wind had been knocked out of her, but she believed herself otherwise unhurt. Still, she deemed it better to lie still until she could be sure of herself. Titan, at least, had not run off. He stood nearby, cropping the grass as his bit jangled between his teeth.

She closed her eyes again and rested while she caught her breath and waited for the shock to turn to pain. Riding Titan had not seemed like such a foolish thing at first. Jumping the fence however... That was perfectly idiotic. Thank heaven no one had seen her! How mortified she would be if they had.

"Miss Durham?" came a voice from somewhere above her, low, gentle, and irritatingly concerned. "Are you hurt?"

She opened her eyes to see her father's hired companion standing over her. Oh why, out of anyone, must it be him? "Of course I'm alright, Mr.-" Oh, blast! She'd forgotten his name again.

"Holbrook."

"Yes, of course."

"Let me help you."

But she didn't want his help. And she didn't want his concern. Or was the furrowing of his brow evidence of his disapproval? What right had he to disapprove of anything she did?

Mr. Holbrook's hand was held out to her, waiting for her to take it. "I can manage," she said. Her head was still spinning and there was a vague ache in one leg. She attempted to raise herself, but thought better of it and sank back onto the ground.

"You are hurt," he said, as if he could just as easily assess her injuries as could she herself. "Please. Let me help you." This time he did not wait. He took an elbow in each hand and lifted her onto her feet as though she were nothing but a child.

"Thank you," she said, though rather tersely, and freed herself from his grasp. "I can manage."

Determined to have Titan in hand and to be on her way before her humiliation utterly overcame her, Laynie took a step forward. As her foot joined the earth, a jolting pain went through her and she collapsed to the ground.

"Miss Durham," he said in an exasperated manner, "what exactly are you trying to prove?"

He did not even attempt to help her now. He just stared down at her as if she were some errant child who needed a good scolding. But she was *not* a child. Not hardly. "I'm throwing myself at your feet, sir. Or can you not tell?"

He laughed a little. "I confess your hostility did not immediately give your purpose away," he answered. "Your ankle is injured, you cannot make it back to the house on your own. Why will you not let me help you?"

"There is nothing at all the matter with my ankle, Mr. Holbrook. I'm grateful for your concern, but it is un—"

"Miss Durham!" came another voice. She turned to see Harry Vaughn running toward her. Why could he not have come five minutes ago?

Harry stopped directly before her and looked at her a moment before glancing at Mr. Holbrook. He ignored the stranger and turned his attention once more to Laynie. "What happened?" he asked, out of breath.

"I'm afraid I've fallen, Mr. Vaughn."

"Jumping a fence." Mr. Holbrook added the unnecessary information.

"And you are...?" Mr. Vaughn demanded.

Mr. Holbrook gave his name. Harry received it without ceremony and after casting a dubious look upon him, knelt down beside Laynie.

"Are you hurt?" he asked her confidentially and pulled a mangled flower from her hair.

She glanced to see Beth, who had followed him, watching with a look half-concerned, half-frustrated. She turned back to Mr. Vaughn, whose appearance was one of unadulterated anxiety.

"I fear I may be," she answered quietly enough to avoid his hearing the catch in her voice. She was on the verge of tears. If Mr. Holbrook should see her cry she would positively despise him.

Without any further delay, Harry scooped her up and carried her toward the house. "If you'll be so good as to bring my hunter, Mr. Holbrook," Harry said over his shoulder.

Mr. Holbrook did as he was bid and took Titan in hand, while Laynie, in Harry's arms, tried to hide from his gaze. She was desperate that he should not see her cry. What a child she was being! And to think of Harry and Beth, and all the trouble she had taken to provide for them a little time together. Only to ruin it by her foolish decision to try to ride a horse far too large for her—and to jump him besides! It was more than she could endure. Mr. Holbrook watching or no, the tears came and they came freely. She buried her face in Harry's shoulder.

* * *

"Good heavens! What has happened?" Mr. Durham demanded as Laynie and Mr. Vaughn entered the house.

"It's nothing, Papa," she said, trying to reassure him and praying he would not be too alarmed at the sight of her. "I'm not very hurt." She dried her eyes and tried to look cheerful.

"Then what in heaven's name are you doing in Mr. Vaughn's arms?" he demanded.

"Miss Laynie took a bit of a spill," Mr. Vaughn explained as he carried her into the drawing room and placed her in a comfortable chair. He drew up a cushioned stool, and Laynie rested her feet upon it.

"I'm perfectly well, Papa. I just need to rest a minute and I'll be good as new."

"A spill you say?" he said to Mr. Vaughn, uncomprehending. "What manner of 'spill' is a young woman likely to have on a walk, can you tell me, Mr. Vaughn?"

"Well," he said, with apparent reluctance, "it seems she thought she might ride Titan, rather than walking him back."

Mr. Durham turned back to Laynie, wide-eyed with astonishment. "What is this? What made you think to ride Mr. Vaughn's horse? And I wonder, sir, what made you think to let her!"

"He knew nothing of my intentions, Papa," Laynie assured him. "I had the opportunity of having the animal at my own disposal, as I was holding him for Mr. Vaughn, and so I found myself wondering what it would be like to ride again."

"And so you thought you might try it? Laynie! It's been a very long time since you've been accustomed to riding."

"Yes, and at times I feel I miss it, Papa. I am sorry. It was simply a temptation too great to be resisted."

"I shouldn't be surprised, I suppose, but I must say your lack of judgment astonishes me."

A movement behind her father caught her eye. She looked to see Mr. Holbrook standing there. He had just entered the parlor from the foyer, where he had no doubt heard the greater part of the conversation. She did not appreciate him playing witness to her scolding. Beth entered and moved to stand at the window, where she alternately watched her sister and something outside.

"Are you certain you're not hurt?" her father asked her.

"I'm not hurt, Papa. Not seriously, at any rate."

"I believe it's her ankle," Mr. Holbrook answered.

Laynie gave him a dour, warning look before attempting, once more, to allay her father's mounting fears.

"I turned it. That's all. I was too close to the fence rail when Titan jumped, and my foot got caught."

"Jumped?" her father said, apparently shocked, and with that same half-condemning look on his face that she had briefly seen on Mr. Holbrook's. "Alayna Durham, what has got into you?"

Laynie was very nearly persuaded to cry once more. Her attention was summoned to the doorway upon hearing the too-familiar tisking of Mrs. Sullivan, the cook. She had entered with Mrs. Fowler whose disapprobation was offered by the silent shaking of her head.

"What have you done now, Miss Alayna?" asked Mrs. Sullivan.

"Miss Durham has fallen," Mr. Holbrook said. "Perhaps if you had some ice…"

She looked to Mr. Holbrook, her eyes large upon seeing him, and then: "Good heavens, yes!" And she left the room.

"I had better look at it," her father said and approached her.

Laynie protested. "It's just a sprain, Papa."

"Now you don't know that any more than I do. I need to know whether I ought to send for the doctor. Now let me see it."

Laynie, feeling compromised, glanced up to find Mr. Holbrook looking keenly in the direction of her skirt hem. His gaze met hers and he averted it to the window, where Harry Vaughn had long since directed his attention.

Her father felt the bone and found that it was sound. Mrs. Sullivan returned with a bundle of ice wrapped, which she placed on her ankle and then covered both it and her injury with her skirt.

With her father's rising, all eyes turned once more to her and there remained for an excruciatingly long time. Mr. Holbrook looked on with that same scrutinizing gaze she was no longer certain she could interpret. Was she a spectacle of curiosity, or was he somehow concern-ed for her? And what right had he to be concerned? She wished he would just go away.

To add insult to injury, Mr. Vaughn appeared suddenly by her side. Beth's face grew predictably redder as she stood in resentful observation of his attentiveness. It had only been Laynie's intention to place him more in the way of her sister, but here he was, attending her as though the guilt were all his to bear. She wanted only to be left alone and she said so. To her utter relief, and yet somehow to her further humiliation, the room began to clear, Mr. Holbrook setting the example by being the first to leave.

It was Beth, alone, who lingered.

"I spoiled your time with him once again. I'm so sorry, Beth."

"You know, Laynie, sometimes I think you cross me on purpose."

"You think I fell on purpose from Mr. Vaughn's horse?" Laynie said, thoroughly shocked by the suggestion.

"I think you planned our outing as a means of securing his attention toward you. You knew little would be accomplished in so short a time as you gave us. And you know how men are about damsels in distress."

"I assure you, Beth, I have no idea what you're talking about."

"Oh yes, you do," Beth hissed. "Don't pretend you don't. You know a man cannot resist a woman he has rescued. Put yourself in his way to be saved and you have all but secured him."

"Beth, no. I don't think so, truly."

"I knew you would betray me eventually, Laynie. I did not think it would come so soon!"

"Beth, please!"

But Beth had turned from her and would not turn back. The door closed with a slam, and Laynie could hear the sound of feet treading quickly up the stairs. Laynie turned once more to the window and, closing her eyes, allowed the tears to fall.

* * *

The afternoon's excitement prompted an invitation for both gentlemen to stay to dinner. Laynie, who had her meal delivered to her where she rested, found she had neither the heart nor the stomach to touch it. At last, when she deemed the company too preoccupied to miss her, and finding a rare opportunity to prey upon Mrs. Fowler's kindness, persuaded her to help her out of doors, where she might sit quite alone and unobserved in her favorite spot beneath the beech tree. There she remained, mercifully undiscovered, until she had very nearly reached the end of her second chapter.

"Are you in much pain?" Mr. Vaughn asked her as he brought a chair near hers and sat down.

"Not much, Mr. Vaughn," she answered him not quite truthfully. She observed his sober countenance. Evidently Beth had not yet forgiven him for his attentiveness toward herself. "I am sorry to have ruined your walk."

"It *was* a pleasant walk," he said and half-smiled, which did nothing to make her feel better, though she was grateful for his honesty. "Perhaps I should be flattered by her jealousy, though I hardly understand it. Truly I would have thought she'd be grateful I came to your rescue. That wasn't why I did it, of course, but a man does like to be thought of as a hero when he gets the chance."

Laynie recalled her sister's words and smiled to herself. How little Beth understood Mr. Vaughn. And how greatly she ought to appreciate him! Would she ever learn to do it?

"She has changed," he observed once again. "And it pains me to see it. She might learn to trust me, though."

"It only requires your patient persistence, Mr. Vaughn."

"Will it be enough, though?" he asked. "I wish I understood what it is that has changed her."

"Cannot you guess?"

"The usual thing, I suppose. Who?"

"Jonathan Hartright. Do you know him?"

"He married Miss Headley, did he not?"

"Beth's dearest friend from childhood, yes. He had given her every reason to believe he meant to make her an offer. In fact he had told her quite plainly he meant to ask her when his family returned from London, where they were to spend the Christmas holiday. When he returned, he was married already."

"I can only imagine her disappointment. I won't pretend I'm sorry she didn't marry him. I am sorry, however, for the pain it must have caused her. Hartright's a fool!"

"Yes, well… She has had a difficult time rallying. She is no longer so trusting. Not of anyone, myself included."

Mr. Vaughn gave her a narrow look. "Why should she distrust you?"

"I have not the slightest idea. Only she does not. Your mother's preference for me does not help things, you know."

"No. I suppose it can't."

"I confess I do not understand it, Harry. Why should she prefer me over my sister? We are both beneath your station. We both have uncertain prospects, little to bring to a marriage, and hardly a connection worth naming."

"Perhaps it's because you won't have me," he said and smiled though a little sheepishly. "But for all that neither would your sister if it were not for the money."

Laynie did not know quite what to say to this.

"I'm no fool," he said. "I know she would not even have given me a moment's consideration were it not for the prospect I might one day be a wealthy man."

"She is understandably nervous about her future."

"And you are not?"

"Of course I am. It's just that I fear more living a life without love than living in poverty. It is irrational, I know. My father often says so."

"Yes, but you see, that is precisely what recommends you to my mother. She married for money, and now she is alone. She doesn't want me to resent my wife as my father learned to resent her." He hesitated a moment, chewing on his next words, but at last spit them out. "I have told Beth that the inheritance is not so certain as she was perhaps led to believe."

"Oh dear."

"I'm aware it may make things more difficult for me."

"And so your brother may be restored? Is it likely to happen?"

"I do not know. He has no respect for my father or his hypocrisies. But if it means losing a fortune, and to his younger brother, who is to say that the ruse will not work."

"And if he does return, Harry, what is to become of you?"

Harry did not answer right away. "I like that Holbrook fellow," he said at last, changing the subject.

"Do you?"

"I do."

Once again, Harry had surprised her. "Are you not worried?"

"Because of Beth, do you mean?"

"Yes."

"He's married, isn't he? What is there to worry about? Besides, he's not Beth's type, is he?"

Laynie laughed. "I'm not sure I even know what that is."

"Of course you do," Harry said. "It is the glittering Adonis, I think. Not the powerful Hercules. It's a good thing Titan wasn't injured or he would have needed to be carried, as well. And I believe the fellow could have done it, too. He did seem a little put out not to be the one rescuing you."

"He did not! He was put out that I fell and interrupted his time with Papa, that's all."

"Well..." Harry said and attempted to stifle the impish grin he wore. "It cannot matter anyway."

"And why is that?"

"Because he's a man of honor, remember. He'd have been sacked his first day had he hefted you as I had."

56

"Hefted?" Laynie said, affronted by the implication of the word.

Harry laughed. "Forgive me, but I like the sound of it. It makes me feel rather manly, you know." Laynie, too, laughed, and Harry arose. "I had best be off. Beth's not likely to come down so late, and Mother will be worried I was gone so long. I'll see you, Miss Laynie."

"Soon, I hope," Laynie answered him.

"Of course," he said, tipped his hat, and disappeared into the house once more.

It was not long after that her father found her sitting beneath her favorite tree.

"You did not eat," he said.

"I'm not hungry."

"You can't just skip meals when you're out of sorts, you know. You'll waste away." He took a seat beside her. "Mr. Vaughn played quite the dashing hero today, didn't he, my child?" He was simply full with the idea of it, and Laynie hated to deflate him, but deflate him she must.

"You know I esteem Harry Vaughn as one of the kindest and most worthy men I know, and he is a dear, dear friend. But, truly, Papa..."

"Shhhh," her father said and placed a hand on her uninjured ankle. "It will come in time. Now off to bed with you."

Frustrated that her father simply refused to listen to her or to believe that his desires might not be in line with her own—or even with the reality of the situation—she simply stared at him, unmoving.

"You are right," he said, and she thought for an instant she had at last made him see. "I really ought to get someone to help you." He stood.

"Not if it's Mr. Holbrook!"

Her father chuckled. "He's been gone this half hour, my dear. But why do you both seem to despise my hired companion so?"

Laynie thought the question puzzling. Beth had certainly shown no signs of despising him. Of jealousy, perhaps, but even that, or so Laynie presumed, was aimed toward Mr. Vaughn rather than Mr. Holbrook. Or was it? As the question applied to herself, well... Did she despise him? She wasn't sure she would use so strong a word as

57

that. She resented his having seen her in her humiliation, and she resented more his patronizing and condescending manner, but she did not despise him. Still, she did not much care for him, either, and that was as it should be. That was as it would be. She was quite determined.

"Well, whatever the reason for your disapproval of him, don't be too unkind, will you? He is traveling a great distance to see me, and I dare say the job will be more of a nuisance to him than a pleasure. But while he comes, I mean to keep him coming if I can."

"Yes, of course, Papa."

"Now I'll go get Mrs. Fowler, and between the two of us I think we can get you to your room."

It took the both of them to do it, too, what with the stairs and the awkward passageway at the landing. Laynie was anxious to retire, to rest and to think undisturbed, but she was also anxious to speak with her sister. She was consequently disappointed to find, upon arriving to her room, that Beth was already asleep.

* * *

The position for which Mr. Durham had hired Daniel Holbrook truly was a simple one. Daniel was certainly qualified—perhaps he was overqualified. But it could not be said that the job was without its challenges. If his employment meant contending with accident-prone and vitriolic women on a semi-weekly basis, he was not so certain he was cut out for it.

But there was no turning back. At least not so soon. The terms had been agreed upon; it would be ungentlemanly, unmanly even, to allow himself to be scared off so soon. Surely things must settle down. It wasn't possible every day held a misadventure of the sort he'd witnessed today. The scene rather haunted him, and he could not say just why. Good Lord! The girl might have been killed! The vision of her lying there—broken, fallen in the grass, her brandy-colored hair unpinned and framing her head like a halo, the poppies blooming round her like blood stains on a green carpet—would not go away.

How to get rid of them?

He'd have a drink when he got home. A drink and a good night's sleep, and that would clear his head. But first he must endure an hour's train ride. An hour at least of visions of poppied fields and fallen women. Perhaps it was the metaphor that made him so uncomfortable.

Chapter eight

FOR FOUR DAYS PEACE AT the Bowery was uninterrupted by the ringing of the doorbell. The absence of any visitors was a reprieve for which Beth was at first grateful. By the end of the third day, however, her anxieties had mounted to an alarming pitch. Was it for Harry Vaughn she felt such anticipation and uncertainty? And why should he have such an effect on her? She had reasoned with herself that, after Laynie's accident, there was little chance that he would come to call upon her now. Would he not then come to call upon Laynie? It had not been so, and so his absence, as it grew more prolonged, both gave her cause to hope and to fear.

When the reprieve ended, and the doorbell at last announced the arrival of a visitor, it was all Beth could do to keep from running to the window to see who it was that had come. She waited, not quite patiently, for Mr. Vaughn to be announced.

"Miss Annabelle Sharp and Miss Harriet Fisher to see you, Miss."

Beth's heart sank. "Please show them in, won't you, Mrs. Fowler?" she said as she pasted a smile on her face and tried to welcome her friends with the warmth she knew she ought to feel.

"My dear Bethany," Miss Fisher said and approached to plant a kiss on each cheek.

Miss Sharp followed her companion's example. "How are you? You left the ball so suddenly last week and we've been hard pressed to come up with an explanation."

"It was Laynie, as usual," Beth answered. "She'd gone out in the downpour and so we had to come home early."

"Oh, that *is* a pity," Harriet answered and looked knowingly to Annabelle. "And to think what an opportunity you threw away to make an impression on Mr. Vaughn."

Beth sat up a little straighter. "Who is to say I did not make a greater impression by leaving early?" she said, echoing Laynie's opinion on the matter and hoping very much that it was true. "And I did dance with him. We did speak."

Once again, Harriet Fisher gave her companion a knowing and not altogether reassuring look.

"He has come to call," Beth added as if this alone were proof. Was it not?

"Who hasn't he called upon?" Annabelle said, taking no trouble at all to offer the reassurance Beth desperately wanted.

"What do you mean?" she inquired.

"It's nothing more than what any of us can have expected," Harriet answered.

Beth did not like the use of the word "us," as if Harriet, too, had plans to play rival.

"The father of every marriageable young lady in the county has called upon him," Annabelle explained.

"And their mothers have called upon Lady Vaughn," added Harriet. "There aren't enough hours in the day nor days in the year for him to return all the calls he has received."

Such explained Mr. Vaughn's absence. It did not offer much comfort.

"Miss Farnsworth's papa has been particularly determined on his daughter's behalf," Annabelle added, as if it were a point of great interest.

"Was it not Miss Farnsworth with whom Mr. Vaughn danced after Bethany quit the ball?" Harriet asked her companion.

"I think it was," Annabelle answered. "The two following, if memory serves. And the last as well."

"The last?" That was three, all told. Beth was not sure how much more she could hear.

"I wouldn't worry," Annabelle said to her, "I doubt she has much of a chance. His mother does not care for her, you know, and so she has no reason at all to hope—" She stopped suddenly and blushed again, as if she had very nearly said something amiss. Her ending her thought so precipitately did nothing to remedy the fact that Bethany was not a favorite of Lady Vaughn and that her friends knew it to be so. Who else knew?

"Of course speculation is running wild in regards to whom his mother will ultimately choose for him," Annabelle continued, as Harriet nodded conspiratorially.

"You do not think he will be allowed to choose for himself?" She knew he must gain his mother's approval, but the idea that the whole thing might be arranged for him had never crossed her mind.

"With a fortune in the balance?" Harriet answered. "I doubt it very much! You do know the reason for William's being cut off, don't you?"

Beth did not answer, only waited for the explanation she knew was coming. If there was gossip to be heard it was sure to be heard from Harriet, for she reveled in such things.

Harriet perched herself at the very edge of her chair. "He engaged himself to a French woman. A governess, whose brother is in some kind of trouble with the law. I doubt very much Mr. Vaughn will be so reckless as to go against his mother when he has seen firsthand the consequences of doing so. But you did not care for him anyway, and so it cannot be a very great loss."

"Oh, it isn't," Beth answered and determined it would not be. Yet no matter how she tried, she would not be quite convinced.

"If your sister will have him, it would be a very good thing for you both, though, I should think," Harriet added.

"And why should Laynie have him?" Beth said, trying to affect enough patience to mask her alarm.

"Because," Annabelle said and laughed as though Beth was the epitome of naiveté, "at the moment she is Lady Vaughn's first choice. You can't be ignorant of the fact."

"I knew that Lady Vaughn was fond of her..."

"Oh, she's more than fond of her," Harriet assured her. "She's made no secret of her preference. In fact she was heard to tell your sister in no uncertain terms how happy it would make her if she would consider her son."

"When? How?" Beth asked but feared she already knew.

"Why, at the ball at Ashworth, of course."

"Whoever would have thought that Laynie would one day prove to be your rival?" Annabelle said as though the idea fairly astounded her, but the mirth in her eyes betrayed the fact that she thought the situation quite humorous.

Beth considered it anything but. In fact she was somewhat dumbfounded. It wasn't as though the idea hadn't crossed her mind. Of course it had. But to hear it spoken of as if the matter were quite set in stone made her wonder anew at what her sister was capable of. She reconsidered her suspicion—that which she had so recently repented of—that perhaps all of Laynie's "fixes" and "accidents" were not quite so accidental as her sister would like to convince her they were. The time to underestimate her was at an end, it seemed.

If Beth had changed in the year that followed her disappointment, so had Laynie. Her sister had once been a clumsy girl with a predilection for getting herself into trouble: falling into streams and ponds, saying just the wrong thing to the wrong person at the very worst time. Why, she'd even been shot at once, having accidentally come upon a hunting party on one of her early morning walks. But Laynie, who had always been considered rather plain and unexceptional, was no longer either of those things. And what's more, people were beginning to take notice.

"She says she does not want him," Beth said, as much to reassure herself as to inform her friends of the pointlessness in Lady Vaughn's planning in behalf of her son.

"Does not want him?" Harriet said as if she did not understand the meaning of the words. "How is that possible? She'd be a fool to refuse him!"

"You said he had come to call," Annabelle said and sat forward in her chair. "Was it Laynie he came to see?"

"He came to see us both. We have long been good friends, remember. In fact I'm tempted to think he came to see me, if you want to know." And she *had* been tempted to think it. Hadn't Mr. Vaughn been a little more attentive to her than to her sister? Had his looks and smiles not lingered upon her a little longer than had those he had offered to Laynie?

"And what does Laynie think of that?" Annabelle asked as if she had read Beth's very thoughts. Of course she hadn't. She was merely asking the next logical question.

"Is she jealous?" Harriet seconded.

"Laynie is never jealous." That was the answer she wished to give, but instead she found herself considering the question a little more carefully. There had been Laynie's evening soak in a late summer storm, there had been Mr. Granger's timely arrival... and there had been a fall from a horse. Would Laynie really have gone to such lengths? Perhaps the better question was, would Beth have done so? The answer, inconvenient as it was for her to admit, was yes.

"I have heard," Annabelle said, speaking more quietly now, "that Mr. Vaughn was quite the hero the other day. That his mother, in consequence, is especially pleased with him, and that the injured party was sufficiently grateful to give all other concerned parties a great deal of hope that the desired union is on its way to being a sure thing."

"I very much hope you are not speaking of my sister, Miss Sharp," Beth said and felt the temptation to redden. Her color, when in consequence of a gentleman's attention, was easy enough to control. When it was attached to her anger, it was nigh to impossible.

"It's like a fairy tale," Harriet said, too wrapped up in the romance of the story to observe what pain it caused Beth to hear her raptures. But then Beth had denied her interest in him. *Was* she interested in him? Perhaps she was, just a little.

"It's as if it were meant to be," Annabelle said, agreeing with her friend.

"No, it is not," Bethany said in rebuttal and with a little less patience than was entirely polite. "What is meant to be is two people in love and prepared to fight against all odds. What is meant to be is that which could never have been without those two people willing to sacrifice whatever they must to be together. *That* is what is meant to be!"

Harriet and Annabelle were both silent after this. At last, and only after a very long and awkward silence, did Harriet dare to speak.

"I did not realize you felt so strongly about the matter, Miss Durham," she said and stood.

Annabelle followed her friend's example. "If I said anything to—" she began but was stopped by Laynie, who, with a book in one hand and a blanket in the other, had just entered the room.

Beth, along with her now reluctant companions, only stared at her, waiting to know what it was she wanted.

"Good afternoon, Miss Fisher, Miss Sharp," Laynie said to them.

They answered with silent curtseys.

"Did you know Mr. Vaughn has come, Bethany? Shall I—"

"I will be ready to receive him momentarily," Beth said and did not mind at all that her voice sounded haughty. "Miss Fisher and Miss Sharp were just leaving."

Harriet and Annabelle looked at each other, accepted their dismissal, and wished Bethany a cool good-day.

"Laynie will show you out. Won't you, dear?"

"Yes, certainly," Laynie said and left the room to do just that. Leaving Beth to do what she might to restore her equanimity before Mr. Vaughn should join her. She was, by now, very anxious to see him.

* * *

"Is everything quite all right?" Laynie asked, concerned by the contention she had apparently interrupted and by the subsequent looks of disapproval and irritation on the faces of Beth's friends as she led them toward the foyer and to the front door.

"Your sister, it seems, is not in the mood for visitors this morning," Miss Sharp answered. "I wish she would have said so from the outset."

"I'm beginning to think she was not quite truthful with us on more than one point," Miss Fisher added.

Laynie only looked at them in confusion and continued to lead the way.

"Are you limping, Miss Laynie?" Miss Sharp asked of her. "Oh, of course. I nearly forgot about your fall!"

Harriet, thus reminded, took Laynie by the arm, but rather than taking some of her weight, she seemed to add to it. "Do tell me about it, won't you? It's simply too romantic to hear in bits and snatches from people who were not even there to see it. How did it happen? Did Mr. Vaughn truly rescue you? And was he as heroic as they say?"

"They?" Laynie asked, and she grew as confused as she was humiliated. "Are people talking about it? And how can 'they' know anything at all of the matter?"

A knock was heard at the door just as Laynie, along with her guests, entered the foyer. She had meant to show them out herself, but perhaps it was best, after all, to wait for Mrs. Fowler, who might show out her sister's friends as she greeted their newest caller. Laynie would then be free to go out—as she had planned to do—to sit beneath her tree. That plan changed the moment the door was opened.

"Good day, Mr. Holbrook," Mrs. Fowler said by way of greeting. "Won't you come in? Mr. Durham is waiting for you."

He glanced at Laynie, who was trying desperately to think of some way to avoid having to face him in the too small foyer.

"Who is that?" Annabelle whispered with apparently great interest.

"Excuse me," Laynie said without answering, and desperate for any means of avoiding Mr. Holbrook, all the more so now she knew the news of her accident had been sounded abroad, "Mrs. Fowler will show you out," and she made her way to the dining room, toward the doors that would take her out into the garden where she would be safely alone.

To her chagrin, Miss Sharp and Miss Fisher followed her. One took her book, and the other her blanket, and together assumed the role of assisting Laynie out of doors. She resented such an affectation of rendered assistance as it portrayed Laynie in rather a more helpless light than she wished to display.

Having arrived at her chaise, having been helped into it, and having her rug placed over her, Laynie prepared to wish the young ladies good bye. Only it seemed they were yet determined to remain. Harriet, taking the chair opposite, sat and encouraged Annabelle to make herself comfortable on the grass. Which she readily did.

"You were going to tell us about your accident," Harriet pressed.

"Oh, yes," Annabelle seconded, as she drew her attention reluctantly away from the house.

"Was I?" Laynie answered, uncertain she wanted to relate her humiliation to the county's most accomplished gossip.

"You were," she said and sat forward, prepared to listen and to do it attentively.

Laynie proceeded to explain how she and her sister were walking with Mr. Vaughn in Jupiter Lane, and how, as the path was not wide enough for the three of them together, Laynie had offered to walk with Mr. Vaughn's horse so that he would not be encumbered by him.

"And you rode him," Harriet said, interrupting her.

"Yes," Laynie said, hesitating. "How did you...?"

"Everyone's talking of it," Harriet explained. "Someone saw you, you know. I don't know who, though I suppose it must have been someone among your staff."

"Our staff? Mrs. Fowler, do you mean? Or—"

"I'm sure I don't know," Harriet interrupted impatiently. "But word got to Elverton and when Mr. Vaughn related to his mother how his visit to the Bowery had gone, the story—which no one quite believed—was corroborated, and the tale of Mr. Vaughn's heroism has spread like wildfire."

"Along with my foolishness, I take it."

"No one blames you," Annabelle assured her. "In fact, to some of us, you are rather a heroic figure yourself."

"Heroic? How so?"

"It's hardly any woman who would fling herself from a horse to win a gentleman's attention," Harriet replied.

"That was not— I did not—"

"Did you really hurt it?" Annabelle asked and looked toward Laynie's covered ankle.

"Yes, I did!" she answered, stopping just short of offering proof by baring the injury for them to see.

"How did you manage it?" Annabelle asked.

"Manage what?"

"To hurt your ankle, of course!"

She was reluctant to say, but perhaps telling the tale, in its bald truth, would somehow strip it of some of its romance and make it one a little less likely to be retold. "When Titan jumped the fence, my ankle caught between him and the post and turned, catching on the post and pulling me from the horse."

It seemed to work. Harriet and Annabelle were no longer so interested in her story. In fact something else entirely had arrested their attention. Laynie looked to see Mr. Holbrook arranging chairs in the formal garden, where, it seemed, he and her father were preparing to read.

"Who *is* that gentleman?" Annabelle asked once again. "And why in Heaven's name did you not introduce us to him when you had the chance?"

"He is only my father's hired companion," Laynie explained. "He's no one of importance."

"Hired?" Annabelle asked, apparently confused—or perhaps disappointed. "Him?"

Harriet, with some difficulty, turned her attention back upon Laynie. "And so it was Mr. Vaughn who found you lying upon the ground?"

"It was not he alone who found me."

"I heard he carried you back in his arms? Is it so?" Annabelle asked, returning her attention once more to the story.

"Yes," Laynie answered flatly. "But it was no more than any friend would do."

"How romantic!" Annabelle exclaimed, as if she had not heard her. "Is that not the most romantic thing you've ever heard, Harriet?"

"It wasn't romantic at all. I felt an idiot."

"I'm sure Mr. Vaughn would never think so ungenerously toward you as that," Harriet said in an attempt to sound reassuring.

"As I said, he was not the only one to come to my rescue. I made a complete fool out of myself. Please, I do not want to talk about it."

"You had *two* heroes?" Annabelle said, completely enthralled by the idea. "Who was the other?"

"How are you today, Miss Durham?"

In her desperation to be at an end with her story telling, she had failed to notice Mr. Holbrook approach.

Her cheeks burned hot as she glanced up at him. "I'm very well, thank you, Mr. Holbrook."

Laynie's companions, too, were gazing up at the great height of the gentleman, utterly transfixed. He acknowledged them with a glance, but the greater part of his attention remained on Laynie. She supposed she ought to introduce him. It was the polite thing to do. She would much rather not.

"Miss Sharp, Miss Fisher," she said, determining at last to be civil if not actually friendly, "my father's hired companion, Mr. Holbrook."

"My pleasure," he said to them.

They giggled and blushed their replies. He took only a passing notice.

"Your ankle still troubles you," he said with a glance at the blanket. No doubt he had witnessed the manner by which she had arrived in the yard. Still, her humiliation was quite fresh. She wished to reassure him, and thus send him on his way.

"On the contrary," she said. "It was not a very serious injury. In fact it's almost as good as new." And, feeling that some proof, this time, was actually necessary, she raised her ankle beneath the blanket and wiggled it. The blanket, in consequence of the disturbance, slipped from her lap and revealed her bare ankle in all its bruised and swollen glory.

"Dear heaven!" Harriet exclaimed, while Annabelle gasped and covered her mouth with one hand. The shock of the injury was quickly replaced with the shock of what she had done—showing her bare ankle to a gentleman. Laynie had thought she was humiliated before. It was nothing compared to this!

"Yes, I see," said Mr. Holbrook, with one eyebrow firmly raised and did not turn away as she covered it once more with the blanket. The effort to replace the blanket succeeded in dislodging the book that had been lying, quite forgotten, on her lap. It tumbled to the ground to rest at his feet. It would have been nothing for either Miss Sharp or Miss Fisher to retrieve it, but, as if they were accomplices to her efforts to charm and attract—and by whatever means necessary—they simply watched and waited for Mr. Holbrook to do it instead.

He took a step forward, knelt and picked it up. In his kneeling position he was at eye level with her. He looked at her a moment, apparently oblivious to the fact that her companions were both watching on as if her embarrassment were a one-act play of high drama.

"Your bruise," he said and handed her the book.

"My—?" she asked but stopped. It was a mistake, and she had realized it in the same moment he did.

The evidence of his realization was in the sudden redness of his face, and in the way he blinked as he stood. "Your book, of course," he corrected himself.

"Yes, of course," she said. "Thank you."

He remained half a moment more, bowed his head to her and then to each of her companions, and returned to the garden where her father was now waiting for him, having returned from indoors with their afternoon's reading.

Her companions tittered as he walked away. Laynie didn't laugh. She was embarrassed, and as much for him as for herself.

"Was *he* the other?" Harriet asked her when he was safely out of hearing.

It took a moment for Laynie to realize she had been spoken to and another to register the question. "The other?"

"Who came to your rescue, yes."

"I—" but she did not want to acknowledge his assistance in so noble a light. He was there, yes, to witness her in her humiliation. He had been there to make her feel just how foolish she had been. "It wasn't like that, you know. He is married."

"He most certainly is not," Harriet said, quite assuredly.

"Of course he is."

Harriet wrinkled one brow dubiously. "Very well," she said. "If you say so."

"Does it not trouble you," Anabelle said, sitting close enough to her to rest her arms on the lounge, "that after all your hard work and sacrifice it is Bethany Mr. Vaughn is presently in company with? Perhaps, after all, it was not *his* attention you sought to win." And Annabelle, with a nod, indicated the formal garden, and the gentlemen sitting within it.

"I assure you, Miss Sharp, if I wanted my father's attention, I need only ask for it."

"It was not your father I meant, Miss Laynie. It was—"

"I know what you meant!" Laynie said, having reached the limit of her patience. "I have a little more self-respect than to risk my neck simply to gain the attention of a gentleman. And I would be very ashamed of myself indeed if I sought by any means to attract the attention of a gentleman who was already married and who my father expressly forbade me to think of."

Harriet's brow knotted more firmly over her close-set eyes. "If he is married, then why would your dear papa feel it necessary to issue such an unnecessary restriction?"

"I—" Laynie began but stopped. "I think I have had quite enough of your impertinent questions for one afternoon, ladies. Good day to you."

Harriet and Annabelle, surprised to be thus addressed, looked alternately to each other and to Laynie. At last Harriet arose. "I think I know when I have outstayed my welcome," she said and helped Annabelle up, and without another word they took their leave, walking away arm in arm and with their heads very close together.

* * *

Beth and Mr. Vaughn had decided upon a walk. That is, Beth had decided. Now she had Mr. Vaughn wholly to herself, she would take no further risks with unwanted company—her sister's included. They had come to the end of the drive and now stopped to stand for a moment beneath the shade of the trees. Beth adjusted her hat and looked up at him from beneath the brim of it. He was not unhandsome. He was no Jonathan Hartright, but he had merit of his own. He had little in the way of charisma, and yet there *was* a certain charm about him. A quiet, unassuming, comfortable charm. What more did Mr. Vaughn possess than these? And what would it take to find out?

"Which way should we go?" he asked her.

"I'll leave it to you to choose," she said.

He looked around, up the lane and down. His attention at last fixed upon a spot not far in the distance, just within view of the house, where a winding, tree-lined path led to a clearing at the top of one of the larger hills. "What about there?" he said, pointing. "Is it a difficult climb?"

"Hangman's Hill? I don't like to go up there."

"Ghosts?"

Beth shuddered. "Even the horses won't climb it. Laynie will, though. In fact it is one of her favorite walks. She goes up to the

71

precipice—God's Precipice, she calls it—to think when things get to be too much for her."

"Is that wise, do you think?"

"I don't know," Beth said, and was tempted to resent his display of protectiveness in Laynie's behalf. "Why shouldn't it be?"

"It only seems to me that, considering your sister's propensity to rush into harm's way," he answered with an air of frustration that was certainly reassuring, "should she find herself overwhelmed by life's difficulties and desirous of contemplating them, she perhaps ought not to be going off alone to some *precipice* to do it."

Beth laughed. "No, perhaps not," she said, grateful to find that his hero's spirit had not been piqued beyond reason. If he could still find fault with last week's damsel, that was a very good thing for her chances. She took his arm. "Shall we walk near the stream? Perhaps you'll spy a place you might like to try at fishing."

"I didn't bring my rod, Miss Durham."

"I didn't mean today, particularly," and she laughed in affectionate deprecation.

"No. Of course not," he said in reply. "Besides. I can think of more pleasant things to do today than fishing."

"Like what, I wonder?" she asked and eagerly awaited his answer.

He looked to the ground, shook his head and looked up again with a coy smile on his face. "Shall we?" he asked, instead of offering a proper answer.

It was not quite what she had hoped for, but it was something. It was certainly something.

"We had begun to fear you had given up on us, Mr. Vaughn," Beth said when they had gone a little way in companionable silence.

"Given up? Certainly not," he said and smiled awkwardly. "That is, four days is hardly an eternity. If I had more time at my leisure…"

"Of course you have been very busy."

"Have I?"

"Well, certainly. What with all your visitors and the calls you must consequently return. You must find it exhausting."

He looked at her narrowly.

"Or perhaps you enjoy so much..." she had planned to say 'attention' but thought better of it, "...company."

Still he looked at her. Was his disinclination to answer a means of avoiding the conversation? Or was it, instead, a sort of rebuke? She did not like to be kept guessing about such things. Were there other young ladies he was considering or weren't there? She decided to take the direct approach. "How do you find Miss Farnsworth?"

He stopped and looked at her. "Miss Farnsworth?"

But Beth offered nothing in clarification, only waited, as silently as he had done, for a satisfactory reply.

"Miss Durham, I'm not exactly sure what it is you mean? My time is not quite my own, it is true, but I'm hardly what you would call busy—and certainly not in paying calls to the Miss Farnsworths of my supposed acquaintance. My mother has been very ill."

"Oh?" Beth said and felt a little guilty. "I hope it is nothing serious."

"To be quite frank with you, Miss Durham, I do not know that it isn't."

She took his arm once more. "I'm so very sorry. If you are here, I hope that means she is recovering."

"She is better today, yes," he said, and his smile seemed to suggest forgiveness. "But not quite recovered, no." They walked on.

"Is there a name for her malady?" she asked, and found herself truly and deeply concerned. Perhaps she did not much like Lady Vaughn, and perhaps Lady Vaughn did not much care for her, but Harry did, and that was what mattered. "What does the doctor say?"

"No name has been given to it as yet. It comes and goes, but the spells seem to attack with increasing ferocity. The doctors do agree that her case is more severe now, exacerbated by recent strain...but then there has lately been a great deal of strain."

They came to a little clearing, where the sun shone down warmly upon them. Beth stopped her walking and faced Mr. Vaughn. "I am sorry about your father," she said. She imagined his mother must have suffered similarly as she had suffered Mr. Hartright's betrayal, only after being married to him for years upon years! "It must have come as such a shock."

"It was a veritable earthquake! It might have been worse had Society not rallied around her. My father's scandal, thank heaven, was entirely his own undoing. She handled it all with such dignity that many have come to see her as a sort of champion of the wronged and betrayed. It does not mean, however, she has not suffered from his betrayal. She's suffered quite acutely, in fact."

"And now your brother has disappointed her."

"It is almost more than she can bear, I fear."

She was sorry for this. Sorrier still for what it must mean for her. She wondered, in consequence, why he wasted his time. What was it he hoped to achieve? Perhaps nothing, after all. Perhaps she was merely an idle pastime for him. Something to do until some more worthwhile opportunity came his way.

"It is good of you to dedicate so much of your time to us. I'm sure there are others who would welcome your company as much as my sister and I do."

"Is that a clever way of telling me my time would be better served elsewhere?" he said.

"That, I suppose, is for you to say."

"No, it isn't," he said, stopping and turning to her once more. "If that is what you mean to say, then say it."

"It isn't. It's just that..."

"Yes, Miss Durham?"

"Your mother is ill, Mr. Vaughn, we do not want to displease her. That she has formed a preference in your behalf is no secret."

Mr. Vaughn stood more upright and seemed to consider; but did he agree with her, or did he find some fault in her assertion?

"Perhaps it is Laynie you came to walk with, after all. I'm sorry her injury prevents her from doing it. I'm sorry it is me you must walk with instead."

"Are you truly angry with me still?" he asked her. "Tell me, won't you, would you rather I had not gone to her that day? Ought I to have remained by your side? Would you have been perfectly satisfied had we together left her to suffer alone whatever horrible fate had befallen her?"

It took her a moment to reply to this. When at last she thought of one, it was a simple truism. "She was not alone. Mr. Holbrook was there."

"But you could not have known that until you had seen him there for yourself."

"She meant to do it."

"What?"

"She fell on purpose. She was jealous of your attention, and so—"

"I cannot tell you how very disappointed I am to hear you say that, Miss Durham."

"I'm sorry, but it's true."

"But it isn't, and I think you know it. Your sister is not the jealous type. She is neither coquettish nor coy. She is never flirtatious or toying, she is never vindictive or cunning. So tell me, will you, how you came to this absurd conclusion?"

There was no answer she could reasonably offer. She had formed the suspicion, she had entertained it and nourished it, and Miss Sharp and Miss Fisher had come this morning with their testimonies to seal her condemnation. And if it wasn't true, and Laynie was none of those deplorable things, then what was she? And what was Beth by comparison?

"I need not tell you, I think, how unbecoming is jealousy, and how, in your case, it is utterly unnecessary."

"But—"

"The bald fact is, Miss Durham, my own preference does not fall perfectly in line with my mother's. I regret it, but there is nothing I can presently do about it. I might suggest, while we are on the subject however, that *you* might."

"Me?" Beth said, stunned by the implication. What could she possibly do to change Lady Vaughn's opinion of her? And if she could, could she change it so much as to persuade her to alter her preference for herself?

"If I have not made my intentions perfectly clear," Mr. Vaughn continued, "it is not because I do not know them or have some desire yet to look about me before I commit to them, but rather, Miss Durham, because I do not feel you are ready to hear them."

75

Beth was taken aback. What exactly was he saying? And how was she to feel about it?

"Until you are certain of yourself, I see no purpose in making any declarations that can only end in disappointment. At the moment, it seems, we are playing a waiting game. I to see what it is you decide you want, and you, I think, to see what I might be worth to you. It is not much of a compliment to me, I'm afraid."

"Mr. Vaughn, I—"

"Take some time, Miss Durham, and consider carefully before you speak. You won't reject me twice, you know. I won't give you the chance to do it. A little time is wanted for us both. And so I'll wish you good day. I have other calls to pay this morning, after all. A great many of them, as you have been so good to remind me."

And without another word, he left her to watch him retreat and to wonder why it was he insisted on torturing her so. Was he not a little unjust? Or was he, after all, stating the matter entirely correctly? And which, when all was said and done, was worse?

For the life of her, she could not say.

Chapter nine

THE WHISTLING OF THE KETTLE awoke Daniel from his thoughts. He looked at the book sitting open and unread on his lap. Sighing, he arose and removed the kettle from the hob, and then he took it into the kitchen to cool. He had changed his mind about the tea. It was something stronger he needed. He poured a glass of brandy, took a sip and then set it down on the table beside his reading chair. He sat again and watched it. The amber liquid was a balm in many respects, a bane in others. The effects of the balm were no longer working. The bane of it threatened him. His father had been an alcoholic. His mother, too. The shrillness of the kettle reminded him of her. The stoic emptiness of the room when the shrilling had quit reminded Daniel of him. Or at least the absence of him. But they were both gone now, drowned in an accident on a seaside holiday. Daniel had been left in the care of his grandfather, and that was where he had remained.

He arose once more and drained the brandy into the slop bucket, having decided upon the tea, after all. He poured the hot water into a teapot and added the leaves, then watched as the water changed in color, first to a pale yellow, then amber like the brandy, darkening until it was just the color of her hair.

Good Lord, what was he thinking of?

He placed the cover on the pot with a clatter and turned to lean against the sink, examining with some dissatisfaction his cramped, little kitchen. It was not a proper gentleman's flat, this. A family had lived here before him, but he had wanted a kitchen. He had grown used to taking care of himself and had no real desire to go out of doors three or four times a day—two at the very least—to get his meals. But the apartment was too large for him. He ought to take a roommate.

He could use the money. At least it would help until he knew just where he stood. His grandfather had left him everything: a house that was falling down, a portfolio of investments that were, every one of them, on the brink of bankruptcy—thanks to a few unscrupulous speculators—and a list of portable property that was more a burden than it was a blessing. At least he could not think of selling it. It would be as one more betrayal to his grandfather who, after all was said and done, had loved him very much.

Daniel, tired of waiting, poured the tea into a cup and returned to the sitting room. He sipped at it as he stood, looking out the window onto the London street below him. He had not particularly wanted to come to Town, but he needed something to do with his time. And yes, a little money, if he could get it. There was not a great deal of work, however, for a man raised to be a gentleman but who had not much lived like one, and who had, in recent years, eschewed all connections in favor of independence—abroad and alone.

He sat down once more and set the tea aside—it needed cream and he had none—and resumed that burdensome occupation of thinking. He was nearing thirty, and yet it seemed to him that he, too, was still a child in many ways. While at Cambridge he had fallen in love and had wished to marry. His grandfather thought him too young. He must take a year abroad first—a year to gain some experience and perspective—and then, if Daniel still loved the girl when he returned, and she him, his grandfather would give his consent. Daniel had returned from his *grand tour* unenlightened and, worse still, un-prepared for the disappointment that awaited him on the docks at Dover. He got no closer to Brookdale (his family home near Cranbrook) than Ashford, where he turned around and boarded another ship.

He'd been gone four years; that's what he told people. But really it had been five. The first year was out of obedience, the subsequent four out of rebellion. The first year was meant to educate him. What were the other four meant to do? He had not used his time well at all.

And now here he sat, as if it would do him any good at all, trying to escape from old memories by entertaining new ones. It was rather working at the moment.

This job of his… He shook his head at the thought. The old man was a loveable eccentric, burdened, as Daniel was, with too much time and—as Daniel most certainly was not—by a family he adored and who adored him in turn. Daniel could not stop himself from thinking of it. And yet he had no right to do it. Mr. Durham almost treated Daniel as a son, like family. But the effort, though it was a sincere and well-meaning one, left him feeling all the more out of place. A man who has willingly and purposefully turned his back on family—on every connection in the world—had no right to claim them later, particularly when they are not his own.

He was torn. A sworn bachelor, resolved to accept that his chances at love had been spent and thrown away, and yet he found himself unexpectedly—inexplicably—tempted…tempted by some vain streak of madness to consider, with no small degree of wonder, the brandy-haired daughter of his employer.

There was only one thing that seemed to keep the past at bay now, and that was contemplating the newness of his present circumstances. Recent events, pleasant employment in the country, an eccentric old gentleman…a horse-flung woman. These were distracting indeed. Perhaps they were too distracting, for they always ended with the same image. An image he ought not to be contemplating at all. Ankles the color of eggplant.

Daniel arose. There were things he needed to do. He had put them off long enough. His past was haunting him for a reason. He had questions, a thousand of them, that would not be answered sitting here, letting his mind roam where it would. Always to the same place.

No, it was Sophie he ought to be thinking of now. Sophie and the myriad questions that required answering before he could ever begin to be at peace with his old life. He arose, took up his coat, and made his way to the station.

* * *

Daniel, not many hours later, found himself standing before a large house of timber and stone, somewhat similar in size and situation to his own, at least as old and nearly as tumble-down.

The door of the house was situated within the shelter of an arched recess, and Daniel stood there a moment or two before at last summoning the courage to grasp the knocker. After the third attempt produced no answer, he went around to the back and startled a woman in the act of plucking a chicken.

"Pardon me," he said to her. "I was hoping I might find Mr. Charles Hamilton at home."

"You might'a done an hour ago, sir," she said as she went back to her work, feathers flying all about her as another, younger woman struggled to coax them into a sack.

"He's gone out," this one said, pointing a downy finger in the direction of the garden gate and the meadow that lay beyond. "He ought to be comin' back any time now. Ye might catch 'im on 'is way."

Daniel thanked her and went off in the direction indicated. How would Hamilton receive him? With pleasure? With shame? With surprise? The last time he had seen him… He closed his eyes against the vision. There was no avoiding it. It must be relived, but he would deal with that when the time came.

Of course memories of Hamilton were not all bad. They had been very close friends at one time. They had first met in public school. The once slight-of-build Charlie Mason—for that had been his name then—was an easy target for the sixth form bullies. Young Hamilton's sensitive nature had excited Daniel's more protective one, and Charlie soon found himself under Daniel's care. The bond remained intact for nearly three years, until the death of the young boy's father required that he return home to live with the aunt and uncle who had given him their name—and the respectability that went with it. Years later the acquaintance was renewed when they'd met again at university. Now though, Charlie Mason was Charles Hamilton, much improved in circumstance and yet still as humble and jolly as ever. Daniel had no reasonable cause to believe Hamilton would have betrayed him. And yet he *had* been there the day of Daniel's first return, four years ago, and he had been there with *her*. What explanation could Hamilton possibly give? And was Daniel prepared to hear it?

He had crossed the meadow and was nearing the copse beyond, when Daniel caught sight of a strange figure emerging from the woods. Whether it was beast or man he could not yet distinguish. There were so many odd angles to it that he couldn't make it out at all. As he trudged on, the shape before him gradually began to take on a recognizable form, and Daniel was relieved to discover that the curious figure was none other than the man he sought, laboring under the weight of some immense burden.

"What extraordinary timing you have," the gentleman said with some trouble—he was fairly winded—once they were at last within speaking distance. His manner, casual and friendly, did not suggest that Hamilton had any reason for shame or guilt. There was not the slightest hint of apology there. Not even, if truth be told, any indication that his friend had observed his absence.

"What have you there?" Daniel asked, nodding to the large gray dog in Hamilton's arms.

"It appears my companion found himself caught between a man and his dinner, likely hoping for his own."

"He's been shot?"

"Front leg."

"It looks serious."

"I suspect he's more starved than injured."

"A wolfhound?"

"Yes," Hamilton answered, straining under the weight of his load. "It seems you've come along at just the right time. Would you mind?"

"Let me," Daniel said and took the burden upon himself, the dog's long legs dangling awkwardly.

"Thank you, Holbrook," Hamilton said, and shook out his arms as he labored to catch his breath. He looked at Daniel and smiled. "I can't tell you how immensely glad I am to see you."

He plainly meant it. Perhaps he felt no guilt because he bore none. Perhaps, after all, Daniel was ready to hear Hamilton's side of it.

"Is he yours?" Daniel inquired, once more nodding toward the dog. He was young by the looks of him, no more than four months, perhaps. Had he been any older, Hamilton would never have been able to carry him alone.

"No. I happened upon him."

"That was rather fortunate, I should think. For him at least."

"Shall we?" Hamilton suggested, and he led the way back to the house. Once there, they entered through the kitchen where Hamilton hastily cleaned off a table, while the cook objected volubly. Daniel set

81

the dog down as directed. The animal lay there quietly, his large brown eyes gazing up at him in a peculiarly fixed fashion.

"How are you, Holbrook?" Hamilton asked as he removed his coat and rolled up his shirt sleeves so that he might examine more closely the dog's injuries.

"I'm well enough, I suppose."

"If you'll just keep petting him while I clean this up," Hamilton said, "he might just stay calm enough to let me do it."

Daniel nodded and Hamilton set to work cleaning the wound.

"The last time I saw you..." Hamilton began and glanced up from his work.

"Was in Dover, yes," Daniel answered. This was why he had come, after all, so why did he feel such apprehension for the subject? Fear, he supposed. The fear of knowing the truth and of it not providing him with the peace he sought.

"I wish you had told me you were returning when you did," Hamilton said, his attention remaining fully upon the dog's injured leg. "I might have done something to prepare you. If I had known where to send to, I might have written."

"You might have," Daniel answered. "But would you have done?"

Hamilton looked up at him and seemed to consider the question. "I don't know," he said. "Who wants to deliver that kind of news? Have you the hot water, Mrs. Huxley?" he asked, addressing the cook who was not at all pleased to have so large a dog in her kitchen, even if he was injured. The water was delivered. "It *was* an astounding coincidence that you should arrive in Dover at the very moment we should be there," Hamilton concluded.

"That is your explanation, is it?" Daniel asked of his friend. At least they had used to be friends. What were they now? "You really mean to tell me that you did not write because you did not believe I would find out until it was too late that you had arranged for the woman I intended to marry to marry another?"

Hamilton, finished washing the wound, looked up at Daniel once more. He then proceeded to dress the injury, and several minutes passed before he spoke again. "Perhaps we ought to take our discussion upstairs," he said and glanced at the cook. "If you were to find him something to eat, Mrs. Huxley..."

With a wry look, she answered him grumblingly but immediately set about the task.

Daniel lifted the dog again as Hamilton led the way, carrying the blanket up to the drawing room where he laid it in front of the fire. Daniel placed the dog once more on his bed, and there the animal stayed, watching the gentlemen as they moved about the room.

The house from the inside confirmed Daniel's suspicion that it was an old one, complete with cracked and peeling walls, doors that did not quite fit their frames and a floor that squeaked loudly however carefully one walked. The walls were sparsely adorned: a few tapestries, a landscape or two, not a portrait in sight. Hamilton was not married, then. No woman would live here willingly. Not without making some necessary improvements. Dark and gloomy as it was, the house's interior was an odd juxtaposition to the cheery disposition of the man who owned and inhabited it.

"This is quite a house," Daniel observed, this time aloud.

"It's a tumbledown pile, Holbrook. But it's the only useful thing my father ever did for me."

The subject had always been an awkward one. Charlie's parents had both disgraced themselves. His mother, first by giving birth to him and then by the manner in which she had ended her own life—an overdose of laudanum to which she was addicted. His father, whose name he had never shared, had fled the country after an attempt at robbery and blackmail had turned to arson and manslaughter. He was found dead on a seashore near Dover a few years later. Dover, it seemed, was home to misfortune of all kinds.

Daniel had not forgotten that other subject. It hung in the air between them like a proverbial bookmark in the conversation.

"We've been friends a long time," Hamilton said, at last beginning where he had left off. "Do you really believe I would betray you in such a way?"

Daniel did not answer him. He prayed it was not so. And, to be perfectly honest, if Hamilton had betrayed him, it had been entirely out of character.

83

The fog of memory parted and revealed the scene in stark detail: the dock teaming with people, she on his Emerson's arm, and Hamilton accompanying them as if to cast his blessing for this betrayal upon them. Daniel had thought, just at first, that they must have come to meet him. He quickly realized his mistake. With their bags gathered about them, it was apparent they were not awaiting some ship newly arrived to deliver home some beloved passenger, but rather preparing for their own departure. Confused, Daniel approached them. Perhaps it was Emerson's smug look of self-congratulatory pride that had drawn him forward. Perhaps it was Sophie herself. He stood there a moment, unobserved. It was she who saw him first. Her face went pale, then blushed crimson. His name began to form on her lips but died there.

"Why, Holbrook!" Hamilton had said upon observing him. "What a surprise!" Judging by the look on his face, however, it did not appear to be a pleasant one. It seemed he was struggling for some explanation. Daniel didn't care who gave it, he only wanted one. He turned to Emerson—his old friend—who greeted him with little more than nervous laughter before turning to avoid Daniel's questioning gaze. He addressed the first passing porter and directed him to make the final arrangements for their luggage.

Perhaps the explanation ought to come from her, after all. He looked once more to Sophie and waited, willing her to say something that would make sense of what he was seeing and could hardly dare to believe. The explanation was given, though not in words. A look of regret and perhaps even of reproach was in her eyes. Her hand was at her throat, he caught the gleam of a ring. A wedding band! He understood. With a look that begged her to deny it, he raised his gaze to meet hers. "I'm sorry," her look seemed to say.

The crowd that gathered from the disembarking ship pushed him onward. He let it. He had to move, and keep moving, away from the betrayal and the disappointment and confusion and utter despair that was now washing over him like an ocean tide. He moved on and kept moving, but he stopped again before reaching home. He could not go back there. Not now. He had only gone away for one reason and that was so that he might have *her*. But that hope had been dashed, and so what was there for him? Nothing. The next day he boarded another ship bound for the continent, determined never to set foot in England again.

"I returned to find you," Hamilton said at last, waking Daniel from his thoughts. "That day in Dover, I saw them onto the ship and then came back to find you."

Daniel only looked at him.

"You asked me to watch over her," Hamilton reminded him.

"I did."

"And that is what I was doing."

"I don't see how. Did you usher her into that fellow's arms? Did you do nothing to protest?"

"What was I going to do? She considered herself in love with him."

"She professed to be in love with me!"

"He was persuasive," Hamilton returned. "And you were gone."

"For a year. One year!"

The dog sat up and looked worriedly to the two gentlemen as their voices raised.

Daniel calmed himself a little, but he was determined, now the subject had been broached, to see it through. "Was it really so long to wait?"

"Long enough, my friend, I regret to say. Just long enough. If there was anything I could have done, I would have done it. I *am* sorry."

Daniel looked to his friend. He had prepared one last rebuttal, but the look on Hamilton's face stopped him.

"You know my story," Hamilton said. "You know that the only reason I sit before you now is because I was rescued by a woman who was rescued herself. I never would have allowed Miss Warren to come to harm."

"Of course not, Hamilton. Forgive me."

"Oh, my friend, there is nothing to forgive. I do wish you had not been away so long, though. It should never have taken this long for you to decide to put the past behind you. And it wouldn't have, had you been here all along."

"Who says I'm putting the past behind me?"

"Aren't you?"

"I don't think I'll ever recover from that, Hamilton. She was to be my wife. Her and no one else."

"If you say so, Holbrook. If you say so. Let me get you a drink."

Daniel meant to decline. It was too early yet for that, and the drinking did not comfort him as it used to do. It hounded and pestered him instead. Hamilton handed him the half-filled glass and Daniel took it, as if it were a draft prescribed from a doctor. Would it be all right to take it for medicinal purposes? Or was he not administering it for that purpose already? If it were medicine and not vice, would it pester him still? The answer was yes, for the brandy looked him in the eye as he raised it to his lips and asked him questions he could not answer. *Will you be like your father in ten years' time? Will it be five before you can't put it down? Or maybe you were born to it and you can't stop even now.*

"I'm truly sorry about your grandfather," Hamilton said to him. "Did you make it back before—"

"No," Daniel said, cutting him off. "He died two days before I arrived." He placed the drink on the table beside him and walked away from it, sitting himself down in a chair on the other side of the room where he could not see it and would hopefully forget it was there at all, staring at him, mocking him. Begging him to lose himself in its amber comfort.

"It's a pity he didn't send for you when first he fell ill."

"He did," Daniel said, as matter-of-factly as he could manage. "I didn't come."

"I'm terribly sorry," Hamilton said and appeared to be waiting for some explanation, something to make it all sound a little less cold-hearted than it was. But Daniel had no excuses to offer.

"Tell me," Hamilton said to him with a look half-worried. "What are your plans now you are home? Are you at Brookdale?"

"No," Daniel answered. "Not so near as that, I'm afraid. Brookdale is uninhabitable at present. If I can get some capital, I'll need to put it back in order. And then, no doubt, I'll have to let it."

"Let it? Things can't be as bad as all that. You were happy there as I remember."

"I was once. That life, everyone in it, they are gone. The house only reminds me of my pride and ingratitude now. I don't know that

I shall ever live in it. But neither can I quite let it go. It's my albatross, I suppose. No, I'm in Town, actually. I've taken employment, you see. In Surrey. I was hoping for something more lucrative, but…"

"In Surrey?" Hamilton repeated, apparently surprised.

"Yes, I've taken a position with a gentleman of somewhat humble means, reading with him thrice a week."

"In Surrey?" Hamilton seemed to think the notion curious.

"It keeps me occupied, until I can find something else. I must be busy, Hamilton. I cannot—I will not be idle."

"Very well…" Hamilton said, but the business of houses and employment seemed trivial and banal after the subject just left off. In fact Daniel was not entirely through with it. There was a question more he must ask. He swallowed hard and summoned the words. "Do you ever see them?"

Hamilton was understandably confused. "Who?"

"*Them*, you know who I mean."

"Oh, yes, of course. That is… Well… Once shortly after. Since… Never."

A long silence extended between the answer and the question that must follow. Who would be the one to utter the words first?

"You had heard, of course," Hamilton inquired cautiously, and Daniel braced to hear the word spoken. "You heard that she had…"

Daniel felt that familiar pain in the area of his chest. Though Hamilton had not spoken the word, the implication was yet a blow. "It is true then?"

"Yes."

"When?"

"A year ago, I think. She was ill, you know, and…"

"Yes. That is, I *had* heard. I did not want to believe it."

"I'm sorry, Holbrook."

Daniel sat and rested his head in one hand. He would not cry. He had shed quite enough tears for her, foolish woman!

"I'm glad you are facing this. I had worried…"

"Is that what I'm doing?" Daniel asked with a breath of mirthless laughter.

"I certainly hope you are. You're a young man still, you know," Hamilton observed, "but growing older before your time with the burden of this. Put it behind you."

"If only I could."

"You have begun to do so already. I can see it. At least a part of you wants to do it."

"How can you know such a thing?"

"You are here, aren't you? You came for answers. Some part of you must want to resolve this history. Forgive him if you can. Move on. Love again."

"Never," Daniel said. "It's impossible."

Hamilton looked at him long and hard, until at last Daniel relented.

"Just say what you have to say, Hamilton."

"Forgive me, my friend, but this brooding is unworthy of you. Tragedies such as these can ruin or make us. Which will it do for you?"

Daniel looked at Hamilton a long time. He was not prepared to answer so provoking and pointless a question. The entrance of the cook, who had come with the dog's meal, rescued him from having to attempt it. Daniel arose, thanked Hamilton for his time, bade farewell to the dog, and took his leave.

*"Please tell me you are not going to climb that
ladder, Miss Durham."*

Chapter ten

DANIEL ARRIVED ON THE DURHAM'S front step to find Harold Vaughn already there and studying the door. The two gentlemen greeted each other, and Mr. Vaughn returned to his business of contemplating the barrier before him and the various means by which his presence might be announced. Daniel, amused, contemplated him. Vaughn was something of a comical fellow. That he held a special interest for one of the Durham sisters was patently obvious. Which one, however, was somewhat harder to guess.

Daniel, with a look only, begged Mr. Vaughn to make a decision. There was little point just standing there, after all. Daniel had come on business and did not like to keep Mr. Durham waiting. While Vaughn prevaricated, Daniel struck the knocker. Mr. Vaughn, with a wrinkled brow, looked at Daniel as if he'd committed some sort of betrayal.

Footsteps were heard within, the sound of voices talking, yelling even. And then there was silence.

Together they waited, though Vaughn's patience was apparently, and very quickly, eroding. When he took out his timepiece, Daniel reached for the knocker again. Mr. Vaughn, observing Daniel's inten-tions, dropped his watch—leaving it to swing by its chain—and rang the doorbell. The two summonses were executed at so nearly the same time that Daniel could not help but wonder what the impression would be upon those within. He was tempted to laugh at the fellow beside him. He checked himself with a clearing of his throat and kept one eye on Vaughn in the event it became necessary to seize him by the collar. If Vaughn should lose courage and decide to take flight, Daniel would not appreciate being left to look the lone and too-eager caller.

It had been several days since Daniel's last visit. He had found it necessary, considering his contemplative tendencies of late, to take a short break. The time away had given him the opportunity to come to sort of tentative terms with his past; to come to terms, even, with his present and how that past was irreconcilably a part of it—never to be forgotten, perhaps never, despite what Hamilton had said about the matter to be overcome. The reminder was necessary, for it had served a double purpose in cementing in his mind the responsibilities he had so recently undertaken and the obligations that came with them. He was prepared now, perhaps more than ever, to keep his attentions upon the job at hand and to resist other distractions, however distracting they might be. Yes, he was much stronger today, much more fit to deal with the changeable moods and unpredictable dramas that must arise in a house of head-strong and silly young women. He laughed to himself. He was no Harold Vaughn, that was for certain, moony over fresh-faced girls who were far too young, far too naïve and inexperienced in the world to tempt him. It was laughable, really.

He considered trying the knocker one more time. The family was at home, he could hear them within. If Mrs. Fowler would only open the door, he would be out of their way in an instant and safely closeted with Mr. Durham. He was growing impatient at the thought of it.

Daniel prepared to knock again, and had just raised his hand to do it, when the door opened. It was not Mrs. Fowler who stood there, but the younger Miss Durham herself, fresh-faced as ever and a little out of breath.

"Good morning, gentlemen," she said and opened the door wider that they might enter.

Daniel, a moment ago eager to pass through the house as quickly as possible, now hung back. He had thought himself prepared for today, but he was no longer so certain. He was not displeased to see her. Hardly that! But there *was* something in her present attitude that struck him uncomfortably. What had happened to Mrs. Fowler?

He gestured for Vaughn to enter first and took advantage of the opportunity to observe his manner toward his employer's younger daughter. Truly there was nothing immediately apparent that would suggest that Mr. Vaughn's state of nervousness had been elicited by his impending interview with the younger sister. Their conversation was all easiness and comfortable familiarity—as would be that of two very old and dear friends.

"I'm afraid my sister is indisposed at the moment, Mr. Vaughn. If you would care to wait in the parlor, I'll be happy to join you as soon as I may."

So it was the elder sister for Mr. Vaughn. Daniel's amusement was tinged with the slightest hint of relief.

Miss Durham turned then to Daniel, prepared to address him. She was interrupted, however, by Mr. Vaughn, who stepped between them. It seemed he had something more to say to her. Daniel was a little irritated, and though he knew it was petty to feel so, bad manners were bad manners; Vaughn, the gentleman he was, ought to have known better. With his back to Daniel he spoke confidentially to Miss Durham, but not so confidentially that Daniel could not make out his words.

"Don't fetch Beth just yet, if you don't mind," he said. "I'd like a word with you first if I may."

If Daniel was confused by the request, and by Vaughn's fervent manner of making it, he was all the more confused by the look Miss Durham flashed him in consequence. He had heard, she knew he had heard, and she was silently rebuking him for doing it. It was not his fault that Vaughn did not know how to whisper properly.

"Very well, Mr. Vaughn," Laynie answered him. "Mr. Holbrook," she said in a manner mildly irritated, "if you will come with me, I'll take you to my father."

He bowed his gratitude and followed. She was silent, perhaps irritated still, which was wholly unnecessary to his mind. He had supposed nothing of the exchange, he knew none of them well enough to do it. What her father would make of it—if Daniel decided to tell him—there was no need to guess, for Daniel had heard his opinion on the matter often enough. Vaughn was meant for Miss Laynie, and it was a union that showed every promise of materializing.

But *would* Daniel tell him what he had witnessed? Was that not part of his responsibility to her father? Strictly speaking it was not, for Daniel had been hired to read and to philosophize, not to play spy. And yet so much of their time was taken up by Mr. Durham's speculating on the marital enterprises of his daughters that Daniel could not be quite certain.

The corridors were not well lit, supplied, as they were, with only the occasional gas jet. And Daniel observed, as they made their way in silence, how even such meager light set the polished wainscot gleaming, as it did similarly for Miss Durham's brandy-colored hair as it hung in a chignon down her back.. He was tempted to reach out and touch it.

She stopped and turned to him, examining him in the pale light of a wall sconce. He watched her watch him, her green-brown eyes flashing with the flickering of the gas jets, and wondered what she was thinking. It was hard not to wonder what she was thinking when she looked at him that way. It was as though she was looking into him rather than at him. What could she see? And did he mind that she saw it?

"You do not usually come on Sundays," she observed at last.

The observation rather surprised him. He did not think she had taken any notice of his comings and goings, save, perhaps, when he was in her way. "No," he answered. "I don't, as a rule. But since I did not come at all last week—"

"No you didn't," she said, interrupting him and nearly throwing him from his train of thought.

"Something came up," he said, and then recalling that it was not to her he need make excuses but to her father, he went on with what he had originally intended to say. "Your father wrote. He thought I might make up the time by spending the day today."

"I see," she said. "I'm glad of it."

"Are you?" he asked aloud and in a tone suffused with the confusion he felt.

"Yes, of course. It will make him very happy." She turned and led him once more along the corridor to the rearmost section of the house. It was not an extraordinarily large house, but the way it wound about—one addition oddly connecting to another, sometimes by narrow corridors, more often by one small room that ran into another-- it at times felt that way. She remained busy as they walked, here and there running a finger along a piece of furniture, checking it, he supposed, for dust. Or she would stop to take up a stack of discarded papers, or a neglected book, that she might return them to their proper places. It struck him again, as it had struck him upon first seeing her at the door, what it was about her present office that disturbed him so. The library door was now in view and he stopped.

"I come," he said before she could knock, "as it is desired I should—by your father," he added as if the clarification were necessary. It was not. "But I do sometimes worry it is an unnecessary burden."

"A burden?" she said and clearly did not understand him.

"A strain, you know."

"On his mind do you mean?" she asked.

He was not doing a very good job of making himself clear. "No, not exactly," he answered. "I'm more concerned about his resources."

She looked up at him with narrowed gaze. There was a little more color in her face than had been there a moment before. "Do you fear not being paid, Mr. Holbrook?"

"No," he said and hesitated to go on. At last he deemed it necessary. "I rather fear the consequences to you—and to your sister—when I am."

"Oh!" she said and blinked as she seemed to recount what evidences she had provided for his believing it to be so—an accident while engaging upon an exercise she was no longer at liberty to enjoy, the shame of having to open a door for a servant who was otherwise engaged… These seemed to him to suggest that greater sacrifices were being made for the sake of his employment—and her father's enjoyment—than were worth it to her welfare or to his conscience.

It was plain by now that she understood him. How greatly had he transgressed in mentioning it at all? She had shown herself to be a woman quick of temper. He was taking a great risk with it now. But her manner was suddenly relenting, pleading even. "No," she said to him. "Please, Mr. Holbrook, don't concern yourself on that account. Your company makes Papa so happy. Consequently, I too am…"

But she stopped. What were her more personal feelings on the matter? He very much wished to know. "Yes, Miss Durham?" he prompted her.

"Nothing," she said and shook her head. "If Papa is happy, then so are we, you may be rest assured."

But he was not satisfied with that. She had distanced herself from her answer with the proverbial "we". Was *she* pleased by his coming? It was rather a surprising notion, for he had believed until that moment that she actually despised him. He was tempted to stall her with another question, anything... But it was too late. She knocked upon the library door. Her father begged her enter and she opened it, blinding Daniel with the light that shone through the uncovered library windows. She was silhouetted against it now and he could no longer see her.

"Mr. Holbrook is here, Papa," he heard her say.

"Oh, good, good!" the old man said. His chair squeaked as he arose from it.

Daniel stepped into the room and felt he was doing her a great disservice by allowing her to announce him as she had done. Her father did her a greater disservice yet if he was creating the conditions for such a necessity.

"Anxious to get started, are you, Holbrook?" her father addressed him with a laugh.

The question surprised him. He looked from Miss Durham, to whom he had just offered a nod of gratitude, to her father. "I'm sorry, sir?"

"The bell and the knocker too, eh?"

"Oh, that," he said. "I arrived at the same time as Mr. Vaughn. He chose one mode of announcing us. I chose another. I apologize if we caused any unnecessary excitement."

"Not at all, Holbrook," he answered. "At least not more than we're used to. Are we, Laynie, my dear?" He grew suddenly scolding. "But what the devil is going on upstairs?"

Laynie looked a little ashamed. "Beth decided she would like to try a fringe." She indicated her meaning with one hand as she swept aside the stray curl that lay against her forehead. It returned immediately to its place.

"A fringe? And what of that?"

"Mrs. Fowler was busy and so Beth took the scissors to her own hair. I'm afraid she's made rather a mess of it."

"And so Mrs. Fowler is trying to fix it, is she?"

"Yes, sir. I'm afraid she was occupied when the gentlemen arrived."

"So you answered, did you? I don't like that. It gives the wrong impression, you know."

"Yes, Papa. I think I do." And she flashed the briefest glance at Daniel.

He returned it with a look that he hoped expressed the regret he felt.

"I'll have to talk to Mrs. Fowler," her father said. "See that it doesn't happen again, won't you?"

"Of course, Papa."

Mr. Durham's countenance suddenly grew a little brighter. "Mr. Vaughn is here, is he?"

"Yes, Papa."

"Well… Don't keep him waiting!"

"Papa, please," she said and sounded as exasperated as she looked ashamed.

"Go, my dear. And if you love me like you ought, you'll have some good news to share with me this evening."

"I doubt very much, Papa—"

"Go, go," he said, interrupting her, and he shooed her away with a flick of his hand.

The door closed, and Daniel took a chair before Mr. Durham's desk as he prepared himself to listen, once more, to the oft repeated ambitions of an anxious father for his capricious and hard-to-please daughters.

* * *

Laynie returned to the drawing room to find Mr. Vaughn at the fireplace, leaning against it and examining a figurine which he held in his hand.

"Hello, Mr. Vaughn," she said.

Startled, he attempted to replace the figurine on the mantelpiece but dropped it instead. "Oh dear!"

"It is nothing, Mr. Vaughn." She took up the hearth brush and bent to clean up the mess.

"No," Mr. Vaughn said, and refused to let her. "I'll do it." He stooped to pick up the pieces and to place them into a handkerchief, which he folded up carefully and shoved into his pocket. "I'll have it repaired. I'll repair it myself if I have to."

"Please, don't trouble yourself over it, Mr. Vaughn. It was not an important piece."

In reality, it had been her mother's—a silly statuette of a young woman with an odd-looking sheep—but she was not very attached to it. "What is it you wished to speak to me about?"

"Can't you guess?"

"Only vaguely, Mr. Vaughn. In the meantime you are rather alarming me. Will you sit? Beth is likely to be detained for some time."

He released a breath and looked, in consequence, somewhat deflated. "Yes, all right," he said, but waited for Laynie to be seated first. She chose her favorite chair. He took a place on the sofa. "You are limping still?" he observed. "You were not limping earlier. I hoped it meant you had recovered. Have you not?"

"No," she answered him. "Not much, at any rate."

He looked at her strangely. "Were you disguising it? For Mr. Holbrook's sake?"

"Not for his sake, no," she answered. "That is, I do not like the attention and so sought to avoid it."

"*His* attention?"

"Now you're being ridiculous."

"Am I?" But he was not teasing her. He simply seemed unable to understand.

"I'd disguise it now, Mr. Vaughn, only I find it's not in me to do it at present." She raised her ankle to rest it upon a nearby stool. "Please. Tell me what it is that is troubling you."

"I think I just did."

"No, Mr. Vaughn. You didn't. It was about my sister, I believe?"

"Oh, that!" he said and seemed to recall himself. Perhaps it was not so momentous after all. "I'm in a bit of a fix," he continued. "On my last walk with Beth, I nearly made my confession."

"Did you?" Laynie said and sat up rather than sitting forward, for her ankle combined with her corseting would allow for no such freedom of movement.

"Yes, but I'm certain she would refuse me if I put such a question to her now. She requires more time. I only fear she is waiting for some assurance that is never to come."

"From you?"

"No. I— I fear, forgive me for saying it, that she is waiting to know that the inheritance is sure."

"And you are uncertain it will ever be?"

"Not exactly. It's only that the assurance of it I cannot give. I won't," he said as if it offered some clarification. It did not. "I wonder if you might guide me. Have you any feeling what my chances might be at all should it turn out I am not to inherit? Would she take me as a common curate?"

Laynie's heart sank for him. She wished she had some reassurance to offer. She had none. "My sister keeps her own counsel these days," she said instead. "We rarely speak. Certainly not as we used to do."

"I'm sorry for it," he said and undoubtedly meant it as much for himself as for her.

"And there is your mother to consider as well. Is she aware of your feelings?"

"Yes, she knows."

"And?"

Harry shook his head as he looked down at his hands.

"Is she really so immovable?"

"I cannot say," he answered. "I'm afraid it is all up to Beth."

"Beth? How?"

But, again, he did not answer her. He merely looked at her as if she might easily come to the conclusion on her own. At last she did. "Do you mean to say that Beth has some power to change Lady Vaughn's mind regarding her?"

Harry looked momentarily hopeful. "Who else?" he said, but the hope quickly faded. "Do you think it possible?"

Truly Laynie did not see how, and yet she hated to tell him so. He required hope at the moment and nothing less.

"Have you considered what will happen if she does not?" Harry said to her now.

Laynie, growing alarmed once more, waited for him to continue.

"I won't cross Mother, Laynie. For all I know my marriage may be a matter of life and death for her. I think you and I would not make each other miserable, but it is, I think, not what either of us wants; but if she sets her mind upon it, if she should get it into her head to speak with your father on the matter…"

"Oh, dear."

Harry arose from his place on the sofa and exchanged it for a spot very near her. He took her hand and held it between both of his. "What are we going to do, Laynie?" he asked her.

* * *

"I believe we are beginning to see some progress at last, Holbrook," Mr. Durham said to him as he turned from the window, where it was just possible to see into the best parlor. His felicity was quite apparent as he folded his hands across his slight protuberance of a stomach and smiled. "We shall have something to talk about tonight, I dare say."

"You are certain she will accept him?" Daniel asked, though cautiously at that. It was a little forward, and he was not entirely comfortable asking the question, but he understood by now what was expected of him, and so he fulfilled his part in the dialogue as faithfully as he could.

"Of course she will. Well, she had very well better!" His brow furrowed as he considered this. "She is not likely to have such a chance as this again, you know. Beth might have anyone, but Laynie… Of course he would no doubt prefer Beth if she would have him, but he is a man of honor and duty. His mother has given her approval already of Laynie, who is not, I regret to say, quite Beth's equal, but there it is. And she knows my feelings on the matter, so it is all as good as done if you ask me."

"You place a great deal of merit in the ability of familial loyalty to determine the course two hearts may take. Such things are not always so possible to plan."

"Now, now, Holbrook, you don't mean to discourage me, do you?"

"Not at all, sir. I only mean to suggest that if, as you say, he would prefer your eldest daughter, perhaps, after all, he does."

"Certainly not. Certainly not!"

"As you say, sir."

Mr. Durham considered this a moment and then offered those thoughts aloud, as if his thinking them must provide convincing evidence. "Laynie may not have inherited her mother's good looks, but she did inherit her sense. Vaughn no doubt appreciates that. She is not very intelligent, nor is she particularly charming in manners," he

added now, as much for Daniel's consideration as his own, "but she is dependable and responsible—most of the time. Her accident was a lapse in judgment, but it certainly did no harm in the end, did it? Every man longs to play the hero, and he did his job well there."

"Very well, sir."

Mr. Durham gave him a suspicious look. "It does not appear as if you quite agree with me."

"It's just that your proof of Mr. Vaughn's attachment to Miss Alayna seems to come with a great deal of qualifiers. She is behind her sister in manner and appearance. She has nothing remarkable about her, as you have said a dozen times before. She is average in every way and particularly wanting in intelligence and charm. And yet you insist Mr. Vaughn has determined to make her his wife. Have you proof of it, sir? Has your daughter told you of her feelings for him? Has he informed you of his own intentions?"

Mr. Durham considered a moment more. "But he is here so very often."

"To a house where two sisters reside, yes, and where one is not so able to go on walks and outings as the other who has no injury to nurse." It would probably have been best for him to remain silent on the subject. It truly was none of his business, but Miss Durham's final objections to her father had seemed significant, as if she were, however vainly, trying to resist the plans her father insisted on making for her. Or was it Daniel himself who was resisting? That was quite impossible. He had no personal interest in the matter. In fact, if he were truly to fill his position as thoroughly as he ought, he would take Mr. Durham's view and adopt the opinion that the youngest Miss Durham was a perfectly suitable match for the wealthy and connected Mr. Vaughn.

So why could he not do it?

Mr. Durham, who had these last minutes been silent and thought-ful, arose from his place to look once more out the window. Daniel joined him there. In the yard, just beneath the beech tree, stood a young man and a young woman, speaking together very earnestly. It was Mr. Vaughn, of course. But it was not Laynie who was with him. It was Beth.

"Excuse me just a moment, will you, Holbrook?" Mr. Durham asked, and then he left the room to go out of doors.

* * *

"You have changed your hair," Mr. Vaughn observed of Beth as she stood before him in the parlor. She fingered the fringes at her forehead. She feared she had ruined it, having cut the curls too short and not entirely even. Mrs. Fowler, bless her, had come to the rescue and had made it all right.

"No doubt Laynie told you what I did," Beth said, certain her sister would be eager to use the opportunity to belittle her in Harry's eyes.

"She said you were indisposed, and that was all."

"Did she?" Beth answered, surprised. Perhaps she shouldn't be, after all.

"You are better now?"

"Oh, yes," she said. "Entirely. Shall we walk outside?" she suggested. "The garden is free, I think."

"Yes, certainly."

And together they walked out, but they got no further than the yard and Laynie's beech tree. Of course it was not Laynie's truly, she had simply laid claim to it by way of it being her favorite spot. The tree was an unusual shape, not tall and straight as are most beech trees, but the branches bent low to the earth, where, in its neglect, vines had been allowed to overrun it and had nearly pulled it to the ground. It had once been a great climbing tree. Beth had never been so adventurous; Laynie had ceased to climb when she had fallen out and dislocated her shoulder. At least Laynie learned from her mistakes. It was more than could be said for most people.

"It *is* a magnificent tree," Mr. Vaughn said, joining her in admir ing it.

"It is, isn't it?" Beth answered. "My father planted it for my mother, many, many years ago. He planted it the day they bought the house. My mother was expecting Laynie."

"A thoughtful gesture."

She looked at him and then down at the tree's trunk as she continued. "It has become a sort of monument to her, which I think my father never intended. In fact he would not go near it for a long time after she died. He dismissed the gardener and the whole yard fell into neglect."

"A little like the East wing at Elverton," he said.

Beth looked at him.

"Not that it was ever a monument to my father," he attempted to explain, "but his library is there, his own private rooms are there... It is shut up now. Even the servants are not allowed to go there. The doors are locked and it is left, I suppose, to ruin."

"Until you take it over."

"*If* I ever take it over," he reminded her.

She looked back to the tree's trunk and said nothing. *If* he ever took it over... What if he never did? Would she have him as a poor man? It was only a relative poverty, after all. A poverty certainly less severe than that which was presently staring her down. But the humble wife of a curate was not what she wanted for herself. She wanted luxury and security. She wanted beautiful gowns and the admiration of all around her. She wanted the sort of life Harold Vaughn of Elverton could give her, not Mr. Vaughn of the vicarage.

"If William should decide to change his way and beg for forgiveness," he said, as if the further reminder were necessary, "it might all be his once more."

"And yet it is your father's fortune, is it not? And if your parents are estranged, then why is it so important I have her approval and not his, I wonder?"

He flinched a smile in answer, but that was all, it seemed, he was prepared to offer. His reticence, this mystery he seemed to want to weave around his supposed fortune, made her feel as though he were dealing not quite honestly with her. Perhaps he had never been intended to inherit at all and this was merely some lie he had cooked up to convince her to give him a chance. The idea infuriated her.

"Is this some game?" she asked him. "Am I merely a distraction to you until you know for certain what it is you stand to lose or gain and what you therefore stand to offer?"

He answered patiently, calmly. "If I were to offer myself alone, would that not be enough?"

She swallowed hard. It was a brutal question and one she could not quite answer, but she had a question of her own to ask. "Let us suppose," she said, "that you and I continue our walks and our visits, and we grow to enjoy each other's company as it is easily supposed we may."

"Go on," he answered cautiously.

"If you should fail to impress upon your mother the merit of your preference over her own…"

"If *I* should?"

"Yes, of course," she said, derailed from the point of her question. If his mother pressed, would he acquiesce and choose Laynie or fight for his own happiness? It was a question she must know the answer to. But he had diverted her, by once again diverting the responsibility of convincing his mother of the merits of his choice over her own. The very idea of it made her angry. "So it is up to me to convince her. Tell me, will you, is it even possible?"

"It's possible," he said with an air of unwavering certainty.

"Will you tell me how?"

"I cannot."

"You won't."

"If you prefer it in those words."

"Do you not desire to help me?" she said, her voice thick with the frustration she felt at the thought of how passive and inactive his admiration for her must really be.

"More than I can say," he assured her.

"Supposing I cannot convince her, Mr. Vaughn—and I certainly have no hope of succeeding without your help—then what do we risk?"

"We?"

"Not together, you and I. But individually."

"What would *you* be risking?" he asked, putting the responsibility of answering the question, once more on her. Or was it, after all, the very same as the last? She was no more likely to answer now than before. "I won't be made a pauper, Beth," he said, mercifully answering his own part. "I may not have a grand house. You may not have quite all the luxuries you want, but I would still be able to take care of you."

She blinked at him. Was this, then, his confession? And where were the words: *I love you, have me, come what may?*

"And if I am unsuccessful?" she tried again. "If I try with all my might and she will not budge, then what?"

He approached her, took her hand in his and held it to his chest. "But you will be successful, my dear Miss Durham."

Her heart beat a little more quickly. How was it possible that the awkward, unassuming and nearly charmless Mr. Vaughn should have such an effect on her? "And what assurance do I have that it will be enough?" she asked him, steadying herself with her still nagging questions. "If I fail to succeed, if Lady Vaughn, on her death bed, insists you marry Laynie, then what will become of me?"

Mr. Vaughn smiled tenderly. He raised her hand, still in his, to his lips. She was about to protest. Or perhaps to ask for something more. Some more solid assurance of his devotion, some word or promise or...

"Mr. Vaughn!"

But the words uttered did not come from her mouth. They had come from her father's, who was quickly advancing toward them, a look of abject displeasure on his face.

"Mr. Vaughn, a word with you!"

Beth backed away, making room for her father and uncertain if she ought to intervene or if it would only make matters worse.

"It has occurred to me, sir, that there are entirely too many unmarried men in my house just now and that perhaps I ought to rid myself of one of them. Mr. Holbrook knows what is expected of him, and—"

"Mr. Holbrook?" Beth asked, as Mr. Vaughn cast a confused look upon both she and her father in turn. "Mr. Holbrook is married... Isn't he?"

"I may have exaggerated a bit on that point," Mr. Durham answered as if that were a perfectly logical explanation, "but the point

104

of the matter is, he knows what is expected of him and he holds that expectation as a duty. You, sir, are a nuisance, and until you make up your mind—"

"Papa!" Beth objected. It was time her father properly understood how things were and stopped imagining them to be what he wanted. But he would not listen, he only kept going on about his hopes and expectations for Laynie and how Lady Vaughn would be so bitterly disappointed to know her son was leading both young ladies on at once, and how no gentleman of honor—perhaps there no longer were gentlemen as honorable as Mr. Holbrook—would dare to attempt such a thing right beneath the nose of their father.

"Papa!" Beth shouted, trying once more to intervene.

At last her father seemed to hear her. He turned to look at her as if she had been a barking dog and nothing more.

"In the house with you, Beth. I'll have something to say to you later."

"Papa?" she begged.

"Go this minute!"

And Beth, seeing no other choice before her, left Harold Vaughn to the mercy of her father and his misguided wrath.

* * *

Daniel, intrigued by the scene a moment ago, found himself unwilling to play witness to another man's humiliation. He took up the book he and Mr. Durham had been supposed to read—and which they had not yet begun—and took himself into a more remote corner of the room. He found a chair and sat down to distract himself with the philosophical poetry of Milton. No sooner had he opened the book than he heard the door open. Had Mr. Durham returned so soon? From where he was sitting, in a shelf-lined alcove, he could not quite see.

He began to rise from his place but stopped himself. The youngest Miss Durham had entered and now stood in the center of the room. He ought to make himself known, but it would be better, far better, if she conducted her business and left again without observing him. Was she looking for her father? No doubt that was her purpose. She would quickly see that he was not here and she would leave again.

Only she didn't. She stood a moment, watching without, and then approached the desk to lean upon it, as though the scene she was witnessing was a physical weight upon her shoulders. He was tempted to ask what it was, exactly, about the situation that troubled her so. But it was none of his business, and he reminded himself once more of the fact.

At last it seemed she could take no more and turned from the desk to approach one of the book cases that flanked it. One directly opposite him. Her limp, now, was more pronounced than he had previously observed. Had she disguised it from him earlier? And at what cost?

In her hand she held a book. It was the book she had dropped before his feet on his last visit, no doubt. She opened it, scanned the last few pages, and with a sigh closed it again. She looked up, contemplating the highest shelf and the gap in the stack of books where hers presumably fit. She studied the ladder next, and with her free hand, clutched at a handful of skirt.

"Please tell me you're not thinking of climbing that ladder, Miss Durham," he said and arose.

"Mr. Holbrook!" She turned around with a start, but otherwise did not answer him. She simply looked at him with those too-seeing eyes of hers.

"I don't suppose you would allow me to replace your book for you?" He might have approached to take the book from her, but, recalling his past efforts to offer assistance, he thought better of it. He waited for her to accept his offer. Of course she mightn't accept it at all. She might storm from the room, or worse, throw the book at him.

She did neither, however, but smiled gratefully and handed it to him.

He approached and took it. He required the assistance of the first step only, and quite effortlessly set the book in its place upon the shelf.

"If you would be so good," she said before he had quite finished, "would you mind fetching me the one next to it?"

It pleased him to do so. It pleased him more that she had asked. He retrieved the requested book and handed it to her. She took it from him, examined the cover and then looked up at him once more. "Thank you," she said.

Part of him—the rational part—hoped that, her business now concluded, she would turn from the room and leave him once more to himself. Another part—the part that found her just a trifle fascinating—began searching for something to say that might keep her here a moment or two longer.

"You've finished with your book, then?" he asked her, and regretted the patent banality of the question. Of course she had finished it. Why return it to its shelf if she had not?

Her answer, however, surprised him. "My bruise, do you mean?"

She was teasing him, reminding him of the mistake he had made when he had returned her book to her a few days before. He had no reply to offer. His faux-pas was an embarrassment and all the more embarrassing for knowing she understood him to be a married man. And so he was necessarily tongue-tied by the lie that had been told for him, if not actually by him. Perhaps it was better that it had been. No, it was certainly better.

"I'm sorry," she said and looked actually repentant. "I should not make fun of you."

"You have every right to do it. It was idiotic of me."

"No more idiotic than trying to jump an unfamiliar horse and then refusing to accept help when I plainly needed it."

It sounded very near an apology, and Daniel accepted it with gratitude.

"I do have a habit," she went on, "or so some say, of getting myself into fixes."

"I've known you all of three weeks, Miss Durham, but I would have to second the evaluation."

The smile of good-humored self-deprecation faded into a look of disappointment. Had he, by agreeing with her, caused her offense? He sincerely hoped it was not the case.

She glanced at him and looked once more toward the window, though there was nothing but landscape to be seen from where they stood. "I wonder what it must look like to you," she said at last and thoughtfully. "How foolish and inconstant we must seem, my sister and I. And poor Harold Vaughn."

107

Why should such a thing concern her so? And why, in turn, should he be concerned by her concern? This was all becoming too complicated. And it was not what he was here for. He brought the rational man resolutely forward, gave him a sound talking to, and told him precisely what to say. "Truly, Miss Durham," he said, "I would discourage you from troubling yourself over what I might think. I would beg you not to do it." Would she heed his counsel, understand it as the plea it was?

No. Apparently she would not.

"I know what my father thinks of me," she said, still looking out the window. How was it she could speak with such emotion and yet stand so exquisitely still like that? "I know he thinks me incapable of stringing two comprehensible thoughts together. Perhaps all women imagine themselves more intelligent than they are, but I am not simple. And I am not a tease. I have not toyed with Mr. Vaughn's feelings.

Though we have been friends for a decade or more, he does not feel for me what he feels for Beth." She looked at him then. "And I am glad of it."

But why did she want so badly for him to know it? "Miss Durham, truly, none of this is any of my business. I don't know why you feel it necessary to offer your explanations to me."

"Because my father will not listen, Mr. Holbrook," she said and looked at him.

Ah, yes. Yes, of course. He understood her now. He was her father's emissary. No more to her than that and no less. He tried to feel flattered by the idea.

"He sees what he wants to see," she went on, "and nothing more. He wants for me to marry Mr. Vaughn. He has set his hopes upon it."

"And yours?" But was he asking for Mr. Durham or for himself? Of course it was for Mr. Durham. He did not care that she felt desperate to be rescued from her father's designs for her. Why should he?

She closed her eyes briefly and cleared her throat. "My hopes are quite simple," she said more calmly. "Perhaps they are unreasonable, as my father would no doubt say, but I don't think they are." She looked to him again, and her words were as a challenge. "I want..." she said, and hesitated a moment before continuing, "...I want someone to understand me."

He supposed it was not so uncommon a complaint. Did fathers ever really understand their daughters? Did men ever truly understand women? He had thought so, once. In fact he had once congratulated himself on being able to figure most women out at a glance. He believed he understood her sister well enough. But her? She was a sea of complicated emotions, and he feared he understood her as little as her father did. The only difference was—for right or for wrong—he wanted to.

"I want someone to value me for being me and not because..."

"Because?" he prompted her, and felt that perhaps he should not have done. This was not the sort of conversation a single man, young or old, should be having with a single woman. But then...he was not single. Not in her eyes. And the words she was flinging at him were meant, after all, for her father, not for him. They were the words he imagined she had wished to utter a thousand times, and perhaps had done, but which would fall, or possibly had fallen, on deaf and unwilling ears.

"I know that I am not my sister's equal," she said looking at him with a conceding tone that suggested she felt it a point of argument her father would no doubt make. One she had heard time and time again. It was not an argument he would think to make, however. Partly because it was not his place to make it. More especially because it was not true. "I know that I have little to offer. But I do have hope. I believe that there is someone for everyone, especially designed for them and for no one else. I believe that there is someone for me, and whatever risks I run in waiting for that someone...I simply must wait. And I will."

From another woman, Daniel might be tempted to think her plying for compliments—for reassurances. He had not even the slightest suspicion that such was her motivation. She was airing her frustrations to the only ears that had ever been willing to listen, and that was all. But it was a great deal, and he understood it to be so. He had no reply; none was expected of him. It did not mean, however, that he had no reassurance to give—it was simply not his place to do it. And even if he were foolish enough to make the attempt, he did not believe she would accept it. Not of him. Perhaps not of anyone.

He watched her a moment, in silent exasperation. He felt that exasperation emanating from her as though it were a part of his own. Perhaps it was in a way. Her father thought her lacking. She was anything but. And the greater pity was that she had learned to believe him. She might, he supposed, be considered average, but only if one were to use the description by its most precise definition. She was average in height, neither tall nor short. Her build was somewhat on the slight side, but she was not thin and certainly showed no tendencies toward plumpness. Even her eyes could not make up their mind between green and brown. Her hair, neither curly nor straight seemed more inclined to behave in a manner somewhere in between the two. The color of it, though, was a perfectly decisive brandy amber. Perhaps by such a description she might be considered average. Ordinary, however? Not by any means! There was a depth to her that was positively unfathomable, but it was companioned by an openness of character he found both welcoming and...well... disturbing. He feared himself unworthy of what she had just given him. He felt that he could not quite get enough of it.

"Forgive me," she said with a heavy sigh and moved toward the window. "I have no right to burden you with my trivial cares."

Again he had no reply to offer, only this time he wished he had, or that it was his place to do it. Had he not gone too far already? And him a married man! The lie was a necessary protection. He was beginning to despise it.

She was watching them once more, Mr. Vaughn and her father, as she stood in a wash of sunlight. Daniel watched her, but at last dared to look for himself at the scene without. Vaughn was enduring his scolding like a man, but like a man whose soul was being torn from his body. Laynie closed her eyes and turned away. Her father had finished. Vaughn was dismissed and was making his retreat. He picked up a stick and swatted it at the garden gate as he passed through it. It shattered into a dozen pieces and he threw the remnants from his hand into the shrubberies.

"Will your sister be very disappointed?" Daniel dared to ask her. It was none of his business, but he wanted to know, and he didn't believe his interest in the matter would be unwelcomed. Not after the speech she had just made.

"I don't know," she said. "I wish I did. Would you think me capricious if I confessed to you that, while I hope she is not very disappointed, I rather hope, at the same time, that she is?"

"You have no desire to see your sister hurt. And yet you want her to care for him as he cares for her."

"Yes," she said and looked at him as if it were an idea completely novel that anyone should understand her.

"It isn't caprice," he said. "It is evidence of a sincere concern for two people for whom you care very deeply."

Again she gave him that look. It lingered and gradually softened into a smile of gratitude. He felt unworthy of it.

"I hope you will forgive me for burdening you as I have done," she said.

"It has been no burden, Miss Durham." And he truly wished for her to understand that it was not. He was not certain how many of these conversations he could endure. He had an obligation to her father to keep himself aloof. It was proving devilishly difficult to do. He watched her quit the room and was still standing there a moment later when Mr. Durham returned.

"I'm telling you, Holbrook, you ought to count yourself lucky you have not daughters of your own to contend with. Something must be done. I have done all I can on my own."

"What do you mean to do, sir?" he asked, both out of obligation to fill his part and also out of a keen, if unreasonable, interest of his own.

"There is only one thing for it," Mr. Durham answered. "I think I must send them away."

The idea was perplexing. Perhaps even shocking. "Is that not a little extreme?"

"Eh?" He looked up at Daniel from the depths of his thoughtful stupor. "Extreme? Not at all. Not at all. I have a sister in Gravesend. My girls are in desperate need of a woman's guidance. Nothing I say is getting through to them. Nor is it ever likely to. They must marry. I must see them provided for. Time is getting on." He sighed and rubbed at his head. "Yes, yes. A holiday in Gravesend will be just the thing. A fortnight should do it, don't you think?" He looked at Daniel, a glimmer of excitement in his eyes. "And while they are away, you and I may read to our hearts' content, for there will be no interruptions to distract us! Just think of that, eh?" And he clapped Daniel on the arm.

"It will certainly be much quieter," Daniel answered with a smile, and regretted very much that he could not share in the old man's enthusiasm for his plan. Two weeks without the Miss Durhams? An hour ago such news would have pleased him to no end. Now, however...

"Is something the matter, Holbrook?" Mr. Durham asked him with a look of concern.

"No, not at all," he answered. He was a man who prided himself on his honesty. If he had realized beforehand just how many false-hoods his employment would require of him, he might have thought twice about taking it.

Part two

September 1897

Chapter eleven

B ETH'S FEELINGS IN REGARD TO her father's decision to send his daughters to Gravesend were mixed. She did not particularly wish to leave home just now. She was comfortable in the knowledge that Harold Vaughn wanted her, and with that fact now established she did not like the idea of having to quit the field, particularly with so many obstacles before them—Lady Vaughn and her father not the least of these.

Neither did Laynie wish to go. She had made her objections clear —at least she had made it clear she had them, if not exactly why—but it had done little good. Her father had made up his mind, and that was that. Laynie had always been a little funny about leaving home for any reason. On this occasion, however, she was more than usually reluctant to do so, for Aunt Phillips had promised—as an especial favor to their father—to encourage her to consider the benefits of marriage to the wealthy and connected Mr. Vaughn.

On this subject Beth had heard quite enough already. But what were Laynie's feelings on the matter? They had not done much in the way of talking lately and so Beth could only guess at what her sister was thinking. Was it for leaving Mr. Vaughn that she was so reluctant to go? Beth was tempted to consider it the case, but then this holiday was meant to encourage her to consider him. What need was there of encouragement if Laynie had formed an attachment to him?

"Laynie, dear," Beth began once they were comfortably seated on the train. The carriage smelled of stale perfume, smoke, and dog. She arose, let down the window and sat again. "I think you are not looking forward to this holiday. Would you mind telling me why?"

"I'm simply not, that's all," she said and picked at the trim of her travelling cloak as she stared petulantly out the window.

"Has it something to do with our aunt's promise?"

Laynie's gaze shifted from the window to Beth. "You know I do not like to be told what I should do."

"You truly have no interest in Mr. Vaughn for yourself? Despite what our Papa and Lady Vaughn might wish?"

Laynie leaned forward in her seat. The look on her face was almost desperate. "I don't, Beth. Truly, I don't. I love him as a dear, dear friend, but I cannot think of him as more. And you know I want more—so much more! And I think...that is I dare to believe you are fond of him. Are you?"

Beth did not like to give her secrets away, and yet her last interview had apparently been witnessed by more than her father alone. If she wished to have him, and she was not entirely certain she did, she would have to lay some formal claim upon him. "I do care for him, of course I do. I've known him too long and too well not to. If I knew I was free to think more of him, then perhaps I would." It was not quite a confession, but it was something.

"Don't hold yourself apart from him on my account, Beth. Please, don't."

"Oh, I don't!" she said, which was not exactly true. If Laynie did not want him it did not mean she would not, in the end, have him. "I simply am not certain of him yet, that's all."

"Because of the—"

But Beth would not stand to be accused of being a mercenary twice. "Because he has not proved himself to me yet, Laynie. That is why. Do you know he expects me to convince his mother to change her mind about me? That is quite a responsibility, do you not think?"

"I suppose so. Only I think, in this case, it is possibly the—"

"How am I to do it? Can you tell me?"

"No," Laynie said and sat back in her seat.

"I think it wrong of him to expect so much from me and to be willing to do so little. And now I must sit and listen to a fortnight's worth of speeches from our aunt as to the merits of *your* marrying him. Why should I even be tempted to believe I have a chance? I don't see how I have any chance at all."

"But you do. Of course you do! It is you he wants, after all, that is something. It's a great deal, in fact! And I mean to make our aunt understand how the matter truly stands. I only hope I can do it sufficiently that she might persuade our father to give up on the idea. He must see reason. And he must see it before he and Lady Vaughn have the chance to put their heads together on the subject."

"Perhaps it is a good thing she does not care much for Papa."

"Perhaps it is," Laynie answered with a reluctant smirk.

"But you are right, Laynie. This is for you to accomplish. You know I will help you where I can."

"By assuring Aunt Phillips that you care for him?" Laynie said and arched one eyebrow.

Her sister knew her well, it seemed. "We shall see. If it comes to that. But think," she said, grasping upon the idea and running with it, "if you can convince Aunt Phillips it's a hopeless case, and if she can convince Papa, can you not then go on to convince Lady Vaughn?"

"Me?" Laynie said and seemed to find the idea a ridiculous one.

"Yes. If she'll listen to anyone, it's you."

"Beth, I'm not so sure that's—"

"It must be done, you know, and who better to do it than you, whom Lady Vaughn is already so fond of?"

Laynie seemed uncertain and turned to look contemplatively out the window.

"Perhaps," Beth said, changing seats to sit beside her, "if you were to meet someone else on our holiday, you might make your point all the more evident."

"And who am I likely to meet at our aunt's?"

"Who is to say! No doubt there will be dinner parties, and there is to be a ball."

"Guested by people we are never likely to meet again. What good is that to either of us?"

"There is Ned."

"Our cousin?" Laynie asked, apparently disgusted by the idea.

"He sometimes brings friends home to visit."

"Friends as charming and well-behaved as he is, Beth? No, thank you."

"Even if it's to make a point?"

"I cannot imagine a circumstance in the world dire enough to persuade me to consider one of Ned's friends, Beth. Besides, he is supposed to be on holiday in France. I have it from Aunt Phillips herself that we are not to be worried by him or his 'friends'."

Beth sat back hard against the seat. "That is a pity," she said and was tempted to pout. "Still, there is the ball, and who knows who may drop in to wait upon our aunt while we are there," she said, brightening somewhat at the thought.

Laynie only answered with a dismissive shake of her head. She took out a book and began to read it. On the seat between them was a newspaper that had been left behind by a previous passenger. Beth picked it up and began looking at the pictures.

* * *

Upon arriving at their aunt's home in Gravesend, the girls were welcomed by their aunt and uncle and shown to the room they were to share by a taciturn housekeeper. It was there their cousin Grace found them half an hour later, effusive with happiness and fully prepared to show it off.

"You have come just in time!" she said and beckoned them to her own room. Beth followed in wonder, dragging Laynie along beside her. Though Grace was Laynie's age, it was she who had formed the close bond. Laynie, by Beth's assignment, had been relegated to the role of the younger, pestering sister, and so had never formed a bond with their cousin. Laynie, therefore, tagged along only reluctantly.

Grace showed them into her room, which had been recently made over and was decorated in the latest style: pale green damask wallpaper, blush colored drapes, and bed curtains in silks and moirés. Upon her bed were boxes and packages, apparently newly arrived, and of which she was particularly proud.

"Look," she said. "Mama and I have been shopping in Paris, and the packages have just arrived in time for you to see what we bought."

Laynie sat, apparently disappointed and not altogether interested in her cousin's desire to show off her finery. Beth was interested but perhaps not gleefully so. It was all a painful reminder of what she did not have and what she wanted desperately—what she might have if she were to marry Harold Vaughn, and then only if he should come into his inheritance. The "if's" were mounting against her, it seemed, and they, together with her hopes for what might be, caused her increasing turmoil as Grace opened her packages and

118

displayed their treasures, holding each up and describing where she had bought it and how she had found it and what else they had seen and done during their stay. Shopping in Paris! To think of it made Beth want to weep.

"And you can see we've had the room done over," Grace said when all the dresses and hats and gloves and parasols and shoes had been opened and shown, and as the excitement of these began to wear off and she yet wanted more to offer for display. "It's a pity Mama should undertake it so late. I've been asking her for years, but... well... it may not matter much longer."

"Why is that?" Laynie asked, only half interested.

Grace answered with an impish smile.

"Have you met someone?" Beth pressed.

"I have, indeed!" Grace said and beamed. She sat at her dressing table and examined her reflection in the mirror. She made a few careful adjustments to her hair and smiled at the result. Her fringe was perfect, of course. Her hair, a little lighter than Beth's, was piled high on her head, expertly arranged and hardly a strand out of place. And as Grace freshened her appearance, she described her young gentleman: he was handsome and charming and would one day—perhaps one day soon—be very well to do.

Beth wished, with a certain degree of envy, that she could share her own news: that a gentleman of means and family wanted her, and that she might learn to want him, and that he was to be very wealthy, or might be wealthy *if*... And again that "if" which prevented her from sharing any of it. Not a word, for it was all too humiliating. Is that not why they had come, after all, so that Aunt Phillips might persuade Laynie to love him, or at the very least to marry him, with or without love? Beth smoothed her own hair, but did it blindly, as there was no mirror convenient to her.

"Are we to meet him?" Laynie asked.

"Oh, indeed! In fact I expect he will be at dinner tomorrow evening," Grace answered, at last satisfied with her appearance. "You will see him for yourself. But you must keep my secret. You will, won't you?"

"Aunt Phillips does not know?" Laynie asked her.

"She has observed his attentiveness toward me," she answered, "and my eagerness to receive it. She knows, I think, that I am fond of him, but beyond that she is unaware."

"There is an understanding between you," Laynie concluded.

"Oh, yes, indeed!" She seemed to consider a moment. "That is, there is an understanding of sorts. It all depends on a very great deal," she said, which Beth understood all too well. "We have some work to do, I think, to convince Mama. But we will convince her. I'm determined to do it."

"Does she not approve of him?" Laynie inquired, quite puzzled by the intrigue.

"She does not disapprove, exactly. She has a reservation is all, but we will conquer her, just you wait and see. Only you will promise not to say anything quite yet, won't you?"

"Yes, of course," Beth said, quite happy to be privy to an intrigue, even if it wasn't her own.

"Laynie?" Grace said, waiting for her younger cousin's promise.

Laynie offered it with a nod.

A bell rang somewhere below.

"That's the dressing bell," Grace said and arose once more. "Mama will want you dressed for dinner." She led the sisters back to their own, much more humbly-appointed room and opened the wardrobe that stood on the far wall. "There," she said, and looked quite pleased with herself. "These are for you. Last year's things. I don't want them any-more. I thought you might like them."

"Thank you, Grace!" Beth said, nearly overcome, and embraced her cousin warmly before she quit the room to return to her own.

Beth returned to the wardrobe, encouraged to see that Laynie appeared pleased by their cousin's show of generosity. She was examin-ing the dresses and gowns, one by one, but only to reject each in turn. She sat in a nearby chair, as glum and petulant as before.

"You don't like any of them?" Beth said, unbelieving. Neither was she certain how to deal with her sister when she was behaving so uncharacteristically. It was as if she were pining for someone. If not Harold Vaughn, than who?

"I like them all," Laynie answered, "but they are not likely to fit, are they?"

"Why ever not? We are nearly enough the same size as Grace."

"Grace is two inches taller than me at least."

"They can always be hemmed, you know."

"But not before dinner."

"Did you bring anything that would suit?"

"Do we own anything that would suit?" Laynie returned.

"You must make some effort, Laynie. Your happiness is at stake, as well as my own. Aunt Phillips isn't likely to be persuaded by a down-at-the-mouth and petulant young woman. She's as likely to think you are brooding over Mr. Vaughn as dreading having to discuss him. Are you?"

"Brooding? No!"

"Then prove it," she said and pulled from Laynie's own trunk her best muslin gown. It was not much, but it would have to do. Beth helped her to dress and together they went down.

* * *

Laynie put on a brave face as she entered the dining room. Beth had been right. Laynie must prove that she knew her own mind, which must mean she knew and understood her own heart and that she was completely in command of it; but she did not want to be here, and no amount of pageantry could convince her otherwise.

"Bethany, my darling, you are a vision!" Aunt Phillips said upon observing her in pale blue satin. She then observed Laynie. Her welcome was not quite so warm. "Do Grace's things not suit you, Alayna?" she asked, evidently prepared to be disappointed in her young niece.

"They are lovely, Aunt, thank you. I think they are likely to be a trifle too long, however. I thought I'd wait until tomorrow and see what might be done in the way of hemming one or two of them. Will you help me to do it? I'm afraid I've never learned to sew well."

"And Beth has not taught you?"

Laynie demurred from answering this. She might have if Laynie had possessed an ounce of patience for learning the skill or Beth for teaching it.

"Oh, my darlings, how *have* you survived without a mama! Yes, of course, Alayna. Certainly I'll help you."

Grace entered in a gown of pale yellow, and with her arrival the meal could begin.

"Sit, do," Aunt Phillips urged the girls, and showed them which chairs were to be theirs. "And afterwards," she said, stopping to place a confidential arm around Laynie's shoulder, "you and I will have something to talk about, won't we?"

The sisters were helped to sit by the footmen, one of them particularly very tall and handsome, and Laynie chided herself for thinking to form any opinion at all of the servants, who were meant to be all but invisible. If her aunt knew, she would be quite beside herself.

"How does your father get on these days?" Uncle Phillips inquired.

Bethany answered in the usual way. "He keeps much to himself. He potters away his time with books and learning, even in his advanced age, and retains little of it because of it."

"Such was the case until lately," Laynie offered. "He has been much sharper of mind recently, I think."

"You know, I think you are right, now that you mention it," Beth concurred.

"And is there a reason for his sudden improvement?" Aunt Phillips wondered.

"He has hired a companion," Laynie answered.

Aunt Phillips laid down her soup spoon. "A what?"

"A companion," Laynie explained. "A gentleman who comes to read with him two or three nights a week."

"He pays this gentleman?" Aunt Phillips asked.

"Yes, of course," Laynie said. "He is an educated man. He keeps Papa happily occupied and that, to my mind, makes him well worth the money."

"Yes, my dear," Aunt Phillips said now with a scoff she attempted, if weakly, to stifle. "But with *what* money? There is so little of it left. Has he thought what he is to do when he runs out? Have you thought what *you* are to do?"

"Perhaps that's why he's in such a rush to see us married," Beth suggested and not without her own hint of disapproval.

"Yes, perhaps it is," Aunt Phillips agreed. "I'm very surprised to hear this. Very surprised indeed. Have you not objected?"

"It's difficult to object when it does do him so much good."

"What makes him happy," Laynie added, "makes us happy."

"That's a very right and proper answer, my dear," Aunt Phillips said, as their uncle listened on. He was draining his second glass of wine. "But it does little to solve the problem at hand, does it?"

"Papa is occupied," Laynie returned, "he is content, he therefore has a great deal less to fuss at us about."

"Well, that is until lately," Beth added with a dour look that reminded Laynie why they were here at all.

The conversation was concluded with Aunt Phillips' express wish to continue it later, at a time and in a place where talk of money and retainers was more appropriate than at table.

When dinner was over the ladies withdrew. Aunt Phillips desired that her counsel to Laynie should be conducted confidentially and so requested that Beth and Grace find something to play at the piano.

"Now, my dear," she said when she had Laynie quite to herself, "I want to hear all about this Mr. Vaughn, who has caused so much excitement between you and your sister. And some rivalry, I trust, yes?"

Laynie glanced to her sister, who was standing at the piano, prepared to turn the pages for Grace, who seemed content to turn them for herself. The conversation with her aunt would be confidential only so long as the piano kept playing.

"Truly, Aunt," she said, when once they had begun, "there is much less excitement than you suppose."

"That is not what your father says."

"Perhaps then the excitement is all on his side. You know how anxious he is to be rid of us."

"Now, now, my dear, he wishes to see you well provided for while he still can. There is nothing wrong in that. And here is a worthy prospect, a gentleman with family, with connections, and with some money! Why should you not think as well of him as he thinks of you?"

"But that's just it, Aunt," Laynie said, grateful for the opportunity to make herself understood. "We are friends. Neither of us particularly wishes for more."

Aunt Phillips appeared confused. She shook her head just enough to send her sapphire earrings swinging. Laynie watched them as her aunt made, what no doubt seemed to her, the most valid of objections. "His *mother*, my dear, has expressed her pointed preference for you. Why should not the son?"

"We have long been very close friends," Laynie explained, "but I hardly think it enough alone." Laynie glanced to Beth, who quickly looked away. "In truth," Laynie went on, more confidentially now, "he has confessed his preference for—"

But she did not appear to be listening. "Just think, my dear, of the opportunity you throw away! If you can secure a husband of means and property and family, then by all means do it! And, if you want my advice"—which Laynie did not—"without waste of time. He may decide he prefers someone else, after all, if you make him wait around too long."

"That's just it, Aunt. He does not want me."

"He will have you, and that's very nearly as good."

But Laynie did not quite agree.

"My dear," she said, more confidentially still, "I did not think I wanted my husband when I married him. And where do you think I would be now had I refused him?" She asked as if Laynie knew the answer and could measure it as logical evidence for her claim. "Such an opportunity does not come along twice in a lifetime, I can assure you."

Laynie thought of Mr. Hartright and wondered how her aunt's argument might be swayed with the reminder of Beth's disappointment. She didn't dare mention it, however.

Aunt Phillips looked at her as if she were quite the thing to be pitied. "My dear Alayna, you are still so young. Perhaps you are too young to understand how these things work."

"Perhaps I am, Aunt," she answered and considered her aunt's reasoning; how, if it being the same as her father's, made so much sense to her Aunt and so little sense to herself, then she certainly must be very, very young indeed to be playing at this game of love—and almost love, and not quite love—and marriage.

"It is not so bad, you know, to marry young. Men like innocent wives. And your father wishes to see you married while he lives. I offer the warning not for his sake alone. Your chances while you are young are so much greater." She paused a moment to allow Laynie to consider her words before adding, once more, the appellation: "If you wait too long…"

Laynie had no further argument to make, neither did there seem any point in trying to make it. Her aunt, as her father did, saw and believed what she wished and little else mattered.

"Love is a matter of chance, my dear," Aunt Phillips continued. "Marriage is a business and you are only setting yourself up for disappointment if you allow yourself to think of it as anything more. You may choose a man you think you might love, only to learn that you don't or cannot. You may refuse a man you think you cannot love, only to learn when it is too late that you might have done it—or worse, have done it. Oh, my dear, how I do wish you would let me guide you." She looked at her gravely. "It would be so much better for you and for your poor father, who worries so, if you would put your fanciful pride behind you and make a sound choice."

"Of course I am happy to be guided by you, Aunt," Laynie said with some measure of reluctance and yet knowing she ought at least to express her gratitude, even if she did not feel it.

Aunt Phillips pressed her hands together as if to quell her excitement. "I'm so glad, my dear. I'm so very glad. And the opportunity to benefit by that counsel is shortly to come."

"Oh?" Laynie asked, somewhat confused and a little apprehensive.

"There is to be a ball next week, and I mean for you to be at your very best, though we will have to work hard if we mean to prepare you properly."

"Prepare me?" she asked, confused. "For a ball?"

"No, my dear," Aunt Phillips said and laughed. "For marriage!" And as if it were all decided she turned to Grace, who was just finishing up her selection on the piano. "Why do you not play that new Serenade for your cousins, Grace? You sing it so well, you know."

"Very well, Mama," she answered with a self-satisfied smile. "If you wish it."

And so began an impromptu recital, wherein Grace played and sang several pieces, where even Beth played twice and sang to Grace's playing. Laynie, with a sense of uncharacteristic gloom, sat and only listened.

"I think you are not looking forward to this holiday."

Chapter twelve

LAYNIE AWOKE BEFORE THE REST of the house had arisen. She had not slept well. Her aunt's appeals, her promises and warnings, had resonated through her mind so that her dreaming was disturbed and interrupted and her waking fitful and nervous. She longed for a solitary walk in the early morning quiet.

She arose, dressed and went out.

The rear gardens were very formal and intricately laid out, and Laynie would have liked to examine them closer. Perhaps she might take a tip or two for her own ever-evolving garden at home. But the rear gardens were also very open and she wished to remain undisturbed as long as circumstances would allow. She chose, instead, the garden that was situated to the west of the house. Here there had once been an intricate maze, but her aunt, upon marrying Mr. Phillips, had determined that her home would be a respectable place, and so the maze, save for its outermost border of boxwood and cypress, was done away with.

Laynie entered and began her leisurely stroll—as leisurely as was possible on an injured ankle; but the garden was not empty. In one corner, standing beside a boxwood that had been cut and sculptured to resemble something like a great cake, stood a gentleman enjoying a cigar. She thought to turn and make her way back, to find some other place to sit and meditate upon her present circumstances, but she had not accomplished half the distance again before he saw her.

"Don't go," he said.

Laynie turned to him. "I'm sorry," she said. "I did not know the garden was occupied."

"If you want it, I'll be happy to forfeit it to you." He dropped the cigar and stubbed it out with his foot.

"No," she said, "I do not mind. I can easily use another of the gardens."

"Are you certain?" he said and a look implied her injury. "You are limping, I think."

"Only a little."

He smiled and exhaled a laugh through his nose. "Or a lot. Sit, won't you? Do you mind awfully to have company?"

She examined him. Who was he? He was very handsome. Alarmingly so, with hair as fair as Beth's, though not so fair as Grace's, and blue eyes that sparked with a sort of reluctant merriment. "No, not at all," she said and sat.

"What did you do to your foot?"

"I fell," was her simple answer and hoped it was enough.

"From?" he pressed.

"A horse."

His brows raised. "You ride?"

"I used to."

"Before your accident?"

"No, before we had to give up our horses."

He examined her narrowly, apparently amused, and walked a slow circle around the stone bench upon which she sat. Having made a full round of it, he sat, too. "You were riding someone else's horse, then," he said eventually.

"Yes."

"The animal was dangerous?"

"No, I jumped him."

"That was very brave," he said and looked at her seriously. "Or very stupid."

If he told her how lucky she was not to have been hurt worse, or even killed, she would get up and walk away from him. She could not stand to be patronized any more about it.

"You did not make your way back home alone, I take it. Someone was with you?"

"No, I was found."

"That was fortunate."

"It was my father's hired companion who found me, actually."

"Fortunate for him!" He smiled belatedly. Did he think this a joke? It seemed he did. His smile broadened. And then he laughed. Gently at first and then with increasing mirth. He was not laughing at her so much as with her. And she could hardly blame him. It was a ridiculous predicament. She recalled it, recalled her humiliation, and then tried to see it from another's perspective. How had it looked to Mr. Holbrook? She dared not think of that. Or of him. She tried, instead, to see it through Mr. Vaughn's eyes, who had seen her in a hundred predica-ments before.

Yes. Yes, it was funny, she supposed. Laynie laughed, too. It felt good to laugh, to make light of something that had once seemed so serious. She laughed the harder for his laughing and continued to laugh until tears began to stream.

He stopped before she did. He examined her a moment, pulled a handkerchief from his pocket and handed it to her.

"Thank you," she said and wiped her eyes. It was only then she looked at it. It was bordered with a black band.

"Are you in mourning, Mr.—?"

"Emerson," he said. "Frederick Emerson. It is an immense pleasure to meet you, Miss—?"

"Alayna Durham," she answered him. "My friends call me Laynie."

"Is that an invitation?"

"I suppose it is, of sorts," she said and wondered just how far he would accept it.

"Miss Laynie, then," he said, as was right and proper. "Thank you."

"For what?"

"For the laugh. It's been a long time. I forgot how good it feels." He smiled, but it faded and a sort of haunted look replaced the mirth that was there but a few minutes ago. "Yes, to answer your question, I am in mourning."

"May I ask for whom?" She wondered if it was someone close to him. A parent or a sibling, perhaps.

"My wife," he answered, which answer Laynie was unprepared for.

"I'm so terribly sorry, Mr. Emerson. May I ask how long it's been?"

"Nearly a year. Just short of it, actually."

"How very tragic. Again, I'm terribly sorry." He was silent then, and Laynie felt it necessary to say something more. "I know it is not quite the same, but I lost my mother."

"We are both familiar with loss, it seems."

"But my loss was some time ago. I know it is not the same. I have had some time to get used to her absence. The loss of a spouse, though... I don't know how you get over that."

"They say time heals all wounds. I think sometimes it only makes us strong enough to bear them."

"Not in a year's time, though."

"No," he smiled kindly, but his eyes remained full of loss. "No, not so quickly as that."

"It's been ten years since my mother passed. I don't know that my father ever really recovered. He is terribly lonely at times."

"But he has you."

Laynie shook her head. "I'm still very much a child in his eyes, I'm afraid."

"He needs to have his eyes opened, then."

She was surprised by this remark and its implications. She looked at him and found him looking very intently at her. Was it quite appropriate to be talking about his loss one minute and receiving such flattery—was that even what it was?—the next?

"Are you a guest here, Mr. Emerson?"

"Yes, in a manner of speaking. That is, I'm staying nearby."

She arose from her place. "Then perhaps we will meet again."

"I hope very much that we will," he said without answering the question she dared not ask—was he Ned's guest? Grace's? Merely a neighbor come to visit?—and smiled once more, a kind, sad smile.

"Until then, Mr. Emerson," and she turned and left him, and tried not to think more about him.

It was difficult to do. Perhaps, after all, Beth had been right. Perhaps the best way to prove to her aunt the futility in her father's plans for her was to show her how capable she was of finding altern-atives. Might Mr. Emerson be an alternative? She considered his handsome face, his kind, sad eyes, his vaguely flirtatious words, and thrilled just a little at the thought.

* * *

Laynie returned indoors to find Beth just coming down the stairs.

"Where have you been?" she asked her. "I've been looking for you everywhere."

"I went out for a walk," Laynie answered.

"A walk? Alone?"

"Yes, of course alone," she lied and did not know why she felt the need to do it. "Did you expect I had taken a companion? I don't usually, you know."

"It's just that I cannot find Grace, either."

"Oh?" Laynie said and wondered if her absence was significant.

"I suppose she'll turn up, but Aunt is anxious that you and I should spend some time with her this morning."

"Whatever for?" Laynie asked a little impatiently. She was not quite prepared to listen to another lecture on the merits of accepting Mr. Vaughn, the only gentleman who was likely to be daft enough to marry her, whether he wanted her or not.

"She wants to give us some instruction at the piano. Evidently she wasn't overly impressed by last night's performance. She's hoping Grace can take one of us, and she the other. But Grace cannot be found."

"It is curious, don't you think? I wonder where she can have gone."

"I'm not sure I'm all that eager to find her, if you want to know. Enduring Aunt's lessons is tiresome enough without having to bear Grace's condescension on top of it. Come, won't you?"

Laynie, with a nod, allowed herself to be led to the morning room, where their aunt was waiting for them.

Aunt Phillips' lessons were nothing new. It seemed she felt it her duty to make up for the neglect the sisters must necessarily suffer by the loss of their mother. Laynie was grateful for the trouble taken, and yet the lessons were no more easy to endure for her gratitude. Their first lesson at the piano evolved—as her lessons so often did—into one for voice, which somehow evolved into instruction in diction. A lesson in poise and carriage followed, of which Laynie, for obvious reasons (or so her aunt declared) was in desperate need. The fact that Laynie's ankle made it difficult to walk at an even gait proved a source of profound irritation to their usually mild-mannered aunt. Aunt Phillips feared—or so she stated quite plainly—that Laynie was determined to lay waste to all her hard work by insisting on the malady. Was there not some unguent she could try? Laynie knew of no remedy but rest. At last, interrupted by tea and apparently frustrated by her nieces' inability to grasp in one afternoon the finer points of playing and singing with the skill of a virtuoso or speaking and walking as elegantly as those born into a sphere considerably higher than her own, Aunt Phillips dismissed Laynie to rest her injury and Beth to keep Laynie company. Laynie, with a book in hand, did rest, but Beth kept herself busy fussing with Grace's cast-off gowns, trying to decide which she should keep, and better yet, which she would wear during her stay.

Laynie was awakened from her nap by the maid who had come in to light the gas jets. She was otherwise alone.

"It's nearly dinner, Miss," she said. "Shall I send someone up to help you dress?"

"There's no need," Laynie said, "but thank you."

The maid curtseyed and left her once more to herself. It was only then she realized her mistake. The wardrobe had been locked, the key taken, and lying beside it was a gown of heavily pleated dove grey. She could tell by looking at it that it was too long. She might wear one of her own gowns, but those, upon being unpacked, had been placed in the wardrobe along with Grace's things. There was nothing for it. She must wear the grey.

It looked well on her, Laynie had to admit. It was quite the finest thing she had ever owned, and it fitted her well, save for the length of it. She would have to make do, and certainly if she was careful enough she could avoid getting caught up in the hem. She required a little help managing all the buttons, however, and so opened the door to peek out into the hall, hoping to find a maid or Beth, or failing that, perhaps she might go to Grace's room to see if she had returned and if she might have her help in dressing.

As luck would have it, the moment Laynie stuck her head out the door the servants' passage opposite creaked open. It hesitated, then at last opened wide. Standing there in the doorway, looking both ways to be sure the way was clear, was her cousin.

"Grace! What on earth are you doing?"

Grace started, turned crimson, and placed one finger to her lips. She looked again to be sure they were alone and then tiptoed across the corridor to Laynie, pulling her into her room by the arm and securing the door. She placed a hand on her chest to still her heart and stood a minute to catch her breath.

"Where have you been?" Laynie asked her. "And what on earth is wrong with you?"

A smile slowly crept across Grace's face as her color restored itself to nearly a normal hue. "I've been out," she said with a flick of her eyebrows.

"Yes, I know. But where? Are you really only just returning? Your mother must be truly anxious for you by now."

"Do you think so?" Grace asked and appeared only mildly worried.

"She's been looking for you all morning. Will you help me?" she said, remembering her buttons and turned to offer her back to Grace. "Where have you been?" she asked once more.

"Can I trust you?" Grace asked her and nimbly began fastening the buttons.

"Yes, of course you can."

"You promise you won't tell Mama?"

"No. Not if you don't want me to, but do explain yourself. You are behaving very strangely."

"I know it," she said and sounded as though she were proud of the fact. "The truth is…I've been out with him."

"Him? Do you mean…?"

Grace nodded enthusiastically. "But you cannot tell Mama," she said more seriously. "He is to come to dinner tonight, and it will be difficult enough to act as though nothing has happened."

"And what *has* happened?" Laynie asked, and, her buttons fastened, she turned to face her cousin. "Will you tell me?"

"Oh, everything!" Grace said and held her hands before her. "But don't worry. It won't be a secret much longer. You shall soon know everything! And so shall Mama. I do hope she is as happy for me as I am. But good heaven!" Grace said and looked suddenly alarmed. "I must dress for dinner or I'll be late!" She turned from the room, but stopped again before the door was quite closed, and, placing a finger to her lips once more, reminded her: "Not a word, remember?"

Laynie nodded her agreement.

Laynie was understandably curious upon going down to dinner to discover just who it was that was the source of all the mystery regard-ing Grace and her secret love. She entered the dining room to find that there were more gentlemen than one in attendance. Ned was there and two other gentlemen besides. Had Ned brought a friend, then? Laynie hoped very much that he had not brought two. One was a stranger to her and stood beside the fireplace mantel as he spoke with Uncle Phillips, while Beth listened on in divided interest as her attention shifted between that man and the other who was in attendance. Considering all the recent anxieties caused by the pre-carious nature of Mr. Vaughn's suit, Laynie had hoped her sister might be a little more reserved where eligible and unarguably hand-some young gentlemen were concerned. Of course she was not.

The second of their gentlemen guests stood at the far end of the room, looking contemplatively at the drinks table and trying to decide what he should have. He chose a brandy and caught her gaze as he took his first tentative sip of it. He smiled with his eyes, a look of recognition, but made no effort to approach her. They had not been formally introduced, after all, and so, until the problem was remedied, they must behave as strangers.

Laynie turned again to examine the gentleman with whom her uncle was speaking, and wondered what evidences of his attachment to Grace he might display. Until Grace arrived none, it seemed. And if he should prove to be Grace's beau—and Laynie believed he must be, at least she hoped very much it was so—she did not like to think what difficulties it might cause between the cousins should Grace find Beth in such pointed attendance upon him.

135

But if this stranger had come to dine with Grace, did that mean then that Mr. Emerson was a friend of Ned's? And what was she to make of that? He did not seem at all like her cousin. He was so well behaved, so exceedingly polite and well mannered—not like Ned at all. She looked to Ned, as though doing so might give her the answer. She instantly regretted it. He met her gaze and winked impertinently.

Beth, having observed her, approached her casually, and only when she was standing very close and holding on to her arm did she speak. "Which is he? Can you guess?"

"Is it not he, with whom our uncle is speaking?"

"I cannot tell!" Beth said in an excited and yet somewhat frustrated whisper. "If only I could!"

Such was Laynie's thinking as well as she examined both gentlemen, comparing them to each other—and to what little she knew of her cousin's taste. The gentleman with whom Beth had so recently been speaking was well looking enough, very tall, but stiff and formal, his manner affected. It told her nothing. Truly it did not seem likely that Mr. Emerson should be Grace's suitor. He had hardly behaved this morning as a man already spoken for; there had been something—or so she felt—shared between them. If he were not already claimed by Grace—and oh, how Laynie prayed he was not—then perhaps Laynie and Beth would soon find themselves at odds. Why should she always play second to her sister? Perhaps, after all, she had had enough of that.

"What are you two carrying on about?" Ned said, interrupting them.

Laynie hoped very much he had not heard their conversation.

It seemed he had, or he could guess at any rate. "Let me introduce you to my friends. Emerson, Jones, come here a moment, won't you?"

So they were both of them Ned's friends. Was it possible?

"I'd like you to meet my charming young cousins, Miss Bethany Durham and her younger sister," Ned added with a flick of his eyebrows, "Miss Alayna Durham. My dear friends Mr. Frederick Emerson and Mr. Walter Jones."

Mr. Jones bowed long and deep, and before he straightened he looked at Laynie, then at Beth, and then at Laynie again before offering a thin smile. "An honor to make your acquaintance," he said.

136

Laynie decided there was something she did not quite like about the hungry gaze he had cast upon them. She hoped, for her own sake, that he should prove to be he in whom Grace had placed her happiness. Did she dare hope such a thing for Grace?

It was Mr. Emerson's turn to address them. "Miss Durham," he said and bowed. "And Miss Alayna. Miss Laynie, I believe you are called," he added and gave her a knowing look.

"Yes," she said and smiled, and understood that his reason for knowing such a thing was a secret between them. Did she have a secret of her own, then? She rather liked the thought of that.

"It is a pleasure! Phillips has told us a great deal about you," he said, more to Laynie than to Beth.

Laynie looked to Ned. "Do I want to know what my cousin has said of me?" she asked.

"All lovely things, Miss Laynie," Mr. Emerson assured her. "Lovely things, indeed. Have no fear."

The conversation was interrupted by the entrance of Aunt Phillips, followed directly by her daughter.

"There you are, my dear! I've been looking for you all day."

"Have you? Why I've been in my room with a headache, though I'm much better now. You dear thing!" Grace said, looking at her mother sympathetically and then kissing her on the cheek. "I'm terribly sorry to have worried you."

The diversion worked, and her mother, absorbing the rare gesture of appreciation, smiled and tutted, and then she invited the party to be seated.

The handsome footman once more appeared to push Laynie's chair in, but Mr. Emerson beat him to it. She was not sorry. She felt the weight of someone's gaze on her and looked to find Ned raising his eyebrows at her. Was he trying to indicate some observed interest? And on her part or Mr. Emerson's? Or was he merely being impertinent?

Mr. Jones, preoccupied by a speck on his boot, was last to be seated. He did so hurriedly and nearly pulled the cloth from the table. "My apologies," he said and haphazardly straightened his own silverware while the footmen repaired the rest of the damage. "I say," he said to one of them, indicating his foot, "would you speak to the boot boy. This is very shoddy work."

The handsome footman nodded. "Of course, sir," he said and returned to his place.

Laynie offered him an apologetic look, which he may or may not have seen. Dutiful as he was, his attention was on no one and nothing in particular. To his master and mistress he was meant to be all but invisible. Laynie oughtn't even to be contemplating him. So why was she?

She turned from him to see that she herself was being observed, and by all but her uncle, Mr. Jones, and her sister (who was busy watching Mr. Emerson). Grace was watching her with a knowing and conspiratorial look; Mr. Emerson, with a questioning look that seemed to imply he had witnessed her gesture to the footman and wished to know what it meant; Ned, who was always watching her with that insipid, too familiar look on his brow; and her aunt, who appeared to be on the brink of saying something important.

"You do look lovely tonight, Alayna. The dress suits you well."

"Thank you, Aunt. I believe Beth chose it for me."

"I beg your pardon?" Beth said, having awoken from her daydreaming by the mention of her name.

"You chose the dress, I think? My dress?"

"Oh," she said and giggled. "That was rather wicked of me. I locked the wardrobe so she had no choice."

"I do wish I'd had a chance to hem it first."

"You will just have to mind where you put your feet," her aunt said, as if it were the simplest of tasks.

Beth laughed again. "People should tell her that more often," she said. "It might save us no end of anxiety. Do you know how she hurt her ankle, Aunt? Laynie and I had decided upon a walk, and—"

"Are you sure that's wise?" Laynie said, interrupting her. "Don't forget to include why we were in Jupiter Lane, and whose horse I rode, and why I happened to have him in my possession."

"Oh, I like the sound of this," Ned said and took an eager sip of his wine as he turned his attention full upon Beth. It was an almost welcome reprieve, or it would have been were Beth not so eager to make her look a fool in front of their newest acquaintances.

Beth was considering Laynie's warning, perhaps considering the story and how there was no way to tell it without confessing she had an admirer already. Laynie hated to sacrifice Mr. Vaughn in such a way, but if it meant escaping being made the punch line of one of Beth's cruel jokes, she would do it.

"Perhaps it's a story for another time," Beth at last demurred.

"Don't tease," Ned pleaded. "Do tell us the story."

She considered her way out of this. "Perhaps another story? There are at least a hundred of them."

"Oh, yes, anything will do," Ned said, too encouragingly.

"There was the time she was nearly shot..." Beth said with a glance at her sister that suggested she would have her way yet.

"Shot?" Aunt Phillips said in shock.

"What is this?" Uncle Phillips seconded. "*When* was this?"

"Years ago," Laynie tried to assure him.

"It was last year," Beth corrected, "and I can't believe you've not heard it already."

"Perhaps it's best saved for another time, then," Laynie suggested with waning patience.

Beth, it seemed, was prepared to ignore her. "You see, it all happened when one of our neighbors had announced a hunt. Papa had asked us to stay home, and—"

"I believe your sister begged you to reserve your story for another time, Miss Durham," Mr. Emerson said. "Are you really so eager to cause her embarrassment? Ned had told me you were very fond of each other. I'm tempted to think he was not entirely truthful."

Beth, ashamed, took up her fork and prodded at the roast that had just been placed before her. She put her fork down again and did not eat.

Laynie cast a very grateful look upon Mr. Emerson, which he received and acknowledged with a slight shake of his head, as if to say, "It was nothing."

But it wasn't nothing. It was a great deal. No one had ever stood up for her before and the feeling was quite novel. It was a little thing, certainly, but it was hardly nothing.

"When do lectures commence, Ned?" his father asked him.

"In another week, sir," was his answer.

"And you will apply yourself these final terms, I hope."

He did not answer him, and so Laynie took the opportunity of posing her own question, which she wanted very much to have answered. "Does that mean, then, you will not be here the entire fortnight of our stay?"

Ned gave her an injured look, but whether it was sincere or mocking, she could not tell.

"If he's not there for the opening lecture, I'll have something very particular to say about it," Mr. Phillips said and seemed to have some especial meaning in mind that Ned quite plainly understood. Perhaps his dourness was on this account and not on Laynie's at all.

"You are friends from University, then?" Laynie asked the three gentlemen at once.

"Yes," Ned said, nodding to Mr. Jones, "and no." He indicated Mr. Emerson with a second nod of his head. "Jones and I shared rooms last term and will share rooms again the next. Emerson and I were at school together. We've recently been reacquainted, as luck would have it."

This explained a great deal. At least it gave her reason to hope—indeed to believe—that Mr. Emerson was very different from Ned and his usual sorts of friends.

"Do you remember, Emerson, that time at King's when we instigated a rebellion against the Praepostor?" And Laynie watched on with great interest as Ned and his two friends recounted certain episodes in their school days. But as she could follow very little of it, with their Latin nomenclature and public school rhetoric, she ceased after a while to listen. It was only when Aunt Phillips spoke again that Laynie's interest was reawakened.

"Of course you will, Mr. Emerson," she was saying now. "A gentleman in such a position as yours, with an education and with so many noble qualities, *must* marry again."

Laynie was suddenly aware she had missed something important. What was the impetus for this consolatory speech? Had Grace made her confession and her mother her answer? What was it she had missed?

Emerson received his counsel with a somber smile that was directed at his plate.

"But not soon, I think," Aunt Phillips added.

His brow knotted and he looked up. "I have no intention of being disrespectful to my wife's memory, ma'am, but truth be told, I am a little anxious to no longer be alone."

Laynie and Beth exchanged a puzzled look. Beth's countenance was first of surprise and then of pity. Laynie looked next to Grace but her attention was full upon her mother. If only she had been paying closer attention to the conversation.

"It is a greater trial than perhaps you can imagine," Mr. Emerson continued, "being alone when you have grown accustomed to having someone always there beside you. It is, at times, unendurable."

Aunt Phillips reached out a hand and patted Mr. Emerson's arm. "You will find someone, Mr. Emerson. Never you fear. And when the time is right, you will know it. When it is the right person it won't be a day or a moment too soon."

Mr. Emerson flinched a grateful smile once more in the direction of his plate. Laynie was feeling all the more confident that it must be Mr. Jones whom Grace favored, but her hope was soon dashed. While the conversation slowly began to reawaken around them, Laynie observed that a look was exchanged between Mr. Emerson and Grace, a long, meaningful look that spoke of hope on her side and doubt on his. Grace, her face suffused with color, shook her head almost imperceptibly and offered him a reassuring smile. He accepted it, perhaps gratefully, and went back to his meal. He lifted his glass, took a sip, and met Laynie's gaze ever so briefly. Not a hint of recognition was in his look, nothing of apology or regret, nothing to hint of bad timing or star-crossed fate. It was as if nothing at all had transpired between them. Perhaps, after all, Laynie had merely imagined it.

Yes, of course she had. Only…

"What do you say, Laynie?"

"What was that?" she said, waking a second time from her stupor.

"Ned has proposed a game," Grace explained.

"A game?"

"When dinner is over, yes. Rather than us withdrawing, Ned thinks we should all have a game."

"Oh, yes! Let's do!" Beth exclaimed and clapped her hands together.

"What game?" Laynie asked cautiously.

"Hide and seek?" was Ned's suggestion. The gleam in his eye was just a little too mischievous.

"That's a child's game," Laynie objected, though that was not her real objection at all. "I think not."

"The Blind Postman, then," Ned offered as an alternative.

"Oh no, Ned. No, not that game. Think of my ankle."

"There's nothing wrong with your ankle," he said. "Everyone else wants to play. You're the one being the child if you won't join in."

And Laynie, apparently defeated, reluctantly acquiesced.

The Blind Postman was a simple parlor game, though it allowed—as all Ned's favorite games did—for a fair bit of not-quite innocent roguery. The larger the party the better, but it would work well enough with the six of them, so long as Uncle Phillips would serve as master of ceremonies. It was he who would decide which countries the remainder of the players would represent. They, seated in chairs placed around the periphery of the room, would wait for their country to be called out, at which time they would trade places, crossing the room in such a way that he who was "it" must try, while blindfolded, to catch one of them before the seats were exchanged.

Uncle Phillips assigned each of the party a country, by which, for the remainder of the game they would be known. Grace was given Spain; Beth, France (a notion that gave her no end of delight); Laynie was Switzerland; Ned was Denmark; Mr. Jones was Prussia; and Mr. Emerson, Belgium.

Uncle Phillips then found some straws, by which the first Blind Postman was to be selected. Grace chose the shortest straw. She was blindfolded, while everyone else chose a place to sit. She stood in the middle of the room and waited for her father to call out the first countries.

"From Belgium to… Oh, dear. I seem to have forgotten which countries I've assigned to whom," he said and laughed.

"To France!" Beth said, calling out her own name and rising, a little more enthusiastic to join in the fun than was quite appropriate. She and Mr. Emerson crossed the room to exchange seats, all the while teasing the postman who must try to catch them. Beth seemed always to be in Mr. Emerson's way, running into him on accident and crossing his path so that he must find a way around her. Laynie was a little embarrassed for her sister, who evidently had not noticed the look exchanged between Mr. Emerson and her cousin and who was trying a little too hard to gain his attention.

"Excuse me," Beth said to him and giggled.

The sound of her voice alerted Grace to her whereabouts and she approached. Beth squealed and held to Mr. Emerson as if he were a sort of shield between herself and Grace who was quickly, if blindly, advancing. What Beth did not see in her flirtatious half-attempts at evasion was the surreptitious gesture made by Mr. Emerson, who lightly touched Grace's hand as she came nearer. She felt the gesture and grasped to take a better hold of him just as he moved away. It was Beth she latched onto instead.

"I have you!" Grace said and whipped off the blindfold. A look of slightest disappointment passed over her brow. "You are it," she said, quickly recovering and evidently happy to give up her "postal" responsibilities.

Grace tied the blindfold and made sure Beth could not see, and then turned to her father whose duty it was to call out the next two names. He was fast asleep.

"Oh, Papa," Grace said, scoldingly. "Shall I call out the countries, then?"

"From Belgium to Prussia," Beth called out before Grace could do it. But Mr. Jones, it seemed, was uninterested in playing. Ned took his place and together he and Mr. Emerson approached Beth so that they came up behind her on silent feet as she strained to listen for their movement. Like twin shadows they followed her about the room, making wild gesticulations and comical faces that made the entire party laugh. She seemed not to know they were there, but she was a good pretender—she always had been—and when they had begun to get comfortable with playing her shadow, she spun on her heel and caught them both at once. Mr. Emerson slipped from her grasp. The other she still held firm, and with a victorious look she removed her blindfold.

"Ned!" she said and with a look challenged his right to be there.

Ned laughed loudly and took the blindfold from her. She was out, but she was apparently consoled by the fact that she was now to sit side by side on the sofa with Mr. Emerson. Laynie watched with increasing unease as Beth took her place beside him, smiling and giggling and making chit-chat. He was all politeness and charm, but one look at Grace told Laynie instantly that Beth was crossing a line, even if she did not know it was there.

"From Switzerland to France!" Ned said before the blindfold was quite secure.

Laynie was certain it was not tight enough to truly blind him. She arose and carefully tiptoed along the perimeter of the room, while Beth sat chatting animatedly with Mr. Emerson, utterly oblivious that she had been called to participate.

"I have you, Laynie!" Ned said and made a quick and direct approach toward her.

"You're cheating, Ned!"

She tried to evade him, but he quickly had her cornered.

"You're cheating. Stop where you are and tie your blind properly."

He did not stop, however, but kept advancing. She had one chance to escape him, and that was only if she could manage to push a chair out of her way. It would not budge.

Ned reached out a hand and pretended to feel blindly about for her, but she knew very well he could see her. He might have taken her quite easily by the arm, but it seemed he was not satisfied with that. Instead, he came nearer still, his arms open wide as though he meant to throw them around her. Desperate to be away from him, she attempted once more to move the chair. It slid just enough, but as she tried to slip between it and the wall, her foot got caught in the hem of her dress and she toppled down, pulling the chair down with her.

"What the devil have you done now?" Ned said, removing his blindfold. "You're all right. Get up," he said and lifted the chair off of her. He took her by the arm and raised her, a little too forcefully, to her feet.

She stood, more embarrassed than actually hurt, and waited for Ned to let her go. He didn't and so she shook him off with a jerk of her arm and gave him a menacing look. He rolled his eyes in answer and handed her the blindfold.

"I think I'm finished, Ned."

"Nonsense. It's your turn," he said and attempted to tie the blindfold for her.

Laynie refused and stepped away from him, limping more now than she had in days. It seemed she was not entirely unhurt, after all.

"If you don't take it you'll have to give me a forfeit."

"I don't have anything to give you, Ned."

"Sure you do," he said with a wicked wink, and he advanced once more to take that forfeit—in the form of a kiss—whether she wished to give it to him or not.

"That's enough, Phillips," Emerson said and arose. "You never do know when to quit."

Ned, looking plainly disappointed, released her, and Laynie, seeing an opportunity for escape, took it. Only it seemed she really had reinjured her ankle.

"Allow me, Miss Durham," Mr. Emerson said and took her arm so that she might lean upon him. She stopped again when her foot threatened to become entangled once more.

"I have an idea," he said and helped her to sit. He rang the bell and met the footman at the door, to whom he offered some words of whispered direction. The footman disappeared for a moment and returned shortly with another. The two of them together approached Laynie's chair and between them lifted it from the ground as Laynie let out a little squeal of surprise.

"Not to worry, miss," said the handsome footman. "We have you." And with the chair held quite securely between them she was carried to her room, while all watched on, some more happily than others.

Ned appeared impressed and a little put out for not thinking of it himself. Grace seemed to be truly concerned for her, and delighted, at the same time, with the gallantry of her beloved Mr. Emerson. It was Beth alone who seemed to disapprove of the scene. She glared at her with a look that suggested Laynie had done something truly outrageous, perhaps even despicable. As Laynie was carried from the room on her makeshift sedan chair, Mr. Emerson followed and stood at the base of the staircase supervising her removal and looking very much like a knight in black gabardine armor. How lucky was Grace to have won the admiration of such a man!

Having reached her bedroom, the chair was deposited just inside the doorway, and the footmen left with it the moment Laynie arose. Beth, who entered just behind the footmen, faced her sister squarely, her face red with frustration.

"That was very well done! Are you truly hurt?"

"Not severely, I think. You needn't worry—"

"I have to wonder, Laynie, how it is you always seem to find a way to demand everyone's attention!"

"You don't think I meant to do that?"

"Yes, if you want to know, I do think you planned it. You are jealous!"

"Not of you," Laynie said and instantly wished she had considered her words a little more carefully.

"Not of me?" Beth returned coolly. "Of whom, pray?"

But Laynie did not feel inclined to answer.

Beth waited, tapping her foot on the floor. "If not me," she pressed, "then whom?"

"I wonder," Laynie said instead of answering the question, "if you observed any sign of Grace's attachment to one of her guests tonight."

Beth reddened just a little. "I perceived none. I don't think her attachment to him can be very great if she was able to disguise it so completely."

"I'm afraid it may be the reverse, Beth," Laynie answered.

Beth sat down upon her bed. "It isn't Mr. Jones, is it," she concluded.

Laynie shook her head.

Beth minced her mouth to one side and looked truly disappointed.

"What of Mr. Vaughn, Beth? I don't believe you are so changeable that you would throw him over so easily as that."

"I haven't. That is, I don't think I have. But, oh, Laynie, Mr. Emerson is so..."

"What? What is he?"

146

"I don't know, exactly," Beth said and studied her skirt. "He is not Mr. Vaughn, is he? He's handsome, charming, gregarious, elegant. He's…"

"Go on," Laynie urged her.

Beth looked up from her lap with a look of anguished hope. "He reminds me a very great deal of Mr. Hartright."

Laynie felt suddenly very sorry for her sister. "Oh, Beth," she said and could think of nothing more.

Beth, with a sniff, regained her composure and arose to examine herself in the mirror. She was one of those rare women who looked well with tears, her eyes brighter, her complexion more radiant. And yet she frowned at what she saw: a great deal of wasted effort. She had taken so much care with her dress and appearance, and now she must quit the party to wait upon her accident-prone and once-again-injured sister.

"You needn't stay, Beth. If you like you may go back down. I don't want your company and I know you do not want mine."

Beth's reflection perceptibly brightened. She turned to look at Laynie, approached her and kissed her on the cheek before leaving the room.

Laynie, upon the closing of the door, let out a long sigh and returned to her bed, determined not to think. Her aching ankle recalled her humiliation. She consequently recalled her rescue and smiled to herself. But the smile quickly faded. Mr. Emerson was Grace's. When would it ever be her turn? And could not that turn, when at last it came, be free from rivals and melodrama? There was only one way that was likely to happen, and that was if Beth married first.

Laynie arose and prepared for bed, and she prepared herself as well to be patient. She was growing tired of being patient.

Chapter thirteen

LAYNIE AND BETH WERE AWAKENED the following morning by the entrance of the maid, who entered to announce the arrival of the doctor. It was kind of Aunt Phillips to think of sending him, but Laynie was certain it was entirely unnecessary. The maid helped the sisters to dress and when that was done he was allowed admittance.

He entered, examined Laynie's foot, felt the joint, frowned, and stood, his arms folded across his chest in thought. "When was your initial injury?" he asked.

"A week or two ago, I suppose," she answered him.

"It's been nearly a month since your accident, Laynie," Beth corrected her.

The doctor frowned more determinedly. "And you turned it again last night?"

Laynie nodded her answer.

"It will not heal if you do not stay off it."

"Aunt will not like that answer, I'm afraid."

"No more Blind Postman, then," Beth observed.

The doctor looked to Beth and then scowled again. "I may have something," he said at last. "Your aunt believes in the merits of volatile oils and unguents. They are sometimes known to work." He opened a large leather case, and, with a finger held up, searched for the bottles he wanted. He removed two, mixed them together into a smaller bottle, corked it and handed it to her. "Thrice a day, if you will, and as much rest as you can give it. And no more parlor games," he said with a serious look.

She smiled her gratitude and took the bottle. She uncorked it and cautiously smelled. She was not sure what she had expected. The usual oils administered to her were of the fish variety. This was something else entirely. It was a rich, heady mixture of pine needles and citrus—like Christmas in a bottle. And it reminded her of something. Or someone.

"It smells of Mr. Holbrook," Beth observed. "Close it, will you? The last person I want to be thinking of right now is my father's charmless hired companion."

"He's not charmless."

"Isn't he?" Beth said as if Laynie's defense of him should be somehow significant.

"Thrice daily," the doctor reiterated, "and perhaps I'll see you again before you quit your Aunt's. Will you show me out, Miss Durham?" he asked of Beth.

Beth grudgingly agreed. "I suppose it's time for breakfast," she said. "Have you eaten, Doctor?"

"Oh, yes. Hours ago," he said and followed Beth out.

The door closed. Laynie applied the oil to her ankle and felt the warmth of it spread across her skin and into her joints. The door opened again and Grace appeared, still in her nightgown, her hair a disheveled mess about her head and shoulders. She stole inside, closed the door and approached the bed, a giddy look upon her fair face.

"Good morning, Grace," Laynie said, greeting her.

Grace stopped before Laynie's bed and sniffed the air. "It smells like a forest in here. Have you been chopping wood?"

Laynie laughed and set her bottle aside. "You look well this morning."

"Oh, I *am* well!" Grace said and sat down upon the bed. "I am so exceedingly well I don't know what to do with myself!"

"May I ask why?"

"Last night, of course. You heard her, didn't you?"

"Her? Do you mean Aunt Phillips?"

"Yes! At dinner. Did you hear what wonderful encouragement she gave us?"

"You and Mr. Emerson?" Laynie asked. She felt it was time to have the question answered once and for all.

"Yes!" Grace answered gleefully. "Mr. Wonderful Frederick Divine Emerson!"

Laynie smiled despite herself. "That is quite a name, Grace. Will you be Mrs. Divine-Emerson, I wonder, or only Mrs. Emerson?"

Grace swatted at her playfully. "You're teasing me."

"I am, rather."

"Oh, but I am so happy to know that Mama approves!"

"But, Grace, are you quite certain that was what she meant to say?"

"Yes, of course! You frighten me a little with your enduring uncertainty, Laynie. Even Mr. Emerson was not quite sure of her meaning, but I assure you I know Mama and I know when she approves. She would not have given such encouragement if she did not."

"If you are quite certain, then I'm sure you must be right."

"Oh I am! Of course I am!" And she was silent for a long and contemplative minute. Laynie was beginning to wonder what more there was to say, when Grace at last revealed her real purpose in coming. "He has promised to speak to Papa today."

"Today?" Laynie said, surprised and not a little disappointed. "So soon?"

"Yes. And I'm so nervous I think I may be ill," which said more than anything about the true nature of Grace's certainty. "I hope I was not rash. He thought we should wait just a little while to be sure, but we both want so badly to be married. I can hardly wait, and I think he is as eager for it as I."

Laynie wanted very much to ask what she would do if her Papa refused him, but it seemed the question did not require asking.

"We'll elope if we must, you know."

"You would defy your parents?"

"Truly I hope it does not come to that. But I will marry him. I am absolutely determined!" Grace took Laynie's hands in hers, a pleading look upon her face. "Go to Mama, will you, Laynie? Try to persuade her to see how fond of each other we are, how necessary it is to his happiness he marry again, and how necessary to mine to have him. Will you? I know she will listen to you."

Laynie wondered what evidence she had for this, unsuccessful as she was in convincing her aunt to believe she could not be happy marrying Mr. Vaughn. She made no argument, however. What would be the point? To do so would only add to Grace's anxiety. She nodded her agreement and arose. She hesitated a moment. What would be her pretense in going? Standing upon her ankle provided an immediate answer. She went to the wardrobe, took out the dove-grey gown she had worn last night, and with it draped over one arms she supported herself with the banister as she hobbled downstairs.

Aunt Phillips was found supervising the breakfast table. Ned was at breakfast with Mr. Jones and so Laynie lingered in the corridor waiting for her aunt to emerge. At last she did and started upon finding her there.

"It is bad manners to linger in doorways, Alayna. What have you there?"

"I was hoping you might help me to hem it, Aunt. It's such a fine gown, and I would like to wear it again, and to do it without fear of injury."

"Oh, my darling. You are quite the limit sometimes. It is impossible not to love such a dear sweet creature, however." She kissed Laynie on the head. "Yes, of course I will help you." And she gave instructions that her sewing things might be brought to the morning room, where she then led Laynie.

"The doctor has been, I think?" she said while they waited for the sewing basket to arrive.

"Yes, Aunt. Thank you. He gave me something to put on my ankle."

"Good," she said with a satisfied smile. "Dr. Harris is a wonder with his cures. It will help, I know it will."

The sewing basket arrived and was placed on the floor between them. Aunt Phillips took out a very small pair of scissors and a hook used for unstitching, and together they began pulling the ruffles from the dress's hem, the first of many tasks to be undertaken before the skirt could be shortened.

For a time they worked in silence, but Laynie knew they would not be alone long. She opened her mouth to speak.

"You know, Alayna," Aunt Phillips said before Laynie could summon the words, "I was watching you last night at dinner..."

Laynie felt her throat get dry. Had her aunt observed her admiration of the handsome footman? Or had she, instead, observed her in observation of Mr. Emerson? Either scenario was equally unwelcome to consider.

"It occurred to me how very much like your mother you have grown to look."

"Truly, Aunt?" Laynie said, both surprised by the statement and touched by it at the same time.

"It's true. I'm not sure how it is I had not noticed before. Perhaps because you have changed a very great deal since last I saw you."

"Have I?"

"What has Laynie done now?" Beth said, entering the room and taking a seat opposite her aunt.

"Perhaps you have some sewing project you might work on while I help your sister to hem this dress," Aunt Phillips suggested.

Laynie hoped very much that Beth would find the idea a good one and would return to her room to retrieve something. To Laynie's relief, she arose. But instead of quitting the room, she pulled her chair closer to her aunt.

"Perhaps I'll help you instead," Beth suggested.

Aunt Phillips found another pair of scissors and gave them to Beth with a warning to use them very carefully.

Beth took them and proceeded to snip away at the ruffling and ruching that was in the way of the hem.

"It's true," Aunt Phillips said, as if there had never been any interruption at all to their conversation. "You have changed a very great deal. It was but a year ago you were here last and you were still a child."

"It was two years ago and I was seventeen."

"Were you?"

"Yes, Aunt," Laynie said and laughed.

"You have some growing up to do yet, I perceive, but you have every chance of doing as well as your sister. Perhaps even better if time continues to deal with you as it has lately done."

Beth's scissors hovered, unmoving, above the fabric of Laynie's dress.

"What is wrong, dear?" Aunt Phillips asked of Beth, completely unaware she had caused her offense or why such a thing should ever be.

152

"Nothing," she said and went back to her snipping, not so carefully now.

"If you would only consider this Mr. Vaughn," Aunt Phillips continued, addressing Laynie once more, "I really do think he will make something far greater of you than you could ever have hoped to imagine alone. You would be well advised to take your opportunities as they come. The same is true for Bethany, as well. Perhaps truer, since she is the older. Your beauty won't last forever, you know."

"That's just it, Aunt," Laynie said, grateful for the chance to make her understand. "Mr. Vaughn is very much attached to Beth. And Beth, in turn, is fond of him. Why should they not make each other happy? I have ages upon ages before I'll be ready to make a choice."

Beth laid the scissors in her lap. "Who says I want Mr. Vaughn at all, Laynie? You are quite eager with your assumptions. If Papa wants him for you and he's willing, I don't see why you shouldn't marry him after all. You are at least very good friends."

"But, Beth… It was only three days ago that…" But she daren't remind her sister of the promise that had been extracted from her. Beth was indeed changeable, and Laynie was sorry to see it. She was sorrier still to find that Grace had joined them and was now standing beside her mother listening in rapt attention.

"Why didn't you tell me you had an admirer, Laynie?"

"Because I don't, Grace. He admires Beth. And I thought, but a few days ago, that Beth admired him. I'm very sorry to say I appear to have been mistaken," she finished wryly.

"Is it true?" Graced asked Beth. "Do you have an admirer?"

"A man of wealth, family, good breeding and connections, too," Aunt Phillips added and tisked as though those virtues were to be entirely wasted on Laynie and her sister. "But why did your father not tell me he preferred Bethany?"

"Why do you not accept him?" Grace said as though she could perceive no possible reason on earth for Beth to hope for better.

Beth lifted her chin. She examined Grace a moment. "What of you, Grace? We have yet to learn anything of your gentleman. You have one, I know, but what of him?"

Grace, stunned by this, turned to Laynie, who could do little more than offer a helpless look. She had not betrayed her to Beth, but then neither had she succeeded in persuading her aunt to consider her daughter's desires. She'd never even broached the subject. If only Beth had not returned from the breakfast room so early.

"I'm not sure how much there is to tell," Grace said and appeared to be struggling to subdue her alarm as she took a seat.

"What is his name?" Beth pressed.

Grace looked from Beth to Laynie to her mother. "His name is Mr. Emerson, if you must know," she said and blushed. "He was at dinner last night. But I told you that already."

"You did not tell us his name before now," Beth observed, "which I consider very ungracious of you. If you are so in love with him, and he with you, why are you not more open about it?"

Grace was silent, and with her hands folded before her she seemed to study them as if they might, eventually, offer some answer. Laynie felt a little sorry for her. What could she say without revealing more than she wished to about the hopes and plans she had begun to make with Mr. Emerson?

"Grace is afraid she will offend my sensibilities," Aunt Phillips said at last, surprising Grace and Laynie both. Aunt Phillips knew of the attraction; that much was apparent. But just how much more did she know?

"No, Mama," Grace answered nervously. "I was merely uncertain, until last night, if you would approve of my marrying a man who had been married already."

"But of course I have my reservations," Aunt Phillips answered.

"And mercifully have overcome them. You have always been very generous in that way, Mama."

"Not so fast, Grace. I am aware of your preference for him; I have seen as much, and perhaps more, than you realize. I perceive that you consider yourself in love with him. I also perceive that he wishes to marry again, and perhaps a little too hastily if you ask me."

"But, Mama! You were so very encouraging of him last night. And because of your encouragement he is to go to Papa this very evening! I hope Papa does not entertain the same prejudices you do."

"I'm not prejudiced against him. I simply know that a man who has been married before has more reasons than one to marry again, and they may not all be quite as selfless as his reasons for marrying in the first place."

"Is not love always selfish in some respect, though, Mama?"

"I certainly hope you do not hold that as truth, my dear, or you will find yourself a very unhappy bride."

Grace returned her attention to her folded hands and looked as though she were about to cry.

"My 'prejudices', as you call them, might be overcome in time, when he has had the opportunity to prove himself. You have some time yet before you will be able to make so great a commitment as marriage, so I do not see the need to rush things along."

The sitting room door opened a little wider. Grace looked up and back down again. Laynie turned to see that Mr. Emerson had entered and was looking a little unprepared to face the conversation that was apparently about him.

"Time?" he inquired and advanced, his attention on Grace and Grace alone as if she had some very serious question to answer to. And yet the question that followed was asked casually, as if it were intended as little more than coy flirtation, which, now acknowledged, might be carried out in the open. "Why shouldn't you be in the greatest hurry to do everything, Miss Phillips? You have the world before you, after all, and only so many years to conquer it. They slip by faster than one would suppose." He punctuated this last with a meaningful look offered to Aunt Phillips.

"However quickly she may wish to conquer the world, Mr. Emerson," answered Aunt Phillips, "she cannot commence upon that errand until she is twenty-one at least. She will not come into her money until then."

"Mr. Emerson does not care about the money, Mama."

"Is this true, Mr. Emerson?" Aunt Phillips inquired of him.

"I do expect to come into some money of my own. I had every reason, until this morning, to expect it might be soon. Now, however..."

"But you said—" Grace said and stopped, apparently confused.

"It is not quite so simple as one might wish it, Miss Phillips. Complications have arisen, it seems."

"Well, then," Aunt Phillips said, as if Mr. Emerson's half-confession provided some sort of proof of his un-readiness to marry again. "But even if it turns out that he should find himself financially independent, if he's a gentleman, and I believe you are," she said with a nod in his direction, "then he will care very much about the feelings of his bride's parents. Money or no money, you will not have our blessing before your twenty-first birthday."

"Mama, please!"

"That is my final word on the subject."

Grace looked to Mr. Emerson, who turned his back upon her. She arose and moved toward the door.

"You will find that your father and I are in perfect agreement, my dear...in the event you meant to go to him."

Grace stopped a moment and turned once more to face her mother. Aunt Phillips had had her say and would not so much as look at her now. Grace turned instead to Mr. Emerson. "Frederick?" she whispered, though loudly enough that he ought to have heard her. He made no acknowledgement. She turned and quit the room.

Mr. Emerson picked up a book of poetry and moved to the window to examine it in the light.

Aunt Phillips sighed heavily. "Now, my dear," she said to Laynie as if it were just the three of them once more, "where were we? Ah, yes, we were on the subject of Mr. Vaughn, I believe."

Beth glanced at Mr. Emerson, then looked up at her aunt. Her face grew red, and she looked back down at her work, stabbing at the stitches as if they had caused her some great offense. "Why have we not touched upon the subject of Laynie's admirers, I wonder?" she asked. "Mr. Vaughn may not exactly be counted among them, but she has them nonetheless."

"Bethany, whatever can you mean?" Laynie said and felt the heat rise in her face as Mr. Emerson stood not far off, listening and pretending not to as he leafed blindly through his book.

"There is our father's hired companion, for one."

"Bethany! What are you talking about? He is a married man."

"No, he's not. Papa lied."

"What?"

156

"He lied," Beth said again. "Father did not want us pestering him, and so he told us his companion was married."

"To marry so humbly, Laynie... I know you are prepared to do it, but..." Aunt Phillips did not finish her thought but shook her head and clicked her tongue in hypothetical regret.

"I wouldn't consider it lowering myself if I loved him," Laynie answered and observed her aunt's look of horror. "Which I do not, of course!"

"And a man so much older..." Her aunt raised her eyes to the ceiling as if the very idea caused her dread.

"But he isn't old," Beth said. "I'm sure he isn't thirty. Laynie's ambitions are not great, I think you'll find, Aunt. Why I think even your footman would do. The dark-haired one, you know."

"Beth, you are very cruel," Laynie said and found herself on the verge of tears.

Aunt Phillips seemed to be considering very seriously. "I had observed your attention towards him myself, dear. He may be handsome, but one does not fraternize with the servants. Oh, dear, what a tragic situation your mother has left you in. And your father... He is my brother and so I can say it, he is utterly incompetent when it comes to raising young ladies. You would learn a great deal were you to come live with me for good, Alayna. Perhaps Bethany will do well enough if she considers Mr. Vaughn, but...."

"But I—" Beth began, plainly livid to be excluded from her aunt's consideration. She was cut off, however, by Laynie, who, though unused to interrupting people, felt it rather necessary at the moment.

"I won't leave my father," she assured her aunt. "Nor my sister. I'm grateful to you, but I can't even consider it."

Bethany seemed only slightly placated and lifted her chin in unnecessary solidarity with her sister. But she was still implacably angry, and even Laynie was not certain quite what had inspired her indignation. Beth slowly arose from her chair. The scissors which had been resting in her lap began to slip from their place, making a plunging dive toward Laynie's injured and slippered foot. A hand appeared from nowhere and grasped the scissors before they made contact with their target.

"Do take care, Miss Durham," Mr. Emerson said to Beth and returned the scissors to her aunt. "Some injuries are more difficult to heal than others. Excuse me, if you will," he said then and turned from the room.

Beth did not seem to take kindly to Mr. Emerson's counsel, though Laynie would have given just about anything to know what it was he meant precisely. Beth remained, standing mute and silently fuming while she considered what she was to do now.

"Perhaps you would benefit from some practice at the piano, Bethany," Aunt Phillips suggested. "Gentlemen are always fond of ladies who can play well."

Bethany approached the piano, sat down at it, struck three chords and arose again. It seemed she, too, was in the mood for a walk. She quit the room and the house as well, and then it was only Aunt Phillips and Laynie alone, who, now silent, recommitted themselves to the task of hemming Laynie's dress.

Chapter fourteen

BETHANY WALKED THE LONG DRIVE that led to her aunt's house. She knew she was being unreasonable, but there was no use for it. She felt slighted by her aunt's remarks, by her offer to take Laynie under her wing, by her suggestion that her sister was becoming a rival to be contended with. She had known it was coming. She had watched the evolution for herself and knew that one day others would observe it as well. One day. Not today. Not by her aunt who might make a very great deal of Laynie's talents and virtues and, yes, beauty.

It seemed desperately unfair. Beth had never been anything but beautiful. Laynie had never been anything but unremarkable. Why could she not remain unremarkable? And now Aunt Phillips wished to do something for her? For Laynie! Not for Beth, no, who might do well enough on her own. Well that had worked out brilliantly so far, hadn't it? Would it work brilliantly still when her looks had faded and her impatience had turned to desperation?

Was she not just a little desperate now?

Oh why could she not just make up her mind to accept Mr. Vaughn! She knew why. His mother, firstly, who, as far as she could foresee, would never give Beth her approval. And secondly...there was Mr. Emerson to compare him to. Beautiful, charming, elegant Mr. Emerson! Who, she felt, was just a little desperate to be married himself. But what did that matter if he had already chosen to marry Grace?

Well, if it should turn out he could not have her then perhaps a very great deal.

If only she could know what Aunt Phillips' news had meant to him. Did he love Grace enough to wait for her? Did he love her at all?

Beth had never seen any evidence of it. Perhaps she simply had not wanted to do it.

She stopped upon passing the rose gardens to hear the sound of voices. She could not see who the voices belonged to, but there was little need to guess. She looked about to be certain she could not be seen, concealed herself more completely behind a row of boxwoods, and there she listened.

"But you promised! 'What fun it would be to be all on our own,' those were your words!"

"I said it was an idea worth considering. But your mother is right. There is nothing respectable in running off together. I've done it once already, remember. I'd rather do it right the second time around."

"Is it about the money? I wish you would say so if it is. Is it because I won't have it if I defy them?"

"I'm not quite a mercenary, Grace. I'll have enough by and by, so long as, when I do marry, it is done respectably."

"When *we* marry, I think you mean," Grace said, correcting him in a huff. "You sound as though you mean to do it all on your own." There was a slightly teasing quality to her tone, but the silence that followed it could not have offered her anything in the way of reassurance.

"You *will* wait for me," she said. It was a question but one she evidently expected to have answered in one way only. "If we cannot elope, you will wait."

"Two years," he said. It was not a question at all, but a blunt statement of a fact that seemed to suggest an insurmountable obstacle.

"It is a long time, granted. It is not an eternity."

"Cannot your parents be swayed?"

"You heard her. She means what she says. Not a day before my twenty-first birthday, Frederick. Not a day. Say you will wait?" she asked, an air of desperation in her voice.

"I can't, Grace," he said in what was almost a whisper, as if the words, uttered so softly, would soften the blow.

"What do you mean you *can't*?"

"It is as I said. I cannot tell you why. I am not entirely my own agent in this."

"Are you so desperate to replace your wife that you'll take anyone?" Grace hissed.

"That isn't quite how it is. I can't explain it more than I've done. I'm sorry, Miss Phillips. Sorrier than I can say."

"Miss—?"

"Will you shake hands?"

"Shake hands? Like mere acquaintances? I gave you my heart! I gave you—"

"I don't know what more to say than I'm sorry," he said, beginning to lose his own patience now. "I haven't a choice, do you see? I'd keep my word to you if I could, but I can't. Without your parents' blessing..."

"Frederick?" Grace said, her voice cracking with emotion.

"I'm sorry, Miss Phillips."

"Frederick, please."

And silence again, though for a moment only. Beth did not hear the sound of his retreating steps on the carpet of grass, but there was an emptiness to the air that suggested Grace was now alone. The stillness was interrupted by the sound of wracking sobs and the long groan of a breaking heart. Beth wanted to go to Grace. There was no way to do it, however, without revealing that she had been listening the whole while. Mightn't she go to Mr. Emerson, though? Was not he in as great a need of comfort as was her cousin?

Beth tore a twig of boxwood from a branch and began plucking it of its leaves as she thought. Were those thoughts carrying her in the direction of betraying her cousin? And was it really a betrayal? It was not her fault, after all, that Grace could not marry him. It was all misfortune of circumstance, misaligned stars—Grace's own impetuosity. Perhaps her loss would be a blessing to her one day. Perhaps Mr. Emerson's loss, so soon on the heels of another far more tragic, might serve as a caution to him to take note of all possible impediments before he went too far. But there were no impediments, none whatever, to Beth's marrying whomever she wished.

But no, she was going to offer consolation, nothing more. Or perhaps not much more. Would it be so very wrong to drop a hint, just the merest hint, that he might be welcome to consider her instead of she whom he could not have? It was perhaps not the best timing, so soon after his disappointment. And yet, if all was over with Grace, how much longer was he likely to remain? He was a friend of Ned's but that alone would not keep him, not when there was awkwardness and hard feelings to face. And hadn't her aunt just minutes ago admonished her to take advantages of her opportunities as they came? Truly, it seemed if she wished for any chance at all, perhaps it was now or never.

Beth heard the sound of rustling skirts as Grace arose from her place. She heard the sound of feet on the pebbled path as Grace walked slowly toward the house, and, at last, she heard the sound of the door opening as Grace returned indoors.

And yet Beth remained. Here was an opportunity, but was it truly hers to take? She thought once more of Grace, of her suffering. She understood that suffering all too well. But it was not Beth's fault Grace had lost him. Neither would it be her fault if she won him. She could hardly be blamed if he found himself attracted to her. How much was it her fault if she threw him a crumb or two? And really, what choice did she have? It was try for him or go home to marry Mr. Vaughn—or worse, to watch her sister do it, all because Beth wasn't good enough for his mama. And while she was not entirely opposed to Harry, why should she settle for mild sentiment and merely passing good looks when she could have the inarguably handsome and radiantly charming Mr. Emerson?

She felt that panic of desperation rise and made her move. There was no point waiting longer. He might be gone already for all she knew, back to the inn where he was staying, and then...? But perhaps, just perhaps, he was here still, walking the grounds, brooding and contemplating—and in need of consolation. If nothing else, mightn't she offer him that? There was nothing wrong in that, surely.

At last Beth found him, standing by the goldfish pond in the rearmost garden, quietly tucked away in a sheltered corner, contemplating the fishes and apparently seeing and hearing nothing.

"Are you quite all right, Mr. Emerson? You appear to be out of sorts."

He looked up at her, apparently surprised.

"Out of sorts?" he asked as if he were not quite aware of himself or his surroundings. His brow furrowed heavily over his blue eyes.

"Yes, I suppose you might say that." He shook his fisted hand before him, something rattled within it. He opened it to examine the pebbles that were there and then began throwing them, one by one, into the pond as the fish dodged and dived to avoid the projectiles.

"Is there anything I can do?"

He looked at her as if she were daft and looked away again, but he turned and gave her a second glance. "Not unless..." He examined her a moment and turned away again. "Never mind," he said.

"I hope something is not the matter between you and Grace."

He gave her a fleeting, narrow look. "There is nothing between us at all...now," he said and appeared more frustrated than actually pained. He threw the remainder of his pebbles into the pond and walked away.

"Mr. Emerson," she said, stopping him. "If you ever need someone to talk to... I am told I am a very good listener."

For the briefest moment it appeared he had some retort to make, and one that was perhaps not entirely polite. He stopped himself short, however, sniffed, cleared his throat, and answered her. "You are very kind, Miss Durham. Perhaps another time."

"Will there be another time?" she asked before he could turn from her again. She was uncertain how to ask the question she most wished to know, but ask it she must. "You do not mean to leave us now, I hope?"

"Regrettably no," he answered, to Beth's relief. "As I am Phillips' guest, I'm somewhat obligated, as awkward as my presence must no doubt make things, to remain the week."

"I, for one, am glad of it. Perhaps I might do something to relieve the awkwardness."

"I don't see how."

"At least I might do something to ease your discomfort."

"Again," he said, one eyebrow raised, "I fail to see how —"

"I'm also told I can be very resourceful."

"I have no doubt of it whatever, Miss Durham," he answered cautiously, perhaps not quite comprehendingly. He bowed his head politely, and walked away. A moment later he looked over his shoulder, a contemplative look once more upon his brow.

Beth offered a smile and waved, but felt a little discouraged by the interview. Had she done enough? Said enough? But he was a man deeply disappointed and, at least presently, preoccupied in that disappointment. But it could not last. At least she hoped it would not. She had done her work. No doubt it would give him some little food for thought, by and by. If he was as desperate as she believed him, the seed would take root. She only needed to wait for it.

Bolstered by these thoughts, she returned to the house and to her room. Grace was there, weeping inconsolably in Laynie's arms. Beth watched them a moment, watched as her sister, so naturally empathetic, soothed and comforted her cousin. How Beth wished she had that gift. Laynie had certainly provided a soothing balm to her when she was going through her disappointment. But having lived it once she balked at reliving it again, even if it was vicariously. Grace must suffer as many a woman do. It was the way of things in a man's world. And yet Beth was not entirely unfeeling. She approached, laid a sympathetic hand upon Grace's shaking shoulders, and uttered her apologies. And then, after gathering Laynie's sewing, she went downstairs—to wait.

* * *

Though Mr. Emerson had assured her that he did not intend to quit the neighborhood quite yet, neither did he spend much time at the house. Ned was rarely there, after all, for there were plenty enough diversions away from home to keep them busy. For entertainment, Ned and his friends took long walks and rides, went hunting and fishing, they had even gone to the races, or so Beth had overheard. And while the time was short, so very, very short, she kept an eye out for any opportunity to lay claim upon Mr. Emerson's attention, if not actually his affection. She suspected such a thing would be far more challenging a feat than what her few remaining days in Gravesend would afford her. It did not mean she did not intend to try.

She found her opportunity one afternoon when the gentlemen had returned from an early morning hunt. Ned and Mr. Jones had arrived at the house for a late breakfast while Mr. Emerson remained outside, no doubt hoping to avoid any awkward encounters within.

Beth, upon realizing that Mr. Emerson was there but that he meant to linger out of doors, laid down her plate and made a surreptitious exit from the breakfast room. She found her bonnet, a basket, and a pair of gardening shears and headed out into the rose garden, hoping that, at some point in his wanderings, Mr. Emerson might happen her way. She did not leave him without some encouragement to do it.

At the entrance of the rose garden, she laid down her hat, she left the gate open, and just beyond it, where a wooden bench had been placed, she laid her apron, veritably creating a path by which she might be found, if he so wished to find her. And if he didn't… But that was silly. He was a man, and a lonely one. She was a woman, and a beautiful one. It was only a matter of time before he found her.

Despite her confidence, she was immensely relieved when at last he did find her.

"Ah, it is you, Miss Durham. I thought it might be."

"Oh, Mr. Emerson!" Beth said and disguised her relief as surprise. To enhance the effect, she dropped her pruning shears and her basket of flowers.

"Allow me," he said and knelt to pick them up.

She joined him there, kneeling upon the ground. "How foolish of me."

"Nonsense. I startled you. Forgive me, won't you?"

"Of course," she said and smiled up at him. "I already have."

The flowers were rescued, and the shears, too, and as she arranged the flowers in the basket she made sure to prick her finger on the thorn of a rose. She cried out.

"Are you hurt?" he asked and stood to watch as she removed her flimsy glove to examine the damage.

"Roses, for all their beauty, are somewhat more dangerous than one would suppose," Beth said and smiled painfully as a drop of blood oozed from the wound.

"I think that may be true of all beautiful things, Miss Durham," he said with a lopsided smile. Did he mean to suggest herself included? He extracted a handkerchief from his pocket and wrapped the injured finger in the cambric square as he held her ungloved hand in his gloved one. "Better?" he asked.

"Yes, very," she answered and then, observing the black trimming of the handkerchief: "I forgot that you were in mourning,

Mr. Emerson. I'm so terribly sorry for it. And now you have this most recent injury to suffer as well. How do you bear it?" she asked and looked up at him through blonde lashes.

"It is a trial, Miss Durham, make no mistake. But I suppose one grows used to one's trials after a time. Life is full of disappointment, after all. One would be foolish to imagine he deserved better." He looked to see if the bleeding had stopped. It had. He returned his handkerchief to his pocket and released her hand. She was reluctant to take it back and let it linger in the air between them a moment more. At last she lowered it to hang limply at her side.

"But you do deserve better, Mr. Emerson. So much better. You will be happy one day, I know it."

"I do hope you are right, Miss Durham."

"If only there were something I could do," she said very earnestly and, by stratagem, dropped her glove.

He stooped to pick it up. She held her hand out that he might put it on her hand for her. It was a little forward—perhaps she was a little desperate to make an impression on him—but it was a desperate moment, an opportunity that might not come her way again. She must make the most of it.

Her glove was replaced, very gently and deftly, and when her hands were once more her own, she examined the rosebushes that stood before them. The largest was trellised over a wooden arch and had grown so dense it appeared as though they had formed a great hedge of their own. She had nearly picked all the good blooms already, but there were a few up high that she might have if he would help her to get them.

"Would you mind?" she said and pointed to the topmost part of the hedge. "Just there. I cannot quite reach."

He took the shears from her, their hands touched briefly, and she made room for him to work as she watched him. His coat somewhat restricted his movement, so he removed it and unbuttoned his sleeves.

"I do hope you intend to go to the ball tomorrow evening."

"Phillips has invited me, so I suppose I shall."

"You do not sound very enthusiastic about it."

"No doubt you can understand why. It's likely to be very awkward, considering."

"It doesn't have to be, you know." She paused a moment to be certain he was listening. "I'll be there, after all."

He smiled broadly to himself as he cut the blossoms, three of them, and then turned toward her so that he could place them in her basket. "Is that all, Miss Durham?"

She pointed to another. He saw it, nodded, and reached to cut it, too.

"You and Ned must be very close."

"Must we?" he asked and returned the last flower to her.

"Certainly you must. You've known each other ever so long, after all."

He seemed to consider his answer. It intrigued Beth that it was apparently not a simple one to give. Was he preparing to confide in her? And might she take encouragement from such a confidence?

"Forgive me for the impertinence, Miss Durham, but to own the truth, I find Ned rather a bore. I believe you share the opinion."

"Me? Why should I have a low opinion of my cousin, Mr. Emerson? He has never been anything but kind to me. Perhaps you know something about him I don't?" she added, wishing to sound co-conspiratorial rather than defensive.

"Your sister certainly finds his attentions plaguing," he said without answering the question. She did not like the idea of drawing Laynie into the discussion.

"She pretends to object to them. That would be right and proper, after all. But in truth, I suspect she secretly likes the attention."

"Does she?" he asked dubiously. "That seems uncharacteristic of her."

Beth laughed to disguise her alarm. "You speak as though you know my sister, Mr. Emerson. You have not, I think, had the opportunity of becoming much acquainted with her."

"We've had our little garden tete-a-tete, much like this one," he said as if he actually meant to provoke her. "And I'm a very good judge of character. Besides," he continued, "generally speaking such coquettishness is out of character for someone who is spoken for, as I believe you meant to imply the other day."

This string of words was not only provoking, it was worrying and, even just perhaps, conveyed a hint of warning. She would not be discouraged. There was no time for that. "Oh yes," she answered him. "That is, my father has someone in mind for her."

"Not his hired companion, I think," he inquired with a teasing look.

"Well, no. That is…"

Mr. Emerson smiled. It was a too-understanding smile, as though he had seen right through her attempts to mislead him into thinking her sister was unavailable to him. Just how much thought had he given to the potential availability of her sister? The idea was troubling in the extreme.

"There *is* a gentleman, both of means and family," Beth explained, "who my father would very much like her to marry. He is above us in station, but Laynie is, to my father as well as his mother, the preferred choice. Papa would have her marry him tomorrow if he had his way."

"And if she had her way…?" he asked. He cut another blossom, one he had chosen on his own, and handed it to her.

She took it from him. There was something in the gesture that suggested a compliment, a kindness—a pointed show of attention. And yet…considering the conversation, she could not quite take it at face value. Not really.

"It seems to me," he said, "if she were inclined to accept him, there would be no need to employ your aunt to try to persuade her to do it. That is the real reason you have come, is it not?"

"How do you know this?"

"Grace. Of course."

Beth resisted the temptation to glower. It was time to put the question of Laynie's eligibility to rest once and for all. "To be quite honest," she said, not quite honestly, "my sister has formed a secret attachment. You may indeed be surprised to learn it is someone far beneath her. That is why she will not consider Mr. Vaughn, though he is a worthier fellow by far."

"Your father's companion, then?"

"I never said so, Mr. Emerson," Beth said and took a seat on the bench. She let the suggestion, and his own presuming, answer the rest, and then presented another topic.

"Will you tell me about your wife, Mr. Emerson?" she said. "I would like to know of her."

"It's a very painful subject," he answered with a flinch of a smile.

"It eases one's pains to speak of it, you know. I'm not a stranger to loss. I know what good it does to confide in a listening ear."

"You mean your mother," he said and sat. "You must have loved her very much. It was some time ago, I understand."

"Grace told you, I suppose," she said, disappointed not to be the one to forge the bond of sympathy between them.

"No. It was your sister who told me, actually."

Of course it was! She ought to have known. And yet, she still could not quite comprehend how it was that Laynie had found the opportunity of speaking with him. When had she managed it? What had they discussed? And what impression had she left upon him? A significant one, it seemed.

"Loss is a great thing, Miss Durham, and must be shared. She did not know I was a widower then. It was the handkerchief that inspired the question, which thus led to my explanation and ultimately to her own confession. I take it your mother is not something she is much used to speaking about."

Beth looked at him a long time. There was a proper response to his explanation. She could not think what it ought to be. She could not think beyond Laynie's duplicity. "Did she cut herself? It *would* be like her!"

"Cut herself?" he asked, apparently puzzled by her assumption. "No. We had been laughing, actually," he said.

"Together?"

"Indeed. She laughed till she cried, and so I lent her my handkerchief. She inquired about the border."

"And you told her."

"Of course I did."

"But you will not tell me. Do you not trust me, Mr. Emerson?" she asked and tried not to show the indignation she actually felt.

"There is nothing I told her that you have not already heard spoken of by your aunt and cousin—perhaps *cousins*," he added somewhat resentfully, "I'm quite certain."

She tried once more to recover her more consolatory manner. "There is a great deal I do not know," she said, "and of which I am most interested in hearing." She smiled as becomingly as she knew how. "How did you meet, for instance? What was she like?"

He seemed to hesitate still. At last he smiled, though briefly, and surrendered to her request. "We met while I was at University," he said at last and began to list off the facts of the matter as if they were a recommendation for employment. "She was the governess to the family of one of my professors. She was not happy there. He was a very strict fellow, and it was not a happy home, not for her or anyone, from what I'm given to understand."

"You rescued her?" Beth asked, with a look that suggested she was impressed by his heroism.

"I suppose, in a way I did. I had not come into my money then, and her family did not think it wise for her to leave her position, not for me, at any rate."

"You eloped? Oh, tell me you eloped, Mr. Emerson. It's so romantic."

He smiled. "We eloped, Miss Durham, and found a little cottage by the seaside in France, where we lived quite happily, until…" But he did not finish. His countenance grew once more guarded and he stood straight to smooth his waistcoat and sleeves.

"I'm so sorry," Beth said and arose to lay a hand on his arm. "You will find another, by and by, who will make you as happy as your late wife did."

He had been smiling a moment ago. The look on his face now was one that matched quite exactly his mood when she had discovered him by the goldfish pond but a few days ago. Frustrated, pained—even angry.

"Have I said something amiss, Mr. Emerson?"

"Please forgive me, Miss Durham," he said. "It's too much. I'm grateful to you for your interest, but I can't bear it. Excuse me, will you?"

* * *

Beth watched Mr. Emerson's retreating figure. She was conscious she was missing an opportunity of admiring it. Instead she could only think of Laynie. She remained where she was only long enough to ensure the way was clear. She took up her basket and made her way back to the house and then to her room.

Laynie was there, standing before the mirror wearing, once more, the dove-grey gown, only this time it fit her perfectly, both in circumference and length.

Laynie caught her sister's reflection in the mirror as she entered and turned to face her. "Oh, Beth, I'm so grateful! What got it into your head to finish my hemming for me? And you did such a good job of it. I can't tell you how—"

"You've been speaking with Mr. Emerson."

"What?"

"When did you contrive to do it, Laynie? Did you meet him somewhere by accident or did you plan it? Why would you hide such a thing from me?"

Laynie's gaze darted about the room, landing, very briefly, in one far corner before returning to meet her own once more.

"You lied to me, Laynie. At least you concealed it. I never before thought it like you to do such a thing. Tell me, will you, where did you meet him. And when!"

Laynie paled slightly, stammered, and then: "I met him by accident."

"Oh, of course!"

"It was our first morning here. I had gone out into the garden, and he was there. I didn't know who it was."

"You never exchanged names? You spoke. You laughed. But never exchanged names?"

"Of course we did. But I did not know he was...him...until that evening at dinner. How could I?"

"Wait a minute. Was this the day that both you and Grace disappeared? The day I asked you where you had been and you said you had gone out and quite alone?"

"Perhaps," Laynie answered. "I don't remember."

"Of course you can! How can you lie to me? And when you knew I liked him, too!"

"But I didn't then. Neither had you yet laid eyes on him. It was very innocent. I swear it."

"Is that so? Was it as innocent as...?"

"As your pursuing him when you knew very well I was all but engaged to him?"

Beth spun on her heal. It was Grace. She had been changing behind a screen and had gone unnoticed until now.

"If Laynie says it was an accident, I believe her, as should you. I do wish he had told me of the interlude, however," she said and flashed a regretful look in Laynie's direction. "But while it might not be like Laynie to deceive, it is like you to cross and double cross. I knew better than to confide in you."

"Then perhaps it's your fault I did not understand how things stood. I would not have pursued him if you had only—"

"Wouldn't you have done?" Grace challenged her. "Why do you come to your sister now, Beth? Are you disappointed not to have caught him and won him just three days after I had lost him?" And Grace punctuated her question with a sob, which she stifled.

"It isn't quite like that, Grace," Beth said and took a step back, and then another as she blindly reached for the door.

"What is it like, then, Bethany? Would you mind explaining it to me?"

Beth looked to Laynie and then back to Grace. "I'm sorry, Grace," she said and actually felt guilty. She had a reason. It was a good enough reason. Grace would understand it herself if only Beth could explain it plainly enough—if only Grace could imagine herself in Beth's shoes. But that was quite impossible. So Grace was not to marry for two years. So what? She would still live in luxury, and when that two years was up she would likely marry someone ten times better than Mr. Emerson, and she'd then have all the wealth and liberty her inheritance and twenty-one years would afford her. Beth had no such future to look forward to. Her hand at last found the door. She turned the knob and let herself out.

Having escaped, she wondered what she ought to do with herself now. She was hungry. She had not yet eaten breakfast. Perhaps there was still a chance if it had not been cleared away already. She went down to the breakfast room, and there she found Ned, loading his plate, and likely not for the first time.

"Ah, Bethany, you've come to grace us with your presence, I see. I'm alone, I'm very sorry to tell you."

172

She answered with a narrow look and took up a plate. Thank heaven there was one sausage left and a cracked and over-boiled egg, but Ned had taken the last of the bacon already. The toast was cold, but she took a slice anyway.

"I wonder what you make of my mother's news," Ned said off-handedly once Beth had taken her seat.

Beth laid her napkin across her lap before answering him. "What news might that be?" she asked, only half interested.

"Why, that Laynie is to stay on with us, of course."

Beth laid her fork back down and stared at him. "I didn't think she was serious."

"Oh, she was serious, all right. She wouldn't joke about such a thing as that."

Beth lifted her chin. "It makes no difference anyway, since Papa will never agree to allow it. And neither will *she* agree."

"Of course she will. Why wouldn't she?"

"Well, Ned," Beth answered archly, "because she does not like you, if you want to know."

Ned sat up a little straighter and shifted in his chair. "Don't say that, Bethany. You quite dampen my hopes. If mother wants her, she'll have her, and that will be that. But don't say she does not like me. We have long been very close friends."

"You can't possibly hope for more than that anyway. You're cousins. Cousins don't marry anymore."

"You know what I think?" he said and patted his mouth with his napkin. "I think you're jealous."

"I'm not jealous, Ned. I just don't understand what all the fuss is about Laynie these days. Yes, she needs help and a great deal of it if she ever hopes to marry well, but my path has not been all roses, you know."

"Then you *are* jealous. You can't be blind. You see her every day. Tell me, Beth, confess it, has she not changed utterly since last she was here? The alteration is remarkable. She is remarkable!"

"Remarkably naïve? Remarkably accident prone?"

"Remarkably beautiful!"

That was the last outrage Beth could endure today. She arose and threw her napkin onto her plate.

173

"Don't be angry, Bethany."

"Oh, I'm not angry, Ned. It's just that I see now why she despises you as she does. You ought to know, were she to stay, she'd be a hundred times more likely to marry your friend Mr. Emerson than to ever consider you, if that's what you were thinking."

"Emerson?" Ned said as if the notion were absurd. "Emerson'd marry anyone who'd have him so long as they were willing to do it quick. But he also knows where I draw the line, and he knows good and well not to cross it."

"What does that mean, 'as long as they did it quick'?" It had been her own impression, but she would very much like to know the reason for it nonetheless.

Ned was suddenly dismissive. "I can't tell you that, but I will tell you that if she won't have her fancy man in Surrey, my mother will find one for her. And why shouldn't it be me?"

Beth had had quite enough of Ned's absurdities. "I suppose it has something to do with the fact that you are a bounder, Ned," she answered him and turned to leave.

He laughed loudly. Too loudly. The sound of it in the vaulted and marbled breakfast room was jarring. "I'll be bound, Beth! I'll wager you don't even know what the word means."

"You might be surprised, Ned. I know a great deal more about the world than you suppose."

Beth met her aunt quite unexpectedly in the corridor. She felt the heat rise and prayed she had not heard any of their conversation.

"There you are, my dear," she said. "I was hoping to find you here. Where is your sister?"

"She's upstairs, with Grace, I believe."

"Oh, what luck! Come with me. We must begin to prepare for the ball. I want to make sure your gowns are chosen and everything is just right. There's no sense waiting until the very last minute, is there?"

Very reluctantly, Beth followed her aunt back up to her room. Together they entered, and Aunt Phillips announced her intentions as she opened the wardrobe and began removing gowns, one by one, and holding them up to each of her nieces, all the while asking her daughter's opinion as to which would suit best and never once observing that Grace was in a bad mood. Perhaps she expected her lowered spirits, but this was something else entirely. Neither was Laynie looking particularly cheerful. Her face was red, her eyes wet with newly shed tears. It was a very somber mood indeed that prevailed. The only cheer to be had was found in their aunt, who was gleefully choosing gowns for her beautiful, if pitiable nieces—in the hopes that some miracle would be bestowed upon them all and husbands might be found for each. And all owing to some fine gowns and an annual country ball. Why not?

Beth could answer that.

In a huff of resignation, she sat down hard into a chair and listened as Grace offered her facetiously-formed opinions—at least as far as Beth's dress was concerned—to her mother, who had no ear for such falsehoods and took the advice as quoted gospel.

The remaining seven days were going to be very long indeed.

Chapter fifteen

THE ANNUAL BERESFORD BALL WAS held out of doors, on a platform erected beneath a canopy of trees. It was a magical sight, for the limbs and branches of each tree were decorated with luminaires of blown glass in which candles had been placed. It was as a scene out of a fairy tale, and Laynie was struck with wonder at the sight of it. The carriage let them out at the front of the house, but they were soon guided to the garden entrance, which led, by way of a vine-covered arbor, to the lower lawns where the festivities had been set up.

Beth, who was all excitement and hopeful anticipation—despite being made to wear a sickly shade of green—took Laynie by the arm. She allowed herself to be led thus, while Grace trailed along behind, reluctant and brooding. She had begged to remain at home, desperate not to have to face Mr. Emerson, her brother, or anyone at all who was presently privy to her humiliation. Tonight was a perfect opportunity, or so Aunt Phillips proclaimed, to make Mr. Emerson feel his loss by showing him just how desirable a companion she was. Why she might win any number of admirers tonight, as no doubt would her nieces, if they would only exert themselves.

Uncle Phillips, as the girls led the way, explained to them the tradition of the Beresford ball. Laynie tried to listen, but was distracted by the magic of the scenery about her and by Beth who kept pulling at her sleeve to show her each and every spectacle, from the candle-lit luminaires—an amber one and then another of iridescent violet—to the arbor itself, and the myriad plants and flowers that had grown to construct it.

It seemed this annual event was held as a sort of nose-thumb at St. Swithin's Day. It had originally been in honor of the holiday, held indoors as it ought to have been, but one year, just days before the event, a fire had broken out and the ballroom had been damaged. Rather than cancel the ball and disappoint the county families, they held it out of doors. It was tempting fate, and Lady Beresford was well aware of it. Only it hadn't rained, and so the family—all of them a little rebellious by nature—thought to take the chance again the following year. Twelve years later, the outdoor event had become a tradition, one much talked about and very much looked forward to.

Uncle Phillips went on, telling a story or two of near misses with thunderstorms, of guests who had disappeared during the evening only to reappear the following morning, having slept it off alone—or not alone—in the shrubberies...but Laynie had ceased listening, and before long she and her sister were far enough ahead that it was no longer possible to hear him. They stopped again when the arched pathway opened out onto that large expanse of lawn that had been visible to them from the drive. Here the guests had gathered. Here there was dancing and refreshment and a hundred or so people talking and laughing, enjoying the company and the music and the clear and moonlit night.

Beth, eager to be a part of the merriment, began to lead them on again. Laynie hung back, reluctant to join the throng and finding herself more nervous than she supposed she would, or perhaps should, be feeling.

"What is it?" Beth asked impatiently.

"You walk too fast. My ankle."

"Your ankle is just fine. That putrid concoction the doctor gave you seems to have been working."

It was true. Her ankle had improved considerably, but it had not healed entirely, and Laynie meant to use it as an excuse tonight. She did not wish to dance. She did not wish to attract attention— particularly that of Mr. Emerson, whom, considering Grace's disappointment and her sister's unpredictable temper, she thought it best to avoid. Laynie was exhausted from the rivalry with her sister and impatient with the constant effort it required to keep all around her happy. She was homesick, and though there was nearly a week remaining, she felt that the end of her holiday could not come soon enough.

"Have it your way," Beth said when Laynie offered no rebuttal, and so she went on ahead alone. Grace clung to Aunt Phillips' side, and they quickly caught up to her.

"Why do you not join them, Alayna?" her aunt asked.

"They walk too fast. That's all."

"Oh, my dear," Aunt Phillips said, "I do hope you will not disappoint me tonight. I had rather hoped your ankle had healed."

"It was getting better, but..."

"You must overcome it. It may be difficult, but look about you. Consider all the work and effort—and expense—that have been undertaken to ensure you have a good time tonight. You have an obligation to make the most of it. It is not every day you have such an opportunity as this."

"I know, Aunt. I will try."

"Now, my dear," Uncle Phillips said, addressing his wife, "even if she sits out the whole night, she is sure to attract more attention than she knows what to do with. Must a gentleman dance with a lady to get to know her? Is not conversation every whit as effective to accomplishing that end?"

"Perhaps. But a young lady who purposefully excludes herself is only begging to feel slighted."

"Nonsense!" Mr. Phillips said. "And I'm prepared to prove it. Come along, my dear," he said and offered Laynie his arm. Together, with Aunt Phillips and Grace following behind at their own pace, they made their way to the dance floor, around which, and arranged between and around the trees that bordered it, a number of chairs had been placed—some more comfortable than others. Uncle Phillips spied a couch, and so aimed himself and his niece in that direction.

"This will do very well. You will see," said Uncle Phillips and sat down upon the couch, taking up very nearly the whole of it and directing Laynie to sit beside him in an armless dining chair. "Any fellow who wishes to dance with you may—and will—come to you, you may be sure, and if he wishes for an introduction, I am right here to give it!"

And so the experiment was tried, but they had not been seated for a quarter of an hour before Uncle Phillips began to nod and then to snore.

Laynie sighed and looked about her. It was bound to be a long night. But at least Ned was not here, nor his friends. Where had they gone to? There was no point missing them now. She was grateful for whatever distraction had come up to take precedence over the ball. She only regretted she had ever met Mr. Emerson in the first place. Had she never run into him to begin with, had they never spoken, she could never have formed any thought of him at all—a thought that, now, must be given up entirely. Why was it proving so difficult to do?

Uncle Phillips' snoring grew louder, and Laynie became aware that he was drawing attention and not all of it of the most encouraging kind. Quietly she arose and stood to look into the light-bestrewn treetops. It was as if the stars had fallen from the sky to catch themselves in the branches. They were hypnotizing, and they drew her toward them. She wandered into the wooded thicket until the sound of music and laughter were somewhat muffled. Apart from the crowd, alone, and surrounded by the comforting glow of the fairy lights, she imagined herself safe and protected.

"What are you doing out here, Laynie?"

She turned with a start to find that Ned had joined her. He had come after all, had seen her, she supposed, as she had wandered off and had followed her.

"Are you hiding from someone?" he asked.

"No," she answered, facing him squarely. "If I were, the first person I'd be hoping to avoid would be you."

He tisked at her scoldingly. "That's not very generous."

"It isn't meant to be."

"Oh, come on. Dance with me."

"I can't. My ankle."

"You're lying. I saw you walk out here without a sign of a limp."

"That doesn't mean it won't hurt when you step on it."

Ned smiled. He seemed to think her protestations a game. He held out his hands, one in the air, one at the level of her waist. "Please?" he said. "I promise I won't pester you the rest of the night if you only dance with me just this once."

It seemed a fair exchange. And the song was half over, at any rate. "Very well," she answered reluctantly and joined her hand in his. He pressed his other hand gently to her back and they danced a slow and careful waltz between the trees, as the breeze occasionally caught at wisps of her hair and threw Ned's alcohol-laced breath in her face.

"That's not so bad, now, is it?" he said eventually.

It wasn't pleasant, either, but she felt it wise not to say so. "You're never so bad when you are behaving yourself. I know better than to think it can last."

"Laynie," he said as if begging for pity. He looked at her long and hard, and she began to feel uncomfortable. "You've grown up, haven't you?"

"It is the natural way of things, Ned."

"I wasn't sure you would ever grow out of that awkward phase of yours."

"Is this some strange form of flattery?"

"I mean it, Laynie. I never would have guessed it, but you have grown into a rather captivating young woman."

Laynie was struck a little speechless and utterly uncertain what to make of Ned's half-drunken ramblings. Did he know what he was saying? And what did he mean to achieve by it?

It seemed he was about to say something more, something a little too earnest to make her quite comfortable, when he was interrupted.

"There you are, Phillips." It was Mr. Emerson. "Is that you, Miss Durham?"

She instantly separated herself from her cousin and felt the blood rush to her face. Thank goodness for the near-darkness that might just prevent him from seeing it.

"Is everything all right here?" he asked.

"Yes, of course," Laynie answered and would have felt more grateful for the interruption if she were not so anxious for what it must look like to him.

She waited for Ned's similar assurance, and when he failed to give it, she looked up at him. He was positively livid. She felt a rush of fear spread over her. What had Mr. Emerson interrupted? And how had he known to do it?

"You are missed, Miss Durham," Mr. Emerson said. "Your sister is looking for you. Your aunt, too. She wishes to introduce you around."

She was not certain whether she should be grateful for this deception—she knew it was not true—or ashamed of having been found in so compromising a position. She acknowledged his statement with a nod and left the two gentlemen to themselves.

"What the hell were you thinking?" she heard Ned say. "I told you before..." But she had moved out of hearing before he finished the sentence. She felt that she had had a close scrape and so returned to the crowd which had gathered at the edge of the dance floor, not to sit beside her sleeping uncle but to stand and, yes, even possibly, to dance were she to be asked.

A pair of gentlemen approached, and the second to pass her by hesitated half a moment. She thought perhaps he was considering asking her to dance but ultimately chose not to do it. Instead he offered her a friendly nod and a half-smile and followed his companion, who looked enough like him that he must have been his elder brother.

"Have you seen Mr. Emerson by chance?" Beth asked offhandedly. Laynie felt more than a little disconcerted at her sister's exaggerated and, what seemed to her, ill-timed interest. "He is here, I believe. At least he said he would be."

"I've not seen him," Laynie said, and once again could not explain her impulse to lie.

Beth looked at her closely for a minute. "Why are you so flushed? Have you been dancing? I thought you said you didn't mean to." Her questions were asked with an interrogating quality that suggested Beth was secretly glad Laynie had professed to hold herself aloof of the gaiety. Would Beth be angry if she changed her mind?

"I've not been dancing, Beth. I'm sure I'm no more flushed than you are. What is your reason for it, I wonder?"

"I see them!" Beth said and was suddenly excited and ignoring her question. "I knew they must be here somewhere." She was just as suddenly sober again. "I thought you were going to sit and rest your ankle."

"I'm tired of sitting. And Uncle is snoring so abominably it was drawing attention."

"I've never known anyone to sleep so much as he," Beth said. "I think there must be something wrong with him."

"Something wrong with whom, pray?" Grace asked archly. She had just returned from the refreshment table with a glass in each hand. She handed one to Laynie. "Of whom were you speaking so, I wonder? I hope it was not of someone to whom you are in any way indebted. It's bad manners to speak ill of anyone in public, more so if it's someone who has been kind enough to host you in their home."

"What are you suggesting, Grace?" Beth asked.

"I think you know." Grace raised her chin, averted her gaze, and suddenly went rigid.

Laynie followed her gaze and observed her brother and his friend, who were standing together on the opposite side of the dance floor and not looking entirely pleased with each other. Emerson and Grace exchanged brief glances, and Emerson turned away while Grace began searching the crowd just around them. She caught the eye of the brothers and, with a bat of her eyelashes and a flutter of her fan, summoned them. Unfortunately there were two brothers and three ladies to choose from. The younger brother, with his eye on Laynie, issued a request for a dance, but Grace, apparently anxious to test the merits of her mother's suggestion, offered herself in Laynie's place, excusing Laynie by reason of her injury.

The elder brother consequently requested the favor of Beth's company. Reluctantly she gave it and Laynie was once more left alone. She retreated to make more room for the ever-growing crowd of dancers, and when she had found a safe place from which to observe, dared another glance in Ned's direction. Mr. Emerson was no longer beside him.

"I think, Miss Durham, it's just possible you are in my debt."

Laynie turned to find that Mr. Emerson had approached her unawares.

"How so, Mr. Emerson?" she asked him, and felt the thrill of flirtation and the shame of it at the same time.

"I rescued you, didn't I?"

"Did you?" she asked. She felt perhaps he had known beforehand what Ned's intentions had been. She wished she fully comprehended them herself, now that she was out of danger.

"I don't think I'm wrong in believing you do not approve of your cousin's manner toward you. I've seen for myself how you shrink from him."

"I don't approve, you are right. But I'm not certain it could be said I shrink from him."

"Your objections are offered with enough courage, to be sure. But you are rather transparent with your inner thoughts and feelings."

"Am I?"

He looked at her for half a moment before answering. "I certainly hope so."

What he meant by it she could not imagine. At least she feared to do it. She certainly was not going to ask him, which seemed to be what he meant for her to do as he continued to study her.

"A simple thank you would suffice," he said at last.

The pressure to answer him, to pursue with the pointless flirtation, was suddenly lifted. "I'm sorry," she said. "And I'm grateful. I did not think I was in danger until you arrived. I— I'm afraid I can be a little naïve at times."

He turned to her and smiled. "It's an admirable quality in many respects."

"It often makes me feel a fool."

"No," he said. "It means you have a trusting nature, which is a good thing."

She was tempted then to abandon what remained of her reservation. She looked to the crowd of dancers. Grace was surreptitiously looking for Mr. Emerson still, while she chatted and flirted with the younger brother. She was looking in the direction where, a few minutes ago, he and Ned had been standing, and where neither of them could be seen any longer.

"Your ankle is bothering you, I think," Mr. Emerson said to her.

"It is a little," she answered. It was not an outright lie. It was healing, but it was in fragile condition still.

"Will you sit and talk to me?"

She did not wish to refuse him. In fact she wanted very much to sit and talk with him, though she did worry what it might look like— what her sister might think, or worse, say. And what of Grace? And yet she hadn't the heart to deny him. She simply couldn't do it. She nodded her answer and allowed him to lead her to a nearby chair, where he sat beside her and together they watched the crowd and did not speak. But it was a comfortable silence and she was grateful for the opportunity to collect herself. If she was sometimes reckless and impulsive in action, she did not wish to be so in speech.

"Is it a ruse?" he asked her quite unexpectedly.

"I beg your pardon?"

"Your ankle? Is it really still injured, or is it a ruse to escape from having to dance?"

"Oh. That. It is much better. I prefer to be careful with it. How long have you suspected me of lying?"

"Oh, I didn't. I merely hoped. You see, now I've sat I'm beginning to think I'd much rather dance with you."

She felt the compliment and resisted smiling in consequence. "Considering Grace and... Well, considering all, I'd much rather not."

"Very well, then," he said and seemed satisfied to relent. "Perhaps another time."

She took pleasure in the implication but was not certain what to make of it. "Is there likely to be another time, I wonder?"

Once more he looked at her before answering. "Are there no parties or country balls in your little part of Surrey?" He smiled, revealing a dimple in one cheek. He was really too charming and the effect of his words and his looks upon her made her wonder if she ought not to be a great deal more careful with him, her sister and cousin notwithstanding.

"I'm afraid after tonight I am swearing off balls and dancing. And perhaps dinner parties as well. At least for a time."

"Why ever would you do such a ridiculous thing as that?"

"I think..." Did she dare say it? Did she dare lay her objections before him? It did seem like the right thing to do, the honest thing, even if it were not the kindest thing. "That is, I have determined myself to wait until Beth is married before I go out in any kind of society."

"You are a good sister," he said, looking at her as if he were weighing the merit of her sacrifice—and her dedication to it.

"I love my sister. I would do anything for her."

"At the risk of letting your own opportunities for happiness pass you by?"

Laynie hesitated. And then nodded.

He took a moment to examine the crowd and perhaps to think over her words. Did he believe in her resolution? She was tempted to ask him but feared what answer he might give—and that he might be right.

He spoke this time without looking at her, with his eyes instead on the crowd upon one or two of the dancers. Upon, perhaps, one pair. Was it her sister he was watching now?

"You will forgive me if I have reason to doubt you. Not your resolve," he said as he tipped his head in her direction, his eyes still on the dancers before him. "That I believe in quite wholly. It's your power to withstand the will of your father I doubt."

"My father?"

"He has someone in mind for you. The fellow's of family, has a fortune, would no doubt marry you in a trice. Why won't you have him?"

"I don't love him," she answered simply. She longed to add more—that he loved Beth, and Beth had given her every reason to believe she might love him in return, every reason, until they had arrived here. Until Beth had met Mr. Emerson. True though it was, she could not do it. She could not betray Beth in that way. "How do you know all this?" she asked him. "Did Ned tell you?"

He looked at her. "No. Your sister did. You won't have him?" he asked after another long pause, during which his eyes danced over her face, her hair, her mouth, and held her gaze quite securely. His look was one vaguely regretful.

She could manage, only, to shake her head.

"Poor fellow."

Laynie suddenly felt a little breathless. "I'm not sure we should be speaking of such things, Mr. Emerson. You have very recently been disappointed. I wish to keep the peace with my family. Anyone who wished to appeal to me would have to wait a very long time for the privilege."

"Is that so, Miss Durham?"

"It is, Mr. Emerson. I'm sorry, but I feel I should be frank with you."

He smiled, then exhaled a laugh through his nose.

"What is so funny?"

"I don't think you *are* being frank with me. There is someone else. Admit it."

"There isn't, Mr. Emerson. Just because I feel it necessary to refuse your attentions doesn't mean I intend to seek them elsewhere."

Mr. Emerson's face flushed ever so slightly underneath the luminaries. "I'm sorry, Miss Durham. I think there has been some misunderstanding."

"Oh?"

"I hope you were not under the impression I meant to apply to you. Not so soon after—"

"Of course not, Mr. Emerson," Laynie assured him, thoroughly embarrassed. "I only thought it best to be certain my circumstances were understood. I would not wish to lead you a dance as Grace has done."

He looked at her questioningly but said nothing.

"She ought to have told you from the start she could not marry you until she was twenty-one. Why you will not wait for her is no business of mine, but though my father has placed no such restrictions on me, I have placed them on myself."

"For the sake of peace," he said, dubiously.

"For the sake of peace."

He arose. "I want to thank you, Miss Durham."

"For what?" For being straightforward with him? She doubted that was the reason for his expressed gratitude. He seemed rather to resent it than be grateful for it.

"For being so generous as to recognize that I was not entirely in the wrong for recanting on my promise to Miss Phillips."

"When there is disappointment, I think there is rarely only one side at fault."

"Still," he said, "I do know how it might look to some. I'm not easily changeable, Miss Durham. Like you, I have certain standards and restrictions—some imposed, some self-imposed—and, like you, I cannot be tempted to deviate from them. It was a pleasure knowing you. I hope you will find happiness, however long you may have to wait for it."

He turned from her before she could decide whether or not to thank him. Though his words were kindly and respectfully offered, they did sound vaguely as a rebuke. Had he called her a temptation? No. Certainly she was imagining such a thing. Her vanity had been piqued by his attention and now that it was at an end she wished to believe she had, if even for a moment, held some power over him. No. Such a thing was never to be. She would do well to forget him, to do anything she could to distract herself from thinking of him.

"Might I have the pleasure of the next set?"

It was the younger brother. She gave him her hand.

* * *

Beth had seen Mr. Emerson watching her. It did not absolve him of the fact that he had been sitting with her sister. Was he trying to make her jealous? Well, she wouldn't let him. But Laynie knew how Beth felt, and she knew, just as well, what trouble it would cause if Grace saw them. Was Laynie really growing so brazen? It was so easy to believe in her innocence, in her sweetness. She wore them like a favorite frock. It was so rare she was anything but those things that it was too easy to forget she knew how to be conniving and man-ipulative in her own right. Beth would have to learn to be ever vigilant. But where was Laynie now? She was dancing. She had promised she would not! And there she was with the gentleman Grace had so recently been dancing with. Did Laynie know no bounds at all?

More importantly still, where was Mr. Emerson?

"Might I beg for the honor of a dance, Miss Durham?" The sound of his voice thrilled her in the very same instant that it roused her ire. He had some explaining to do. At least, if he wished for her audience now, he was going to have to work for it. She pretended not to hear him, but continued to search the crowd, from one corner of the lawn to the other, her head held high, looking at everyone and everything and seeing nothing.

"Did you not hear me, Miss Durham?"

"I heard you," she said.

"Ah, I see," he said. "Well, then, a simple 'No, thank you,' would have made your refusal a little clearer. Forgive me for troubling you." And he turned to walk away.

"Mr. Emerson," she called out to him. He turned but seemed reluctant to return.

"Forgive me. It's just that…well…I fear, you know, what Grace will say. I don't want to cause trouble."

"No, of course not," he said and did not just at first seem to believe her quite entirely.

"I'm sorry," she said, a little more desperately. Her usual coyness did not seem to have the effect on him it had on others. "I do not always know what is the best thing to do or say in such awkward situations. I do hope you'll forgive me."

"You are forgiven," he said, with a bow of his head. "But, if you will not dance, would you consider walking with me instead?"

She looked around, at the trees that lined one side of the dancing area, then toward the lawns that spread out between the dance floor and the house, the open well-lit gardens that flanked each side of it.

"Certainly," she said, deeming it safe enough should they walk in that direction.

He smiled and led the way. Side by side, but not too closely, they walked toward the copse of trees—not toward the house at all—and toward the private shelter they might find within. Beth was not entirely certain so secluded a walk was really wise, but, fearing to offend him irrevocably by refusing him a second time, she swallowed her objections.

They walked in silence, and Beth felt the opportunity slipping from her. Ned had been invited to the ball, but he was expected to return to University in the morning. There was no reason for Mr. Emerson to remain beyond that.

"I am sorry about Grace," Beth said, desperate for conversation and meaning several things at once.

"About her jealousy, do you mean?"

"No. I mean with you and her. That it did not work out."

His brow furrowed. He looked angry, but he said nothing. It was only when they had reached the copse of trees and were hidden from view that he stopped. They had entered a little clearing where the fairy lights lit up the treetops and cast a faint glow upon the ground. And upon them. His look was brooding, dark.

"Mr. Emerson?" she said.

The faint sound of rumbling thunder could be heard in the distance. As if the angry sky had somehow encouraged him to anger too, he turned from her.

"Dash it!" he said, and then: "Oh, forgive me, Miss Durham. I don't know what I'm about. I'm a fool. I've been too long alone and I don't know what is proper to feel in such a situation as this. But I *am* disappointed. Indeed, I am angry!"

"I'm sorry, Mr. Emerson."

"If she couldn't have married me right away she ought to have said so from the beginning! I've been wronged, and there's nothing I can do about it."

"I agree, Mr. Emerson. It *was* wrong of her. But to be fair, she did believe she could convince her mother to make an exception."

"For a man who had been married before and who had perhaps been the cause of one wife's death already?"

Beth was shocked at first by this suggestion. No refined person would ever even imagine such a thing of anyone, least of all Mr. Emerson. She approached him and laid her hand on his arm. "Don't say that, Mr. Emerson. No one thinks that. My aunt may be strict, but she is not so cruel as to think something so horrid of you."

"Perhaps not," he said and shook his head; he appeared for a moment as though he might cry. "I'm sorry. It was ungenerous of me to suspect such a thing of her. She never showed me anything but kindness. And I have lost my temper. You must think me a monster."

"There, there, Mr. Emerson," Beth said, and took his hand in both of hers. "It will be all right. You will be happy again. And Grace is so changeable, so moody and petulant, I'm sure she would never have made you very happy. It is cruel of me to say, but I know her well. She was not right for you. You are too sensitive, too feeling for the likes of her."

Mr. Emerson nodded silently. At last he took a deep breath and steadied himself. "You are right, Miss Durham. Thank you for your kindness. I have suffered a very great deal these last months. I don't know how much more I can bear."

"If there is anything I can do…"

It was he holding her hand now. "You have been so kind to me. I don't know how I can thank you. I only regret I may never see you again. And it gives me pain to know it."

"Is there nothing at all that might bring you to Surrey?"

"I can only think of one thing."

"And what is that?" she said, hopeful it was something that might, indeed, give him reason to seek their society once more.

"I fear you will think me a cad for saying so."

"I doubt very much I could ever think anything so ungenerous of you, Mr. Emerson."

"It's just that I know two very charming sisters who live—"

"Two?"

"Well," he said and laughed, and, how he dared to do it she did not know, he pressed her hand to his lips. This was more than she could have hoped for! "Perhaps one in particular." His eyes glinted in the lantern light. "I've made you blush," he said, observing her color. She freed her hands and held them to her cheeks.

"I'm surprised there's enough light that you can see."

"Oh I can see, all right," he said. "Yours isn't the only blushing face I've seen tonight."

"I hope you have not inspired another, Mr. Emerson," she said and took a step away from him.

He advanced and put an arm around her waist. "Dance with me," he said, and he began spinning her around to the music that could only be faintly heard through the trees.

"You didn't answer my question."

"I don't intend to."

"Why ever not?"

"You might not like the answer."

She freed herself once more. "Does that mean you did?"

He laughed, somewhat irreverently. "Not on purpose," he said. "I happened upon someone who was trying to carry on a romance in a lovely little clearing in a quiet little wood. Forgive me if it gave me an idea."

Beth blushed again and allowed him to take her hand once more, to place his arm very gently around her waist. As the music played, he hummed its tune in her ear.

The sky rumbled again. It shook the earth, while her heart beat very quickly. She did not want to part from him. Not so soon.

"Will you come?" she asked him. "Will you come visit us in Ashworth?"

"Is that an invitation?"

"It is. Of course it is."

"I don't know."

She looked up at him.

"I fear I may be setting myself up for disappointment. I don't know that I can bear any more of that, Miss Durham."

"Why should I—we—cause you disappointment, Mr. Emerson?"

"Well, considering what great efforts your father is taking to arrange for his daughters to be married, I may arrive too late."

"Then you must come with all haste," she said, teasing him in turn.

"I'm afraid it's going to take a little more persuading than that, Miss Durham."

"And how am I to persuade you, then?"

"I can think of one way." He looked at her, very intently. A heavy silence hung between them. She did not know what more to say. She suspected he wished for her to do something, but she did not know what, or rather feared to misunderstand, to hope for too much.

His head lowered, she felt the brush of his lips against her cheek, slipping across the corner of her mouth as though hoping for a little something more than she was willing to give him. There was another peal of thunder and great drops of rain began to fall, here and there, upon the ground.

Mr. Emerson offered her a look of regret. The sky would soon open wide. They could not remain. He took her hand and together they made their way back through the thicket. They came to a sudden stop upon coming to the edge of it. A man was standing there, very red of face and looking altogether displeased.

"Uncle!" Beth cried in surprise and freed her hand from Mr. Emerson's.

"What is going on here?" he demanded of her. And then, of Mr. Emerson, "I demand an explanation, sir."

* * *

The first set had ended and Laynie found herself dancing with the elder of the two brothers. In fact she was not so certain which was older and which the younger now she had had the opportunity to speak with them both. Perhaps they were the same age—twins. They were both handsome enough, but the conversation was so stilted and trivial as to make it nearly unbearable. How did she like the party, where was her home, did she enjoy living in Surrey, and did she know the famous Mr. Meredith personally? These were the questions put to her, and they were so easily answered and reciprocated with the same that, at the end of it, she felt she knew the gentlemen no better and that their design was not truly to learn anything significant of her but simply to fill the time.

In her boredom, she began watching the other dancers. Was Beth dancing? She could not find her. Not anywhere. Strange, that. Where had she gone? Neither was Mr. Emerson anywhere to be seen. Was it possible they had gone off together? Her attention was arrested by the sight of a familiar figure, tall and broad and yet elegant in his evening clothes.

She felt a jolt in her chest and it drove her forward. She abandoned her formation and crossed the floor, giving little thought to what she was doing, only that if he were here, she would like to know it. She should make herself known to him. She was at his side now, as he waited for the ladies in his square to turn their circle and rejoin their partners. She touched his elbow. He turned to her, a puzzled, uncomprehending look on his face.

"Can I help you, miss?"

It was not Mr. Holbrook. Why had she thought it might be? His height, the length and curl of his brown hair were similar, but there the similarities ended.

"I'm sorry, no. I mistook you for someone else. Forgive me." And she turned away, to find a place where she might sit. No. No, she did not want to sit. She wanted to be away, to go home. At least to be by herself.

192

"You are a funny one," Ned said and took her arm. He escorted her back to her own square, which had rather fallen apart in her absence. He dismissed the brother—was he the younger or the older? She could not remember and no longer cared. "What were you doing?"

"I don't know," Laynie said and only finished the set by following Ned's exact directions, his pushing and pulling of her as if she were a puppet on a string. Perhaps she *was* a puppet to him. Perhaps she was a puppet to her father, to her sister... Why was she even here? In Gravesend, or...Beresford, or...wherever they were.

The music at last ended and Laynie headed once more for the lawn and the peace and quiet of solitude that she wished desperately to find there. But Ned quite unexpectedly had her by the arm.

"No, you don't," he said. "I rescued you from very nearly creating a scene. You're going to dance with me now."

"Oh, Ned. Not a polka. Please, my ankle can't take it."

"Balderdash!" he said a little more loudly than necessary and with the smell of brandy so thick on his breath it made her feel sick. "I've been watching you all evening. There isn't a thing wrong with your ankle. You're only being difficult."

He took her hand, placed his other on her back, a little too firmly, and they began. She really didn't have the energy for it, and Ned had not the self-discipline, it seemed. His hand slid, by degrees, to rest at her side beneath her arm. In this way his hand brushed against her in a most distressing fashion as she turned to complete the movements. She stepped away from him, gave him a warning look, and allowed him to return his hand to its proper place.

"You're no fun anymore."

"It's because I've grown up and I've realized what a scoundrel you are."

"You're very cruel to me, Laynie. I don't deserve it."

"I think you do."

He was quiet for a moment only and then: "I return to University tomorrow, you know."

"Yes, thank heaven!"

"Don't say it like that. I haven't been able to spend the time with you I wanted."

"Funny. I was feeling I'd had rather too much of you."

"You are very hard on me. Why are you so hard on me?"

"Because you are an impertinent scoundrel, Ned. It's really quite simple."

"Listen, you. I want a chance to say goodbye."

"Fortunately for you, I believe in efficiency. Goodbye, Ned."

"Not like this," he said and held her closer, which was unnecessary. As much as she wished to be away from him, she was not going to leave him standing alone on the dance floor. She doubted she'd be able to accomplish it without making a bigger scene than the one she had very nearly escaped a few minutes ago. "Before I go will you grant me half an hour?" He had said it in a whisper, and his breath, as he did, brushed her neck. He was far too close.

"Not alone," she insisted.

"Yes, of course alone. How else?"

She did not answer him.

"You do try my patience, you know."

"Consider it fair turnabout for all the fretting you make me do."

"I don't know what you mean."

"Your toying. Your empty flirtations. You're always touching me. It makes me feel cheap. Like I'm an amusement to you and nothing more."

"I'm actually rather fond of you," he said as if she'd caused him real injury. "Perhaps it's merely out of habit I tease you. You were always just little Laynie to me. My shy, awkward cousin. I feel like I hardly know this woman you've become. I'd like the opportunity. I think you owe me that much."

"I disagree. Considering all, I don't think I owe you anything." She found it necessary to move his hand once more and stepped away from him. "Really, Ned. If you cannot treat me with a little decency, I want nothing at all to do with you."

She managed at last to free herself and turned to walk away, but his hand was on her wrist and holding it a little too tightly.

"Let me go," she said to him.

"Not until you listen to me."

"I've listened. I'm finished now. Goodbye, Ned."

But he did not let her go. There was a sound of rumbling, like a hundred chairs being moved at once across the floor. Were they drawing such a spectacle as that? She had to end this and end it quickly.

"I will give you this last warning, sir," she said as quietly as she could manage and still get her point across, "to unhand me and to leave me in peace."

He laughed loudly. "Or what? Come on, Laynie," he said and pulled her close enough to almost kiss her. Was he so drunk as that? His breath and his roughly whiskered chin brushed her cheek.

She responded in the only way that seemed appropriate. She slapped him hard across the face. There was a flash like lightning, a clap of thunder, and the rain came pouring down. Her hand ached fiercely. Her bracelet was gone, having unclasped itself when she struck him. There was a scratch on his cheek and a row of tiny red drops formed on the surface of it. He reached up to touch it and examined his finger. A look of anger flashed in his eyes. Would he retaliate? In the safety of a closely-watching crowd she had thought not, but now that the crowd was dispersing, running for cover from the deluge and leaving her quite alone with him, she could not be so certain.

"What is going on here?" Aunt Phillips demanded, appearing suddenly at her side and looking like a drenched poodle, her frothy muslin dress hanging as limply about her as the hair on her head.

"May we go home now, Aunt?" Laynie said and wished she could travel home to Surrey this very night.

"I think we must!" she answered with barely subdued anger. She turned to look about her. The other guests were heading for the house, taking chairs and sofas and tables with them. "Where is your sister?"

"She's here," Uncle Phillips said, holding a sodden and very blushing Beth by the wrist.

"And where have you been?"

"You don't want to know," was Uncle Phillips' answer.

"Well, then," her aunt said and grew rigid as the rain poured down and began dripping from the end of her nose. "I really think I had better, don't you?"

Uncle Phillips grew suddenly reticent as his daughter joined them. "We'll discuss it later." He took his son by the collar. "Home with you. Now!"

"Come, Grace. We're going." Aunt Phillips took both nieces by the arm and followed her husband toward the house and the carriage that awaited in the drive. Ned was placed quite briskly into one carriage, the girls were handed into the other and the door was closed upon them while their aunt and uncle had a very brief conference in the rain. Laynie heard not a word of it, only saw their lips moving through the window.

"What is going on?" Grace asked. "What has happened? Why must we leave now? I was having such a lovely time."

But neither sister was inclined to answer.

Uncle Phillips, at last having his say, joined his son in the other carriage. Aunt Phillips stood a moment in the cooling rain before at last climbing in. She looked at her nieces for a very long time. It was only when the carriage jolted into motion that she spoke.

"Remind me never to bring you to another ball," she said. "I don't know why I even bother to take the trouble to help you. What were you thinking, Laynie? To cause such a scene! I'll never live it down! Never! And you, Bethany. We shall have private words in the morning. I am beside myself with disappointment. And after all the trouble that was taken." She took a deep breath and seemed to hold it forever, as if she were trying not to cry. She let it out at last and contemplated the fogging glass of the window as they made their way home.

As the carriage at last began to amble down the drive toward the house, she spoke once more, this time much more calmly. "I must write to your father. I think it will be best if you return home tomorrow."

Laynie tried very hard to maintain the look of regret and alarm she wore upon her face. She did regret. And she was a little afraid of what more her aunt and uncle might have to say to her—not to mention to Beth, whose transgression she could not begin to guess. But, in truth, she was very, very glad to know she would be going home. Oh, very glad indeed!

196

Grace tried one more time, upon returning home, to discover what it was that had caused such a fuss. Laynie was not inclined to tell her she had struck her brother or why, and Beth was equally silent on the subject of her embarrassment. Even when they were alone and the door shut securely Beth remained silent, alarmingly so. The girls changed out of their wet clothes and Beth was the first to crawl into bed and turn out the light. Laynie lingered for a little while before the fire. She was sorry for the trouble she had caused and for the disappointment, but if she had known striking Ned would be her ticket home, she would have done it the first day he'd arrived.

Chapter sixteen

THE GIRLS WERE HOME, AND though Mr. Durham was happy to have them safe and sound under his roof, he would have been happier still to know that some good had come of their holiday, short as it was. And though he did not yet know the reason for their early return, he trusted it would all come out sooner or later. His sister had said little in regard to her reasons for returning them home early, only that her nieces were perhaps better suited to the company of their father than anyone else in the world. Apart from that she had hinted that some further advice regarding his parenting methods might be expected from her by way of post in a day or two—after she had some time to sort out just what it was that had happened.

Mr. Durham smiled to himself. He knew what had happened. His young and lively daughters had caused some excitement amidst his sister's Gravesend society. It did not surprise him. It was to be expected, after all. He was rather surprised his sister had been so unprepared for it. But was the holiday a complete failure? What had been the effect upon Laynie in respect to his sister's appellations in behalf of Mr. Vaughn? That was the real reason they had been sent. Was Laynie more inclined now than previously to accept Mr. Vaughn? And what of Beth? She was petulant and dour. Was it owing to his sister's success? Or had some other unfortunate gentleman found his way into her path?

Perhaps he ought to be disappointed to have them home so soon. Perhaps he was just at first, but though Mr. Holbrook kept him occupied three times a week, he had the other four days to consider his loneliness. To be quite honest, he was very pleased to have his children home. Indeed, he was not certain he would like to send them away again.

Upon receiving them he was greeted with tear-filled hugs that went a long way to placating any frustration and alarm he might initially have felt. He kissed them and sent them to their rooms to rest and unpack. They did so without argument, and all seemed to be well. Two hours later, however, Mrs. Fowler came down to tell him Laynie had caught a cold and must keep to her room.

A portion of that former annoyance returned. Had she not learned her lesson already about getting caught in downpours? Ah, well, there was nothing for it. Perhaps his sister's letter would tell him all he wished to know.

It came, of course, and rather than elucidating him, it left him more perplexed than ever.

> Dear Nathaniel,
>
> You will no doubt be put out with me when you read what I have to say, but it cannot be helped. I have endeavored to educate your girls, to train and guide them, and, as you yourself begged me to do, to counsel them as to the wisdom in marrying well, and in so doing, laying aside their more selfish desires. I have done all I can. I fear — that is I am now convinced — it will never be enough. If only their poor mother had lived to guide them through this delicate age perhaps all would be in hand and just as it ought to be. As it stands, they are willful and headstrong, and require the sternness of their father to rein them in before it is too late. I regret to say, dear brother, that you have never been one for sternness. I always thought it one of your most endearing qualities until now.
>
> As to why they have been returned to you early, while I did and do feel it necessary, I'm no longer so certain it was entirely their fault. I am still laboring to get to the bottom of what happened on their last evening with me. Suffice it to say a scene was caused — and perhaps more than one — embarrassment was felt, and, I regret to say, at least one heart was broken. If your daughters seem to you a little downcast upon their return, consider it a practical and much needed lesson to us all (yourself included) and leave it at that. I doubt you will get more out of them than I have been able to do. Young people these days are so tiresomely willful!
>
> One last thing, brother. On the subject of this Mr. Vaughn, I do believe you will get nowhere. If the fellow fancies the older of your daughters, and if she can be persuaded to care for him in turn, why should they not be allowed to have their way? Far worse things can befall Bethany than that some wealthy and connected gentleman should wish to marry her. In any event, it will be one less thing for you to worry about. As for the approval of Lady

Vaughn, where a favorite son is concerned, a mother's heart can always be swayed.

> *Your affectionate sister,*
> *Eloise Phillips*

* * *

Laynie's indisposition allowed Beth some much needed time to think. She was confused, and aware of being confused in a way she had never before experienced. As the peace and quiet consequent of Laynie's recuperation dragged on, Beth began to grow uneasy. What did Mr. Vaughn's prolonged absence mean? She had gone to Gravesend determined to forget him, and as much as it was possible, she had. It was easy enough to do when Mr. Emerson was about— handsome, charming, broken-hearted Mr. Emerson. She had been wholly fascinated by him. She had been a little afraid of him, too. He excited her in a way she was not certain was entirely proper, and though she had not been his first choice it seemed she had at last convinced him that she was, of the three young women, the one most worthy of consideration.

And yet there still remained the problem of Harold Vaughn. Her time in Gravesend, her efforts to win over Mr. Emerson, and her apparent success in doing so had not quite convinced her to give up on Harry. While Harry's greatest flaw was that he was not Mr. Emerson, it was true that Mr. Emerson's greatest flaw was alarmingly, even ironically, similar. Mr. Emerson, when all was said and done, was not Harold Vaughn. He had not Mr. Vaughn's sincerity, his intelligence, his steadiness, or his depth of character. And yet it remained—perhaps it always would remain—that poor Harold Vaughn had not Mr. Emerson's charm, good looks, or winning ways. Mr. Vaughn was not exciting. And Mr. Emerson was not here. Neither of them were, for that matter. So what was she to do about it? Nothing. Nothing, but wait. That old, familiar occupation.

Beth, sitting in their bedroom, watched her sister sleep. She had been resting for three days uninterrupted. She needed the rest. But what more did she need? What was it that Laynie truly wanted? Was it Mr. Emerson? Was it, in fact, Mr. Vaughn? Or was it just as she had said—that her heart had not yet been inspired to yearn for anyone? Beth felt a little repentant about the harder feelings she had been tempted to entertain for her sister in Gravesend. Even still, she knew Laynie had not been entirely honest with her in many respects. Had she lied about that, too? Had she some secret attachment to someone? Or had she merely a wish that her heart might be awakened to love? Who, Beth wondered, would be the one to do it? It might be anyone, after all. She might yet be persuaded to love Mr. Vaughn. It had occurred to Beth on more than one occasion that her sister was far more worthy of him than she could ever hope to be. And yet the idea of choosing Harry now, when any day Mr. Emerson might come to call, seemed utterly impossible.

If only she could think of some means of distracting Laynie until she had made up her mind what to do and whom to love and what to think or feel about any of it. But there were not many distractions available here. Hardly any at all.

The doorbell rang.

Quietly Beth left the room and slipped down the staircase landing to see who it was that had come. She sat in disappointment to find that it was only Mr. Holbrook.

Mr. Holbrook? An idea struck her and she pondered upon it. She smiled to herself. She really could be very wicked when she decided to be. But it was not wickedness for wickedness's sake. She had a purpose. A necessary purpose. And no harm would come of it, she was sure. What harm could there possibly be?

* * *

Laynie arose on the fourth morning after her return, much refreshed and feeling quite recovered. Even her ankle seemed at last and wholly restored. More than anything, she felt her mood had improved. The lethargy of illness and the idleness of rest had her feeling low in spirits. But today, with the sun shining brightly through the parting clouds, she was beginning to feel more like her old self. She was home, after all, where there was relative peace and where she could, for the most part, do as she liked. She had had enough of resting and felt the need for some occupation that would allow her the luxury of her own company and yet would keep her actively occupied. The solution was immediately apparent upon reaching the dining room. She stepped out into the yard to find that a week and a half was just enough time for the weeds to run rampant, the grass to grow too long, and for the hedges to look unkempt. She returned to her room, where she changed into her outdoor clothes and where she stopped a moment to examine the gowns she had brought from Gravesend. It was for they alone she regretted having no one to impress. Other than three very fine gowns she would never have occasion to wear, she was relieved that it was so. If she had ever entertained aspirations to live a life of privilege a week at her aunt's had cured her.

Laynie returned downstairs, took a hurried breakfast, and went out into the yard. But where to begin? The lawn could wait. There were ways to deal with that. One of the neighbors owned a mechanical lawnmower, and occasionally she hired one of their boys to mow the small patch of grass that surrounded her favorite tree and which served as a favorite gathering area for her father's guests and for the rare garden dinner party her father occasionally held. As for the shrubberies, they must be clipped and sheared and shaped before anything more could be done.

She went to work on these, and once finished, she stood back to examine her work. The idea had occurred to her to expand the present design to match one of Aunt Phillips' formal gardens. To create a formal border would require several more boxwoods, but there were starts enough to choose from, and so she began by digging these up and setting them aside. Next she marked where the holes would need to be dug for the new plantings, and, taking up the shovel, prepared to begin. The sun was warm, though there was a refreshing breeze. Still, she felt herself beginning to perspire. At least, private as the garden was, she was not likely to be seen.

"Good morning, Miss Durham."

Laynie turned to find that Mr. Holbrook had entered the garden.

"Forgive me if I startled you. I'm looking for your father."

She was aware she must look a sight to him. It was a good thing she did not care what he thought of her. But then if she didn't, why did she feel the heat in her face so? The sun, perhaps. Yes, of course it was the sun. "Do you usually look for him in the garden?"

"No," was his simple answer. He appeared as confused as she.

"And yet you look for him here?"

"It is where I was told I would find him."

"By Mrs. Fowler?"

"No. By your sister."

Laynie looked toward the house in time to see the parlor curtain drop. Why would Beth do such a thing? "I'm afraid she was mistaken. Or..."

"Or?"

"Nothing," she said. "My father is in his library, as he usually is. You may go through the dining room, if you like. It's shorter."

He nodded in acknowledgement but remained where he was. "You know there is..." he said, pointing to a spot on his face and taking a step forward. He stopped again. "Do you need help?" he asked her. "Do you want it, I mean?"

She had dug the first hole already, and there were at least a dozen more to go. It was not hard work, but stepping down on the shovel did seem a strain on her newly-recovered ankle. Would it be wrong to say yes?

"My father is waiting for you, I think," she said instead.

"Of course," he replied. "Excuse me."

She watched him go, and when the door had closed upon him she leaned her shovel against the fountain and rested there. He must have startled her more thoroughly than she had first supposed. Or perhaps she was not so recovered, after all. Her heart was pounding harder than it ought to be. She was a little shorter of breath. She looked at her reflection in the fountain's surface. It was not running today and so the reflection was undisturbed. Or nearly so. A great smear of dirt stretch-ed from her cheek to the bridge of her nose. She threw off her gloves and found her handkerchief, which she dipped in the water and used to wash her face, first just the spot and then the whole of it. She took off her hat, dampened her neck and smoothed her hair.

Good heavens, she was a mess through and through, and she felt it besides.

* * *

Upon entering the house, Daniel stopped at the window and watched a moment. Why had Bethany Durham told him her father was in the garden? She must have known her sister was there. Was it a contrivance? And what was the purpose of it?

He watched the younger Miss Durham as she washed the spot of dirt away. It did not belong there, marring her lovely face like that, and yet he was a little sorry to see it go. He had very nearly offered to wipe it away himself. Was this, then, the sum of his determination to consider himself a confirmed bachelor? He would never forget Sophie. He had a duty to carry her memory with him. He had a duty to abide by the promise he'd made Miss Durham's father. And to these duties he would be faithful. But was it wrong to take a little pleasure in such pleasant company as hers?

Daniel arrived at the library door and was just about to knock when Mrs. Fowler appeared.

"Miss Bethany is with her father just at the moment, Mr. Holbrook. I'm sure he will be ready to receive you shortly."

"Thank you, Mrs. Fowler. Will you tell him I'll wait for him in the garden?"

"Yes, of course, sir."

And Daniel, as if a slave to impulse, left the house once more. She was sitting on the bench, apparently deep in thought and drawing her dampened handkerchief blindly through one hand and then repeating the exercise with the other.

He removed his coat and placed it on the bench beside her. "Are you certain you don't want help?"

She looked up at him and appeared nearly as surprised this time as she had been but a few minutes ago.

"Your father is otherwise engaged, it seems."

"With whom, I wonder?" she said, apparently confused.

"Your sister, I believe."

Her brow wrinkled over her perfectly formed and dirtless nose.

"How was your holiday?" he asked her.

"Dreadful, if you can believe it."

"May I?" he said and gestured toward the shovel.

She nodded her grateful acquiescence.

"Might I ask why?"

"Perhaps I was simply determined not to enjoy myself. I never really wanted to go. I would have been perfectly content staying at home."

He wished to know why again but refrained from asking. It was vain and he would no doubt be disappointed by her answer.

"My aunt is kind and well meaning, but we will never be quite fit for her set. I should be grateful, I suppose, that she continues to try, though I doubt very much she will ever take the trouble to do it again."

"And why should she give up on you now?" he asked. "Here?" he inquired and pointed toward the ground, beside which a little shrub-bery start had been placed.

"Yes. Thank you," she said and nodded. "My aunt is quite certain my father is a horrible parent. I don't see that she's been any more successful with her own children. My cousin Ned, in particular, is quite unbearable."

He dug the first hole in two shovelfuls and looked up at her. "Go on," he said.

She did not appear to want to expound upon the subject further. She reddened slightly and straightened her apron over her lap. "That's it, really," she said dismissively. "But for all her good intentions, she was no more successful in convincing me to do my father's bidding than he has been."

"You refer, I think, to the unfortunate Mr. Vaughn."

Laynie nodded her answer.

"So nothing has changed in that respect, I take it," he said and tried to disguise his pleasure. He was almost successful. "It is as it was when you left. Mr. Vaughn would like the pleasure of applying for your sister's hand. Your father would prefer him for you. I do wonder why he is so determined to that end."

"He is afraid of Lady Vaughn and knows an advantageous opportunity when he sees it."

"And you?"

She shrugged slightly. "My aunt says I'm willful."

He stopped only long enough to glance at her. He wished, in this case, she would continue to be. "And what say you?"

"I have unrealistic fancies."

"I believe that's your aunt speaking again."

Miss Durham exhaled a laugh. "I suppose it is. If I were to offer some defense I would say that I hope to marry for nothing less than sincere affection and admiration—even respect. I care very much for Mr. Vaughn. He is one of my dearest friends. But I do not love him."

"How do you know?"

This seemed to strike her momentarily speechless. She blinked her eyes and opened her mouth. "I—" But she said nothing more.

"Forgive me," he said. "I'm prying. No doubt you will know it when it comes."

"I think I *am* the type to make a friend first and then fall in love later. Certainly I am one to make up my mind very slowly. But Harry? If I don't love him by now, I'm not likely to, I think. I'm in no hurry for it, at all events."

"There's no reason you should be. Yours is a very sensible plan."

"Is love ever sensible, Mr. Holbrook? And is it sensible at all that I should be speaking of it, who never was in love? And with you who are—"

But she stopped suddenly. He set the shovel in the earth and looked at her. He very much wished to know what she had to say. "Yes, Miss Durham? What am I?"

She blushed crimson and looked away. He waited, grateful for the excuse to stand there looking at her for however long it took to persuade her to say what she meant to say.

"I was going to say married," she said very quietly and not looking at him. "I know you are not." A glance. "I think it is not right for us to be speaking so openly with one another this way."

"Perhaps not," he said with some measure of regret. He had begun very much to enjoy the conversation. But she did have a point. He stopped again before the shovel had penetrated the earth. "For the record, I did not intend to misrepresent myself."

"I know that, Mr. Holbrook," she said reassuringly. She arose to attend once more to her shrubberies and said nothing more.

He dug her holes in silence and did it more slowly now, hoping to draw out the interlude as long as he might. In time she caught up to him. She placed a bundle at his feet and looked up at him as she knelt on the ground.

"How many holes would you like, Miss Durham?" he asked her.

She stood and brushed the dirt from her apron. It seemed she had stood too quickly and was a little light headed. He took her elbow to steady her. She thanked him and held onto the shovel's handle as he held it in his hand, the blade resting securely on the ground. She was standing so very close to him now. No, it could not be right to take so much pleasure in her company. He released her elbow. She shook her head to clear it and pointed. He watched her instead and tried to listen.

"You see, there's a marker for each one. It goes all around the fountain, in a circle."

She was not wearing a hat, and her hair was coming out of its plaits, hanging haphazardly about her face, falling over her shoulder, clinging to her fair and sunburning neck...

"Do you see them, Mr. Holbrook?"

She was looking up at him, waiting for an answer, or some acknowledgement he understood. Belatedly he looked where she had pointed. There was indeed a marker where each hole ought to go, a rock set on the grass, quite easy to overlook if she had not pointed it out. There were a dozen more perhaps. He might remain here all day, digging and quite happy to do it. When he turned back to face her she had moved away from him. Her face was red again, but whether she was blushing or it was the effect of the sun he could not tell.

"Please sit, Miss Durham." He helped her to be seated and retrieved her hat. He found her handkerchief lying on the bench, wetted it and returned it to her. And then, quite reluctantly, he returned to the shovel and the holes that had yet to be dug.

"You know I thought I saw you there. In Gravesend."

"Did you?" he said and wondered.

"There was a ball in Beresford. There was a man there, very tall, very..."

"What, Miss Durham? Do finish."

But she continued on as though she had said the words and he had merely failed to hear them. "I don't know why I thought it was you, but I did. It was a quadrille. I broke my formation to say hello."

"Did he appreciate the gesture?"

"No," she laughed. "I don't think he did. Neither did my partner, nor my cousin who came to my rescue."

"I'm sorry for that. I hope they were, none of them, ungracious."

"Only my cousin, as I refused to accept him as my partner after that. But that is his way. He is either impulsively presuming or uncompromisingly angry. Always one or the other. Do you think a man can change, Mr. Holbrook?"

"I certainly hope so," he said, and wondered what her cousin had made her endure and what the experience had taught her about human nature.

"You asked a question earlier and I did not quite answer it. You asked why it should be that I will likely never go to my aunt's in Gravesend again. You see, my cousin has always paid me a little more attention than I would like him to do. It was always idle teasing before, a flirtation to him. It meant nothing, I'm sure."

She was quiet for a moment, but he feared to prompt her. He feared what she had to say or that she might not say it after all.

"It turns out he has formed some sincere feeling. Or at least he declares it to be so. I think he meant to offer to me. And while his attentions may be sincere, they are still unwelcome. At least his manner of delivering them is not always quite delicate, or even, for that matter, decent. I put an end to it, you see."

"You refused him?"

"I struck him."

"You don't say," he said in wonder. "For all to see?"

"For all to see." She cocked her head and gave him a sideways glance. "It seems that is rather frowned upon in certain circles."

"I should say so," he said. "Still, I congratulate you."

He watched her smile, then laugh at the thought.

"And will that be an end of it, do you think?"

"Yes, since I won't be returning. As for him, I think some men do not change," she said. "I don't think they can."

"Some men, perhaps. I hope you don't believe all men incapable."

"I don't know," she said. "I haven't any reason to believe it."

He continued on with his digging. If she had any idea the wrongs he had committed… "Perhaps," he said, struggling for any excuse to persuade her to think it possible, "perhaps you have given him reason to do it. Now."

"It does often fall on us, doesn't it?" she asked a little resentfully.

"You are, by nature, the gentler, the more nurturing sex. You set the standard. You provide the inspiration."

She sat forward on the bench. He thought—perhaps hoped—she would rise and approach him. But she remained there, intent and very serious. "But that is such a great charge, don't you see? It leaves us no room to make our own mistakes. We must ever be perfect. When we fail to be we are condemned. How lovely it would be to be a man and to do whatever one wanted without recourse."

"I assure you, Miss Durham, there is always recourse. Consequence is a faithful companion in all deeds, whether good or bad, and it can teach us like nothing can to change our ways when we have done wrong. Besides, if there is no repentance, then what was the point of God's great sacrifice?"

"I do not know," she answered flatly. "Perhaps it is possible, under very extreme circumstances. But a mistake is one thing. Wickedness in character is quite another. A man who lies will lie again. A man who is unfaithful, who is ungrateful, who takes pleasure in tormenting another, he remains the same at heart, I'm sure of it."

Was it possible she was speaking of him? Had she learned something of him that he would not wish her to know? And if so, then how? Or was she merely punishing him now for maintaining a lie, even if it had been told by another? "Have I done something to offend you, Miss Durham?"

"Heavens no," she said and stood, appearing a little alarmed at the thought. "I was merely thinking aloud. I do tend to say too much when I am with you, don't I?"

"I don't know that I would say that."

"It's a bad habit I am forming, I'm afraid. I wonder why it is so."

"I consider it a compliment, actually."

She did not say anything for a long moment. She looked up at the sun, very warm and bright, and at last back at him. "My holiday has left me feeling very tired. And perhaps a little cynical. If I have caused you any distress, I do hope you will forgive me."

"Always," he answered her.

"I think I ought to go back in."

"Yes, of course." He moved to help her but was stopped again.

"Holbrook!" came Mr. Durham's voice from beyond the shrubberies. And soon the man himself appeared, his arms waving and a book in one hand. He stopped short at the sight of Daniel, dirt

209

on his hands and on the cuffs of his trousers. "What are you up to? What is this? You are digging holes?" he said. "Holes?"

"I'm planting more boxwoods, Papa," Laynie informed him and sounded tired. "It's to be an Italian garden like those Aunt Phillips has in Gravesend."

"Shrubberies are fine for you, Laynie, but I do not pay Mr. Holbrook to dig holes. Come Holbrook, time is getting on." And the old man walked off, perfectly confident in Daniel's obedience.

Daniel hesitated a moment. He did not like to leave her thus. He took up his coat and turned, quite reluctantly, to follow Mr. Durham who had already made his retreat.

"Thank you for your help, Mr. Holbrook."

"It was a pleasure," he answered. It was agony, too, but a pleasure certainly and one he would willingly repeat, however unwise it might prove to be.

* * *

"Well?" Beth asked upon joining Laynie as she made her way back to the house.

"Well, what?

"Did you speak to him?"

"You know I did. You watched me do it."

"And?"

Laynie did not answer and so Beth pressed on.

"Do you still find him dull?"

"I never found him dull. You did, remember? But why do you care what I think of him?"

Beth gave her a noncommittal shrug in answer.

"Good heaven, Beth! What *can* you be thinking?"

"I was just curious, that's all. He *is* very handsome, don't you think?"

It was a question she refused to answer aloud. It was a question she had tried to avoid asking herself. But now it was there and couldn't be ignored. Yes. He was handsome. At times, distractingly so.

"You do like him, admit it."

"I like him very much, Bethany, but for far better reasons than his beauty alone."

"Beauty?" Beth echoed and seemed to make a little too much of the word.

"You know what I mean. But I won't think of him as more than what he is. I can't."

Beth was quiet a moment. They had arrived at the house. Beth reached for the door's handle but did not open it. "And what is he, exactly?" she said.

"You know what he is, Beth. Now can't we just go in? I'm hot and very tired."

"Not until you tell me what he is—or may be—to you."

The simplest answer would have been 'nothing', but Laynie could not quite say it. She had shared too much with him, she had grown to think of him as something more significant than merely her father's hired companion. Was he a friend? She very much hoped so, but somehow felt it was presuming to say so. He was nothing more than that of course...and yet when she thought of her friendship with Harry, they were very, very different things entirely. She enjoyed Harry's company, but she did not revel in it. She did not think of him when he was away. If she saw him in a crowd of strangers, would she have broken her square to approach him?

Bethany still was waiting for an answer, and Laynie found herself suddenly without patience. "Why did you do it, Beth?"

"Do what?"

"You know what. You told him Papa was in the garden when you knew he was not. You pushed him into my company when that was not what he wished for."

"But it was, Laynie. He saw you through the window, and—"

"Stop it, Beth! I won't be a pawn in one of your silly games. I don't know what you are up to, but I won't have any part in it. I consider this joke of yours a very cruel one, indeed." She reached for the door and pulled it open for herself.

"Laynie?" Beth called after her, but Laynie had nothing more to say on the subject. "I meant no harm."

Chapter seventeen

"WELL, HOLBROOK, IT SEEMS THE holiday I took such pains to provide for my daughters was a complete waste of time," Mr. Durham said almost the moment Daniel had sat down.

"I'm sure it wasn't an utter waste," Daniel answered him.

"No?" Mr. Durham returned. He removed something from the lining of his coat and handed it to him. "Read it."

And Daniel did. Upon finishing it, he looked up at his employer and very much wished to ask a question—or perhaps several. "A scene? Embarrassment? Do you know to what she is referring?"

"Not a clue. I've spoken with Beth but there's no getting anything useful out of her. Evidently she and her sister were separated, she did say that much, but whatever it was they suffered—or perhaps caused—Beth won't say. And if Laynie got into some trouble—and knowing her, I think it rather likely—Beth says she does not know what it is. I'm inclined to believe her."

"And have you spoken to your younger daughter?"

"I should. Perhaps I'll send for her." He arose to do just that but Daniel stopped him.

"Sir. It's just possible I know what it was about."

"Oh?" Mr. Durham said, puzzled.

"She mentioned a cousin."

"Ned?"

"She said he presumed upon her. I'm not entirely certain what that means, but it was plain she did not welcome the attention. I believe she said she struck him."

"Struck him, what!" Mr. Durham said in surprise. He considered it a moment, and then laughed out loud.

"I'm not certain she would have liked for me to tell you, but I thought you ought to know. If there was an embarrassment, your sister, from what I can gather, is right to doubt that it was Miss Alayna's fault."

"No doubt she led him to it, though."

"Do you truly think so?" Daniel asked and waited for Mr. Durham to consider and to answer.

"Perhaps not in this instance," Mr. Durham conceded and sat back down in his chair. "Imposed, did he? You know she never did like him. I don't know if I ought to be proud of her or disappointed."

"She is spirited, as your sister states it. I'm not convinced it's entirely a bad thing, considering."

"No…perhaps not. But that is only part of the problem, isn't it?" Mr. Durham observed to his friend. "My sister thinks I ought to abandon the idea of Mr. Vaughn for her. She was equally as unsuccessful in convincing her to see reason. And that, too, is spiritedness—and not for the better, I should think."

"If there is no especial attachment between them, nor likely to be, then perhaps she is right to have made up her mind so uncompromisingly." Daniel was aware he was making an argument in whose outcome he had some little interest.

"But what am I to do now?" Mr. Durham turned to look out the window. Laynie, of course, was no longer there, but it was hard to look anywhere in that garden and not think of her.

"Is it necessary you do something? Time usually has a way of working these things out."

"Not just anyone will do, you know," Mr. Durham said and turned from the window to face him.

"I should hope not."

"I'm not certain just anyone would take her. She is a handful. Perhaps you've noticed."

Daniel was uncertain how to answer this without giving away the fact that he'd actually given the matter some thought. "She'll settle down in time. She is anxious, and considering the pressure presently upon her to make a decision she is not ready to make, I'm not sure it fair to blame her."

213

"But it does make things difficult, don't you see? What are the chances, do you think, that another like Harold Vaughn might come along?"

"I suppose that depends on what you mean, sir." But he thought he understood already.

"To marry so far above her, and to have the wholehearted approval of his mother besides …it's unlikely such an opportunity will come her way again. Of course he needn't own a castle to be worthy of her. I'd be foolish to set such high standards as Vaughn or anyone like him. But I do want to see her taken care of. You understand."

"Yes, of course I do."

Mr. Durham minced his mouth thoughtfully to one side as he looked out the window. He seemed suddenly to realize something. He turned to Daniel. "Laynie confided in you, did she?"

"She did," Daniel answered somewhat cautiously. It was not the first time, either, and while he was rather flattered to know she trusted him, he was not certain her father would approve of it.

"That is significant, don't you think?"

"I don't know." He did but was afraid to say so.

"I think it is. She has no one to talk to. She and her sister do not confide in one another as they used to do, and you know she will not talk to me."

Daniel ventured to guess it had more to do with Mr. Durham's unwillingness to listen than his daughter's unwillingness to speak.

"I wonder," Mr. Durham continued, "if you could speak to her—about Mr. Vaughn, I mean. She might listen to you, who knows?"

"I'm afraid that's quite impossible, Mr. Durham. I've already given my opinion on the matter. If she does not care for him, it seems to me the matter should be abandoned."

Mr. Durham appeared disappointed. "I suppose you're right, Holbrook," he conceded reluctantly.

"But all is hardly lost," Daniel reminded him. "If he cares for your eldest daughter, is that not nearly as good a solution?"

"Yes, yes," Mr. Durham said. "If Beth should decide she wants him, then of course there is that settled. But there is Lady Vaughn, as well, to consider in the matter."

"But why should she approve of one and not the other? I'm not sure I understand."

"I would like to chalk it up to eccentricity, Holbrook, but I know the woman too well. And I know my daughters, besides. She has a soft spot for Laynie, I'm not certain I can tell you just why, but I think Bethany has rubbed her the wrong way and not without reason. If you ask me, I believe Bethany means to hold herself apart from Mr. Vaughn until his inheritance is certain. She's wise to do so, if you ask me, but from Vaughn's point of view, or his mother's, it isn't very flattering."

"I see," Daniel said and wondered.

"Bethany is getting on. She won't be young and beautiful forever. It will be good to have her settled if it can be managed, but, truth be told, I'm not so worried for her as I am for her sister. Beth might catch anyone. Laynie, however… Perhaps when Beth is settled it will be easier, but while there are both girls to choose from, why would any fellow choose Laynie?"

Daniel could answer this quite easily enough: her kindness, her sincerity, her stark individualism… Yes, Daniel could see why this last might be problematic for some, but, as someone who had gone against the grain himself, he rather admired it. She would be a handful, it was true. If one could manage to keep her from flinging herself from horses and otherwise placing herself in peril, she would make an admirable companion, but there was no doubt that the fellow, whoever he should prove to be, would have to stay on his toes. Of course, he could not speak any of this aloud, and so he said nothing at all.

"You aren't giving me much reassurance, Holbrook. And that, after all, is why you are here," Mr. Durham said and laughed self-deprecatingly.

"It's readily at hand, sir, if you truly want it. I think you're wrong."

Mr. Durham seemed instantly taken aback. "Sir?"

"Miss Alayna is not so behind her sister as you suppose. I think, while you've been fretting over the disparagement between them, she's grown into something extraordinary in her own right. I think she will do very well, by and by. There is no hurry, and why should there

215

be? When the time is right, just the right suitor will come along, and you'll be glad you did not rush her to make a choice before she was ready to do it."

Mr. Durham looked at him half-suspiciously and then sat back. "You..." he said, and did not say anything more for a moment or two, which made Daniel not a little nervous. "You believe I am worrying for no reason?"

"I do, particularly as it regards your younger daughter. She will do well for herself, you will see."

"Perhaps if I made a greater effort to show them about..."

This did little to offer Daniel any comfort, but at least he could rest assured he had not said enough to make Mr. Durham suspicious of his weakness. "Perhaps you might let Mr. Vaughn know he's free to return. That will help things along, I think."

Mr. Durham sighed. "And I was so enjoying the peace without him."

"Perhaps the time apart has given Miss Bethany an opportunity to feel his absence."

"You do have a point, Holbrook. I suppose it ought to be tried. But only if he has made up his mind. I can't have any more of this indecisiveness. It sets the girls too much against each other."

"I don't believe he was ever truly indecisive. It's my opinion he was merely trying to keep all parties happy."

"I'm tempted to call him spineless, but as I'm one of the parties in question, I suppose I must give him some credit for trying."

"I have no doubt, sir, that his intentions are in the right place."

"I hope you are right, Holbrook. And I suppose, so long as no one comes to usurp his place, all—as you say—will work itself out in time."

"I have no doubt of it, sir."

* * *

Daniel arrived in London that evening to find the post waiting for him, and with it a letter from his grandfather's solicitor. It seemed an inquiry had been made regarding Brookdale. Would Daniel consider letting it?

He lowered the letter and thought. Brookdale to let? It was not an idea that sat quite comfortably with him, and yet he could do with the income. It would certainly be wise to do something in the way of improving his circumstances, even if some investment must be made at the outset. There was some money. The stocks he had inherited had not all turned out bad. The canal ventures had gone belly up, and those, too, in foreign railway. London rail, particularly underground, were making slow but steady gains. It was those in automotive that had surprised him the most, for these had begun to bring in a steady sum. He had not been prepared to spend it. He was not confident enough in them to take the risk. Until now.

Mr. Durham's speech this afternoon had inspired Daniel to do something more in the way of shoring up his finances. Laynie had confided in him, her father knew it and considered it a good thing. Daniel knew his place and had no intentions of betraying the old man's trust, but certainly, given time, Mr. Durham would warm to the idea.

Yes, Mr. Durham had set him to thinking more seriously about his circumstances, and to providing that he was secure in them. The solicitor's letter certainly gave him the impetus to take some decisive action toward that end. Whether or not the house would be let, it must be restored. To have the house habitable again seemed to him wise. It was a way to repay his grandfather, if only posthumously, for the faith he had placed in him. And who was to say what might come of it in the end? Daniel, after all, might one day decide to make his home there, not alone, no, but... The idea rather pleased him.

But when to begin? Soon, he thought. Not just yet. But very soon.

Not-quite innocent roguery.

Chapter eighteen

L AYNIE STARTED AND SAT UP in bed. Her heart was pounding, and so was her head. It was light out. How long had she slept? She recalled the dream that had awoken her; it loomed before her still. She was at a ball held out of doors. She saw someone she knew, felt compelled to approach him, even if it meant breaking formation and abandoning her partner. She touched the arm of a tall stranger and he turned to her. It was Mr. Holbrook. The rain was pouring down upon him, pouring down upon them both. He begged her to dance. She accepted, but he would not put down the shovel he held in one hand. She took hold of the handle as he held it. And they danced as the rain poured and pelted. He was looking at her so intently, so tenderly, as though she were something fragile and he feared to break her. She said something, she could not recall just what, and his look of cautious admiration changed to one of regret, perhaps even reproach.

The bell rang. Laynie looked to Beth's side of the room, but she was not there. What time was it? She checked the clock on her night table. It was nearly noon! She threw the covers off and arose, but she stopped as her head spun and ached. She waited for the spinning to stop and for her vision to clear. At last it did. She dressed, but hesitated at the door. Who had come? Was it Mr. Holbrook? Did she wish more to see him or to avoid him? And how was it possible to want to do both? The bell had rung, but in the time she was ready to go down, he would be safely closeted away with her father. If he was with her father, would she not see him at all?

It was this question that drew her from her room.

Downstairs, the house was quiet. Perhaps she had imagined the bell, after all. She went to the parlor and thought, at first, that it was empty. But no, standing closely together before the empty grate were her sister and Mr. Vaughn, speaking very warmly and, or so it seemed, confidentially. Perhaps his time away had done them some good. They looked up as Laynie entered and made a little more room between them.

"It is so very good to see you, Mr. Vaughn," Laynie said and approached him. "We were wondering when you might come again."

"Your father sent word this morning I might come," he said. "In fact, he's invited me to dinner this evening."

"That is very encouraging news," Laynie said and looked to Beth. "Isn't it?"

But Beth said nothing.

"How are things at home?" Laynie asked him in an attempt to fill the silence. "How is your mother?"

He seemed disinclined to answer and only turned toward the mantle. "I've returned it."

"Returned it?"

"I promised I would."

In the center of the mantle, between Mr. Vaughn and her sister, was the statue that had belonged to her mother which Mr. Vaughn had broken. It had been repaired. Only...

"I had it mended. I ought to have had it done properly, I suppose. It's been hard to get away. I had one of the servants fix it. He didn't do a very good job of it, I regret. I *am* sorry."

He had begun his explanation with a certain amount of enthusiasm. By the time he had finished, he actually sounded as if he regretted the attempt to repair it at all. No doubt his change in manner was inspired by Laynie's reaction. She regretted very much that every thought and feeling she had was so obviously displayed on her face.

"I'm grateful to you, truly, Mr. Vaughn. In fact I'm sorry you went to so much trouble. It really wasn't valuable, you know." And truly, until she saw it thus, she had regretted the loss of it very little. Now she found it rather tragic. It was a strange piece to begin with. The girl, a young woman, was very delicately and admirably done. But her companion, an oddly proportioned and rather sickly looking sheep, made the whole thing seem strange and haphazard, like a work of art that was only half finished, or finished by someone with considerably less skill than he who had begun it. It was flawed, and so she had only admired it for her mother's sake. Now there was little to admire about it at all, and it only served as a reminder that her mother was dead and she had one less thing to remember her by.

It was unlike Laynie to be so trivial, and she did not know what had come over her. Perhaps it was the haunting effect of her dream. She feared it must be an omen, and here was the grotesque figurine as evidence to support the idea.

"I should have just bought a new one. You are disappointed. I don't blame you."

"No, Harry—Mr. Vaughn. I—I'm afraid I've just awoken from a very strange dream is all. I'm sorry. I'm not feeling quite myself today."

"I'm surprised you slept at all," Beth offered. "You tossed and turned all night. And you usually sleep so soundly. Is something troubling you, I wonder?"

Laynie ignored the question. "You did not tell me how your mother is, Harry. I hope she is well. I think I ought to visit her. Perhaps Beth and I together," she suggested aloud.

Beth did not appear to be too thrilled by the idea, but Harry was encouraging. "My mother would consider that a very great kindness, Miss Laynie, Miss Beth. I do hope you will. And soon."

Laynie understood his enthusiasm. The greatest impediment to any future happiness that might be found between Mr. Vaughn and her sister was presently his mother. And with Lady Vaughn's condition apparently a chronic one, it seemed there was little time to waste.

"We will be sure to do it this week," Laynie assured him.

Mr. Vaughn, grateful, glanced at Beth. "We had just decided upon a walk," he said, still speaking to Laynie. "Would you care to join us?"

Laynie looked to the clock. It was not Mr. Holbrook's day, but he had been coming more often of late. Did she wish to be here when— and if—he arrived this afternoon? No, she thought. It would be best to be away.

"Actually," she said, "it's been some time since I visited the precipice."

Harry scowled at this idea.

"But if you don't mind," Laynie said, "I might accompany you to where the path splits off from the road."

"Of course," Mr. Vaughn said and looked pleased at the prospect.

Beth turned up her chin and left the room to get her hat and shawl. She might have retrieved Laynie's as well, but she did not. Harry did it instead and helped her on with her things, which was wholly unnecessary and perhaps contrary to his efforts to please Beth. Harry offered his arm to both ladies, and Laynie, instead, took her sister's and led her out of doors, leaving Harry to follow behind. He caught up to them on the path, offered his arm to Beth alone, who took it, and the three of them ventured off together.

The fresh air and sunshine did Laynie a world of good. Her headache eased a bit, and she considered the beauty of the countryside, something she never tired of doing.

"I hope you'll tell me all about your holiday," Vaughn said, initiating the conversation.

Laynie glanced at Beth. She appeared to have complete control over her complexion and began to list for him all the very most boring parts of their stay in Gravesend. There was no mention made of Mr. Emerson. None, even, of Ned. Beth described the ball as a pointless affair, unmemorable save for its being rained upon, and that all she could think of the whole time was getting home to her dear Papa and her beloved Beeches.

Laynie herself had done little in the way of contemplating her holiday. She had gone, she had returned home, and that was an end of it. In fact Beth's recitation matched more closely Laynie's experience than it had Beth's own, and Laynie wondered if the deception were for Harry's sake or if Beth had simply found the whole vacation, now it was over and done with, a complete disappointment. Had that disappointment inspired her to try all the harder to persuade herself to think well of Mr. Vaughn? Laynie hoped very much it was so, and so she persuaded herself not to mind at all that she was now being quite neglected from the conversation. Perhaps it was for the best. While Gravesend had not been unmemorable, she would prefer not to recount it, particularly as Beth seemed to be doing it for her, though ascribing Laynie's experience as her own. It was perhaps better if Laynie chose silence rather than taking the risk of contradicting her sister's version of the story.

Nothing very memorable had happened in Gravesend, after all. Her return home, and the events of the last day or two previous were of more import to her than had been anything she had experienced during her time in her aunt's home. But was that quite as it ought to be? Why was her interlude in the garden—that which she had shared with Mr. Holbrook—so very significant? Had something happened to draw her closer to him? Or he to her? Or was it merely Beth's ill-timed question? What did she think of him? And what might he mean to her? She resented ever having been asked that question. It nagged at her to be answered.

The idea of loving anyone frightened her, particularly the idea of loving anyone as unobtainable as Daniel Holbrook. The thought was a little ridiculous. He was her father's companion—his friend. He was so much more experienced, wiser, more educated. She was but a child compared to him, and his employer's child at that. But perhaps more importantly to be asked, why should any of these obstacles cause her even a moment's uneasiness? She ought not to be thinking of him at all. And no doubt never would have begun to do it were it not for Beth and her meddling.

What sorts of meddling might Beth have engaged in had they remained in Gravesend as had been the original plan? Certainly Beth would never have pushed Mr. Emerson into the garden with her. She had met him there nevertheless. She thought of him, standing on the other side of that garden, alone but perhaps not quite wishing to be. He was standing perhaps the same distance away as was that gentleman lingering there at the roadside, watering his horse in the stream. He looked a great deal like him, too. Was it possible?

"Is that you, Mr. Emerson? Can it be?" Beth said and released Mr. Vaughn's arm to approach him.

Mr. Emerson looked up, examined each member of the party that had just happened upon him, and smiled with apparent pleasure. "Why it's the Misses Durhams together. What a lovely surprise. I was not prepared for you to welcome me."

"We can't have done, silly," Beth said, "we did not know you were coming."

"That, I believe, may be a point of some debate," he said and gave Beth a rather knowing look. He glanced at Laynie then looked to Mr. Vaughn.

Laynie thought to introduce him, but Beth, upon anticipating Laynie's intention, undertook to do it first.

"Mr. Emerson, may I introduce to you our dear friend, Mr. Harold Vaughn?"

Mr. Vaughn shook Mr. Emerson's hand then turned to Laynie as if she hoped to have some explanation offered him. Of course she could not give it.

"So this is the famous Mr. Vaughn, is it?" he said, offering Laynie a brief but knowing smile.

"Famous? Why should I be famous to you, Mr. Emerson?" Harry asked, confused and apparently a little affronted.

No one seemed inclined to answer him.

"We were just taking a walk, Mr. Emerson," Beth said. "Won't you join us?"

Mr. Emerson took another look at the party, as if he were weighing the merits of such company.

"Perhaps he's tired, Beth," Laynie suggested. There was no telling how long he'd been travelling, though he appeared quite fresh and well groomed, as did his horse.

"It's a fine animal," Vaughn said, perhaps just for the sake of conversation.

"Hired, but thank you," he said and turned back to Beth. "I was looking forward to meeting your father, Miss Durham."

"He's busy at present. His hired companion is here. He does not like to be interrupted."

Laynie was not aware that Mr. Holbrook had come. Perhaps she simply did not wish to return to the house quite yet. Not with Mr. Emerson and Harry, too.

"Then perhaps a walk is just the thing. You're sure my horse will be safe if I tie him?"

"Quite safe, Mr. Emerson. Come, won't you? I'll show you about the neighborhood."

Mr. Emerson, quite pleased to agree, tied his horse and followed as Beth led him. Laynie and Mr. Vaughn remained where they were, looking alternately from Beth and Mr. Emerson to each other, each with a store of unaskable and unanswerable questions.

At last Beth turned back. "Are you not coming?" she asked impatiently.

Mr. Emerson paid them no mind. It was as if Laynie were not even there and Mr. Vaughn hardly worth considering.

"I was never going with you anyway, remember," Laynie said. "I think I'd much rather go back home."

"Suit yourself," Beth said. She addressed Mr. Vaughn with a look that implied the same question. He did not answer it but shook his head and followed Laynie back the way they had come. Beth looked a trifle disappointed. Perhaps she was actually sorry for slighting poor Harry in this way. Laynie hoped she was sorry; she ought to be.

"If you want to go to the precipice, Laynie, don't let me stop you," Harry said as they neared the drive that led through a tree-lined alley to her house. "It sounds like the very place to be at the moment, if you ask me."

"I'm not certain I'm up to it after all, Harry. I've not been well lately, you know."

"Are you ill?" he said, catching up to her and gracing her with a look of sincere concern.

"I was. I'm still a little weak, it seems. I really just want to go home and sit quietly for a while. You are welcome to sit with me, if you'd like."

Harry thought this over and then, "Who is he?"

"Mr. Emerson? We met him at my aunt's in Gravesend."

"I don't like the idea of them walking off alone together like that."

Laynie looked at him. He was plainly a man in torment. "I don't either, Harry, but I know when I'm not wanted. I think if I were you I would have stood my ground, though. At least I would not have retreated."

"So he does mean to play rival, does he?"

Laynie sighed. The very idea made her feel heavy with regret— and for more reasons than one.

"He'd heard of me. How?"

"He overheard my aunt discussing you as the gentleman my father would have me consider."

"Beth did not correct her?"

Laynie looked at him a long time. She did not know how to answer this. "Neither of us did, Harry. I'm sorry." She walked on and a moment later realized he was no longer following her; he had remained where he was and was watching her walk away.

"I wish I had some encouragement to offer." She thought a moment. "Except…"

"Yes, Laynie?" He was a man in desperate need of encouragement. He'd take anything.

"If you want to win the battle that may—or may not, for all I know—be ahead, you must prepare to fight. The victor of any contest is never one who stands aside to watch, you know?"

"I know," he said, and she believed he did.

Laynie turned back toward the house, more disappointed in Beth than in anyone or anything else. Was she sorry Mr. Emerson had not come for her? She felt the slight, and yes, she was a little disappointed, but not so much as she might have supposed. What was it that had softened the blow? She knew the answer and dismissed it in the same instant. She would not think of that. What she had do was find a way to help Harry to prove himself to Beth. Perhaps, after all, Mr. Emerson was as changeable as was her sister. If only Beth's friends would come around to meet him. What might happen then? Laynie cringed to think of it, yet hoped for something, anything, that would give Harry, once more, the advantage.

* * *

"So *that* is the famous Mr. Vaughn, is it?"

"It is," Beth said and thought to offer a deprecating look in Harry's behalf. She could not quite manage it.

"If I did not know better, I'd think he was not making a very great effort to win your sister. In fact, I'd be tempted to think his affections lie elsewhere."

Beth merely shrugged, grabbed at a bachelor's button and pulled it from its stem.

"Has your sister decided to accept him, then?"

"Oh, I don't know what Laynie plans to do. No one ever does."

226

Mr. Emerson, as they walked, examined Beth a moment.

"I don't want to talk about my sister and Mr. Vaughn," she said haughtily.

Mr. Emerson reached to take Beth's hand and extricated the flower from it. He slid the flower into his button hole.

"And I suppose you'll say I gave it to you," she said, looking at him and smiling reluctantly.

"I might at that. But I doubt very much that, between us, I'm the only one who can twist a truth," Mr. Emerson answered.

"I don't know what you mean."

"Yes, you do. Who is Mr. Vaughn truly? Your father may want him to marry your sister, but that isn't *his* intention, is it?"

"Perhaps not. But it's hardly my fault if you understood it differently."

"I'm not so certain about that."

"I hope you are not the jealous type, Mr. Emerson. I'm afraid you'll have a very hard time of it if you are."

"Because of all your admirers, do you mean?"

"Oh, not mine alone. Laynie has several of her own."

"Your father's hired companion, I suppose," he said as if the subject bored him. "That's nothing."

"Isn't it?" Beth said and feared to know his meaning.

He stifled a smile. He was clearly enjoying this game. "I thought you said you didn't want to talk about your sister," he said.

"Is it Laynie you came to see?" she asked him and stopped as if to turn back. "If it's so, then I have no wish to waste your time—or mine—by keeping you from her."

He too stopped, laughed, and folded his arms over his chest. "I beg your pardon, Miss Durham, but who is jealous?"

"Not I, I assure you. Shall we?" And she pointed the way back home.

"Not just yet, if you please. I've not seen enough of your lovely countryside by half. Besides, now I'm here I was hoping you and I might continue where we left off."

"And where was that, sir?"

He stopped once more. Looked at her knowingly. Too knowingly. "I think you know." He leaned toward her, but she stopped him with a hand on his chest.

"Where I'm from, a kiss is a token of intention and is not so easily granted as I think you would wish it to be. Besides, I believe you yourself said that respectability is of paramount importance to you. Am I mistaken?"

He looked at her narrowly. "Not mistaken, exactly, though perhaps you misunderstand my intention. You thought I was going to kiss you?" he asked as if the idea were laughable.

"Why not? You've done it before, after all," she answered. "At least it was my impression you mean to try. I had no reason whatever to suppose you'd be successful."

"Is that so?"

"Do you really mean to tell me that wasn't your intention just now?"

"My dear Miss Durham. Whether it was or it wasn't, I can't possibly think of compromising you and your hallowed 'respect-ability'."

"Perhaps you had best make your intentions clear, Mr. Emerson. Before either of us gets ahead of ourselves."

"Perhaps I don't know what my intentions are just yet."

"Then let me decide them for you. I believe you are walking with the wrong companion." She stopped and turned back toward the house.

He took her arm and turned her to face him. "I'm not here to play games, Miss Durham. I want to marry. So, I think, do you. Shall we not give ourselves a chance to see if our aims are compatible? Don't tell me I came all this way for nothing."

Beth thought long and hard. She could not give him any commitment, but she had to give him something. She needed to be sure of him. She wanted, at least, the chance to know just how committed he was to his intentions insofar as they involved her. But she knew just as well that she must be very, very careful not to try Harry's patience beyond its limit. If only she knew what that limit was.

* * *

Laynie entered the house with the intention of returning to her room to rest, but upon passing the parlor, she was stopped by the sight of her mother's figurine. It really was grotesque. She almost wished she could get rid of it, but such would seem ungrateful after all the trouble Mr. Vaughn had taken over it. She approached to examine it closer. The head of the girl was somehow spared any injury, but Laynie suspected that the fellow Harry had employed to mend it had actually glued the sheep's head on wrong. Was it upside down? It didn't look like a sheep at all, really. She picked the figurine up and studied it. It was so very tall for a sheep, and its wool was really more like coarse hair than wool at all.

"How are you today, Miss Durham?"

She started. The jolt in her chest was actually painful. The figurine slipped from her hand to crash on the tiled hearth.

"Good heaven, I'm sorry." In three great steps Mr. Holbrook was beside her. "Forgive me," he said, plainly regretful, and knelt to pick up the pieces.

She swallowed down her nerves—why should he make her so nervous?—and found the words to answer him. "There's nothing to forgive, I did not much care for it. Please, Mr. Holbrook, I'll get it. It's best to throw it away, I think."

He looked up at her with an expression of such regret she wished very much that she had never cared at all for the statue. But it was not his fault she had dropped it. It was her own carelessness and nothing more.

"You were studying it very carefully for something that you profess means very little to you. Are you certain it was not important?"

"It was my mother's."

The furrow in his brow deepened.

"But I never liked it," she tried again. "It was broken already. Mr. Vaughn had it mended, for it was he who broke it first you see, and…"

But he did not appear to be listening. He was busy sweeping the pieces up with the hearth brush. Before sweeping them into the pan, however, he picked up the head, which had once again escaped entirely uninjured, and placed it in his pocket. She wondered at it but did not ask. She knelt to pick up the pan so that she might take it out, but he stopped her with his hand, which he placed over hers very gently. She saw their hands together, saw the shattered remnants of her mother's figurine and recalled the dream.

She arose to her feet.

"Forgive me," he said, "I—"

"It's quite all right, Mr. Holbrook," she said but could not decide if it were not in fact all wrong. She wanted to fly from the room. She wanted to remain here with him indefinitely. What was wrong with her? "If you will excuse me."

"Are you unwell, Miss Durham?" he asked, stopping her.

"I have a headache. That is all. I haven't been sleeping well."

"No nightmares, I hope?" he asked congenially.

Could he know about the dream? The idea alarmed her. But no, that was quite impossible. "Perhaps," she said.

"Will you tell me?"

And she wanted to do it, just as she always wanted to tell him everything that was troubling her. But this was not something to be shared. How would she go about it? *I had a dream of you last night, Mr. Holbrook, and…* Good heavens! It was too mortifying to even consider.

"Are you quite all right? You look a little—"

"You are kind to be so concerned, but it is unnecessary. Excuse me, won't you?" And she practically flew from the room, not thinking what impression she must have left on him.

It was certainly not one to offer much in the way of encouragement.

Chapter nineteen

"YOU'RE NOT SLEEPING *AGAIN*?" BETH said upon entering their bedroom that evening. "What is wrong with you?"

"I'm not sleeping. Only thinking. Or trying not to, rather."

"And what great philosophical conundrum are you trying *not* to ponder tonight?"

Laynie, from her prone position on her bed, answered Beth with a glance and then looked away again.

"I hope you're not angry with me? I could not help it that he wanted to walk with me alone."

"Harry, do you mean?" Laynie said, sitting up. She knew very well whom her sister meant but wished to make a point.

Beth rolled her eyes and turned away.

"So what do you mean to do now he's come? Do you mean to throw Harry off completely or is he merely to stand aside and wait for you to decide whom you prefer?"

"You make me sound quite heartless, Laynie. It isn't as if I don't have a right to make up my mind and to be certain of it."

"You knew he would come, didn't you?"

"I thought he might," Beth answered with a dismissive glance. She opened the wardrobe and inspected its contents. At last she chose a gown and held it up to examine in the mirror.

"Is that why you pushed Mr. Holbrook into my company? Not because you suspected he betrayed some slight interest in me, but so that I would have something to distract me while you prepared yourself to receive Mr. Emerson?"

Beth turned to her and smiled stiffly. "You ought to dress, Laynie. He's coming to dinner, you know."

"Papa has invited him?"

"No. *I* invited him, and he's promised to come."

Laynie felt a little sick at the thought of both Mr. Emerson and Mr. Vaughn staying to dinner. She had just begun to congratulate herself on escaping her father's designs for her. Would he take up the cause again now someone else had come to play rival for Beth's attention?

Beth selected a green gown with a very low neckline and presented it to Laynie.

"I have a headache, Beth. I think I would really rather remain here this evening."

"You have to go down. Papa will insist, and so do I. You can't leave me to face both men alone."

"It's a problem of your own creating, Beth. I'm sorry, but I can't help you out of it."

"And what of Harry?" Beth said and feigned a look of real concern. Or perhaps she *was* worried. There was no telling. "Mr. Emerson, I fear, is prone to jealousy. If he makes Mr. Vaughn feel uncomfortable I may lose him for good."

"And you don't want that, I take it."

"Certainly not."

"And in the meantime, I'm to keep him entertained while you enjoy yourself without a moment's thought as to the pain you cause him?"

"Oh, Laynie, please say you'll come down."

Laynie considered. She did not want to give in. If Beth was left to feel uncomfortable, then she deserved it. She thought of Harry, however, and felt herself begin to relent. "I'm not wearing that," she said. "It hasn't been hemmed."

"I hemmed it."

"Did you?"

"I did." And she thrust it forward.

"The neck is far too low, and you know green isn't my color."

Beth lowered the dress in frustration and returned to the wardrobe. "Here," she said at last and brought forth the dove-grey gown. "This was very lovely on you at our aunt's house. And it will fit you now. You needn't fear humiliating yourself in it tonight."

But it was those very words that made Laynie hesitant to try it. She had been humiliated in it before. Was she destined to do it again, hemmed or not? And is that what Beth wanted? Reluctantly she took it.

"Thank you, Laynie," Beth said and appeared truly grateful.

"I'm not doing it for you, Beth. I'm doing it for Harry," Laynie said and began to dress, otherwise preparing herself for a very unpleasant evening.

* * *

A knock on the study door interrupted Mr. Durham from his reading.

"What now?" he demanded of no one in particular.

Daniel could not have answered him at all events.

Mr. Durham sighed and arose to see who it was.

It was the housekeeper. "Forgive me for the interruption, sir, but there seems to be a bit of confusion in the kitchen. Is it one extra to dinner tonight or two?"

"I have invited Harold Vaughn, Mrs. Fowler. What is so confusing about that?"

"Mrs. Sullivan says it is her belief that another gentleman has been invited besides."

"Mrs. Sullivan's eyes and ears are once more doing her greater service than her position demands. I know of no other gentleman, Mrs. Fowler."

Mrs. Fowler cleared her throat. "I believe there may be some truth to it, sir. A gentleman has come, though I have not received directly any notice of his staying to dinner. I was rather hoping you could enlighten me. If you cannot then I'm afraid the confusion remains."

"Who is this fellow?"

"Someone with whom the girls were acquainted in Gravesend, I believe. He has arrived this afternoon to reacquaint himself, as I understand it."

"Why has the fellow not been introduced to me?"

Mrs. Fowler cleared her throat. "He wished to introduce himself earlier, sir, but you know you do not like to be disturbed." She darted a glance in Mr. Holbrook's direction.

Daniel nodded politely and tried to appear as though he was not listening. Of course he was.

"He has not received the invitation from me, Mrs. Fowler, though it shouldn't surprise me that the invitation was offered nonetheless. I suppose we had best count on it," Mr. Durham said and turned to Daniel. "I suppose we had better make a party of it. What say you, Holbrook? Will you stay?"

"Certainly, sir. If you wish it."

"I ought to have you more often, really. A meal is so much more enjoyable when there is some sensible conversation to be had. It seems that will make three extra to dinner, Mrs. Fowler," he said, addressing her once more. And he shut the door before she had quite turned away. "Well, what do you make of this, Holbrook?"

"I hardly dare to imagine."

"I suppose the fellow has come for Beth."

"Presumably, sir." At least he hoped it was the case. Miss Laynie had mentioned no other gentlemen acquaintances besides her cousin. That did not mean there had been none. And why should she mention it to him if there had?

"And here I was just beginning to think we had everything settled," Mr. Durham continued. "What will this do to upset things, I wonder?"

"I cannot guess," Daniel answered, and truly he could not.

"It's not impossible he's come for Laynie's sake, I suppose. Then all will be as it ought to be, and I can quit worrying about them, eh?"

Daniel had no answer for this. It was presuming a very great deal that any gentleman who might appear would be the answer to Mr. Durham's prayers. Of course the fellow might have come for Laynie. He'd be a fool not to have done.

"I do hope this will not cause trouble. I suppose it must, mustn't it?"

"Really, sir, I haven't the faintest idea. Though I'm rather inclined to pity poor Mr. Vaughn about now." It was better than pitying himself, after all.

"Well, it's a good thing you are too sensible for my girls, isn't it? Or you might very well be in the same boat. It was why I warned you off them, you know. And I'm glad I did!"

"Yes, sir, of course."

"Well, you and I at any rate will have a pleasant evening, I dare say."

"I expect so, sir," Daniel said and prayed it would be the case. It was bound, however one looked at it, to be awkward. Well, at least there would be no excitement where he was concerned. He had entertained a passing fancy for the younger of his employer's daughters. He had known it was foolishness. He had best prepare himself for a very awkward evening indeed. Far better to expect the worst than to be surprised by it.

The two gentlemen returned to their books and continued their reading until the bell rang and Mrs. Fowler returned to announce that the first of their guests had arrived.

* * *

Perhaps it was ungenerous, but Daniel took some encouragement at the sight of the plainly downtrodden Mr. Vaughn standing in the foyer. Vaughn was aware already, it seemed, of their visitor and had been left dispirited by it. It could only mean one thing: the usurper had come for Beth.

"Come in and sit down, won't you, Mr. Vaughn?" Mr. Durham asked him and led the way to the parlor. "Will you have a drink?"

"Perhaps just a small one," Vaughn answered and sat, slump-shouldered upon the sofa.

"You, Holbrook?"

"No, thank you, sir." Daniel approached Mr. Vaughn and offered his hand. "Mr. Vaughn. How do you do?"

Vaughn bowed his head, took Daniel's hand and released it again to take the glass Mr. Durham offered him. He nodded his gratitude and tossed the drink down in one swallow.

"May I?" Daniel said and gestured toward a chair adjacent.

"Of course, Mr. Holbrook. Please," Vaughn said and tried to look a little more interested in the company.

Daniel sat and thought to strike up a conversation but could think of nothing. There was no mentioning the topic most heavily weighing upon them—who was this fellow and what had he come for? And so Daniel submitted to the necessity of silence. Awkwardness threatened, while Mr. Durham lingered over the drinks and inspected the condition of the tumblers. The silence, however, was broken by the sound of feet upon the stairs in the hallway. The girls were just coming down. Daniel stood; Vaughn, preoccupied, seemed not to notice, and so Daniel nudged him.

Vaughn stood, straightened himself to his full height, and put on a brave face.

The girls entered; first Beth, with apparent relish for the attention and happy to be shown in her finest: a pale-blue gown with a rather low neckline; Laynie entered after, looking a little more reluctant to do so and dressed in a perfectly fitted gown of dove gray. Daniel wished he had a right to approach her, to take her by the hand and to encourage her to enter with a little more confidence. Would she be more confident on his arm? It was a pointless thought and he tried to dismiss it as Mr. Durham greeted them.

"Ah, there you are," their father said to them. "I half expected you'd be late coming down so as to make a grand entrance. It's grand enough, I suppose. You *do* look well! Where did you get these?" he said, referring to their gowns.

"Oh, Papa," Beth said and, passing her father by, entered the room.

Laynie alone stopped, gave her father a kiss and whispered something into his ear.

"Ah," he said, "that was generous of your aunt. Very generous. You look lovely, my dear. All grown up, eh?"

She smiled, blushed a little, and followed her sister, still hesitantly, as Beth approached the gentlemen. Laynie stopped to stand before them, apparently, and quite suddenly, too shy to speak.

"Miss Durham, Miss Laynie," Mr. Vaughn said, greeting them when once they were standing side by side and doing it as though both were of equal esteem to him. Perhaps they ought to be, after all, but Daniel did not quite wish it to be so.

Daniel greeted them likewise. "Good evening, Mr. Holbrook," Beth said and gave him a coy look. "Doesn't my sister look well?"

Laynie shot a scowl at Bethany and turned to whisper some words of encouragement to Mr. Vaughn. Daniel heard them. Perhaps they were intended to be heard. "Stand your ground, Harry. You've earned it, after all."

"Good evening, Mr. Holbrook," Laynie said to him and did not quite look him in the eye. "Would you like a drink? I'll get one for you."

"That's quite all right, Miss Durham," he said, stopping her. "I don't drink, but thank you. Sit, won't you?"

She did, and he thought to start a conversation, while her sister sat very near Mr. Vaughn and plied him with her most engaging looks. He could not hear their conversation. He could think of any number of topics he might like to discuss with Miss Laynie and had just decided upon one, when Mr. Durham joined them.

"Now, Holbrook," he said and sat, "we did not get to finish our discussion of *Don Juan*. You are a man of the world, are you not? You've done your share of travelling, of roving about." He laughed irreverently.

Daniel was not certain this was the sort of conversation they ought to be carrying on with the ladies present. There were certainly many things about Daniel's past that he would be ashamed for Miss Durham to know. He remembered her speech at the fountain and felt his unworthiness.

"Come. Don't keep your adventures to yourself. Admit you know a little of what it is like to be the roving adventurer."

Daniel smiled stiffly and snuck a glance at Laynie. She was trying to listen, it seemed, to her sister's conversation with Mr. Vaughn. She looked up at the clock, and then at Daniel. She looked away again and pressed her hands very tightly together so that the knuckles shone white.

"It is possible, sir," Daniel answered as confidentially as he could manage, "that when I embarked upon my pilgrimage so many years ago that I left in the spirit of *Don Juan*. I assure you I returned in the attitude of a world-weary and repentant *Childe Harold*. I'm not proud of my time abroad."

"It was over a woman, I wager!" Mr. Durham said a little too loudly.

Laynie was suddenly on her feet and crossing the room.

"Where are you going, my dear?"

But she did not stop to answer him. She simply walked out of the room. A moment later one of the outer doors was heard to open and to shut again.

"What did you say to your sister, Bethany?"

"Me, Papa? Nothing at all, I assure you!"

"Hmm," Mr. Durham said and considered. "The fellow's not even here yet and we are already having temper tantrums. I wonder what can be the matter."

Daniel merely shook his head, unprepared to speculate and feeling that none of this was a good omen. He looked to Mr. Durham to find his employer watching him keenly.

"You know..." he said and thought a moment. "You said, I believe, that my Laynie has once or twice confided in you."

Or a dozen times. "Yes."

"It might be helpful to know just what it is that's eating at her. Is she anxious for this fellow, or is it something else, do you see?" He paused again and Daniel waited for the question he both dreaded and longed to have asked. "Do you mind?"

"No, sir. Not at all." And Daniel arose to see to the errand.

"You might try beneath the beech tree, you know. That's where she is usually to be found when she is in a mood."

Daniel nodded and left the room and then the house, exiting through the dining-room door. It was growing dark, but there was still some light left. He closed the door very quietly and walked on grass-silenced steps to the edge of the tree's cover. She was standing there, her back to him and leaning against the trunk.

"Is something the matter, Miss Durham?"

She turned slowly to look at him, offered him a solemn smile, and looked away again. She was facing him now, however. She would answer him eventually if he did not press. And though there were a thousand questions he wished to ask—*Who is this fellow who is causing so much excitement? Is there some rivalry between yourself and your sister? Are you in love with him?*—he said nothing and only waited.

"I'm being unnecessarily moody and petulant, Mr. Holbrook. You are kind to be concerned, but I'll overcome it in time."

"In time for you to receive your guest?"

"I certainly hope so."

"You do not seem to me to be looking forward with much pleasure to the evening ahead." It gave him some comfort, but he nevertheless was made anxious by her anxiety.

"I can tell you what will happen, Mr. Holbrook," she said looking up at him. "He will arrive, Beth will fly from Mr. Vaughn to the new arrival as if Harry never mattered to her at all. And she can do it, too, because she is so certain of his fascination for her. Perhaps it's because Mr. Vaughn is so old and close a friend that it pains me so. Perhaps it is that I know him to be one of the most worthy men of my acquaintance. Or, just perhaps, it's that I know what it feels like to be set aside as if I do not matter. I'm tired of being overlooked in favor of her. I'm tired of cleaning up her messes. And poor Mr. Vaughn!" She took a great breath, which caught in her throat and was silent for a minute as she tried to calm herself.

Daniel took a step forward, reached out to her, but then stopped himself.

"It is wrong of me to speak so ungenerously of my sister. Forgive me."

"There's nothing to forgive," he answered. "This fellow, though, he has come to call upon Miss Bethany," he concluded with a measure of relief and felt he hated the man nevertheless.

"Yes. It appears that way."

The fact that she was not quite certain made him wonder if she was not, after all, a little disappointed.

"Who is this fellow? You met him in Gravesend, I understand."

"Oh. Yes," Laynie answered thoughtfully. "He is a friend of my cousin Ned."

"If you don't mind my saying…"

"Yes, I know," she answered, anticipating his thought. "It doesn't speak well of him, does it? But he isn't like Ned. I think they were friends as boys and only recently reacquainted. He did not seem to approve of Ned's manner toward me. He actually rescued me from him more than once."

"Your cousin imposed himself more than once?" Daniel asked, his temper rising at the thought.

Laynie blushed and looked to the ground.

"Forgive me, Miss Durham. I do not mean to pry."

"No," she said. "I told you of him. Perhaps I did not tell you the whole of it, but…well, I do not like to think of it, much less speak of it."

"Of course. You were telling me of…"

"He was Ned's friend, as I said. But more than that, he was the gentleman my cousin Grace proclaimed she meant to marry. It was supposedly all settled between them. I, myself, had thought him rather charming, but of course when I learned of Grace's attachment to him, I abandoned all thought for myself. Beth, however…"

Daniel struggled to keep up with her. "Go on," he said.

"Well, she didn't. And when it came out that they had been carrying on a romance, Grace and Mr. Emerson, I mean, my aunt put her foot down. The affair was broken off, and Beth, without a moment's hesitation, began to pursue him. Why am I telling you all this?" she said and suddenly seemed ashamed of herself.

"Because I asked, I suppose. And you have done me the honor of explaining the trouble between you."

"It's Harry my heart breaks for, Mr. Holbrook. She ought not to be toying with him this way."

Daniel agreed but thought it best not to say so.

"This Emerson fellow—that was his name, did you not say?"

"Yes, that's right."

Daniel knew the name too well, but certainly it couldn't be the same. "He followed you here? You or…your sister? Forgive me if it's prying, Miss Durham, but in a week's time do you feel you really had the opportunity to know him? It does seem awfully quick work for him to turn from one woman, whom, by all appearances, it seemed he was to marry, to another he had just met."

"I— I don't think we know him very well at all, really. I do know he was married once," she said, as if she'd just remembered the fact and offered it as something significant to his history.

The pronouncement nearly knocked Daniel off his feet. "A widower?"

"Yes."

"His Christian name?"

"Frederick, I believe it is."

Daniel was silent a long time before he realized Laynie was looking at him. "Do you know him?" she asked.

"Just possibly, Miss Durham. I can't say for certain until I lay eyes on him, but...it's just possible."

"I'm sorry," she said.

"Whatever for?" he answered.

"For once again unburdening myself to you. You're going to learn to fear talking to me at all."

"There's not a chance of that, I assure you."

The bell was heard. Excitement from within. The door was answered and Beth's voice spilled out of the house and into the falling night.

"You have come, Mr. Emerson! Let me introduce you to my dear Papa."

"I suppose we had better go back in," Laynie said, plainly reluctant to rejoin the company.

But he was not ready. He was curious, certainly, though at the same time he feared having his worst fears confirmed. He wished to remain out here with her. Could he dare detain her? He thought of it, thought of reaching out to her, holding her here where they might remain, together, until they were called in or the fellow left. But no. No, it was impossible. *He* would not be guilty of imposing.

She turned from him. He hesitated a moment but at last followed. She stopped to wait for him at the door. He joined her there, looked at her a moment as she looked up at him. It seemed an opportune time to say something. To make some confession, perhaps, that would, if nothing else, give her a reason not to think of this Emerson fellow. It seemed to him that, for half a moment perhaps, she was waiting to hear what he had to say. But this was not why he had been sent by her father to speak to her. To even think it was a betrayal. He opened the door and they returned to the drawing room, entering together side by side.

"Ah, here is Laynie. I had wondered where you had got to!" Beth said. "And let me introduce you to my father's hired companion."

Mr. Emerson looked up at him. It had been four years since he'd seen the fellow last, but it was certainly him. But how, in the name of all that was good and holy, had he found his way here! Was it coincidence alone, or was it something else?

"Holbrook!" Emerson said, greeting him. "Of all the lucky co-incidences! It's jolly good to see you. How long has it been?"

Not long enough, Daniel would have liked to say but thought it best to put on a brave face, to stand his ground as perhaps Laynie might have advised him to do. If he had spoken a moment ago, he might have the right to take her hand now. But it was presumptuousness to think she would advise *him* to take a stand for his right to her. He had none, after all, nor was likely ever to have it.

"It's been five years, I think, has it not?" Emerson insisted. Daniel had no doubt he knew precisely how long it had been in years and months and days—in hours, even.

"Something like that," Daniel said.

"Won't you shake hands?" Emerson said next, as if his refusal to do so had been Daniel's idea all along. He had not offered his hand. He was guilty of that much, but no more. Emerson's hand was presented. Daniel took it. "There," Emerson said and looked relieved. "I was afraid for a moment there was bad blood between us. But you were never the sort to hold a grudge, were you?"

"You know each other?" Beth said, fairly astounded.

Laynie was slightly less surprised, having been warned of the possibility already. She appeared to be, if anything, disappointed in Daniel's lack of enthusiasm for the re-acquaintance.

Beth, as Daniel had been warned, took command of Mr. Emerson's attention and led him to the sofa, where she begged him to sit and where she sat beside him while Vaughn skulked off to watch, glowering, from a far corner of the room. Laynie had just moved to join him when Daniel, at last succumbing to impulse, reached out a hand to stop her. But what to say?

"Did you mention to him you knew me, by chance?" he said, choosing that question out of a hundred he might have asked. "When you were in Gravesend, I mean?"

She looked awkwardly from Mr. Emerson and back to himself. Emerson was watching them. "Though you did come up in conversation," she said, "I don't recall ever mentioning you by name. Is there some history between you?"

Daniel released her, sighed, and straightened. He could not answer her now. Not here. Perhaps not ever. Why had he chosen *that* question? Why had he stopped her at all?

"Go to Vaughn," he urged her, though he did it with some measure of reluctance. "He's in need of your company."

She looked at him a moment, perhaps disappointed her question was not to be answered, and crossed the room to sit beside Mr. Vaughn where they talked, or she talked, and no doubt encouraged him to endure this trial with grace. God willing, it would not last long and he would be victor again. But then what would that mean for Mr. Emerson? Would he just move along to the next most available prey? And would that be Alayna Durham?

The idea enraged him. It was agony to stand in the same room as him, to smile and pretend all was well. It was impossible to look at him and not see Sophie. It was impossible to be in the room with Laynie and not think of her. If only he could make his excuses and go. But that would be ungentlemanly.

"Can I get you a drink, Mr. Emerson?" Mr. Durham offered.

"Yes, thank you," he said.

Mr. Durham arose, nodded to Daniel and poured the drink. "Why do you hold yourself apart, Holbrook? Come join the conversation. Here is a fine fellow," he said more confidentially. "What do you think?"

But of course Daniel could offer no reply but a forced smile and a nod. Reluctantly he followed and took a seat a little distance off, where he could listen to the conversation and where he could watch while Laynie worked her magic on Vaughn as well. It seemed Miss Bethany, too, was aware of her efforts in that quarter, though perhaps not the motivation behind them. She threw a scowl over her shoulder then looked at Daniel and raised her eyebrows as if she meant to suggest some kind of sympathy of feeling. She was something, Bethany was. It was a wonder two women could be so closely related and yet be so entirely different from one another.

"So you are acquainted with my sister and her family, I understand," Mr. Durham observed to Mr. Emerson.

"Yes, sir. An old friend of your nephew, actually. Ned and I were at school together."

"And you are acquainted with our friend Holbrook as well. That is a remarkable coincidence."

"It is, isn't it?" Emerson said and sat back, as if the question were something to consider.

"How *do* you know each other?" Beth asked, plainly curious.

"Well…" Emerson said, and Daniel could see the wheels turning in his head. How was he to tell all their history? And would he even dare to do it? Daniel felt it wise, perhaps, not to give him the opportunity.

"We were at University together," Daniel said.

"A Cambridge man?" Mr. Durham asked, impressed.

Mr. Emerson offered Daniel a brief but indecipherable look and smiled stiffly as he answered Mr. Durham. "Indeed, sir."

"And your family? Where are they from?"

"I'm from Kent originally, sir. Portsmouth. By and large I am in London these days. I have an uncle there from whom I am soon to inherit."

"Indeed!"

Beth, who had been looking over her shoulder at the conversation going on between her sister and Mr. Vaughn behind her, seemed suddenly interested in this revelation. She was too predictable. Poor Vaughn. If only his fortune were certain. She didn't know what she had in his admiration. Would she know before she lost it?

Daniel himself had begun to focus his attention on the dialogue going on in that far corner. It was quite all he could stand listening to Emerson list off his glowing qualifications and somehow evading the point of having to give any too detailed account of his history. The fact that he was married before never came up at all. For which Daniel was grateful, though he felt it an omission that would, and sooner rather than later, require rectifying.

Daniel arose.

"Is everything all right, Holbrook?" Mr. Durham asked.

"Yes, sir. I think I will have that drink now, if you don't mind."

"Of course. Help yourself, won't you?"

Daniel took himself to the drinks table and chose a decanter. He ought not to be indulging, he knew that, but one drink just to dull his senses was certainly forgivable. One drink to calm him and no more.

"What she wants, Harry," he heard Laynie say, "is someone who is so certain of his regard that he will stand up and fight for her."

"I understand that, Laynie, but you have to understand she has to be equally as certain. When my mother learns of your visitor and who he came to see and why…she won't gain any esteem in her eyes. You must see that."

Laynie, plainly frustrated, sighed and rolled her eyes. In the process she observed Daniel, pouring a drink, which thing he had professed half an hour ago never to indulge in. She gave him a questioning look then turned to observe Beth as she addressed their father.

"You know, Papa, Mr. Emerson is a widower like yourself."

And at last the nail was struck. He was a fool if he thought to escape that subject entirely. He raised the glass to his lips and it slipped from his hand. It struck the table with a clatter and spilled the contents onto the rug. Daniel swore under his breath and prayed no one heard him.

Laynie was suddenly at his side. "I'll get it, Mr. Holbrook," she said and found a rag that was kept in a lower drawer of the cabinet. The glass had not broken, so it was only a matter of mopping up the brandy.

"Miss Durham, please raise yourself. You do have a house-keeper, you know."

She looked up at him as though he had caused her some offense, though his intention was only to offer a show of necessary deference. He helped her to her feet.

"What is the matter with you?" she asked him, her hand still in his. "His presence here has upset you. Why?"

"Ghosts, I suppose."

"Meaning?"

"That's the only explanation I can offer at present."

She looked at him, perhaps trying to decide if the qualifying phrase indicated he meant to confide in her at some future time. Did he? He did not think it likely.

"Miss Alayna," Emerson called to her, "quit playing housemaid with the servants and come talk with me. I'm feeling a little slighted, if you want to know."

Daniel's jaw tensed at the jibe. Laynie slid her hand from Daniel's as if she were suddenly ashamed of its being there, and turned to Mr. Emerson. "Very well," she said, though cautiously, and Daniel watched as she crossed the room to sit near him. She gave him an uncertain glance before taking her seat.

Beth, very quietly, very calmly, changed places to sit near Vaughn, who, despite his apparent turmoil but a moment ago, was all self-possession and indifferent confidence now. And consequently, Beth was clamoring to make up for lost ground while Mr. Emerson, on the other side of the room, had turned his considerable charms upon Laynie—and not without some observable effect.

Daniel found the servants' bell and pulled it perhaps more forcefully than necessary. He then returned to the drinks table and poured himself another drink. This time he swallowed it before it had a chance to spill. And then he watched as Mr. Emerson charmed the younger Miss Durham and while—Devil take the fellow!—she let him. She smiled. She blushed. She listened to him with fascination, laughed at his jokes and answered with one or two clever remarks of her own.

Mrs. Fowler entered, interrupting his observations. She tutted at him and proceeded to clean the mess he had made, ushering him aside as she did to make way.

It was too much. He left the room and returned out of doors for some much needed air. Having closed the door behind him he stood for a moment, his thoughts and the brandy buzzing about his head. Frederick Emerson was here at the Bowery. Was it coincidence? Was it more? And why now, when Daniel had just begun to put his life into some semblance of order? But these answers were not immediately to be answered. He needed time to sort through them. He needed a moment to pull himself together. He crossed the lawn to the formal garden and sat, but the longer he remained the more he knew he could not go back in. He had not the strength to face Emerson and the memories that his very presence must summon. He had not the strength to watch as that fellow flattered and wooed the Durham sisters. And as Laynie received his flatteries with novel delight. If she had not lived her life in the shadows of her sister she would know better than to entertain for even one moment the attentions of someone like Frederick Emerson.

"Dinner is ready."

Daniel looked up with a start. It was Laynie.

"We are only waiting for you. Won't you come back in?"

He stood. "I think, perhaps…"

"Yes?"

"I think I had better not, Miss Durham."

"You're not leaving?" she said, surprised. And perhaps disappointed, too. Under any other circumstances he might have felt touched by the idea. "Will you tell me what is the matter?"

"I want to. Very much."

"You don't trust me?"

"I trust you implicitly."

"But you won't tell me what is wrong. You have some history with Mr. Emerson."

"I do."

"And you do not wish to discuss it."

"I do not."

"That seems unfair."

"Does it?" he asked her. He supposed it was true. He had asked her a dozen or more questions and she had, even if reluctantly, answered them all. "I apologize if that seems the case."

"I unburden my soul to you, tell you everything I'm thinking and feeling—well, nearly so, at any rate. I know nothing of you really and am never likely to, it seems."

"I hope that isn't true."

She offered no rebuttal to this, just stood there, looking at him in the darkness. Was the shining of her eyes a play of the light or of something else?

"I hope, very much, to one day tell you everything you might wish to know. I simply cannot do it right now."

"Why? If you say it's not because you do not trust me, then why?"

"Miss Durham. Do you not remember? You stood in this very spot and declared your steadfast belief that a man cannot change, that he who has done wrong will always do wrong. I have done wrong. I cannot bear the thought that, once you know all there is to know about me, you will never see me the same again. You will never trust me as I believe you have learned to do."

She was silent for a moment, examining him as if she were trying to divine the secrets he was unwilling to divulge. "Mr. Holbrook," she said at last, "I find it impossible to believe you can ever have done something so wrong as to convince me you are not a good man now."

"It's kind of you to say, Miss Durham," he said and approached to stand very near her. "But, if you will pardon me for saying so, I'd rather not take the chance. Give my excuses to your father, won't you?" He stood for a moment—though it felt much longer—and then passed her by on the way to the gate.

"Mr. Holbrook?"

He turned, but she did not speak right away. He waited, hoping she would give him some reason that might make it worth remaining.

"Don't leave."

It was almost enough. Almost but not quite. "I wish you good evening, Miss Durham," he said, and after bowing his head, turned from her.

* * *

Laynie remained there a few minutes more, watching Mr. Holbrook's retreating figure and wondering at his strange and unexpected behavior. What mysterious history had taken place between Mr. Emerson and her father's hired companion? What great sin had he committed that persuaded Mr. Holbrook that he could never confide in her? It was a bitter disappointment to think she knew him so little as she evidently did. It was a bitter disappointment to know he felt he had been judged by her so harshly that he could not confide in her. She was hurt; she blamed herself. She was angry; she blamed him. And what was Mr. Emerson's part in all of this? She turned back toward the house.

"Where is Holbrook?" her father asked her when at last she appeared in the dining room.

"He has left, Papa," Laynie informed him. "I believe he had another engagement."

"Another engagement? What?"

She resented having to lie for him, but she was not about to reveal to her father how disappointingly he had behaved. "He must have forgotten it. He left in rather a hurry."

Mr. Emerson mumbled something under his breath but not so quietly Laynie could not hear him. At least it sounded as though he had said something to the effect that Mr. Holbrook's behavior was typical.

"What was that, Mr. Emerson?" Laynie asked him.

"Oh, nothing," he said.

But Laynie continued to look at him, pressing him, by means of her silence, into explaining what he meant.

"It's just that I've known Holbrook a long time. He was never what I would call reliable. How is it he came into service here?" he asked as the soup was placed before them by the housekeeper.

"I ran into him in London, as a matter of fact," Mr. Durham explained. "I was looking for someone to read with me a few evenings a week, and he presented himself to the task, rather miraculously I might add."

Mr. Emerson seemed inclined to scoff at this, but with a look in Laynie's direction he stifled it.

The meal commenced, and Mr. Durham continued on upon the topic initiated by Mr. Emerson. He explained to him how propitious it was to discover such a man at such a time and in such a place. How he had proved himself trustworthy and wise, an excellent conversationalist and a valued friend and companion to the old man in his advancing age.

Mr. Emerson seemed to think every good word spoken by Mr. Durham doubtful.

"You are acquaintances," Laynie observed to him. "I take it you are not, nor have ever been, close friends."

"On the contrary, Miss Durham. We were very close friends, once upon a time. It's been some years, granted, but trust me when I say I know the man very well."

"Perhaps he has changed since you last saw him."

"It's a happy thought. I rather doubt it." Mr. Emerson looked at her, seemed to watch her while Mr. Durham continued on now in a slightly different vein, talking of books, and men of experience who read and think, and those who write whose words are worthy of discussion by men—educated men—of philosophical and intellectual inclination.

While Mr. Durham was preoccupied by his own soliloquy, Mr. Emerson leaned close to Laynie and whispered confidentially, "I would advise you, Miss Durham, as a well-meaning and not entirely disinterested friend, to forget about him."

"What do you mean, Mr. Emerson?"

"You are attached to him. It's as plain as the nose on your face."

"Mr. Emerson, I beg you."

"There's no use denying it. But I must warn you, it is nothing but a fool's fancy to attach yourself to anyone so unworthy as Mr. Daniel Holbrook. Forget about him, Miss Durham, before you learn to regret it."

Laynie wished very much to contend with him, but found she could not. It was neither practical in present company, nor possible. She did not know Mr. Holbrook as well as she wished to do. She wanted very much to come to his defense, but after tonight she knew she could not. He had not behaved in a manner that made it possible. She looked up from him to her sister, who was glowering at her ferociously. Harry, too, was looking at her and not, it seemed, entirely pleased by what he saw. He should be grateful that, somehow, she had managed to divert Mr. Emerson's attention away from her sister. What was there to disapprove of in that? And if there was nothing, then why did she feel like crying?

She was not sorry for herself that Mr. Holbrook had left. She was not attached to him. That was ridiculous! But there was a sort of strange and distressing emptiness that pervaded the atmosphere now. Perhaps it was merely that an unoccupied place lay unclaimed at the table. Perhaps it was something else entirely. But she was not injured by Mr. Holbrook's sudden departure. If anything she was angry. That was it. She was angry with Mr. Holbrook. She was disappointed in his hypocrisy and in the manner in which he had manipulated her into telling her all and then refusing to tell her anything. She was friends with a stranger, which meant, of course, that they were not friends at all. She could not defend him. He had given her no right, no power to do it. Only to lie for him, to make his excuses, and to wish, very much—oh, why must she!—that he were here to keep them company. To keep her company?

She rebelled at the thought and arose.

"Excuse me," she said. "I don't feel well." And quit the table to go to her own room, where she went to bed and pretended to sleep, even when Beth came in an hour or so later and called her name. She did not want to talk about the evening. She did not wish to think of it. She only wished to escape into velvet darkness of sound and dreamless slumber.

It was not to be.

Chapter twenty

LAYNIE AWOKE EARLY THE NEXT MORNING to find that Beth was already up. She was sitting in the morning room, hard at work on some piece of sewing. As Laynie drew nearer she recognized it as the gown Beth had initially attempted to persuade her to wear last night.

"You are up very early," Laynie observed.

"Yes, I suppose I am," was Beth's simple answer.

"Can I ask what you are doing with that dress?"

"I'm filling in the neckline. I know how modest you like your gowns to be. It isn't exactly the same color, but I think it works. What do you think?"

Laynie did not quite understand the impulse behind her sister's sudden spirit of charity towards her. "Are you sure you wouldn't rather have the dress for yourself? You know green does not look well on me."

"It might, though. If it had a wine-colored overlay, don't you think that would warm the color against your skin? Or perhaps a silk wrap of that color?"

"But we don't have anything like that, Beth."

"Then we'll just have to get you something, won't we?"

Laynie watched her sister work for a long time.

"What is it?" Beth said, glancing up at her over her needle.

"Aren't you angry with me?"

"What for?"

"Well, I don't know," Laynie answered, afraid to offer any evidence against herself. Beth's displeasure the evening before had been quite apparent. How was it possible she had forgotten it overnight? "Are you expecting Mr. Emerson today?"

"You know, I'm not certain," Beth said and offered a weak little smile. "Perhaps. Who knows?"

"I'm sorry I abandoned you last night. I—"

"It's quite all right. You didn't feel well. You hadn't been feeling well all day. I'm not upset with you, Laynie. Really I'm not." She looked up once more from her work and Laynie had to believe her sentiments were offered sincerely.

Laynie sat down. "How was the rest of the evening?"

"Dull, actually. Papa monopolized the conversation until Mr. Vaughn was bored quite senseless. He left not long after dinner, and Mr. Emerson followed shortly thereafter."

"And everyone parted on good terms?"

Beth looked at her as if she ought to know better than to ask such a question. "If you want to know, Laynie, I think your retiring early hurt Mr. Emerson's feelings."

"That's a rather ironic idea. I left— That is…one of the reasons I did not want to remain, besides my headache, of course, was because he was being disrespectful. And forgive me for asking, but if he is displeased with something I have said or done, why should you take exception to it?"

"You put him in a dour mood, Laynie. He wasn't any fun after you left. Neither gentleman was, if you want to know."

Laynie considered this for a moment. "Do you think I ought to apologize?"

Beth shrugged. "That's for you to say, I suppose."

"And he said nothing for certain about returning today."

"He did not commit to anything, but then I did not ask. Papa assured him he was welcome any time. I'm sure he'll come, Laynie, don't worry."

"I'm not worried for myself, Beth. I'm frustrated, if you want to know. I've been taking great pains to keep the peace and it seems whatever I do it isn't quite right. I'm grateful you are not angry with me this morning, but it does seem that you are put out that I have made him unhappy, and I would have thought you'd be glad of it!"

Beth sat up a little straighter in her chair. "You speak as though you think me capricious, Laynie. I'm not certain my own feelings aren't hurt. And to think I've gone to all this trouble to alter this dress for you!"

"I'm sorry, Beth," Laynie said, exhausted from trying, and without success, to please her sister. She arose from her place to take a walk outside.

"Where are you going?"

"I thought I'd go up to the precipice. I keep meaning to go. I really could do with a good think, you know."

"Oh, don't leave me. I thought we might go to visit Lady Vaughn today."

Laynie examined her sister, puzzled. "Truly?"

"Yes, indeed. I'm very worried about her. And I think, if you want to know, it was for worrying about his mother that Mr. Vaughn was so low last night."

Laynie thought this rather a preposterous assumption considering the circumstances, though it was true she did suspect he was more anxious for her than he let on.

"Say you will go with me, Laynie?"

"Yes, all right, Beth. If that's what you want, we can go today."

"Good," Beth said, and with an apparently satisfied smile, went back to her work.

* * *

Mr. Durham put down his reading at the sound of the bell. "What now?" he said to himself.

A moment later Mrs. Fowler announced the arrival of Mr. Emerson.

Mr. Durham, a moment ago annoyed at the interruption, was all excitement now. He begged the housekeeper to show the gentleman in.

"Mr. Emerson!" said Mr. Durham upon greeting his guest. "What brings you to our door this afternoon? I regret the girls aren't at home."

"It's just as well, Mr. Durham. I had been hoping for an opportunity of speaking with you alone. No doubt you have wondered why I have come."

"Well, to be quite frank, Mr. Emerson, it is no very great mystery."

"I wish to be honest with you. I find honesty, after all, is the key to avoiding misunderstandings."

"Certainly, sir. Will you sit? Can I get you anything? Tea or—"

"No, thank you," he said and did not sit. He appeared too nervous for anything but standing. "You know I have been married before."

"Yes, so you said, and I'm sorry for your loss."

"As am I. It's not something a man quickly recovers from, as you must know."

"Indeed, sir," Mr. Durham answered gravely. "I *do* know."

"And yet, though it hasn't been quite a year, I am anxious to marry again. While some may seek to find fault, I do not see anything shameful in committing myself to being a marrying man. It's a far nobler pursuit, to my mind, than the alternative."

"And what is that, sir?" Mr. Durham asked, anxious to know that Mr. Emerson did not mean to find fault with *him*.

"I mean no offense, of course. It is one thing for a respectable and much respected father to devote himself to his daughters rather than hunting out a wife who, for all anyone may know, could never love them as their own mother did. As you do."

"I thought it a sensible course for myself, yes," Mr. Durham answered somewhat placated.

"But for a man still young and with no such fortunate circumstances by which he might occupy his mind and heart, well, the temptation to waste one's energies in ignoble pursuits...you know what I mean."

Mr. Durham nodded sagely.

"Well...sometimes it is a very great burden indeed. I tell you this, sir, because I want you to understand my intentions and to set any concerns aside that my motivations are anything other than honest and well meaning."

"I have no reason to doubt it, Mr. Emerson. No reason at all, I assure you. And I'm grateful to you for your directness."

"And yet, sir, it is true... I feel as though I have been dealt with unjustly."

Mr. Durham straightened. "How so, Mr. Emerson?"

"It was your younger daughter I became acquainted with first. It was not until some time later I was informed she was intended to marry a gentleman of her intimate acquaintance. She never refuted it. Indeed, though Miss Alayna was my initial preference, I stepped aside in respect to him, whom I was given to understand had won the honor already of claiming her affections. I was disappointed, certainly, but I very soon discovered the charms of Miss Bethany, who I had every reason to believe was quite unattached. We parted, as you know, and upon saying our goodbyes, Miss Bethany issued an invitation that, were I ever to find myself in your neighborhood, I should feel free to call. And so I have. I feel it my duty to tell you that, upon arriving, I found Bethany so welcoming, myself so overcome by her manner toward me, that I uttered some rather impetuous words. Indeed, I made it quite clear to her that I wished to court her. She was equally clear that she was willing to consider me."

Mr. Durham nodded, not quite following along, but hoping it would all become clear in time. He stood and began pacing the spot of rug beside his desk, hoping the exercise would help him in that aim.

"Imagine my surprise," continued Mr. Emerson, "when I joined you for dinner last night to find that Bethany has been encouraging the affections of the gentleman to whom your younger daughter was supposedly intended to marry, and that *that* young woman is vainly trying to disguise the fact that an attachment has been forming between herself and your hired companion, Mr. Daniel Holbrook!"

"What, sir?" Mr. Durham said. He sat down hard into the nearest chair.

"If I had known what duplicity and capriciousness I would be met with here, sir, I don't know that I would have come. But dash it if I am not in love with your daughter!"

"Are you?" Mr. Durham said and sat forward. He gestured to Mr. Emerson to take a seat. He did. "It is very good of you. Very generous to be so willing to forgive. My girls are troublesome, I'm afraid, very given to flirtatiousness and jealousy. They've given me no end of trouble, I assure you. May I ask, Mr. Emerson, to which you have formed your preference?"

"Isn't it obvious?"

"Um…well…Yes. Yes, of course," he said, but was not certain it was obvious at all. And yet he did not wish to look the confused old man, and so simply nodded and pretended it was all as clear as water. Surely Mr. Emerson would make himself understood in time. Perhaps he, too, was confused. Who wouldn't be!

"Miss Bethany is beautiful, charming, and full of the grace and elegance I admire so very much in a woman."

"Indeed she is, Mr. Emerson. Indeed, she is."

"And yet I find Miss Alayna to be…unexpectedly, surprisingly captivating in her own right."

"Do you?" Mr. Durham said and wondered.

"She is funny and witty and clever and honest to a fault—save for this matter about this Mr. Vaughn fellow."

"That may be my fault, sir, as it was my intention, while they were in Gravesend, that my sister should try to persuade my youngest daughter to marry her old friend. There was no use in it, after all, it seems, but…I would not fault her if she feared, for my sake, even perhaps her sister's, to deny what Bethany had told you. But, tell me truly…do you really find Laynie all these things?"

"All these and much more! She is unpredictable and exciting. If she is capricious she is so in such a way you don't recognize until much later when her hook is set and secure. Her arts are not of the typical kind, it is true, but she is quite extraordinary."

Mr. Durham was pleased by Mr. Emerson's words, but his words had also unsettled him. Had not Mr. Holbrook said something very similar? And what did that mean in consideration of Mr. Emerson's assertions against him? Had Holbrook betrayed him? He could scarcely believe it.

Mr. Emerson leaned forward in his chair, an intent, determined look on his face. "Sir," he said, "I have to tell you, I am deeply alarmed by Mr. Holbrook's presence here. I know he is a friend of yours, and while it is true he was once a friend of mine, he is no longer. I regret speaking ill of anyone, particularly a friend of yours, but it must be said. It is my duty to warn you—he is not a man worthy of your trust and respect."

Mr. Durham wished to ask the reason for the breach between them but feared the answer.

"You have daughters. It is your duty to protect them. And out of respect for you, and admiration for them, I feel it my duty to tell you what I know, however unpleasant, of the man who has convinced you to place your trust in him."

"Do go on, sir."

"It was perhaps six years ago that Mr. Holbrook and I became acquainted with a very lovely young woman with whom we were both rather enamored. He took advantage of an opportunity—indeed, he took advantage of her. He had promised to marry her, but truly he did no more than seduce and abandon her."

Mr. Durham felt his blood begin to boil. Had he been so deceived?

"It was perhaps a good thing that we were rivals, at least for her affection. I married her to rescue her from her shame, but…in the end it did not matter. She never recovered from Holbrook's betrayal. I did what I could for her. I did *all* I could for her. It was not enough. In the end it was his betrayal that killed her. I have no doubt whatsoever of it. I am a widower because of him. And now…now I find him here! Am I to be betrayed again?"

"No, sir. No, you are not," Mr. Durham assured him, his heart racing and the vein in his forehead pulsing.

"And to think of your poor, innocent, naïve daughters, Mr. Durham. I can hardly bear it!"

"Nor can I, sir," Mr. Durham said and arose. "Nor can I, I assure you!"

"I'm not sure I can stay, sir. I'm not sure I can stand for it. But I have done my duty, and whatever I decide to do, I know your girls are now safe. I only wish…"

"Mr. Emerson. Don't despair. You mustn't go. I will do something about this. You have my word. I cannot believe I have been so deceived, so betrayed. And my poor Laynie! Why, I believe you have rescued her."

"She is not rescued quite yet, is she? Only time will prove that. I can see I've distressed you. I'll go."

Mr. Durham followed him to the door. There was more he wished to understand, more he wished to say. "You will come again?" was all he managed.

"I must think what I am to do. I would regret going now, but I must be certain, you know… I am a man with a broken heart. It cannot be broken again. I could not bear it."

Mr. Durham placed his hand on Emerson's arm. "Thank you for confiding in me, Mr. Emerson. You have my word I will speak to Holbrook when next he comes."

"It is entirely likely he will not come again. I will no doubt have reminded him of his shame and dishonor. He is dishonorable indeed if he dares to show his face here again."

"Perhaps then," Mr. Durham said and felt suddenly very tired and alone, "the problem will solve itself."

"Perhaps it will, sir. I'll need to go to London for a day or two. My uncle, you know. But I'll return, if I may—if I can."

"I very much hope you will, Mr. Emerson. You are welcome here, indeed."

Mr. Durham offered his hand. Mr. Emerson took it and shook it gratefully. He was gone, leaving Mr. Durham alone with his thoughts. For the present he refused to face them. He found the book he had been reading with Daniel. He found them both and tossed Holbrook's into the fireplace. There was no fire there now, but Mrs. Fowler would light one this evening, and if Holbrook should come and see it there before that time, so much the better!

He sat down with his own copy and tried to read, but he could not. The words—both those spoken by Emerson and those printed upon the page—simply refused to make sense.

* * *

Laynie arrived with Beth at Elverton and the two sisters were shown into a darkly-papered and richly-appointed upstairs sitting room, where Lady Vaughn reclined on a chaise lounge in the semi-darkness. Laynie had to wait for her eyes to adjust to the dimness before she dared to navigate into the room. The wall sconces had been lit and there were candles here and there, including one on a table beside Lady Vaughn's place of repose. It was shaded, however, and offered very little light.

"Come in, come in," Lady Vaughn beckoned impatiently and with a voice weak from lack of use.

Laynie entered; her sister, with her hand in hers, followed close behind. Upon the chaise lay Lady Vaughn, devoid of rouge and wig and looking frightfully pale. Beth's hand held to Laynie's all the more tightly. For all of her determination to pay this visit, she seemed quite afraid of her now. Perhaps not without reason.

"Sit," the woman said to them.

Laynie sat and pulled Beth down to sit closely beside her. Beth had reason enough to be frightened of Lady Vaughn, considering the objections the venerable woman maintained for the elder Durham sister, but the ghastly sight of her was positively terrifying, and that terror showed too apparently in Beth's countenance. She would have to put forth some sincere effort if she hoped to gain any ground today.

"How are you feeling?" Laynie asked.

"Much the same," Lady Vaughn answered, which told Laynie very little.

"Are you in pain?"

"Some," she said, "but not severe. It is a dull, persistent thing that pesters even when I sleep."

"We have been very anxious for you," Layne said and looked to her sister. "Have we not, Beth?"

"Yes, of course," Beth answered. "Do the doctors not know what your ailment is?"

Laynie was proud of Beth for thinking to ask and grateful she did not inquire as to whether it was catching, which seemed always to be her first concern whenever she was in the presence of illness.

Lady Vaughn smiled stiffly and did not answer. She reached out for Laynie's hand and patted it. "How are you, my dear?" the woman asked her. "And how is that poor father of yours?"

"We are all well, would not you say so, Beth?" Laynie answered, attempting once more to include her sister in the conversation.

"Yes, ma'am," Beth answered simply and apparently struggled for anything more to say. Laynie wished she knew how to help her. If only there were some pleasant topic of conversation of interest to them all, but even Laynie was lost for suggestions.

Lady Vaughn lay quiet and very still, her darkly circled eyes open and studying both sisters in the pale light. "Sit closer," she said at last, "I want to see you properly."

260

Beth arose to open the curtains, but Lady Vaughn stopped her. "My dear, no! The sunlight is too piercing. Do you mean to kill me?"

"No, ma'am. I'm sorry," she said and sat again.

Lady Vaughn removed the shade from the candle beside her and took up her lorgnette through which she examined both sisters, first Beth, then Laynie. "You do not look perfectly well, my dear," she said to Laynie alone. "In fact you seem a little downcast."

"We are worried for you," Laynie answered.

"Nonsense. It is not for me you are sullen." She lowered her eyeglass and gave Laynie a narrow look. "Harold has been downcast as well. Might I take hope the two of you are at last beginning to see reason?"

"I'm afraid not, Lady Vaughn."

She huffed and held the now folded lorgnette in both hands. "Then what is the matter with you?"

"I don't know, ma'am," Laynie answered. "I'm not downcast exactly. It's just that I've not been sleeping well. I don't know the reason. I wish I did."

Lady Vaughn appeared not to believe her. She examined Beth. "I wonder if *you* know, Miss Durham, what is troubling your sister. I'm willing to bet you know what is troubling my son."

Beth looked down at her hands, and Laynie willed her to say something convincing and sincere.

"Tell me," Lady Vaughn urged. "Why is your sister downcast?"

Beth looked up at her, seeming to have found a little courage. "Laynie *has* been acting strangely of late," she said, "but I'm not certain I can say just why."

"She has not told you?"

Beth glanced toward Laynie. A faint look of regret crossed her brow. "I'm afraid we do not talk to each other as we used to do, ma'am."

"That is a pity. There is no blessing greater than a sister's love, particularly at your age. Life is difficult enough without someone to endure it with."

"I'm sure you are right, ma'am," Beth said, and Laynie was reminded what Lady Vaughn had suffered since her husband had left her.

261

"What of Harold?" she asked then.

"I beg your pardon?" Beth answered, having forgotten Lady Vaughn's original question.

"What of my son? Can you say just what it is that has turned him to brooding? It is owing to you, I take it."

Beth turned very red and did not succeed this time in conquering it. Whether or not Lady Vaughn could see it was another matter entirely. "Perhaps, ma'am," Beth began and her tone made Laynie cringe, "as you won't approve of his choice, his unhappiness is as much owing to you as to me."

Laynie looked to Lady Vaughn and waited for her response. Would she raise her voice in indignation? Would she send Beth from the room?

"You may be right," Lady Vaughn said to Laynie's utter surprise.

Beth looked at her a little less defiantly and yet more confidently as well. Had she gained some respect in Beth's eyes? And could the feeling be reciprocated?

"And do you admit to having some part in it?" Lady Vaughn added. It was a challenge of sorts, and Beth had no choice but to reply.

"I regret that it may be true."

"Regret?"

"Yes, ma'am. I do."

"You're not worthy of him, you know."

Beth was not prepared to accept this at face value, it seemed. "And yet my sister, by some mystery, is."

"It's no mystery, Miss Durham. Your sister is true and honest, sincere in speech and action, a friend to any and all and without condition. You might learn a great deal from her were you to take her example."

Beth glanced at her sister and then hung her head. "You are right, of course," she said at last.

"Good. I'm glad you are at least willing to see reason," Lady Vaughn said. "Will you tell me one thing more, Miss Durham? Why is it my son's suit does not quite please you? You have already acknowledged your unworthiness, but why is it you consider him unworthy of you?"

"I'm not sure that is quite the problem, my lady."

"Then what is, prey?"

Beth seemed to have no answer for this, though Laynie hoped the volley had nearly come to an end. If Beth could find a way to meekly accept Lady Vaughn's interrogation and the counsel she must consequently give, perhaps Beth would succeed in improving Lady Vaughn's opinion of her, even if just a little.

"I know what it is, my dear. I'm not a fool. Harold has told you his inheritance is uncertain, and you are waiting to see what comes of it. Is that not it?"

Beth blinked, but she answered Lady Vaughn directly. Perhaps too directly. "I beg your pardon, ma'am," she said, "but it is not my own happiness I think of. Of course I would like to marry into my security. Who would not? But you have to recognize the difficulty of our position. I may wait for Mr. Vaughn's inheritance to become sure only to find I am the cause of his losing it again. If he is not utterly devoted to me, I do not want him. And yet I would never ask him to cross you. I might not have him as a poor man, but I most certainly would not make him one. Yes. I confess it's a consideration. I beg you to believe me when I say it is not the only one. Not nearly."

Lady Vaughn examined Beth with a narrowed gaze. Beth had stated the matter very well, but it was only one side of the question. Was Lady Vaughn familiar with the other? She was, it seemed.

"Let me see if I understand you," she said. "You expect my Harold to be quite entirely devoted to you, and yet you will not give him the same courtesy?"

"I simply have not decided yet if he can make me happy," Beth answered more humbly, "or I him. I'm afraid I'm rather slow to know my own mind. I regret it, but it is true."

Lady Vaughn smiled, once more stiffly, glanced from one sister to the other, and then asked another question more. One that Laynie was not quite prepared for.

"Tell me, will you," Lady Vaughn began, "of this new addition to your court of admirers. Has he anything to do with your inability to decide? I think it safe to suppose he is a contributing factor to my son's state of sullenness. Am I wrong?"

Beth did not answer, and Laynie certainly wasn't going to try to explain his sudden and, at least for her, unexpected arrival. But how could Lady Vaughn have heard of it?

"You think I don't know what goes on in that house, do you? Need I remind you that my kitchen maid is the niece of your cook? Servants talk you know, and much more than you would think."

So Lady Vaughn had employed a spy in her kitchen maid. It should not have surprised Laynie, but it did. Beth looked positively chagrined.

"What is his name?" Lady Vaughn insisted. "Who is he? Who is his family? Answer me, Miss Durham."

"His name is Emerson, ma'am," Beth answered, though reluctantly. "Frederick Emerson, originally of Portsmouth, though he has family in London. An uncle, I believe, from whom he expects to in-herit."

"Ah, my dear, if we all had such uncles!" she answered wryly. "Emerson. Emerson," she said and seemed as if to taste the word on her tongue. "The name sounds familiar. Fetch me Debrett's, my dear," she commanded of Laynie and waved her in the direction of the bookshelf.

Laynie did as she was bid and sat to wait while Lady Vaughn turned the pages of the well-worn book of heraldry, anxious to know for herself what it might reveal. She watched and waited in mounting anticipation, while Lady Vaughn scanned the pages with the aid of her index finger and her lorgnette. It appeared she required a third hand for the task.

"I hear your father has hired a reading companion," she said, looking up from the book and lowering her lorgnette.

Laynie only wished she would finish with one topic before jumping to the other. "It's true," Laynie said. "He has."

Lady Vaughn closed the book, though she held the place with one finger. "What *can* your father be thinking?" she asked rhetorically. "How can he afford such a thing? I don't expect you to answer that. I already know. He can't! And what are you two to do when he runs out of money, will you tell me?" She freed her finger from the pages of the book and huffed in indignation. "What are we to do with him? If your poor mother were still alive..."

"But she isn't," Laynie reminded her with some regret. She regretted all the more that the book was now closed and the subject of Mr. Emerson seemingly abandoned.

Lady Vaughn attempted to sit up, but finding the effort too much for her, lay back down and closed her eyes. "Oh, how I do wish you would let me help you," she said. "If Harold only had the sense to choose you, Alayna... Or even if..." But she did not finish. What would she have said? If Beth were somehow different? But how different? What was it Lady Vaughn wanted in Harry's bride? "If you would only learn to love my Harold," she went on and seemed to find it a point of immense disappointment, "I could do so much for you. I could do everything!"

"But it isn't me he loves, ma'am. I may be foolish, but I'd like to think someday I might be someone's first choice, not their second."

Beth took hold of Laynie's hand, but whether it was a gesture of reassurance or one of gratitude for making the argument, she did not know.

"Oh, pish!" Lady Vaughn said and then sucked the air in through her teeth as she winced in pain.

"Can I call someone for you?" Laynie said and stood.

Lady Vaughn shook her head, reached for the bell on her table and dropped it. It rattled to the floor, but the nurse was close enough to hear it and quickly came to the aid of her mistress.

The nurse entered and administered a tonic. Lady Vaughn reached to take it and in so doing the book fell from the bed. Laynie moved to retrieve it, but the nurse stopped her.

"You must go," she said. "Lady Vaughn must rest now."

Laynie left the book and she left Lady Vaughn, regretting that she had not come sooner and that Harry's mother must be left to suffer so.

In the entrance hall they were met by a glum Mr. Vaughn.

"Harry, how are you?" Laynie asked him. "Your poor mother. Is she worse?"

"She has been thus for the past week or two, I think. She grows better and worse again. Are you going?" he said.

"I think that we had better," Laynie answered.

"May I walk with you?"

Laynie glanced at Beth, who appeared cautiously hopeful.

"If it isn't too much trouble," Beth replied, "we would be very grateful."

"There is the carriage if you would prefer."

"It's such a lovely day, Mr. Vaughn," Beth said. "Mightn't we walk? I could use the exercise."

Laynie hoped very much that this was an excuse to spend a little more time with him.

Harry nodded. They exited the house and stood a moment in the drive.

"Would you mind," Beth asked demurely, "if I took your arm?"

"Never," he said and presented it.

Laynie walked on ahead, allowing the two of them some privacy and hoping they would make the most it.

There was not much said between the pair. Laynie worried that the short half hour would count for little more than a series of wasted minutes. However, from what she could observe as she occasionally glanced back at them, what few words were exchanged counted for a very great deal.

From Harry's perspective it was especially so.

"I am so very sorry about your mother," Beth said to him after they had walked some distance in silence. "I did not realize she was so ill."

"She does not want people to know it. It hurts her pride."

"I regret to hear that. I was hoping to have improved myself in her opinion. I think I did not succeed."

"And why ever would you want to do that, Miss Durham?" Harry asked, praying for the answer he most desired in all the world.

She did not answer right away, and when she did it wasn't quite the answer he had wished for. But neither did it entirely disappoint. "I beg you will be patient with me, Mr. Vaughn. I need some time yet. I cannot explain just why, but I do have my reasons. I pray you will not give up on me."

He did not know quite what to make of this, but something within him felt a great deal lighter than it had before. He had to stop himself from taking her hand in his and squeezing it. "Never, Miss Durham," he said. "So long as there is a chance."

266

"Aren't you angry with me?"

Chapter twenty-one

L AYNIE entered the foyer, her sister and Mr. Vaughn following closely behind, and stopped in the midst of untying her hat.

"Is that Papa?" Beth asked.

Laynie did not answer but followed the sound of her father's voice, ranting and grumbling loudly, and found him walking slowly and distractedly down the corridor from his study toward the dining room.

"Papa!" Laynie said to him. "What is the matter?"

"Hmm?" he said, looking up at her suddenly. "You're home? Good, good." And he passed her by, mumbling and complaining still, though what he was saying she could not quite comprehend.

"What is it?" Beth asked him as he crossed the foyer toward the drawing room. The three of them followed him there and stopped in the doorway to watch him as he examined the contents of the liquor cabinet. "Has Mrs. Fowler failed to freshen your decanter, Papa?" she asked next. He kept a plentiful store of refreshment in his study. His behavior was alarming.

He examined the decanters and bottles. What he wanted was not there.

"Papa?" Laynie asked, growing increasingly alarmed. "Can I get you something?"

"I don't know what the world has come to," he said, shaking his head as he examined one decanter and then another. "You can't trust anyone these days, can you?"

"Perhaps I had better go," Mr. Vaughn said and began to turn from the room.

Laynie stopped him with a hand on his arm.

"If I had known from the start what I was doing in welcoming that fellow into my home…"

"Whom, Papa?" Laynie asked.

Beth had gone a shade of white.

"Do you know, I think we may never see him again, and good riddance, too!"

Laynie felt a weight upon her chest. "Why do you say that, Papa? What has happened? Of whom do you speak?"

Mr. Durham at last poured a drink. He put the stopper in the bottle and then found a chair. His glass remained on the shelf of the cabinet where he had left it. Laynie picked it up and gave it to him. He raised it to his lips but stopped before taking the first sip.

"Does a man not have a speck of honor anymore? Does he have no respect at all for the word "gentleman"? As if he could pick the title up and put it on him like a hat when he wanted to and then put it down when—" He stopped himself and looked at his girls and then at their companion. "Mr. Vaughn," Mr. Durham said and closed his eyes. "You are here."

It was impossible to tell if the gesture indicated frustration at the sight of him or relief.

"Actually, sir, I was just leaving."

"No!" Mr. Durham said and arose. "A word with you, if I may?"

Harry looked a little worried. "Yes, of course, sir."

Mr. Durham led Harry from the room, and it was just Laynie and Beth alone. Beth closed the door and then turned to her sister. "What does he mean, Laynie? Who is it that has offended him so? Who won't we see again?"

Laynie shook her head. "I fear to guess."

"What can Mr. Emerson have done to anger father so thoroughly that he would send him away?"

"You know how he dislikes indecisiveness," Laynie suggested.

"Mr. Emerson is not indecisive," Beth said, but her countenance faltered as she considered what she had said, what had happened the night before. She closed her eyes and sat.

"He cannot mean Mr. Holbrook," Laynie said with equal uncertainty.

"No," Beth answered. "Certainly not."

"And yet it must be one of them. You saw their reception of one another last night. There is some history between them and it is not pleasant."

"If only we could know what it was."

"Mr. Holbrook would not speak of it to me."

"If it means speaking ill of another, then what gentleman would?" Beth said.

"But someone must have said something or what could Papa have to be so angry about?"

Beth wrung her hands in her lap and thought. Laynie, fearing to consider for herself, determined not to. What sort of conclusion might she come to? And so she watched and waited for her sister to offer some answer. "I cannot think," Beth said at last.

"You would not mind, I think, were Mr. Holbrook to go." It was an accusation, and she expected Beth to reply to it as such, but her manner was calm when at last she did.

"Would *you*, Laynie? I would mind it very much if *you* minded."

Laynie was somewhat perplexed by the question, apparently quite sincerely asked. "And Mr. Emerson?"

Beth arose and crossed the room. She looked out the window and crossed it again, wringing her hands still. "The only thing I can come up with that makes any sense at all is that one of them knows something horrible about the other, and that it has come out."

Laynie felt that she wanted to cry. She feared very much that her sister was right. She feared she knew who it was that was not to return. "Beth? What are we to do if…?"

"Yes, Laynie?"

"If he doesn't come back? What will we do with Papa?"

Beth raised a knuckle her lip.

"Don't say he can be replaced. I know you are thinking it. Harry is with him now. That is not what I want to hear. This is an upset to Father, and—"

"Laynie," she said and stopped her.

"Yes, Beth?"

"I will sort this out."

"You? How?"

"I..." she shook her head. "I don't know. But you are not to worry, do you understand?"

"How can you say such a thing? Of course I'm worried. For Papa, at least."

"Yes, I know."

"Aren't you worried? Don't you fear it's Mr. Emerson who is not to return?"

Beth did not answer for a very long time. "I think," she said, "that we will see them both again. A man always shows his true colors, however briefly, when he has something great to lose."

"What do you mean by that?" Laynie asked and feared the answer. She was not to get it.

Beth approached her, kissed her on the cheek, and sent her up to her room to rest and freshen up for dinner.

"Aren't you coming?" Laynie asked her.

"I want to wait for Mr. Vaughn."

Laynie nodded and went upstairs, and she tried very hard to do as her sister asked. It was impossible to rest. It was impossible not to worry. What on earth had happened this morning to rend in two the peaceful world that was her home?

* * *

Mr. Durham closed the door of his study with a loud bang and proceeded to pace the length of floor before the unlit hearth. Mr. Vaughn watched him and observed as he passed the fireplace the third time that a book lay atop the spent coals.

"I have been betrayed, Mr. Vaughn," he said and glanced at him.

Vaughn said nothing in return, only waited.

"I was taken in, hoodwinked. I gave the man my trust, allowed him free access to my home, to my daughters! And he has betrayed me!" He punched the air with his fist and turned to make another pass of the hearth. "For weeks, months I considered him my trusted friend, my confidante! So completely did I trust him that I did not see what was going on beneath my very nose!"

"You are speaking of Mr. Holbrook, I take it."

"Blast the man! I hope he rots in Hell."

"Sir," Vaughn said cautiously, "may I ask what it was he has done to betray you?"

271

"He lied. He misrepresented himself."

"Forgive me, sir. Wasn't it you who insisted he pretend to be a married man?"

"Dash it, Vaughn! He pretended to be an honorable man. He's as good as killed a woman!"

"What?" Vaughn said and was inclined to think Mr. Durham exaggerating. "Daniel Holbrook?"

"He seduced her, broke her heart, left her. She died as a result of his betrayal. He as good as killed her. And now he's after my Laynie!"

Of all the things Mr. Durham had said so far, this surprised him most. And yet...

"If Mr. Emerson had not come to reveal the truth, I don't know what might have happened."

"Mr. Emerson told you this story?" Vaughn asked with a certain amount of skepticism.

"Yes, yes. He knew the girl. Rescued her. Married her! Too late, it seemed. The poor, poor man. But he is a good fellow, I think. He has decided upon Laynie, and I think she will be a good match for him. She will comfort him in his loneliness. She will be the balm to his soul."

"Laynie?" Mr. Vaughn said, unbelieving. At least uncomprehending.

Mr. Durham looked up at him. "Oh, don't tell me you want her now. Not when we had just got it all settled between you and Beth."

"Sir, my heart can't and won't change, though I think it rather soon to say it's 'all settled'. It's hardly that. But Laynie and Mr. Emerson? Have you spoken to her about this?"

"No, but I mean to. That is I mean to tell her what it is Mr. Emerson has rescued her from. What he is prepared to rescue her from. But it is not a story one repeats, not at least in genteel society. Not to womenfolk, you know, though she must be made to understand the danger she was in."

"Holbrook had feelings for Laynie," he repeated to himself. It was a shock and yet it did seem to make a certain sense. Danger, however... He had a hard time believing that.

"Feelings? Feelings? The man didn't have feelings for her. He had designs!"

"Are you certain of this? You've known Holbrook for months now. Mr. Emerson hasn't been here twenty-four hours and you're willing to believe everything he says? I can't help but suspect he has some motives of his own, and not all of them quite altruistic."

"You mean a rivalry. Well, yes, there is that, of course. But then there was one before, it seems. A man's character may be immediately apparent, or it may take time to reveal itself, but reveal itself it will. And it has!"

"Certainly," Vaughn agreed and yet wondered whose character had been revealed in this instance. He did not know Holbrook well. Perhaps he did not know him at all, but he had a difficult time thinking of him in such a light as had just been painted for him. He neither liked nor trusted Emerson, but then perhaps he had no reason to do so. It was possible Vaughn only wished to believe in Holbrook. Holbrook and Laynie. What an astounding idea.

"Do you know, sir, if Laynie has feelings to return for Holbrook's—supposing it's true?"

"By gad, I hope not! I suppose I should speak to her. I don't know that she'll listen to me. I don't know that she'll make any confession. Not now. She might despise me for all I know. No. I'll let Emerson speak with her. He'll know what to say. Perhaps, by and by, she'll forget about Holbrook as thoroughly as I intend to do."

"Are you sure you're being quite fair, sir? Every story has two sides, after all. Holbrook has never given you any pause for concern before Mr. Emerson arrived. He may very well have an explanation worth listening to."

Mr. Durham looked at him long and hard. It seemed he did not quite believe him. "You may be right for all I know. But I know an honest face when I see one, and Emerson's is the most honest I've met with in an age. He's a heartbroken man, Vaughn. Holbrook caused him the injury. What sort of a man would lie about something like that?"

"I confess I'm somewhat perplexed," Harry said. "When I arrived last night it was quite plain to me that Mr. Emerson was laboring to secure the attentions, if not the affections, of Miss Bethany. It was not until Holbrook arrived that his attention shifted to Laynie. Are you certain you can trust this man?"

"You are biased, Vaughn. You see him as a threat to your future happiness, and I can't say I blame you. I'm not entirely certain he's quite decided. But if he'll take Laynie I mean to encourage him to do it. It will keep her safe from that scoundrel Holbrook."

"Sir, I feel I must tell you I have watched Mr. Holbrook very closely these last many weeks."

"No doubt you have. Yes, yes, you're a clever fellow. You probably saw through him before I did. I think I was too fascinated with the man—I won't call him a gentleman—to see the truth."

"Perhaps I was too, if you want to call it that. I think I rather looked up to him. But I did watch him. And while I think it entirely possible he has developed some tender feelings for Laynie, I have never seen anything untoward or in the least way duplicitous or presuming in his behavior. As far as his past is concerned, I think he deserves the opportunity to respond to Mr. Emerson's accusations. But as for his present conduct, I can see nothing reprehensible in it. I do not, however, like Mr. Emerson. And while you are right to suppose I do have some personal motivation for despising him, the truth is I simply do not trust him."

"Why should you, Vaughn, considering all? Why should you?"

The book in the fireplace was positively distracting. "Sir?" he said and pointed to it. "May I ask?"

"Is it cold in here to you?" Mr. Durham asked, misinterpreting Vaughn's meaning. "Perhaps it has grown a little chilly. I'm afraid I'm too distraught to think of my own comfort just now. I'll ring for the housekeeper to light it."

While Mr. Durham turned for the bell, Vaughn arose and took the book from the grate. He was examining it when Mr. Durham turned back to face him.

"Byron on the coals?" Vaughn inquired. "What did he do to deserve that, I wonder?"

"It's Holbrook's. He left it when he took his rather hasty and unexpected leave of us last night. He won't be needing it again. I won't be needing *him* again."

Mr. Durham reached for it, perhaps to throw it back onto the fire, but Vaughn evaded him. It interested him. Something he had seen in it had caught his eye. "Do you mind, sir, if I take it? I hate the thought of burning books."

"You have a whole library full of them, Vaughn. Why I'll bet you have six volumes of Byron's works hidden about in that great house of yours."

"Even so, sir."

Mr. Durham gave his permission with a disgusted wave. "Get it out of here. Oh, Vaughn," he said, calling him back. "Beth paid a call on your mother today. How is she?"

"Not particularly well, sir."

"I'm sorry to hear that. Is there any chance we'll win the day—regarding Beth, I mean?"

"I do think so, sir. It all depends on her."

Mr. Durham looked doubtful.

"Don't worry, sir. I have a plan."

"Would you mind telling me what it is?"

He considered. Mr. Durham was not known for his ability to keep confidences. "Perhaps another time, sir. Thank you for the book."

"Yes, yes. Good afternoon, Vaughn. And thank you."

"For what, sir?"

"For listening to an old man ramble and rant about his disappointments."

"Any time, sir. Good day."

Mr. Durham nodded his gratitude, and Mr. Vaughn entered the corridor and closed the door. He stood there a moment thinking, then looked at the book in his hand. He crossed the corridor to the nearest wall sconce and opened the book to examine the pages in the light. There were drawings on some of the pages, suggesting Holbrook had not been listening as attentively at times as perhaps Mr. Durham would have liked. Mainly they were little sketches of sunsets and tree-lined views, but as the pages progressed, they grew more focused, more... realistic rather than fanciful. On one page, where a great space of white was left where one poem ended and another began on the next, a small cottage scene had been drawn. The house was a miniscule facsimile of the Bowery, quaintly set against an all too familiar hillside.

"Mr. Vaughn?"

Vaughn closed the book with a snap and turned to find Beth standing in a doorway. "Have you been waiting for me?" he said, somewhat encouraged.

"How is Papa?" she asked him.

"Distraught, confused, angry."

"Did you find out with whom?"

"Will you walk me to the door, Miss Durham?" he asked instead of answering.

"Yes, gladly. That is…I'll gladly walk you. I'm not so happy to see you go."

He smiled his gratitude.

"I'm grateful to you for sitting with him a while, listening to him, you know."

They had reached the foyer. He took up his coat and hat and opened the door, where he hesitated. "Perhaps if you would be so kind as to walk me to the gate," he said.

"Yes, of course," she answered and fetched the shawl she kept nearby.

They did not speak again until they were standing beneath the trees outside.

"It's Holbrook," he said. "Your father feels he's betrayed him."

"Betrayed him? How?"

"There is some history between Mr. Emerson and Mr. Holbrook—"

"Yes, I know. That is, Laynie told me. What it is, she—we do not know."

"It isn't pretty, Miss Durham. It paints Mr. Holbrook in rather a paltry light."

"I'm very sorry to hear that." And it appeared she was.

"Your father is also under the impression that Mr. Holbrook has formed an attachment to Laynie. Something, as you know, he's been forbidden to do."

Beth blinked, swallowed, and nodded her head.

"Did you know this?" he asked her.

"Well, no, not as such. It's possible though that if he thinks well of Laynie it is because I encouraged him to do it. Do you think I placed my sister in any danger?"

"I suppose it's impossible to say. I cannot quite shake the feeling that something isn't right here. That Emerson fellow has formed a preference for her as well, and he has convinced your father to encourage her to think well of him."

"What?" Beth said and looked a little sick. "My father told you this? Mr. Emerson spoke to him about it?"

The day had gone so well until this shock that Vaughn had quite forgot that Beth had openly encouraged Emerson's flirtations. Last night he had been very much discouraged by their apparent intimacy—until Emerson's focus had switched to Laynie. Knowing Beth's tendency to consider her sister a rival, this revelation perhaps might have been spared her. At the very least he might have delivered it with more tact.

She stared up at him, resolute and unmoved, but there was a sparkle of light in her eyes that suggested her emotions were not entirely under her own command. He was afraid to ask what the matter was. He was afraid to say anything more, and so he said nothing at all.

"Mr. Vaughn," she said at last, "you have been very good to be so patient with me. I'm afraid I have asked a great deal of you. The truth is, I may need to ask a great deal more of you yet."

"Meaning?" he asked cautiously.

She looked at him a long time. "You may not like me very well when this is all said and done."

"What are you thinking, Beth?" he asked and worried that her jealousy, her need to be the victor in any rivalry, had turned her to thinking once more of Mr. Emerson.

"I don't know yet. I haven't decided." And yet he feared she had. She put her hand out to him. He took it, reluctantly. "Good day, Mr. Vaughn. And thank you."

"Beth? Miss Durham?" But she was walking away from him and would not turn back. She entered the house and closed the door. Had she closed it upon him?

He walked to the road, his mind heavy with disappointment, with the shock of recent events, and their refusal to make any sense to him. He remembered the book in his hand and stopped. He flipped it open to the back. On the very last page, between the end paper and the publisher's advertisements, were two figures, exquisitely drawn. The first he did not recognize. Beneath her sketched profile were the letters 'S.W.' The other image he recognized instantly. Beneath this was written, very simply yet in carefully executed letters, 'A.D.'

Chapter twenty-two

D ANIEL ARRIVED AT BROOKDALE IN the wind and the rain. The grey stone house looked all the more forlorn with water dripping from the eaves and the stonework stained with wet. Ivy climbed and clung and, left to run rampant, had reached the roofline, crawling through windows and doorways.

Daniel entered through the creaking plank door. There was no butler to open it for him, no housekeeper to greet him. There was no family to welcome him home, no friends—none but one—knew he was even here. He entered the cold house, exchanged his coat for a dry one, and began his thorough inspection of the premises. The house was quiet as death, every footstep, every creak of an opening door echoed through the cavernous emptiness.

Daniel examined carefully the lower rooms, the peeling papers, the cracked and damaged plaster, the broken windows and crumbling chimneys. How quickly a house falls to ruin when there is no one to take care of it.

Upstairs, Daniel stopped at the door to his grandfather's room. He did not like to enter it, but, as it might one day be his own, he thought he had better. It was a long and narrow affair, sparsely furnished with a large bed at one end and a sitting area before the fire at the other. In between these, a wardrobe stood on one wall. Situated opposite sat a chest of drawers crowned by a mirror of monstrous proportions, and in the very center of the room a large table, whereon his grandfather had kept his reading material and whatever else he had employed to stimulate his mind in his spare, often lonely hours. It stood empty now, save for a vase of wilted flowers, placed there, no doubt, before he had died and quite forgotten when his body had been carried away.

Daniel wandered the room, stopping now and then to examine a picture or to look out the window. He avoided the mirror. He had never been particularly fond of them, but in recent years he had spent as little time as possible face to face with his own reflection. He was getting older and he hated to think of it. Thirty in two years. It was a respectable age, but what then? He had little to show for it. He had never married, had no children, and behaved as most expected a man in his position to do, as if he could have no care in the world for these. It was not quite true.

In the still of the room his thoughts were disturbed by a sound. A small, rhythmic pat-pat-pat. It had been here all along, but only in the quiet of his meditations had it penetrated his consciousness. Carefully, he scanned the room, following the sound until he discovered the source. Above the bed the plaster was bowing, and from the very center of it a small hole had formed. As faithful as the second hand of a clock, metered drops of water fell from the orifice onto the canopy of the bed below it. The water pooled there for a moment before finding its way through the fabric of the canopy and then dripping again, just as faithfully, onto the bed itself. Daniel fetched the wash basin and placed it on the bed as the soft slapping of water on wet fabric became a ringing of porcelain. Thus recalled to the immediate needs of the house, Daniel took a more faithful turn of the rooms, even checking into the attic to assess the extent of the roof's damage. The leak above the bedroom proved the worst of them, but it was hardly the only one. It seemed it had been some time since anyone had examined the integrity of the slate, which had a tendency to blow off dangerously in adverse weather. Worse yet, he feared that things had been this way for some time and that more might need to be repaired than just a roof and a little plaster. He immediately set to work making an inventory of that which was most necessary to be done and preparing himself to engage as many tradesmen as required to assure that the house was properly repaired and restored without further loss of time. Under such circumstances, it seemed necessary that he should remain here for the time being. It was a good excuse to be away. As good as any. And while he was not entirely comfortable with the thought of leaving Emerson to run unchecked amidst the Durhams, Daniel simply could not face him. Not just yet.

A great crashing startled him. It repeated and reverberated through the hallways and corridors, into the rooms and shaking the floor. It was merely the sound of a knocker against the door of an empty house, but it was a disturbing sound, like angry spirits coming to claim his soul.

"Holbrook? Are you home?"

Daniel descended the staircase to find Charles Hamilton standing in the entrance hall examining the house, while the large wolf hound who had accompanied him watched Daniel.

"You really *have* let the place go, haven't you?" Hamilton asked him.

"Your dog has grown," Daniel observed in return.

"He's impressive, isn't he?"

"I'm very glad to see you, Hamilton." He shook his friend's hand, ruffled the dog's coat and smiled. "Come into the drawing room, won't you? I'll find you something to drink."

"Your letter sounded urgent, Holbrook. Is everything all right?"

"I'm not certain," he said as Hamilton took a place on the sofa. The dog joined him there, resting his head on Charlie's knee. Daniel examined the liquor cabinet. There was not much left, and what was there looked questionable.

"I don't want anything anyway," Hamilton said. "Sit down, won't you. What's going on? And don't tell me you only wanted to see a friend. I could have come to you in London if it was merely a social call. It would have been much easier than coming all this way."

"All this way?" Daniel said and turned to face him, a half empty and apparently watered-down decanter in his hand. "You're not at home? I could have met you in London very easily. Why didn't you say?"

"I'm very rarely in Kent these days. I have some business in Town, and I find it suits me better to stay near to it."

"Business? What sort of business?"

"Not the sort I'm prepared to discuss at the moment."

"Why ever not?" Daniel said, eager for any distraction. "Is it underhanded? I suppose you are involved in some scandal at present and *can't* talk about it."

"We can discuss it later. Sit. Tell me what is so urgent."

Daniel examined the decanter in his hand, decided it was not servable, and set it down again. And then he stood there, helpless as to how to begin.

The dog sat up and looked at him, curious and perhaps half-concerned.

"Spit it out, man," Charlie said, "you're making me nervous."

"Emerson is in Surrey."

Hamilton sat forward in his seat. He brushed his nearly black hair out of his eyes as though the gesture would help him to better understand. "It sounded as if you said—"

"Emerson is in Surrey. At the home of my employer, yes."

"How the devil did he end up there?"

"It's coincidence, I suppose."

"Balderdash! I don't believe in it."

"That's a rather ironic thing to say for someone whose whole life has been a series of coincidences. No, I think it must be. I can't account for it by any other means." Daniel tested the cushion of a velvet-covered chair and sent a cloud of dust into the air. He remained there, watching it, examining it as if it would provide him with some answer to his dilemma.

"He didn't find you out, come looking for you?" Hamilton suggested.

Daniel looked at him. "'Why would he do that? He got what he wanted from me."

"And lost it again."

Daniel feared to say what he was thinking. Feared more that Charlie might say it for him. Had he returned to take something more?

"It *is* astounding. But I think there is something you're not telling me. How did this come about?"

At last Daniel sat. The dog climbed off the sofa and came to sit at his feet. Daniel stroked his head a moment, as he summoned the words to begin. "Do you remember I told you Mr. Durham has two daughters?" he said at last.

"Yes, of course. Very young, I think you said."

Daniel dropped his hand from the dog's head and closed his eyes in shame. The dog nudged him. Daniel resumed stroking the animal's head. It gave him a sort of comfort to do it. A comfort he needed to proceed. "Miss Bethany is one and twenty. Her sister, Alayna—though everyone calls her Laynie—is not yet twenty."

"Not children, then."

"No. Not children." He laughed self-deprecatingly. "Not hardly."

"Go on," Hamilton urged him, growing apparently apprehensive as Daniel dragged the story out.

"They have an aunt in Gravesend where they recently spent a week. They met him there."

"And he followed them home? That is rather presumptuous. And coincidental. Are you certain he didn't know you were there?"

"Laynie—Miss Alayna, I mean—said she had mentioned me in conversation, but did not believe my name was ever spoken."

"But she is not certain?"

"No."

"It was her belief Mr. Emerson had come to call upon her sister. And to be honest, it did seem that way at first. But the longer I was there, the more I spoke with her, the more determinedly he sought her attention. I cannot help but wonder..."

"Hold on just a moment," Hamilton said, apparently struggling to connect all the pieces. "Let me see if I understand this. These sisters met him by chance in Gravesend. That, at least, is a coincidence."

"I believe so. He had intentions, or so Miss Durham assures me, toward their cousin, but for some reason it all unraveled while they were there."

"Unraveled? Do you know why?"

"Their aunt objected on some grounds or another. After which some tentative attachment was formed with Miss Bethany. The invitation, as I surmise it, must have come from her."

"And you have met him there. He has seen you?"

"Oh, yes. He addressed me as if we were and had always been the closest of friends."

"You *were* close friends. Once."

"Yes, well. The question is, it seems, now what?"

"Indeed. What do you mean to do?"

"What is there to do? I'm not about to keep him company, that's for certain. And Brookdale needs a great deal of attention just now. I might remain here for a time. I don't know how long."

"Do you mean to give up your position with Mr. Durham?"

"I think I may have to, only—"

"Only?"

Only he regretted the idea of it more than he could say and perhaps not entirely for the right reasons. He looked at Hamilton, who seemed to understand that he was keeping something back. Was there any use in concealing it? "It's just that I can't get it out of my head that history is repeating itself. It can't repeat itself, Hamilton, do you see?" he said, rising again to pace the room.

The dog followed him.

"No, my friend, I can't say that I do."

"When I think of walking away, I think of how I left *her*, and how if I had to do it over..."

"Yes, I know. You are not alone in regretting how that turned out."

Daniel walked the length of the room. He turned back and stopped. "When I think of facing him, of sitting in the same room with him... I can't do it. I can't smile and pretend that everything in me isn't simply dying to strangle the life out of him. To stay away seems cowardly. To continue going is madness. It seems everything I do is the wrong thing."

"Holbrook," Charlie began but hesitated before finishing. "Do you mean to say you—"

"Why here?" Daniel asked rhetorically and interrupting the question he could not bear to have asked and was unprepared to answer. "Why now? Why at the Durhams' home, where I have found such unexpected peace and happiness?"

"Is it because of her? Because of one of them? The daughters, I mean?"

Of course there was no escaping the question. Daniel had led Charlie to it, after all. He was not yet prepared to answer it, and yet he wanted Hamilton to understand him. He crossed the room again, the dog following him still, and stopped to stand before his friend. He rubbed hard at his brow in an effort to make sense of all this in his own mind so that he could help Hamilton to make sense of it in his.

"Which one?" Charlie asked him.

"The younger."

"Not yet twenty."

"Yes, I know!"

"I thought you said…?"

"It's forbidden? I did. And it is." Daniel sighed. "I had begun to think I could convince him. It is weakness, Hamilton, and I'm ashamed of it."

"Well I'm not. I mean, yes, it is a bit shady if you mean to cross her father. It is hardly the honorable thing to do. But one cannot always control one's feelings. And to be quite honest, I'm glad of it. I know you were determined not to love again. Even I was not entirely certain you'd ever recover from your loss."

"I'm not sure I have, Hamilton. Certainly I had begun to. The wound seems to have opened anew now. I'm reliving it again."

"And what of Miss Durham? Are you certain for which one he has come?"

"I can't be certain of anything. It did seem, as I said, he had come to call on the elder sister. Perhaps he doesn't know. Perhaps I've changed his mind!"

"He saw your attachment? You are usually so guarded. Perhaps, after all, it was hers he saw."

"That is kind of you to say, but I don't think so. I have formed a connection with her that isn't there with the other. It is a confidence, is all, a friendship and a trust. We had a few confidential words the night of his arrival. It would not be difficult to make more of it than it was."

"Or to make of it what it truly was."

"You are not helping matters, Hamilton."

"I beg your pardon. What of her, then? Can you discern any preference for him?"

Daniel sighed. "She is unused to the attention. She is grateful for it and yet reluctant as well. Any attention he does pay her will likely be met by a great deal of opposition from her sister."

"And what of her feelings for you? Has she anything to return for your regard?"

"I don't know. I had begun to think so. I'm not so certain now."

"Do you not think you had best find out?"

Daniel knew the answer but was avoiding it. "I don't know," he answered at last. "I have workmen coming. The house will soon be under construction. I thought I might wait a few weeks, perhaps a month..."

"I don't understand you," Charlie said and closed his eyes. "You say you cannot leave her there, and yet you make plans to remain here."

"What am I to do?"

"Go. Find her out. Find out, if you can, how she feels about you. If she has feelings, talk to her father. Do *something*, Holbrook. The mistake you made last time was not in not marrying the woman you loved when she might have been yours, it was in waiting too long to make the decision to do it."

Daniel sat again. The dog rested its head on his knee and looked up at him. Daniel rested his hand on its head absentmindedly.

"If there is nothing on her side," Hamilton continued, "it will be at an end and there will be no harm in leaving. If there is, then perhaps you ought to explain—"

"No. I can't tell her that."

"Why not?"

"How do I explain what I did? How do I make her understand? She is so young, so innocent. When I think what I have done with my life, Hamilton, I wonder how I even dare to presume to sit in the same room with her. She wants a noble heart to love her... A noble heart does not abandon the woman he loves."

"Holbrook, you are too hard on yourself."

"I'm not hard enough! And perhaps that's why I should go. If she laughs at me, I have asked for it. If she despises me for my presumptuousness, I deserve it."

"You don't have to make any declarations, you know. Feel her out. It cannot hurt. I think you owe it to yourself. And if, like you say, you fear it is history repeating itself, if you think there is even the slightest chance she feels something for you, you absolutely owe it to her, do you see? And you owe it to yourself, as well."

Daniel thought a moment and at last nodded his head. The idea of her accepting him made him a little giddy. The idea that Emerson sat in the background, ready to devour any good thing Daniel presumed to want, made him violently angry.

"Go." Hamilton stood and handed Daniel a card. "Write to me here. I want to hear from you within the week."

Daniel took the card and examined it. "Newhaven House? What is this? Is this where you live?"

"I'm helping out, in a manner of speaking. I'm not staying there, but I'm nearby. If you write, I'll get it."

"It sounds like the name of a lying-in house."

"It is. We'll talk soon, shall we?"

"Are you not taking the dog?"

"Oh, no. I brought him for you. I can't have a dog that size in the city."

"And I can?"

"You're here. Or in Surrey. I rather think Jupiter would like Surrey."

"Jupiter?"

"Within the week, Holbrook," he reminded him and was gone.

Daniel followed Hamilton into the entrance hall and there remained, looking alternately through the still open doorway, then at the card in his hand, and then at the dog who was yet at his side.

"Jupiter, is it? I hope you'll not prove to be trouble."

The dog wagged his tail and then sat.

"Reformed, are you? Aren't we both!"

Chapter twenty-three

A LATE SUMMER STORM HAD passed overnight, and the grass on the lawn was wet and glistening. Within, all was still. It seemed *that* storm had passed, as well. Beth had come to bed very late, and though Laynie had stayed awake, anxiously waiting to learn what—and who—had been the source of her father's anger, Beth would tell her nothing.

"Good night, Laynie," was the only return she received for her questions.

This morning her sister was nowhere to be found. The house was empty, save for a quietly bustling Mrs. Fowler who was just cleaning up breakfast.

"You've nearly missed it," she said upon observing Laynie in the dining room doorway. "I'll just fix you a plate."

"Thank you, Mrs. Fowler," Laynie said and sat down at the table. "Is Papa at home?"

"He's gone out for a walk in the wet," she answered. "I hope he doesn't catch a cold. I don't know that I'm up to playing nurse on top of all my other duties."

"It's too warm for that, I'm sure. Besides, you were an excellent nurse to me when I was ill."

"Yes, my dear, but that is because you are an excellent patient. Your father, now..." she said and tisked what she felt too disrespectful to say outright.

Mrs. Fowler set Laynie's plate before her and then took up the rest of the dishes to carry out of the room, leaving Laynie alone with her thoughts and a soft-boiled egg. She cracked the shell with her spoon and heard the door open.

"Papa, is that you?" she said and arose to see. It was he. He was sitting in a chair in the foyer pulling his boots off and leaving bits of grass and dirt on the carpet as he did.

"Ah, good morning, my dear. How are you today?"

"I'm all right Papa. … How are you?"

"Hmm!" he answered.

"Papa?"

"Have you eaten?" he asked her.

"I'm doing it now."

"Good. Good. I think I'd like a word with you when you've finished."

"I can come now."

Having removed his boots he looked up at her as he sat in his stocking feet. "I can wait."

"I'm not sure I can, Papa. I'm awfully anxious about last night."

"Are you?"

She nodded.

He put his slippers on and arose. "Very well. We might as well have an end of the unpleasantness as soon as may be. Come along." And he led her to the study, where he gestured for her to sit and where he stood looking out of the window for a very long time, while Laynie waited as patiently as she could manage.

At last he turned to her, his hands folded behind his back. He clasped and unclasped them again. "I'm disappointed in you, my girl."

"Are you, Papa?"

"I am."

"Will you tell me why?"

He was silent again as he walked back and forth between his desk and the window. At last he stopped and looked at her. "I was very plain, was I not, when Mr. Holbrook first came, that you were not to play the minx with him?"

"You were, Papa, but I don't—"

"It is not always possible to know whom to trust in this world," he said and left Laynie wondering if the two things were connected. "You are very young, my dear, and very inexperienced with the world

289

and the ways of men. You do not—cannot—know what danger you were flirting with."

"Danger?" she said, uncomprehending. "I never flirted with Mr. Holbrook, Papa. It wasn't like that."

"He is not to be returning. I have dismissed him."

"Papa...?"

"We have been deceived in him. I have this very morning sent a letter that will end the matter once and for all, and that is all I wish to say regarding the matter. It is at an end."

"But, Papa!"

"That's an end of it, I said! Though there is one other matter I wish to discuss with you."

Laynie did not answer, but waited.

"Mr. Emerson has—"

"Is he the one who has turned you against Mr. Holbrook?"

Her father gave her a narrow, warning look. "Mr. Emerson," he continued, "has spoken to me. He has declared himself quite attached to you."

"To me?"

"You sound surprised."

"I am."

"I'm sure we all expected that he would choose Beth, but it seems that, by some stroke of good luck, it is you he wants."

"Papa, I don't under—"

"He has been quite discouraged by your behavior the other night. I realize you were not yourself, but I wish you would take a minute, Laynie, and put his feelings before your own. I think you would find it the proper way to treat a gentleman freshly bereaved and only just finding the courage—and incentive—to try once more for the happiness so cruelly robbed of him. Your quitting the table last night was both insensitive and rude. If I had realized the extent of his injuries and the torment he was suffering—for you!–I never would have allowed it. You *will* be more encouraging the next time we have the honor of receiving him."

"Papa, I hardly know him. *You* hardly know him."

"That's precisely why he has come. So that we might get to know him. So that you might have the opportunity to prove to him—if you can manage it—that he was not wrong in singling you out."

"Papa, tell me, please, what did he tell you regarding Mr. Hol—"

"I told you we've made an end of that subject, Alayna! Now you will be kind to Mr. Emerson, and you will listen to all he has to say, and you will consider very carefully the honor he is prepared to pay you. It is the very least you can do for all the trouble you have caused—or might have caused—in your reckless flirtations with men you have no business associating with. Do you understand me?"

"Yes, Papa," Laynie answered meekly. "I believe so."

"Good. Now go and let's hope he will forgive you and that you have not ruined all your chances already."

Laynie had no voice left to answer. She turned from the room and closed the door between herself and her father. She stood there and leaned against it.

So Mr. Holbrook was not to return. Not ever. What could he possibly have done to be dismissed so readily and without the opportunity of defending himself? A week ago, perhaps two, she might have reveled in the idea of winning the regard of someone like Mr. Emerson. Now she could only think what she had lost in the trade. And what was that? The echo of Beth's question knelled in her ears. What was he? What might he be to her? She could not answer these questions still. She wouldn't! What was the point?

She heard the sound of the door again and sniffed back her tears. What would Beth think of her father's news as it concerned herself and Mr. Emerson? Or had she been given a clue of that already? Perhaps that was the reason for Beth's reticence last night. Should she face her now and find out for certain? Perhaps she ought to go to her room and prepare herself for her guest—in the uncertain event he should come. Or ought she to try to find something more useful to do while she walked the tightrope that was her duty to her father and her desire to preserve her sister's love? She went to the boot room where she gathered her gardening apron, her gloves, hat, and boots, and went outside to plant boxwoods in holes dug for her by a man she had once had the pleasure of calling a friend. Once. But no more.

Mr. Emerson did not come that day, nor even the next. It was only on the third day following her father's admonition, when nerves were well and truly frayed and the idea had settled uncomfortably upon them that he might not come at all, that at last he arrived. He found her working in the garden.

"What are you doing playing in the dirt, Miss Durham?"

"I'm not playing. I'm gardening." She arose to show him what she had done and what she planned yet to do, but he was not listening.

"Are you not interested in gardening?"

"Forgive me if I find you utterly distracting. You have dirt on your face. Did you know?"

She covered one cheek—the cheek that had once before been found dirt-stained—with her gloved hand.

He laughed. "Wrong cheek," he said. "Will you go in, please, and freshen up? I'll wait."

"Very well," she said and returned indoors and to her room where she washed and changed and repinned her hair, all the time feeling very anxious. It was not exactly the sort of comfortable nervousness she had felt in Mr. Holbrook's presence. This was exciting, even frightening, in an almost nauseating way. The pressure to accept him for her father's sake was so immensely high. The pressure to refuse him for her sister's was equally great. It yet remained her decision, however, and it could not be made until she knew her own feelings on the matter. If only she trusted them as she used to do.

Laynie returned downstairs and stopped at the dining room door. She could see Mr. Emerson idly strolling through the garden. There was something about his presence there that seemed an invasion—a corruption of a memory she preferred to keep untainted. Perhaps she might persuade him to sit beneath the beech tree, but that was little better.

He saw her and left the enclosed formal garden to approach her. "That's much better. But why do you linger in the doorway?" he asked her. "Are you afraid of me?"

"Certainly not," she answered and stepped out onto the grass. He offered his hand; she took his arm. A fluttering of curtain caught her eye. An indication they were being observed from within. Beth, no doubt.

"Shall we walk?"

"Yes, all right," she said.

"Where?"

"I'll let you choose."

They proceeded down the tree-lined lane and stopped again at the road. He looked one way and then the other. "Where does that go?" he asked, looking up toward the path that led to the precipice.

"Hangman's Hill. It's haunted," she said.

"I'm even more intrigued. Is it a difficult climb?"

"In places."

"Are you afraid?" he asked her again. She was beginning to think it was an emotion he wished to encourage in her.

She looked at him a moment. She was not going to the precipice with him. That was her place alone. She nodded her answer.

"Hmmm," he said, observably disappointed. "We might walk toward the village. Perhaps there is something you need there."

She had been thinking about the silk shawl her sister had suggested for her. The temptation to go and look was tempered by the idea that they would no doubt be seen walking out, alone and un-chaperoned.

"There is a pleasant walking path beside the stream," was her suggestion.

Once more he looked a little disappointed, but mercifully he offered no argument. They walked on together in that direction, turning right at the road rather than left toward the village and, beyond that, Elverton.

"Forgive me if I observe that you do not seem as comfortable in my company as you were last time we met."

"That was before you came to cause an upset, Mr. Emerson."

"An upset? You mean that fellow, Holbrook?"

"My friend—and my father's—yes."

"Did your father tell you why he is to be dismissed?"

"He said Mr. Holbrook betrayed him. But he would tell me no more than that. Will you?"

"It isn't the sort of story one relates with pleasure. It isn't a story for genteel company."

"I want to know."

He looked at her a long moment. "Suffice it to say you have had a lucky escape."

"But from what? Papa blames me, I think, for encouraging his attention. What attention he did pay me was never exaggerated. He never betrayed my father's trust in any way that I can see."

"Oh, Miss Durham, you *are* very naïve!"

They came upon the stream and stopped a moment to admire it as the water rippled past almost silently.

"Am I?" she answered him after a moment of thought. "I hope I am if I do not believe everyone capable of evil designs. I was never uncomfortable in *his* presence." She wished to make a point, but it did not seem as though he picked up on the hint.

"And that is the greatest deception!" he said. "He has fooled you, and your father too, into thinking him trustworthy when he is anything but."

"But in what way did he betray that trust? I don't understand."

"Well, thank heaven for that!"

"Mr. Emerson…?"

"Miss Durham," he said and led her onward down the path. "The mere mention of that man's name brings up such unpleasant memories. Won't you spare me and let us speak of other things?"

"Just tell me, please," Laynie begged him, "that he has not gone away because of me."

"Why should it be because of you?" he asked and seemed to be considering the idea seriously.

"Clearly there is some history between you, but that is in the past, is it not? Tell me, then, that you did not vilify him to my father simply because you saw him as a threat."

He looked at her a moment and laughed. "I have no reason to consider him a rival. Not when I know that my right to try for you trumps his. It's possible you tried for him, despite your father's cautions against it."

"I didn't."

"Well, then, let us all be grateful. How much greater the trouble for him if you had, and how much greater the danger for you."

"That's just it. I don't see the danger."

"Trust me, Miss Durham, you do not know the world as I know it. Not everyone is worthy of your trust."

She looked at him, desperate to understand the extent of Mr. Holbrook's supposed guilt, and fearing it would never be.

"Do you know what I think, Miss Durham?" he said, leaning closer to speak more confidentially, though there was no one around to overhear them. "I think you are in love with Mr. Holbrook."

"I told you before, sir, I'm not!"

"No? Then why this insatiable need to defend him? Why this insistence in speaking of him when I've told you quite plainly it causes me great trouble of spirit to do it?"

Laynie stopped and looked at the ground around her, at the late summer flowers that had outlived their prime.

He held out his hand once more to her. "You owe me an apology, I think."

She looked at that hand and then up at him and his dimpled grin. "Do I?" Perhaps she did, but she did not feel very apologetic.

"You lied to me, you know? At least you were not entirely honest when last we met in Gravesend."

"Oh?" she asked and did not understand.

"We had spoken of your father's plans for you. For you, that is, and Mr. Vaughn."

"That was not a lie."

"But you knew very well that you did not intend to accept him."

"That doesn't mean my father—or even Lady Vaughn, who, as far as I can tell, is on her deathbed—would not have insisted upon it. I was powerless to deny it."

"Perhaps," he said. "But I'm inclined to think you did not want to do it."

"It may surprise you to know, Mr. Emerson, that I consider more than just myself in these matters. You know how tenuous my relationship is with my sister. You know what heartache you caused my cousin."

"And do you not think of me and my heartache?"

Her hand was in his now. She freed it and walked on. It was too soon for this. She was not certain she liked Mr. Emerson much less could learn to love him. He was attractive, yes, and she felt herself being pulled toward him. His charm, his attentiveness, his very speech seemed to poke and prod at an aching inside her, an emptiness of which she had never before this week been aware.

"Miss Durham," he said, catching up to her. He was smiling, but it was one of his sad, lonely smiles that expressed more pain than pleasure. "Are you so determined to break my heart?"

"What of Beth? I believe you came here to call upon her. What was it that made you decide you would rather try for me?"

"I told you. It was the very fact that I had thought you unavailable to me that I didn't do it in the first place. And when I learned that it was not quite so... Forgive me, if you deem my actions cruel as they relate to your sister. Miss Durham...Laynie...I find I cannot help myself. Perhaps I did persuade your sister to offer the invitation to come. I wanted to be near you. If she was as close as I could get, then so be it."

"Mr. Emerson!"

"Well, it's true. You asked, and I think you are too perspicacious to be lied to. When I arrived and realized things were not quite as I had been led to believe, forgive me, Miss Durham, if I considered it a second chance to have my first hope realized."

"Don't think that just because the chess pieces have moved that your way is quite clear."

He glowered. "I hope you are not speaking of Mr. Holbrook again."

"That is not what I meant at all."

"Yes it is. Admit it. You made a run at him. He, fortunately for you, hesitated just long enough that someone—you'll remember one day that it was me who rescued you, though you may be ungrateful for it now—came along and exposed him for the monster he is. And now you want to tell me that I don't have a chance because you have thrown your heart away on *him*?"

Until that moment, Laynie had refused to believe that it was in any way possible she had been wrong to trust Mr. Holbrook. But now, seeing the anger, the torment and anguish on Mr. Emerson's face, she was forced to consider that it was just possible. She hardly knew Mr. Holbrook, after all. For all the time they had spent together, she knew nothing of his history. Her pride in this instance was a difficult thing to swallow. But swallow it, it seemed, she must. Her heart, despite her efforts to withhold it, reached out to him.

"Miss Durham," he said, turning pleading blue eyes upon her. "Please give me a chance. You owe me that much. It is not so great a thing I'm asking for. Won't you?"

"Yes," she said, at last having swallowed down that burden and in doing so feeling her heart and spirit relent. "Yes, of course."

"Thank you," he said and smiled briefly. He reclaimed her hand and kissed it, then let it go. And together they finished their walk along the stream, speaking of idle, pleasant things now, of Surrey and Box Hill and fishing, and of trivialities too unimportant to recount, but which, little by little, began to endear him to her, and which persuaded her to believe she was growing to know and understand him. And, yes, even to trust him.

Her heart was feeling very light indeed when they returned to the house. The weight of her cares descended, however, with the dropping of the drawing room curtain.

Beth was watching them.

"Perhaps we had best part here," he suggested with apparent regret and with a glance in the direction of the drawing room window. "Forgive me if I play the coward, but I do like to avoid a storm when I can help it."

"I quite understand, Mr. Emerson. Good day."

He bowed, took her hand, and graced her with a look that suggested he would much rather part with a gesture more meaningful, and then he retraced his steps down the drive on his way back to the village.

Laynie entered the house. She stopped to stand at the drawing room door and waited for Beth to have her say.

"Did you have a nice walk?" she inquired as she put away her sewing things. By all appearances it seemed she had not moved from her chair all morning.

"Yes, very pleasant," Laynie answered.

"Where did you go?"

"Along the stream, toward the bridge, though not so far as that."

"I see. Lunch, I believe, is ready."

"Is it?" Laynie asked and watched as Beth arose from her place. Were they to eat together? And were they to do it so companionably? Where was Beth's anger? Where was her jealousy?

Laynie moved as if to go to the dining room but hesitated. "Yes, do go in," Beth said, observing her uncertainty. "You must be hungry."

She followed her sister's direction, but Beth only followed her as far as the foyer, where she began preparing herself to go out of doors.

Laynie said nothing, only watched as Beth put on her hat and a shawl and then her gloves.

"I won't be long," she said and then left the house, leaving Laynie puzzled and not a little anxious.

* * *

"Mr. Emerson?"

Emerson turned at the sound of his name. He was not entirely disappointed to see Beth. There was bound to be a bit of uncomfortableness at first, but he was confident he could overcome it.

"Miss Durham. How are you today?"

"Did you intend to leave without saying hello?"

"I thought it best to avoid a scene."

"You are very confident in your ability to rouse me."

"I'm merely confident in your propensity to be roused."

"With or without reason?"

"I won't deny you may have reason, just at present. I know what it looks like."

"I'm sure it looks no less than what it is. My father has chosen you as the potential suitor for my sister's hand. I should congratulate you, I suppose. I'd say it's quite an accomplishment but as my father would offer Laynie to practically anyone it isn't quite that. Persuading her to return your 'regard', however, will be. And so I'll reserve the con-gratulations until you've actually done it."

"It's true your sister does appear to be a little more selective than your father."

"She's making things difficult for you. I'm glad of it."

"You are angry. I don't blame you. I may look the roving cad to you, but I do have a good explanation."

"You needn't explain anything to me, Mr. Emerson, you are in a hurry to be married and are simply searching out your easiest target. You were wise to choose Laynie, as you have my father's ready and willing support. I wish I could say I'm convinced you have hers. Do you love my sister, Mr. Emerson?"

"To be quite honest, it's a little too early to say. But I do know when a woman is in grave peril and when she is determined to put herself in harm's way. Until I know my mind for certain, I thought it best to do what I could to preserve her from certain destruction."

"You have a talent for painting yourself as a hero, Mr. Emerson, when you appear to be behaving with dubious intentions. Perhaps you will do me the kindness of explaining just why you felt Mr. Holbrook so eager to condemn my sister to ruin. I have heard, in vague details, of what it is he is supposedly guilty. Is he a serial rogue, or does he simply choose to prey upon those to whom you are drawn?"

"It's a worthy question. I wish I had an answer; I don't. All I know is that he was the cause of my tragic loss, and during his time abroad he very well might have been the cause of countless others. If I had thought her safe from him have no doubt I would have no cause to regret my words to you now."

"And do you?"

"I can't court you both, can I?"

"No, I suppose not."

Beth appeared really to regret it and so did he. "Why?" she asked him.

"I just told you."

"No. Why the hurry? I know what it is like to be uncertain. I have been playing Harry along for such a long time now that I have no reason to suppose I don't deserve the same. But you are in a great haste to remarry, and I want to know why. I know desperation when I see it. This is something else."

"It's not something I like to speak of. It rather puts me at a disadvantage. But you are a young lady of some intelligence. No doubt you can put the pieces together for yourself."

"You mentioned an inheritance. Has that something to do with it?"

"You see? I knew you were very smart. It's true. Should I agree to submit to certain conditions, then I stand to inherit my uncle's fortune and his estate in Kent. His own son died rather unexpectedly, and so I am next in line. He did not approve of my first marriage and so he has made the inheritance conditional on my marrying again. Only this time it is to be done properly, having chosen a respectable woman whom I am to marry publicly and without the vaguest hint of scandal."

"Such as making overtures to one woman, perhaps, and then begging permission to court her sister?"

She understood the matter better than he supposed. He smiled his acknowledgement. It was a stiff, uncomfortable, gesture.

"That does not explain your hurry."

"He is ill, my uncle. Possibly—probably—gravely so. He has been given a year to live. He wants to see it done before he dies. At which time, if I have not married and with his approval, I get nothing."

"I see," she said.

"I'm taking a chance, I know. I think your sister does not give her heart readily. But then neither do you, Miss Durham. Am I mistaken?"

She looked down at her folded hands. Had he been mistaken?

"Miss Durham?"

"I think," she said at last, "I would have said 'no' before these last few weeks."

Was she saying what he thought she was saying? Had he moved her? And had he been just a little hasty in securing himself to Laynie? Holbrook might have been dispensed with without having taken it so far as that.

She looked up at him. "Now, I'm not so certain."

The temptation was too great. He took her hand and pressed it to his chest. As he had hoped, the rest of her came with it.

"Don't dismiss me just yet," she begged him.

"I've already spoken to your father. I confess I did suggest my mind was not entirely made up."

She looked at him, hope swimming in her eyes.

"How could I be certain of anything? The two of you together are enough to make a man mad." He attempted to kiss her, but she pulled herself away from him.

"We do not quite want that, Mr. Emerson," she said with a coy smile and then turned from him to return to her home. She cast another look over her shoulder. "We only don't want you to give up on us quite yet."

"No," he said and smiled to himself. This was possibly very dangerous ground. He could manage it though. Especially now Holbrook was out of the way. He had managed far worse, after all. Perhaps was managing it still.

But that couldn't go on forever, could it?

* * *

Harold Vaughn weighed the riding crop in his hand. He swung it from side to side, then made a quick swipe with it. To be honest, it was not his horse he imagined striking. For a moment it was not even a riding crop but a foil. He stabbed a dress form and sent it rocking on its stand. He righted it as the shopkeeper eyed him narrowly.

Vaughn paid for the whip and left the shop. This was his only errand in Ashworth today and yet the thought of striking that Emerson fellow to the ground was so great a temptation that he dismounted his horse nearly the moment he had mounted.

The inn was across the street. He might just inquire if Emerson was in. If he wasn't, there was no harm done. If he was...? Well, it would be a convenient opportunity to learn what the fellow was about.

The innkeeper was signing in a guest when Vaughn entered. The gentleman scrawled his name and took the key handed him. He nodded politely to Vaughn before following the porter to his room.

At last the innkeeper greeted him with a smile. "Good day, Mr. Vaughn. What can I do for you?"

"Do you have a Mr. Emerson staying with you?"

The innkeeper's smile faded. "He was, yes."

"Was? Has he gone?" And Vaughn felt a sudden surge of exultation.

"He comes and goes. But he won't be lodging with me again if he doesn't square up with that gentleman there. His last lodging has sent a bailiff." The innkeeper nodded to a man in tweed who was sitting in the back of the room reading over a newspaper and nursing a pint of ale.

"He's been here all morning, and he ain't going nowhere either until he's been paid. You can tell your friend that when he's paid *that* fellow," he said with a nod that indicated the bailiff, "he can pay *me* next or find somewhere else to eat and sleep."

"He's no friend of mine," Vaughn said, feeling it necessary to explain how the matter truly stood. "Merely an acquaintance."

"Does he owe you, too?"

"I'm not sure yet," Vaughn said and approached the bailiff. He drew out a chair opposite him but did not sit. "You have some business with Mr. Emerson," Vaughn said to him.

"Are you acquainted with him?"

"I am. What is the nature of your business?"

The bailiff looked at him dubiously but at last answered. "Mr. Emerson is in the habit of leaving his rooms without settling his bills, it seems."

"What does he owe?"

"Are you offering to pay?"

"Perhaps." But why would he do it? Not as a favor, that was for certain. He wanted the fellow gone, certainly, which leaving him to find this man waiting for him might accomplish very nicely. But Mr. Emerson had raised some very interesting questions upon his arrival and Vaughn wanted them answered. He observed the bailiff, his left leg resting on a small chest, his right arm on a pile of letters.

"Are those his effects?"

"They are and restorable to the owner—or to his representative—" he added with a nod in Vaughn's direction, "upon settlement."

The temptation to pay the bill simply to inspect Mr. Emerson's things was almost too great to resist. And yet it was hardly honorable. Did he care? Well…yes, and perhaps a little too much to do him good at present.

"May I see?"

The box slid further beneath the bailiff's chair.

"Might I at least examine the letters?" Vaughn tried again. "They might not be really his, after all. How do I know we are talking about the same person?"

"Mr. Emerson? Mr. Frederick Emerson?"

But Vaughn did not remember his first name and so could not respond in the affirmative. He chose, therefore, not to respond at all.

The bailiff, without taking his eyes off Vaughn, slid the letters toward him.

They were all addressed to an F. Emerson. There was one from Gravesend written in a feminine hand. Beth's cousin? There was one from London. His uncle, presumably. Another not addressed to Emerson at all, but addressed by him and returned. The address puzzled him, the name too. There was no reason he should recognize it, and yet there seemed something strangely familiar about it.

The bailiff cleared his throat and snatched the letters back. He held out his hand for payment. Vaughn deliberated a moment more, but at last paid him. Mr. Emerson's personal effects were now his to dispose of. By law he was supposed to return them. He certainly did not want them for himself, but he could not exactly just hand them back over without some explanation. Vaughn eyed the letter again. Did he dare open it? No. No he would not sink so low. It seemed to him the information on the envelope would be enough to give him a place to start. He copied it down, as precisely and exactly as he could manage, and then returned the entirety of Mr. Emerson's things to the inn-keeper.

"Are you going to pay my bill, too?" the man asked him.

"No," Vaughn, said. "I think I had better not. But I'll pay you thrice what he owes you presently if you promise to forget I was ever here."

"How do I explain these?" he said, gesturing toward the case and stack of mail.

"That's for you to figure out. You're a clever fellow. Do you want the money or not?"

The innkeeper did not pause to think. He nodded. Vaughn paid him and quit the inn, a facsimile of the returned envelope tucked safely into his pocket.

Chapter twenty-four

THE EFFECTS OF LAYNIE'S WALK with Mr. Emerson were multiple and swiftly changing. At first she had returned home light as a feather, imagining at last that someone appreciated and valued her as something necessary to their happiness. That feeling, upon seeing her sister leave the house, changed to one of increasing anxiety. It did not turn to jealousy as she expected it to do, as she began to hope—by the second day following, wherein Beth took a few more mysterious outings—that it would. By the third day the swelling of her heart had suffused and had left an emptiness larger than that which Mr. Emerson's admiration had temporarily filled. Had Mr. Emerson persuaded her to care so greatly for him that his absence was as a hollow in the very center of her being? Possibly. But if so, why was it not he she was thinking of in his absence? Why was it not he that made her solitary hours—something she usually took great pleasure in—feel like condemning and gnawing lonesomeness, made her feel as though she would shrink into herself until there was nothing to see or hear of her, or even to remember?

She had been waiting at home for him to call again, waiting for the reassurance his presence might offer her. But she could bear it no longer. She must be out of the house today. The tranquility of the precipice had been calling her name since she had returned from Gravesend. A great deal of rain had fallen lately and so she had put the walk off. But the sun was shining brightly today, the weather had begun to cool, and it would be a perfect day for such a long-awaited outing.

Before leaving the house she collected her things: a book and her hat. She ought to tell Papa, but it was just possible he would prefer her to spend another day waiting for her absent suitor. She wouldn't spoil another day indoors—not another hour. And so she left without telling a soul.

Though her ankle was now quite sound, the rain had made the path slippery in places. She tucked her book beneath one arm and found a sturdy stick to help her, and with it in hand, she picked her way carefully up the trail. The exercise was exhilarating. The concentration it required almost kept her mind from her worries. At least it was some distraction. Upon reaching the place where the path became shaded by the trees, Laynie looked back. The view of her home from here was quite picturesque and she was reminded how grateful she ought to be to live in such quaint comfort with so many to love her. Perhaps it was ungrateful of her to feel so empty now. But though a desire to love and be loved had been awakened in her she could imagine nothing that would persuade her to wish to leave her home.

She continued on along the tree-shaded path, watching carefully for exposed roots and fallen limbs. Now and then she found it necessary to jump over a little rivulet as it crossed the way At last she reached the top, breathless from the effort and from the view. But then the view always managed to take her breath away. A breeze blew, cooling her, and she let it whip her hair and her skirts about as she stood there admiring the countryside below. She was spent from the climb and so she crossed to the other side of an overhanging rock to sit in the shade of it. And there she rested as she continued to admire the glorious landscape she was fortunate enough to call home. In time she remembered her book, but she no longer wished to read. She was content just to sit here and look out at the world, so peaceful from this height and distance, not thinking, not worrying, just…being. She had not been sleeping well, and with the subsiding of her anxiety came a profound sense of fatigue. She at last gave into the temptation to lie down in the grass, and there she began to doze.

* * *

Daniel had arrived in Surrey with the counsel Charles Hamilton had given him a week ago pounding in his ears. He had come to see just where things stood—or might stand—were he to try for Laynie's heart. He had brought Jupiter with him. Upon leaving the station, Daniel unleashed the dog and let him run ahead on his own. He had been trusted at Brookdale never to run too far ahead and always to come back when called, and so Daniel had no reason to believe his behavior would alter with the altering of location. He was proved wrong when, upon reaching the drive that led to the Bowery, Jupiter did not stop but, with his nose to the ground and his tail wagging, continued on unheeding. He was determined to follow his own course now and would not heed Daniel's calling. He veered from the road to follow a trail that wound up a steep hillside and through the trees. With Jupiter playing deaf, Daniel was powerless to do other than follow.

Upon reaching the top of the hillside, Daniel stopped to admire the view while Jupiter ambled about, sniffing at the ground and relieving himself on the occasional tree. Views such as this were wasted on dogs, but Daniel was awestruck.

Jupiter, it seemed, was preoccupied with something he had found on the other side of a great rock that jutted out over the precipice ledge, his tail wagging frantically with excitement. Daniel approached the dog, making his way around the rock, and doing so cautiously in case it proved to be some wild animal, cornered and prepared to defend itself. What he found quite shocked him. Laynie was there, lying in the grass. Had she fallen? Was she alive? Yes, quite alive, it seemed, and he released a breath of air. He had been just about to do something very foolish: raise her up in his arms, press his head to her chest, speak words he had thought but had never dared to utter.

She stirred in time to save him from his foolishness. Her hand brushed Jupiter's wet nose from her face, and she opened her eyes. "Hello," she said to the dog, completely unafraid.

"Hello," Daniel said, making his own presence known. "You had me frightened for a moment."

"Mr. Holbrook!" she said and raised herself.

He offered his hand to help her and she held onto it a little longer than required.

"I am so immensely glad to see you!" she said to him. "But how did you know to find me here?"

"I didn't. Jupiter led the way. I simply followed."

"Jupiter?" she said and seemed impressed by both the dog and his name. "Is he yours?"

"He is not much accustomed to the city."

"No. I can imagine. And you brought him here?"

"I had thought you might like him. He's quite gentle."

"I can see that," she said and stroked his head.

He watched her admiring the dog, while the dog, in turn, showed his gratitude by letting her. He observed her disheveled state—strands of hair blowing about her face and falling over her shoulders, grass poking out all around her head and stuck to her clothes. And she entirely unconcerned. The effect was bewitching.

At last she looked up at him. "I'm so glad to see you, Mr. Holbrook. Have you come to speak with Papa?"

Did she understand his purpose in coming? And how could she? How could she know that, should she give him any encouragement at all, he would make his confession to her father and request the privilege of courting her? Was this not all the encouragement he needed?

"Yes," he answered cautiously.

She sat down upon the grass and continued petting the dog, watching Jupiter as she spoke to Daniel. "I'm afraid Papa is quite angry with you."

He was instantly deflated. "For keeping away? I apologize. I had some pressing business to attend to. I've been putting it off, and—"

"Mr. Emerson has spoken to him of you."

Daniel was taken aback, though perhaps he should have expected something like this. He sat down upon a large rock and waited for her to say more.

"I don't know what he told him, but the result is that Papa feels betrayed."

"Betrayed by me?" he said, indignant. "In what possible way?"

"I'm afraid it may have something to do with me," she said, glancing at him. And then, coloring, turned back to the dog once more.

He felt guilt and shame and elation wash over him all at once.

"Of course it isn't true."

Wasn't it, though?

"I think perhaps Mr. Emerson observed something he imagined to be more than it was. Between you and me, I mean."

"I understand you."

"I'm quite embarrassed to mention it. It is awkward."

"Don't be. It needn't be."

"We are friends, still, I hope. That won't change?"

Again Daniel did not answer her. If her father was angry, what chance was there of maintaining the friendship he had managed to form with her?

"That isn't all, though. At least, I don't think it is. There is a history between you. I think Mr. Emerson must have related some part of it. I do wish you had told me what it was. Is it so condemning as to persuade my father that you cannot be trusted?"

He looked down at her. She was smiling through the question but he could see real anxiety in her eyes. Was it? Well, certainly Mr. Emerson had twisted it around to sound as condemning as possible. But what could he offer in explanation? Anything that would absolve him? No. "Yes," he answered. "Quite possibly."

His answer plainly disappointed her. She looked down at her hands which she folded in her lap. There was a leaf stuck in her hair, dangling just above her ear, blowing and spinning in the breeze. He wished to pull it free but dared not do it. He had no right to touch her. Perhaps he was wrong to be sitting here now, however innocent his intentions. He took off his hat, laid it aside, and brushed a hand through his hair as the breeze cooled him.

"I am sorry," he said at last. "If I could go back, do things differently..." Then what? Then he would never have met Alayna Durham to begin with. Would he truly wish that? Impossible!

"I have trusted you," she said, her voice catching. "I have not done it unwisely, I hope?"

He lowered himself from the rock to the grass so that he was as near her as he dared. "You are, I think, a good judge of character," he said and waited for her to look at him. "Have I ever made you feel unsafe? Have I ever made you feel threatened? Have I ever imposed myself in any way?"

"No, never."

"Then remember it, I beg you, if ever my character is called into question, if it has been already. If you have known me to behave honorably, Miss Durham, please know it is not because there was nothing here to tempt me."

She looked at him and blinked. Did she understand him? He could not tell. She gave nothing away. "Will you remember it?"

"Yes," she said. "I will remember."

"When I first began coming," he went on, "your father asked me of my history. I did not wish to tell him. I see that I should have now. At the time it was too fresh, too painful to speak of. Being here, knowing your father, knowing you, it has helped me."

"I'm glad of it."

"I wish now I had told him."

"Would it have made a difference?"

"I believe so."

"Is it too late to tell your side of it?"

"I cannot know. If he will listen, it might be worth trying, but it is in the nature of man to believe the first version he hears of any story. I'm hardly innocent. I don't know that my deeds are forgivable. But I was young, impulsive, feeling myself entitled to the world and all the pleasures it had to offer. If only I could have known what pain it would bring, and not to myself alone."

"And I told you I did not believe a man could change," she said in self-condemnation.

"Some don't, and I hope you never forget it. Though, at the same time, I hope you never have cause to remember it." He looked at her. She appeared on the verge of tears and he wished with everything in him he could reach out to her, offer some comfort, some reassurance, offer some proof, any proof, of his honorable, if selfish, intentions toward her. But any move he made to win her heart now would only serve to prove whatever villainy Mr. Emerson had accused him of.

"Miss Durham," he said at last, unable to bear the silence. "I have disappointed you, and I'm sorry."

"No," she said, but he did not believe her. Her disappointment was too clearly written on her face.

"I think I have," he insisted solemnly.

A tear spilled and slipped down her cheek. She buried her face in her hands and cried as he watched her helplessly.

"Shall I go?" he asked her. It was that or take her in his arms. Perhaps, after all, she did not want him.

He really expected her to say yes, but she shook her head and held out a tear-dampened hand. He took it and held it, brushing the moisture dry with his thumb. He looked at it, small and slender and fine, and wondered that he had ever supposed it might be his. But he was holding it now. How long would this last? Mere seconds? Minutes? Who would be the next to hold it? Emerson? He couldn't bear the thought of it. If there was anything he could do to keep her from him, to preserve her, even if it was not for himself—or perhaps... He remembered Charlie's admonition. Was it not the very most of all his own hopes? If there was even a chance...

"I think, perhaps, I should speak with your father, Miss Durham."

She did not seem to hear him, or was slow to do it.

"Miss Durham? Laynie?"

She looked up at him, observed her hand in his, that which had been holding to him every bit as securely as he had held to her, and she removed it. He felt those precious fingers slip from his. But the faintest glimmer of hope was enough to suppress his fear—fear of failure, fear of losing his place here, of losing her.

"Did you hear me?"

"Yes," she said. "Do. Speak with him. Convince him you are not the villain Mr. Emerson would make you out to be."

"And if I can, would you grant me permission to speak to him on another matter?"

"Your employment?" she said and seemed not to understand him.

He laughed uncomfortably, nervously. "It's not my employment I meant." Silly, naïve, darling creature!

"Father has dismissed you. He sent a letter. Have you not received it?"

His hope was extinguished. "No," he answered cautiously. "I haven't been home in over a week. I've had business in Kent. I came straight here. Dismissed?"

"I'm so glad," she said and appeared truly relieved.

"Glad that I've been sacked, Miss Durham?"

"No. Of course not. Only that you did not come knowing you were not welcome."

He arose. He was no longer certain what to do. Was he un-welcomed by her father alone? She had given him no indication she did not wish to see him. Quite the reverse, in fact. But whatever connection there was between them there was apparently nothing like an understanding. She considered him a friend, unaware, it seemed, that he really could have any sincere feelings for her. She had been warned it was possible. Why was she so ready to dismiss it if she had plainly entertained the idea of his guilt in other matters? And yet, here she was, with him, alone and unafraid on a Surrey hillside. What was he to think? … What would her father think?

"I should go."

"No," she said and stood. "Not yet. If you are sent away…"

"Say it, Miss Durham," he said, frustrated with her inability to comprehend what he could not say, and even more frustrated to think she *might* understand him after all and yet lacked the courage to let him know it. "For heaven's sake, just say what you are thinking."

But she didn't. She swallowed it down, whatever it was.

"You are making it very difficult for me to know what to do."

"Speak with him. Do. Make him see."

"And what, precisely, am I to make him see?"

She gave him a look that suggested his question was foolish, that he already knew. "Make him see—at least to remember—that you are good and true and honorable."

"Am I?" And he really began to wonder.

"That he was not wrong to trust you."

Wasn't he? But he said nothing, only looked at her as she pierced him with pleading eyes that begged him for something he didn't understand. Did she want him to revoke what little of a confession he'd made? Was he to assure her father he had no feelings for her? Or perhaps to lie, to deny he had any history to be ashamed of at all. If that's what she wanted, it was quite impossible. Perhaps there was no hope for him. Perhaps he never ought to have come.

"Good bye, Miss Durham. I hope we shall see each other again."

"Mr. Holbrook," she said, stopping him.

He turned, but whatever it was she wished to say, she once again kept it to herself. She hesitated a moment, thinking, perhaps, of something else to say instead. She took a step forward. "At least let me walk with you."

"Yes, of course, if you wish."

They stood there for a moment longer, he looking at her, she returning his gaze for a moment before turning to look one last time at the view. She would see it again, even if he did not, but it was she he wished to remember. Her smile, her face, the length and curl of her hair, the way her eyes looked like two little replicas of the green-brown earth. Nothing else mattered but remembering her. And never for-getting.

"Shall we, then?" she asked him at last.

"Yes. I suppose so."

He did not offer his arm as they made their journey back down the hillside. He thought it best to keep some distance between them. He was mindful of her, however, and warned her of roots and of fallen limbs over which he helped her. He even had the rare and un-forgettable privilege of lifting her over a little stream. For a moment he held her as closely as he had ever imagined doing. And then he had to let her go again.

Near the bottom of the hill, just before the clearing, she stopped and turned to him. "Perhaps I should go on alone."

"I think that would be wise."

She said nothing for a moment, and then: "In case I do not get another chance, I wish you well, in whatever you do. Don't forget me."

"Impossible."

"If your efforts are unsuccessful, please know you will be very much missed."

Was she speaking for her father or for herself? He did not know quite what to say. He feared that to open his mouth would be to confess his every thought and feeling for her. This, here and now, was their ending. An ending before anything had begun. A warm friendship, several weeks of torment, and now...accusations that he could not say were entirely false and which must drive him from her perhaps forever.

"Stay, Jupiter," he said as she turned from him. He took hold of the dog's collar and watched her retreating figure as she made her way down the remainder of the trail. It was not until she had reached the drive and he could no longer see her through the trees that lined it that he continued onward, unable to guess what it was he was walking toward and praying for any opportunity to offer his own side of the story, for whatever it might be worth. He knew it would not be worth much. Perhaps once. Not now.

* * *

Laynie did not turn back upon leaving Mr. Holbrook. She did not dare. She was only barely managing to hold back the tears as it was. What a fool she had been to shed them in front of him! She might have made a greater fool yet of herself. To say more than she ought was always a temptation when she was with him. She had conquered it this time, thank heaven!

She was aware of him following her at some distance behind. She was aware of him watching her and wondered what he thought. How deeply did he regret? But was she not being a little selfish in her desire to be as greatly missed by him as he would be by her? It wasn't her society alone he would be separated from, but her father's too. She could not know how fond he was of her poor, doddering papa, but her father had grown to love Daniel Holbrook very much. How was it his opinion had been so thoroughly altered? She felt she knew the answer to that. Had her feelings not been manipulated as well?

She arrived before the house to find Mr. Emerson there, apparently disappointed to have to wait for her. "Where have you been?" he asked her. "I've been waiting this hour or more."

She wanted very much to point out to him that she had been waiting for him these last few days, but she had no strength for argument.

"Neither your father nor your sister have been able to account for your absence. They're quite worried, you know. I've been quite worried."

"I'm sorry."

"Look at you!" he said, suddenly and quite apparently alarmed at the sight of her. "Where have you been?"

313

She touched her hand to her hair and felt the leaves and grass that were stuck to it. She must have forgotten her hat at the precipice and her book, too. "I went for a walk and fell asleep."

"Do you typically wander off alone without—" Mr. Emerson stopped suddenly upon observing something over her shoulder. She did not have to look to know what—or who—it was.

"What are you doing here?" Mr. Emerson demanded of Mr. Holbrook. "How dare you show your face here!"

It seemed Jupiter did not like the sound of Mr. Emerson's voice and began barking loudly.

Laynie approached the dog and as she did he stopped his barking and began, instead, to pant and wag his tail. "I'll take him," she said to Mr. Holbrook. "Perhaps then you can go in and talk to Papa."

"What are you doing, Laynie?" Mr. Emerson said, using her Christian name for the first time and evidently trying to make a point in doing so. He took a step forward as if he meant to protect her, both from Mr. Holbrook and his dog, but he stopped again as the dog lunged toward him. He was quite safe, however, for both Mr. Holbrook and Laynie had a hold of the dog's collar, their hands touching, his almost holding hers as she held onto Jupiter. Why did she feel safer standing beside her father's former companion—a supposedly dan-gerous man—and hanging onto an apparently vicious animal than returning to Mr. Emerson's side? Was it instinct or sheer foolishness? She wished to believe in Mr. Holbrook, beyond that she knew nothing, really, of him or his supposedly scandalous history. Why did she keep forgetting that?

Mr. Emerson, too, seemed to make something significant of the sight of them together. "Wait just a minute," he said. "Are you just arriving now, Holbrook, or did you accompany Miss Durham on her...*walk*?" He said the last word as if he doubted very much it was the right one to use to describe what they had been doing together.

"I merely happened upon her."

Mr. Emerson blinked as if the pronouncement were a significant one. Whatever it was he meant to say next he was interrupted by her father, who stepped out of the house to see what the commotion was about.

"You, here?" he demanded upon seeing Daniel. "Why have you come? I believe I told you quite plainly I did not wish for you to return. Your employment is at an end, sir! And why do you look that way, Laynie? Have you had an accident?"

"No, Papa, I—"

But Mr. Emerson would not let her answer.

"Miss Durham and Mr. Holbrook are just now returning, *together*, from a long walk."

Mr. Durham looked at Emerson as he said this and then for a moment after, as if waiting to understand the implication of what was being said. Laynie herself was at a loss to understand how her walk, and Mr. Holbrook's happening to find her and to accompany her home, should be interpreted as something so villainous as Mr. Emerson seemed to wish to imply. And as her father evidently considered it now.

"That isn't exactly how it—" Mr. Holbrook began but was stopped as Mr. Durham put a hand up in the air.

"I have nothing to say to you, sir. Except," he said, reconsidering and approaching him, "except to say that you are no longer welcome here. You are forbidden from ever associating with me or my family again. If I should hear that you have so much as thought about my daughter, I will have the law on you. And I guarantee you, sir, if I find that one hand has been laid upon her…" But he was too angry to finish his threat.

"Papa! You are being unfair. Mr. Holbrook deserves an opportunity to answer the questions raised against his character. You have an obligation to listen to him."

"I owe him nothing, Alayna. Your trust is misplaced, but you and I will speak of this later. In the house with you."

"But, Papa!"

"In the house with you. Now!"

And so she went, her heart breaking for Mr. Holbrook. Her heart breaking, just perhaps, for herself. What was it she had done that was so very wrong? What was it Mr. Holbrook had done?

She approached the door to find it was open just a crack, the space occupied by a pair, perhaps two, of observing eyes. She reached for it as the space cleared. Mrs. Fowler opened the door for her as Mrs.

Sullivan scuttled back off toward the kitchen. Beth was standing in the foyer, her eyes large and glistening.

"Oh, Laynie!" she said and nothing more.

"What is it? What is the matter?"

Beth did not answer but took her by the arm and led her to the mirror where, for the first time, she was able to see the effects of her napping on the ever windy precipice. She was a little shocked at the sight of her reflection. She was a great deal embarrassed, too. Mr. Holbrook had seen her this way? What must he think of her!

"What happened, Laynie? Tell me."

"I went up to the precipice. That is all. I fell asleep and when I woke up, Mr. Holbrook and his dog were there. We spoke for a few moments, and then he walked me home."

"Are you certain, Laynie, that nothing more happened?"

"We shook hands. I—" But what more had happened? He had held her hand. Had she given it to him or had he taken it? She couldn't remember. But there was no use revealing so much. There was nothing to be ashamed of. Beth's question seemed to imply there was or might have been. It confused her and alarmed her at once.

Her father's railing had suddenly stopped. All was quiet. The dining room door opened and closed again. There was the mumbling of voices and then their retreat as Mr. Emerson followed her father to the study.

Laynie went to the door to peek out. Mr. Holbrook had gone. She was about to shut the door again when she saw something that made her heart leap. It was Jupiter, sitting on the other side of the gate and peering over it.

"Where are you going?" Beth called after her.

But she didn't answer. She merely walked down the path toward the gate, where Jupiter sat patiently waiting for her. Had Mr. Holbrook really gone without him?

"What on earth is that?" Beth said, having followed her out.

"It's Jupiter," was her simple answer, and she led him through the gate and up the walking path.

"You don't mean to bring him indoors, I hope?"

"I'm not going to leave him alone," she answered and led him past her sister and up the stairs.

"Why would he leave his dog, Laynie?" Beth asked her, standing at the bottom of the staircase and watching them.

"I don't know," she said. "Perhaps he did not want to go with him."

"Perhaps Mr. Holbrook left him."

Laynie stopped. "Why would he do that?"

"From what I could see from the doorway, Jupiter here does not like Mr. Emerson, and neither does Mr. Holbrook. Perhaps it's a gesture."

Laynie could only stand there, mute and staring. She wished to believe it so but wished even more that there was a way to know for certain.

"You had best hide him, though I don't know how you're going to manage it. I'll help you change. Papa will no doubt wish to speak to you once he is done with Mr. Emerson. It will perhaps be best to make you look as fresh and presentable as possible."

Laynie nodded her acquiescence and made room for Beth to pass her by on the stairs. She declined, however, apparently afraid of the dog. But there was no reason to be afraid of him. He was quite gentle and trustworthy. As trustworthy as the man who had left him here? She looked to the door. The door that had been shut upon the man she considered a friend, whom she felt she knew intimately even while she knew him hardly at all. How was that possible? And was he truly never to return? Would she never see him again?

She felt the temptation to cry once more, but there wasn't time for that now. She had to be strong for Mr. Holbrook, who was not to get the opportunity to defend himself. Was she likely to have any success on that score? Would her father even listen? She understood Mr. Emerson's jealousy, but her father's anger surprised her. Why should Mr. Holbrook be made to suffer because she had gone off on a solitary walk and been discovered? It seemed like everyone was making a big deal out of nothing. No. She would cry later. For now she needed to be strong. She did not feel strong, only very, very foolish.

Part three

September through December 1897

Chapter twenty-five

LAYNIE SAT IN A CHAIR before the window and stared at nothing. Her attic bedroom looked out into the treetops and, except for the winter months, it was nearly impossible to see anything else. She liked it that way. From here she could observe the seasons change as they evidenced themselves in the turning of the leaves: first small and fresh and pale, then growing more verdant until, at last, they changed in color from green to yellow then amber before falling to the ground, as they were doing now. She usually looked forward to autumn, when the earth changed its wardrobe to something more festive. She did not look forward to it now. The falling leaves seemed to indicate to her that something was ending and without hope of renewal.

Jupiter, with his head resting on her knee, whimpered. She had neglected him in her distraction and went back to stroking his head while she continued to wait.

At last the summons came. Laynie, now carefully washed and dressed and groomed, followed a sniffing Mrs. Fowler downstairs and to her father's study door where the housekeeper stopped, looked at her a moment, and then, with a stiff and regretful smile, ushered her into her father's study. What on earth was the matter with their beloved housekeeper? Was it some indication of the punishment that waited to be meted out to her by her father? She had gone for a walk. She had been accompanied home by Mr. Holbrook. What was so offensive in that?

Laynie knocked and heard her father's encouragement to enter. She did and hoped very much not to find Mr. Emerson present. He was not.

"Sit down, Alayna," he said to her. Not 'Laynie', not 'my dear', but her full given name. This did not bode well.

She sat and he studied her. In time he removed his spectacles, rubbed his face and put them back on. He cleared his throat. "Have you any idea the shame, the embarrassment, the disappointment you have caused me today?"

She looked down at her hands, folded firmly together in her lap.

"If only your mother were here this would never have happened. Perhaps I was wrong not to remarry. Perhaps any mother would have been better than none at all. Had I taken more care to provide for your guidance certainly you would never have come to break my heart in this way."

"Papa," Laynie said and felt the prick of tears. She felt the shame, but she did not know why she should. Not yet. "I'm sorry, Papa, truly. But will you tell me, please, what I have done?"

"Don't you know?" he said and looked as if he, too, were on the verge of tears. She had never seen her father cry, not ever. "Perhaps you should tell me precisely what happened today. How was it you came to be with Mr. Holbrook at Hangman's Hill? Did he take you there? Or was it your idea?"

"I went of my own accord and quite alone, as I often do. I assure you I saw no harm in it. There has never been any harm in it before."

"My fault, I suppose."

"I did not mean that, Papa, I—"

"Go on. What happened next?"

"Well...once I got to the top I realized I was still very weak and fatigued, and so I lay down in the shade. I fell asleep there, and the next thing I knew Mr. Holbrook's dog was sniffing my face."

"And what then?"

"We spoke for a few minutes..." She recalled the interlude. How much of it should she share?

"What did you talk about? What did he have to say? Did he tell you why he had the presumptuousness to come when he was not wanted?"

"He didn't know, Papa. He has been away for some time and never received your letter. He did not know he had fallen out of favor with you until I told him."

"Likely story!"

"It's true, Papa. He was very surprised by the news."

"The devil he was!"

"Please, Papa. What has he done? Why do you despise him now? You were very fond of him once."

"Not as fond as you apparently are. Are you in love with him, Alayna?"

She did not answer right away. For a moment she was not sure how to.

"Alayna! For heaven's sake, say it isn't true!"

"No, Papa. Of course not. But I want to know what it is he has done. I considered him my friend. I want to know why he is no longer yours."

"Did he touch you? Did he lay a hand on you?"

"No, Papa. I—" But once again, she was not certain that he hadn't. He had held her hand. He had helped her over a stream…

"Alayna. What aren't you telling me?"

"Nothing, Papa. Nothing happened."

"That wasn't what it looked like."

"Then what did it look like? Do you really fear his harming me?"

"I fear his taking advantage of you. And by all appearances, he did!"

Laynie stood. For the first time she considered what it might have looked like to her father, even to Mr. Emerson. She had heard the narrative already. She knew what had happened and what had not. But what might it look like to another? She had been alone with him, had fallen asleep, had returned looking windswept and tousled. She gasped with the realization.

"Oh, Papa! No! No, no. How can you think it?" And she fell back into her chair and cried.

"How can I not think it, Laynie? How do I not worry every day for your safety and protection? But you have always been willful. You have always gone your own way. You are certain nothing untoward happened?"

"Papa, I swear it. Mr. Holbrook has ever behaved the gentleman toward me, whatever it may look like. There has never been anything improper between us. Not ever!"

He shook his head.

"Don't you believe me?"

"I believe you, child, but you will have a much harder time convincing the world of your innocence."

"I don't care what the world thinks. And as for Mr. Holbrook, please don't fault him for my carelessness. He did not know I was there. He was only following the dog. We did speak. I persuaded him to speak to you. He said he would, that he wished to explain, to tell his side of the story."

"Hmm!" said Mr. Durham and lifted his chin.

"He has the right to defend himself, Papa. Considering how fond of him you were and all the trouble he's taken to serve you as you wished, and you turn him away without the opportunity to defend himself. It isn't just, Papa. All he wanted was a chance to be understood. That was why he came today."

But was it the only reason? He had said he wished to speak to her father on another matter, one for which he wanted her permission. Her hands began to shake. She stilled one with the other. For the briefest instant she had thought he was preparing himself to propose. She had dismissed it in the same moment but now wondered anew. What more would he have spoken to her father about? Was there any chance, the least little possibility, that he loved her? The pain in her chest grew almost too much to bear.

"Is he truly never to come again, Papa? Are you certain you can't forgive him?"

"If he steps foot on the property again, I'll have him shot!"

"You don't mean that," she said and felt the drop of a tear on the back of her hand.

"He's not worthy of those, my dear." He stood and handed her a handkerchief.

She took it, sat, and held it to her face as she sobbed into it.

"Oh my child, my child. This will pass. And you'll be glad it did. You are not the first woman to break her heart over such a worthless fellow. He has broken more hearts than you can suppose."

Slowly Laynie looked up at him. "Is that what Mr. Emerson told you?"

"And much, much worse, my child."

324

"Tell me. I beg you. Tell me the worst. Tell me all."

"I can't do it, Alayna. You are so young, so naïve."

"Then educate me. You wish for me to change my good opinion of Mr. Holbrook, then give me a reason to do it, and something more than vague allusions to what another man has told you, who, for all I know, may or may not be telling the truth."

"You cannot doubt Mr. Emerson?"

"And why not?"

"He is bereaved, grieving…"

"And what has that to do with Mr. Holbrook's supposed guilt?"

"Mr. Holbrook once ruined another young woman's reputation."

"Another? Papa, you cannot mean to suggest…?"

"I most certainly do."

Her heart broke a little more. She recalled certain of his words. *I don't know that my deeds are forgivable. I was young, impulsive, feeling myself entitled to the world and all the pleasures it had to offer. If only I could have known what pain it would bring, and not to myself alone.*

It was too much! She stood, paced a portion of rug for a moment and then stopped with her back to her father and a fingernail between her teeth.

"It was Mr. Emerson who rescued her," her father went on. "Mr. Holbrook, who had promised to marry her, would not. And so Mr. Emerson, to salvage her character, did. And, as you know, she died. Mr. Emerson blames Holbrook, as well he should. Mr. Emerson is a good man, Laynie. He will rescue you, too. He has decided to forgive you."

Laynie slowly turned to face her father. "There is nothing to forgive, Papa. I am innocent."

"I know that. Mr. Emerson may well be persuaded to believe it in time, but the world, my dear…"

"The world, Papa? The world was not here to witness what did not happen. It was you and I and Mr. Holbrook and Mr. Emerson alone. You don't intend to speak of it. I don't intend to speak of it. Mr. Holbrook certainly won't speak of it."

"I wouldn't be so sure. You don't know men, Laynie. What looks like a conquest might be counted as a conquest to some."

"Not to him, Papa. I won't believe it."

He shook his head in despair and sat. "What am I going to do with you?"

"Perhaps, Papa," she said as another tear slid down her face, "you will simply dispose of me to the first taker. I believe you have."

"Oh, Laynie," he said and arose again to approach her. He embraced her, kissed her on the head and held her closely. "I only want what's best for you. You must know that."

She nodded against his shoulder.

"Mr. Emerson is a good man, Alayna. He loves you. He would have you if you would accept him."

She pulled away enough to look up at her father. "Does that mean I have a choice?"

He did not answer her.

"Papa?"

"Refusing him would be unwise, my child. You don't know what you may be risking."

"Please promise me, Papa, that you will not force me to marry him—or anyone. I will consider him, very carefully, I promise. But you must promise me you will allow me my choice."

"Within reason, my dear," he said and seemed to think he was being generous. She was not certain it had anything to do with generosity. She feared, after all, that Mr. Emerson had a little too much influence with her father. Would he be able to influence her similarly? She very much feared the answer to that question.

At last he released her and with a hand on each shoulder he looked at her.

"You do forgive me, Papa?"

"Of course, my dear." He kissed her on the forehead. "Only do think how proud you will make me if you agree to marry Mr. Emerson. He is waiting to speak with you. Let me tell him you are ready to see him."

"Papa," she said and tried to stop him. It was no use.

A moment later the door opened again. It was Mr. Emerson.

He closed the door, looked at her a moment, and then walked to the grate. He kicked the andiron with his foot and turned to look at her again.

"Your father has spoken to you?" he asked her.

"And I to him, yes," she said and refused to be intimidated by his distanced and imperious manner.

"He has told you?"

"He told me a great many things, Mr. Emerson. You'll have to be more specific."

"He told you that I will forgive you."

"There is nothing to be forgiven for, sir. You have jumped to an incorrect conclusion. That is all."

He took a step toward her and stopped again. "That may be so as regards your walk with Holbrook. Perhaps it *was* innocent."

"It was."

"On your part. I'm not convinced it was on his."

"You may take my word for it, then."

"I think I won't if it's all the same. He has you convinced he's some god or something and you refuse to see otherwise. Perhaps I should help you."

"Papa told me of what you have accused him."

"I am a forgiving man, to an extent, Miss Durham. I have a difficult time forgiving those who lie to me."

"So you refuse to forgive Mr. Holbrook. That is between you and him. You can't mean to say you hold it against me for whatever wrongs he may have committed against you."

"It's you, my dear Miss Durham, whom I am inclined to believe is the liar just at present."

"Mr. Emerson!"

"You are in love with him. You have denied it. I don't believe you."

She swallowed hard and backed away from him as he approached her. He was too quick, however, and caught her by the waist. She moved to free herself but he held her firm.

"I am prepared to rescue you from the scandal you are so desperate to throw yourself into," he said. "I'll rescue you from what danger you seem to be all too eager to welcome, but I cannot rescue you if you refuse to let me do it."

"I'm not in any danger. He is gone. Never to return, thanks to you."

"So you *do* regret."

"I regret very much that you have your hands on me as you do. Something my father thought entirely improper of another but ten minutes ago."

"And *did* he touch you?"

"I've answered the question already. I won't answer it again."

Despite her protestations he held her all the tighter. "Are you in love with Daniel Holbrook, Alayna Durham?"

She refused to answer the question.

His manner took on a more imploring tone now. "What can I do, Laynie? What can I do to convince you to love me like that, so wholly, so blindly trusting?"

"I'm not in love with Mr. Holbrook, Mr. Emerson."

"I don't know if you realize what has happened today," he said as if she had not answered him at all. As if he knew she was lying. "When I saw you, Laynie, standing there with him, looking as you did... I thought my heart would break."

"That's an exaggeration," she said and at last succeeded in freeing herself from him.

"It isn't, though. Please, will you listen to me?"

She turned to face him. She had promised her father she would listen. She was not heartless, after all. She was not impervious to his pleading.

"What will you do without me, without someone to protect you, when word gets out? And it will get out, my dear, naïve Miss Durham."

"How can you be so certain?"

"Things like this always do. But you must make up your mind to accept me. There is no waiting. If your character is harmed..., it will be too late."

"So you will take me unsullied but in no other way? That's not much of a rescue, is it?"

"It's just that...if my uncle should hear of it. It may be difficult."

"What has your uncle to do with whom you marry?"

"My inheritance is dependent upon my marrying respectably. I eloped the first time, you see, and... well, my uncle knew of my wife's past experience. Needless to say he did not approve."

The reference to Mr. Holbrook reminded her of the wound. Was it true what he had done to that woman? Was it even possible? "So that is your motivation to remarry," she said, actually angry. "An inheri-tance."

He approached her again. She took a step back and he stopped.

"I'm in love with you, Laynie. How many times do I have to say it? I'll marry you. I will. Whatever happens. It's just that…well…it will be difficult for us without the money. I'm not a wealthy man. I'm sorry, but that is the truth of it."

"And so by accepting you now I rescue myself, and by refusing you, I ruin you?"

"Yes. You have that power over me. I see you take pleasure in it."

But she didn't, and it was one more evidence that he did not know her at all.

"Marry me, Laynie, please."

"I want time to think."

"There may not be time."

"I'm not ready to give you my answer."

"My uncle is dying, Laynie."

She felt the need for air, for room and space and time to think.

"I think *I* am dying," he added with a little laugh. "I die a little each day I have to wait for you."

"I need time. A week or two. A few days at least. Please?"

He seemed to consider. "It's just possible I can grant you that, I suppose. As it happens, I have some business that calls me away. It is taking a risk, however…"

"I insist."

"Very well… I have to take care of some final matters regarding my late wife's estate. It will take me a few days, I think. A week at the longest. You will have your answer when I come back?"

But this was not what she had meant by wanting more time. She wanted time with him to get to know him, time to find out if she could love him, if she could trust him, respect him. His going away would not allow her that. But it would at least give her a moment to sort out her thoughts. She would take anything at the moment.

"Yes, all right," she said.

He smiled and appeared quite genuinely happy. He approached her once more, placed a hand at each side of her waist, and then…he kissed her, quickly and not quite tenderly. Then he quit the room. The moment the door shut, she sat. Great day! What had she done?

Laynie sat before the window and stared at nothing.

Chapter twenty-six

PEEKING THROUGH THE CRACK IN the door, Laynie surveyed her room. It was safe. Beth was not here. Jupiter lifted his head as she entered and watched her as she crossed to her dressing table, where she sat and examined herself in the mirror.

"Well?"

She had been mistaken. Beth was here waiting for her, apparently anxiously, in the seat she herself had an hour ago occupied at the window.

"Well what?"

"Don't pretend you don't know, Laynie. What did Papa say? Does he believe you?"

"Yes. I think so," she said.

Beth cast a wary gaze at the spot before the hearth. Jupiter lay there quietly, but even so she walked a wide path around him toward Laynie's bed. The dog followed her with his gaze. "I'm very relieved," she said and sat.

"I should be, I suppose. It all seems so utterly ridiculous! I fell asleep at the precipice, was found by Mr. Holbrook's dog, and suddenly my character is in question? I may never have the respect of any respectable man because I fell asleep on a hillside?"

"Laynie, the world is not so gentle a place as you like to think it. Going out alone, anywhere, is never entirely safe. You should know this. You were nearly killed when you fell from Mr. Vaughn's horse. You were nearly shot in a forest while you were out walking."

"But those were accidents, Beth. This is something else. This is accusing a man of…"

"Yes, I know, Laynie. Trust me, I know."

"Papa did tell me what Mr. Emerson has accused Mr. Holbrook of."

Beth looked at her and waited.

"He says he seduced a woman and abandoned her. That Mr. Emerson married her."

"Yes, I know."

"You knew? And you did not tell me?"

"I didn't want to worry you. I didn't want you—"

"What? You didn't want me to what?"

"To be afraid."

"Of Mr. Holbrook?" she said in surprise. "Do you think now that I should have been? Do you regret not telling me?"

"I don't know, Laynie. I don't know what to believe now."

"How did you learn of it? Certainly Papa didn't tell you."

"No, he told Mr. Vaughn. Mr. Vaughn told me."

"Mr. Vaughn knows?"

Beth nodded.

Laynie crossed to the door.

"Where are you going?" Beth demanded of her.

"I want to see him, to speak with him. Will you come with me?"

"He's not at home just now, Laynie. He's been away for several days."

"Away? Where?"

"I wish I knew."

"Will you tell me, Beth? Does Mr. Vaughn believe what Mr. Emerson has said?"

"I don't know," she said hesitantly. "He doesn't like Mr. Emerson. But why should he?"

"But does he trust Mr. Holbrook?"

"He thought very highly of him. I know that."

"And now?"

"I don't know. I wish I did."

"As do I, Beth. I wish I had his counsel now. I don't know what I am to do. Mr. Emerson says people will be talking about it, but I don't see how. Who else knows besides him and me and you and Papa?"

"Mr. Holbrook."

"Yes, but why would he tell such a story on himself, particularly if it corroborates another story, and one he won't speak of even when it might help him?"

"He won't, Laynie. But he does owe you something, I think."

Something swelled in Laynie at the thought. If only he would offer to rescue her... But then, once more, why was he to be trusted above Mr. Emerson? Was not Mr. Emerson the victim of Mr. Holbrook's nefarious dealings? Try as she might, she could not believe it was true. How she wished she knew his side of it!

"Perhaps that was the point of the dog."

"Jupiter? How?"

"If he does not trust Mr. Emerson, and neither does his dog...it's a little like him being here in proxy when he can't be here in reality."

Laynie looked to Jupiter. It was too easy to believe this. All the more so because she very much wanted to believe it.

"You don't think Mr. Emerson would speak of it, do you?" Laynie asked.

"I don't think so. He has to be equally careful of scandal. I don't see how it could help him."

"You know of the inheritance, too, I take it."

Beth reddened a little, took a shuddering breath, and arose. She crossed to the wash stand, wetted a rag and dipped it in the water, and then she began to wipe her face clean with it.

"Beth, I have to tell you, Mr. Emerson has asked me to marry him."

Laynie stopped as Beth's gaze, in the reflection of the mirror, turned upon her.

"Papa says I should accept him. That I would be a fool not to, and that he is very generous to be willing to forgive me and to rescue me from my supposed shame."

Beth slowly put down her wash rag.

"I had to tell you, Beth. I'm not certain I will accept him, but you deserve to know."

"You *won't* accept him, Laynie. You can't."

"If there are rumors, I'm not sure I'll have the choice. How I wish Harry was here!"

"So you could marry him instead?" Beth said in a very accusing tone.

"That wasn't what I meant, Beth. I wasn't even thinking it." And she hadn't until that moment. She only wanted his counsel, but it was something to consider. "I must do something, don't you see?"

"Laynie, listen to me," Beth said, kneeling before her sister. "You mustn't marry Mr. Emerson, and you cannot tell Mr. Vaughn about Mr. Emerson's offer or what has inspired him to make it. Not yet. I will tell him. And if there *are* rumors, then you and I will bear them together."

"That's easy for you to say," Laynie said, on the verge of tears once more. "It isn't your character that is at stake."

"And neither is yours, yet. And until we know that it is, I see no reason to rush into—"

"Is this simply to preserve your right to both men?" Laynie said, having reached the end of her patience with Beth's games. "You would do this at the expense of my character? At the expense of my future?"

Beth stood. "You think this is about me? You must think me capricious indeed, Laynie, if you think that. And selfish. Am I so terrible a sister as that, truly?" And Beth, too, appeared as if she were about to cry. But there was no use arguing with her. If she had decided to take offense in the midst of Laynie's crisis it was only like her to do it. There was nothing Laynie could do about it. And she did not try, only waited in silence for Beth to have her say or to leave. She chose the latter and left the room with a slamming of the door.

What was she to do now? If only she could know just what was at risk? If she could know what the immediate future held for her. But she didn't; and she couldn't. All she could do was to think and try to make her mind up to marrying Mr. Emerson. She really needed him here, and yet there was something about his presence that seemed to befuddle her. He worked upon her, he bent and twisted and manipulated her feelings until she thought that she really might be in love with him, if even just a little. It was when he was gone, when she was alone like now, that she realized she did not—perhaps could not—love him at all. When she realized she actually hated him.

335

Heaven help her! What was she to do? If only she had someone to talk to. If only Mr. Holbrook had not gone. But what would be the use in that? Could she speak to him of this? No. Certainly not. And yet she could not shake the feeling that she very much wished to. She knew he would not approve of her marrying Mr. Emerson, but then the two gentlemen were enemies. Was his opinion of Mr. Emerson any more sound than Mr. Emerson's opinion of Mr. Holbrook? If Mr. Emerson was the victim in the events that had transpired between the two gentlemen and the woman who had once been Mr. Emerson's wife and perhaps—yes, certainly it was true—Mr. Holbrook's lover, why was it Mr. Holbrook she trusted above the other? It was a question she was desperate to have answered and yet knew no way of doing it.

Her reason was not sound. It was just possible, after all, that Mr. Holbrook was every bit as skilled at manipulating her emotions as was Mr. Emerson. Given time, would she realize she did not care for him at all? Would it take a day? A week? A month? A year to stop missing him? She didn't have that long. She had a matter of days to make up her mind. A week, perhaps, and nothing more.

* * *

Vaughn had been in London for four days. It was longer than he liked to stay away from Beth and that presumptuous, imposing Mr. Emerson, or even from his mother. She was not strong and did not like to be in the house without him, but she was well cared for and expertly attended. He had meant to be gone a day, perhaps two, and no more. He had come in search of Holbrook and his counsel, but the man was not at home. Vaughn had come each evening for the three evenings previous, had knocked at the door, had rung the bell; there had been no answer. This was certainly the place. But then where was Holbrook? Was he really so great a rogue that he was never at home? Vaughn didn't like to believe it, but he was growing increasingly convinced with every new disappointment.

These were gentlemen's lodgings but only just barely. These were not the rooms of the idle wealthy. They were bohemian, dirty and shabby. He had caught a glimpse of a neighbor's rooms as he had come home one evening. It was one of masculine but comfortable humility. Curiosity had gotten the better of Vaughn and he had

336

stooped to peek through Holbrook's mail slot. It was the same, though more spare, a little cleaner, very comfortable. But humble. Not quite embarrassingly so, but nothing to be proud of, either.

No, Holbrook wasn't at home. Where the devil was he? He gave up and turned for the stairs, impatient to have the questions he'd brought with him settled but growing all the more resolved to the fact that they might never be. In his impatience he bumped into another gentleman who was just coming up. He'd seen the man before and glanced over his shoulder to observe him again. The other gentleman stopped at the top of the landing and peered down. They exchanged a look and Vaughn continued on his way.

"Excuse me," the other gentleman called out.

Vaughn turned back.

"I've seen you here before. Are you looking for someone?"

"I am, actually. Do you live here?"

"No, but I'm acquainted with some of the residents. Perhaps I can help you."

"I'm looking for a fellow by the name of Holbrook."

"Daniel Holbrook?"

Vaughn retraced his steps up one or two of the stairs and stopped again. "Yes, that's him. Do you know where I might find him?"

"He's not in London."

That was it, then. Vaughn was prepared to give up. "Thank you for your help," he said and continued down again.

"Might I ask your name?" the other gentleman inquired.

Vaughn, turning back, mounted the staircase once more and presented his hand. "Harold Vaughn of Elverton. Surrey."

"Charles Hamilton. Pleased to meet you. Surrey, did you say?"

"Yes, that's right."

"Do you happen to know Mr. Holbrook by means of his employment with Mr. Durham?"

"Former employment," Vaughn answered, "but yes."

"Former?"

"He was dismissed."

"Great day!"

Vaughn was reluctant to say too much, and yet perhaps here was an opportunity to learn the answers to those questions heretofore unanswered. "There have been some charges laid against him."

Mr. Hamilton offered no reply to this but looked deeply disappointed, not perhaps in his friend but in the circumstances.

"You didn't know of his dismissal?"

"No. For that matter I'm not sure he does. I've come to see if by chance he's returned, but it doesn't seem he has. I grow worried with his prolonged absences."

"Returned?" Vaughn asked.

"He has a place in Kent."

"Kent?"

"I'll give you the address if you like," Mr. Hamilton offered.

He didn't have time for this. He needed to get back home, to his mother, to Beth, and perhaps Laynie, too. He nodded anyway.

"Have you anything to write with?"

He had a pencil. He had brought a few cards, but they were used, slipped through Holbrook's mail slot, under his door, left at the club where he had been staying. All that remained was the scrap of paper he had in his pocket and it had been written on already. Still, he might use the other side of it. Had he any other choice? Vaughn extracted it, folded it in half—the written side inward—and handed it to Mr. Hamilton.

Mr. Hamilton, using the wall to write on, scribbled the directions and then handed the paper back to Vaughn. It was released from Mr. Hamilton's hand a moment before Vaughn had grasped it and it fluttered to the ground to lay open—the written side up—revealing a hand-copied facsimile of an envelope.

Mr. Hamilton picked it up and examined it. He seemed not to believe what he was seeing.

"It's why I wanted to speak with him. I don't understand what it means, but there is something about it that isn't right."

"You copied this?" Mr. Hamilton asked him.

"I did."

"Are you sure you copied it correctly?"

"As well as I could. The first postmark was smudged, I couldn't make it out."

"This isn't possible, you know," Hamilton said, his brow lowered heavily. "It makes no sense."

"It certainly raises some questions."

"Indeed," Mr. Hamilton said and studied the facsimile more closely.

"This fellow, Emerson, he is an acquaintance of Mr. Holbrook's?" Vaughn asked.

"Yes, and mine as well. Unfortunately."

"He has come to Surrey to court the daughters of Mr. Durham, with whom I am intimately acquainted."

"Daughters? You don't mean both of them."

"It does appear that way from where I stand, yes."

"And you have taken this mission upon you? Why?"

Harry did not answer right away. At last, though, it seemed there was nothing for it. He made his confession. "I'm not disinterested in the outcome."

"I see." Mr. Hamilton looked at him a moment, as if trying to divine something further, and then turned his attention back to the facsimile.

"What does this mean, Mr. Hamilton?"

"I don't know yet, but I can tell you we had best find out before it's too late. Are you feeling up to a little travelling tonight?"

"Kent?"

"Kent."

"If you want, you might take the errand upon yourself."

"No, I don't think so. I'm not familiar with Holbrook's employer nor his daughters. You came to play the hero, after all. I'll not take this from you. Have you everything you need?"

"Yes. I believe so."

"Good. We had best not waste any time. Shall we?"

Vaughn hesitated a moment more, then he nodded and followed Mr. Hamilton onto the street, into a cab, and to the train station. It was going to be a long night, but at least he could rest assured his message was soon to be delivered and his questions, God willing, shortly to be answered.

* * *

Lady Vaughn awoke with the parting of the curtains and shielded her eyes from the sun. Her headache had somewhat subsided, perhaps today she might get up and move about. She was tired of lying here; she was tired of being ill. And now Harold had gone, she knew not where. She was willing to bet he had at last had his fill of Bethany Durham's games and had gone off somewhere to sulk. But she needed him. Didn't he know she needed him?

"What time is it?" she asked the maid who was now clearing off her bedside table in preparation for it to be laid for breakfast.

"Just gone ten, ma'am," the girl answered.

Lady Vaughn sat up. "I think I'll dress today. Where is Hannah?"

"Should be finishing up with breakfast, ma'am. I'll fetch her for you."

The girl left and ten minutes later Hannah entered. "Are you feeling better today, ma'am? Susan said you wished to dress. Does that mean you intend to move about the house today?"

"I mean to try it, at any rate. One cannot sleep one's life away. Particularly when they have so little left of it."

"Hush, ma'am. You're not dying. You're too strong for that."

"Strong!" Lady Vaughn repeated and scoffed.

"You are. You haven't let life beat you so far. What are you giving in now for? And with your son home and needin' you."

"But he isn't home, is he? And he doesn't need me."

"Oh, I think he does. And he'll be marrying before long, I'll wager, and then you'll have grandchildren to help raise. You don't want to give up before you get to see them, do you?"

Lady Vaughn cast a look of reserved gratitude at her maid as she helped her to sit before the dressing table, where she began to let down and then to comb her long, graying hair. It was still more raven than white, of that she was glad. Perhaps she wasn't yet ready to give up on life. She had endured much. She did not care to endure much more, but she had long ago learned that she had little choice in such matters. Oh, if only Harold would marry. If only he would marry Alayna Durham! How happy she would be then. She sighed.

"And what is that for, ma'am?"

"Oh, the usual. I don't suppose there's any news from the Bowery."

Hannah glanced at her in the reflection of the mirror and shook her head.

"I know that look. What is it?"

"You won't like it, ma'am."

"Oh, won't I? What is it? Has Bethany gone off and eloped with some gentleman? Has she disgraced herself at last? I didn't think she would be so eager to prove me right on that score."

"It isn't Miss Bethany, ma'am. It's her sister."

Lady Vaughn watched her own color drain in the reflection of the mirror. "Oh?" she asked and tried to sound unconcerned without sounding disinterested.

The maid gave her another sideways glance.

"Say it if you have something to say!"

"Nothing is known for certain, all I heard was what Jane said her aunt, the Durham's cook saw."

"And what did she see, Hannah?"

"She saw, or so Jane said—"

"Yes, yes. Go on!"

"Miss Alayna went on a walk yesterday, quite alone, and returned many hours later looking as if she had rolled down a hill."

"That's it? That is the gossip that has excited the kitchen this morning?"

"That's not it entirely, no."

"Well, do get on with it then!"

"She was not alone when she returned."

"Not alone?"

"There was a gentleman with her."

"A gentleman? Who?"

"Her father's hired companion, recently sacked."

"What?" she said. "I don't understand. Why was she out alone with her father's hired companion? I'm glad to know Mr. Durham has seen some sense and got rid of the fellow, but..."

"Too late, it seems," Hannah said with a raise of her eyebrows.

"What is it you are suggesting, Hannah? Tell me plainly what it is that has happened."

"Well, I suppose there's no saying for certain, ma'am, but when a gentleman and a young lady are seen to have returned from a long

341

and solitary walk, and when one of them returns looking rather buffeted and windswept…"

"Oh, dear," Lady Vaughn said and suddenly understood. She closed her eyes against the image. If those girls only had a mother! If their father had only thought about his children before himself. And what did this mean for her hopes for Harold? "How I wish my son were home!"

"I'm sure he'll be home today, ma'am."

"Oh, you don't know that. You're merely trying to appease me. Dress me. And be quick about it. Then send Jane to me, I want a word with her."

"Yes, ma'am," the girl said and silently finished her work.

Half an hour later, Jane stood before her, trembling. "I understand there has been some chattering in the kitchen as regards the young ladies at the Bowery. I wonder how you can be so careless with a young woman's reputation when any day you might find yourself without a job and without a reference. Have you an explanation?"

"No, ma'am. It was nothing more than what my aunt told me and had seen with her own eyes."

"Which is nothing you have heard and seen with your own, is it?" Lady Vaughn asked rhetorically. "The next time you hear something you think may be of some interest, I expect you will bring it to me first. Do you understand me, Jane? It will come to me and go no further. It might behoove you to know that, should I be fortunate enough to have my way, Miss Alayna Durham will be your mistress one day, and you will speak her name with respect and deference or face dismissal. Do you understand?"

Jane nodded her understanding.

"Have you repeated your story to anyone outside of the household?"

"No, ma'am," she said.

"Do you swear on it?"

"Yes, ma'am. I repeated it to Mrs. Patton as we were preparing breakfast. Perhaps a few of the housemaids overheard, but no one else. I've spoken to no one else, I swear it."

342

"Good," she said. "I suppose that'll do, Jane. You may return to your work."

Jane curtsied and returned to the kitchen.

Lady Vaughn considered it might be wise to repeat the warning—in far more general terms—to the staff at large. There would be no toying with young ladies' reputations in this house. Such things, like the silver, were far too easily tarnished.

Chapter twenty-seven

VAUGHN HAD ARRIVED WITH MR. HAMILTON very late and in bad weather, and so the two gentlemen had agreed to share a room in Hawkhurst, the nearest station to Cranbrook. They spoke of many things during the train ride, but on the subject of the letter, or even of Mr. Emerson, Mr. Hamilton was tightlipped. "We'll wait for Holbrook to explain it, shall we?" was the only answer Vaughn received for his efforts. Regarding the Durham sisters there was a little more conversation, though the questions, in this instance, came from Mr. Hamilton, and the answers, what few he was willing to give, came from himself.

"Forgive me if it's prying," Mr. Hamilton had said when they were some distance into their journey. "You said you were not disinterested in the outcome of this...shall we call it an investigation?"

Vaughn nodded his acceptance.

"May I ask for which of the Miss Durhams you are laboring in behalf of?"

"Both, really," Vaughn answered, and without thinking how it sounded.

Mr. Hamilton remembered the conversation in the stairwell better than he did, it seemed. "Both?" he inquired with something of a sus-picious look. "The same as Emerson?"

"No, not at all," Harry objected and tried to explain. "I'm particularly attached to the elder, but the younger is one of my oldest and dearest friends. There may be no use in it, you know...with Miss Bethany Durham, I mean. But if she will not have me, I would still do everything in my power to keep her from unnecessary harm or heartache. I would do the same for anyone I cared about, and that includes her younger sister."

"Yes, I see," Mr. Hamilton said and smiled sympathetically.

Vaughn was grateful for the gesture but had soon begun to grow suspicious. "I don't suppose Holbrook has made any confessions to you on that score?"

"Hmm," Mr. Hamilton said, which was not really an answer at all.

"I only wondered why you asked."

"Oh, no reason," he said dismissively.

"If Mr. Holbrook has formed his own attachment," Vaughn continued, pressing on though he knew it was possibly pointless, "it might prove very useful…"

"If he has," Mr. Hamilton answered, just as jovially as before but just as dismissively as well, "then it will be for him to say, won't it?"

"If you say so," Vaughn said and gave up.

The following morning came early. Vaughn stretched and yawned, but Hamilton was already up. He had ordered breakfast for them both and had nearly finished his when Vaughn appeared in the public room.

"It's getting cold," Mr. Hamilton said in reference to the plate that sat opposite him. "I've a carriage waiting to take us the rest of the way. It's a few miles yet."

"Yes, of course. And thank you," Vaughn said, finishing his breakfast and resigning himself to waiting for any useful information until they arrived at Brookdale. Clearly Mr. Hamilton was not going to help him any on that subject, and yet, as they made their way to Mr. Holbrook's home, he was as open and communicative as could be desired, at least insofar as any other topic was concerned. He was a friendly fellow and Vaughn liked him very nearly as much as he liked Holbrook. A man with friends to speak for him…that said a lot. Where were Emerson's friends?

At last their carriage entered a park and made its way very carefully down a waterlogged avenue. The avenue ended at a circular drive, in the middle of which was a moss-covered fountain and on the other side of that an enormous house of stone and brickwork. It rivaled Elverton easily in size, though it was rather a shabby-looking sort of place. Not unlike Holbrook's apartment. But a house of this size…it suggested something more of Holbrook than he had ever considered.

"Are you certain we're at the right place?"

"Oh, yes," Hamilton said and had the door open before the carriage had quite stopped. He was halfway to the door before Vaughn was out. He followed and they stood to wait for the door, which Hamilton had already knocked upon, to open.

At last it did but by Holbrook himself.

"Hamilton!" Holbrook said, and then, "Vaughn?" He looked to Hamilton and back again at Vaughn. "Welcome," he said, appearing puzzled and perhaps slightly alarmed. "Come in!"

Vaughn did as he was bid and entered the foyer to stop and stand before Mr. Holbrook and his friend. The poor man looked as if he hadn't slept, as if he had been working day and night on this house which was apparently under renovation. Did he work here, then? When he was not reading with wealthy—and not so wealthy— gentlemen?

"This isn't your house?"

Holbrook laughed. "It is, actually."

He led the way to a poorly-lit sitting room and offered the gentlemen a seat. Vaughn examined a cushion before sitting down on the sofa; it was dusty but it would do. "Have you no staff?" Vaughn asked him next, observing the state of the housekeeping.

"I don't live here now," he said.

"You very nearly have been, though," Hamilton reminded him.

"Yes, all right. I'm used to doing for myself. There was a staff. A few are here still, just to see to the general upkeep. When the house is finished, perhaps. We'll have to see. I'm preparing it to let, actually, but… Well, one doesn't like to let go of the familiar. Why have you come, Vaughn?" he asked, his curiosity at last getting the better of him.

Vaughn didn't quite know how to begin.

"Show him," Hamilton prodded him and so without introduction or preface Harry took the facsimile from his pocket and handed it to Holbrook.

Holbrook reached halfway, looked at Hamilton who nodded warningly, and took it. He opened it and examined it as his brow furrowed deeply. "What is this?" he asked, nearly demanded, of Vaughn.

"It's a copy of a letter I happened to see several days ago."

"Where did you see it? How did you come by it?" Holbrook asked, nearly demanded.

"I thought I'd pay a call on Emerson at the inn in Ashworth. I wanted some answers regarding his presence there. I'll be honest. I wanted some answers regarding his dealings with you..."

Holbrook looked up at him from the facsimile.

"...and the accusation laid against you. Yes, Mr. Durham told me. Upon my inquiring after Emerson at the inn, I was informed that there was a bailiff waiting for him."

"A bailiff?"

"It seems he left Gravesend without paying his bills. I paid them for him."

"Kind of you."

"In exchange, the bailiff let me examine his personal effects. I saw the letter, wondered at it, and made a copy of the envelope."

"And what, I wonder," Holbrook said, "would make it curious to you."

Vaughn chose not to answer this, not just yet.

"It's missing the first postmark," Holbrook observed and seemed to find it a point of immense inconvenience.

"I couldn't read it."

"It's rather important, though. You couldn't have taken the letter itself?"

"No. I thought it best not to."

"I very much wish you had."

"It wasn't the right thing to do, Holbrook."

"Oh, wasn't it!" he said and looked to Hamilton. He quickly went back to studying the facsimile and it was a long time before he said anything more. "I'm reluctant to believe this means what I think it could mean," he said, more to Hamilton than to Vaughn, and looked more haggard and tired yet.

"There is only one way to find out," Mr. Hamilton said, knowingly.

"What does it mean?" Vaughn asked. "Please. I want to know."

"It means Hamilton and I are going to be crossing the channel today."

"I'm coming with you."

"No, you're not. You're needed at the Bowery. If you did not take the original, it means Emerson has it by now. If there's nothing to it, if the letter is an old one, as I think it must be, there is nothing to it and he'll be there when you get there. If the letter is of recent origin however… Well, then he won't be there, and if he's not…"

"If he's not?"

"It means he has something to hide."

Not all Vaughn's questions had been quite answered. For that matter, neither had those Holbrook himself had asked. "Forgive me, Holbrook," Vaughn said. "You asked me a question and I did not answer it. It was the name that caught my attention, the initials. *S.W.* I've seen them before."

"Where?" Holbrook asked, plainly puzzled. Perhaps even a little alarmed.

"Your volume of Byron—I have it. You left it with Mr. Durham; he threw it in the fire and I rescued it."

Daniel took in a great breath, closed his eyes, and then slowly released it.

"He didn't see it, if that's what you're worried about. He never opened it as far as I can tell. I did, though. Idly at first. And then I saw…"

"You saw my scribblings."

"I did, forgive me. Tell me, won't you? 'S.W.' Those initials refer to Mr. Emerson's late wife."

"Indeed," Holbrook answered. "And someone to whom I was once very much attached."

"Is it true you abandoned her? Forgive me, Holbrook, I must know."

Daniel rested his head in his hand and rubbed at his brow.

"If there had been only one image on that page I wouldn't be asking you. I would consider it none of my business. But there wasn't, and so I must know."

Hamilton looked from Holbrook to Vaughn and back again, waiting.

"It comes down to that, I suppose," Holbrook answered eventually. "At least it does in Emerson's eyes. Perhaps it did in hers. It was not my intention. I loved her. I meant to marry her. It was understood, even if I had not formally offered. I left, yes. But I *did* mean to come back."

"But you didn't?"

"I returned too late. She had promised to wait. She didn't."

"Was it out of necessity, Holbrook? Did she agree to marry him because she felt she had to?"

"It was not any necessity I had placed her in. I was to be gone twelve months. I returned at the end of that year to find she was in the very process of eloping with him."

"And it was a year ago she died?" Vaughn asked next.

"Nearly that. Yes," Holbrook answered and closed his eyes at the thought. The pain was obviously very real to him still.

"But if the letter was returned…" Vaughn pressed on. "Does that mean…?"

Holbrook arose and raked his hair. "I'm not prepared to think it out that far, Vaughn. The letter might have been sent months ago and only just returned. If it was sent more recently… the implications, even for me, are… there isn't a word for it. Something between devastating and miraculous. Is there a word for that?"

"Life-altering, I think," Hamilton offered.

"Yes. Good god, yes!" he said and looked as if he might actually cry.

Vaughn, perhaps foolishly, pressed on. "The other initials in that book…?"

Holbrook sighed in frustration and turned towards him. "I think that's enough, Vaughn."

"I'm not asking, Mr. Holbrook, out of idle interest. You know how highly I regard her, how greatly I care for her."

Holbrook nodded his acknowledgement.

"If it should turn out she's in danger of him, I would do anything to protect her. Anything, do you understand?"

"But didn't you say that he was intent on pursuing them both?"

Hamilton had asked the question, but it was to Holbrook Vaughn delivered his answer. "Mr. Emerson quite plainly came with the intent of winning Beth, but the moment, Holbrook, that he saw you there, that he saw the friendship between yourself and Miss Laynie, he has done everything in his power to secure her and to defame you. I don't know why he would do it. I don't know what history there is between you, but I do feel it my duty to warn you I will not stand by and watch him, whom she does not love," he added pointedly, "cajole her into agreeing to something she does not want. If I must come between them, I will."

"At the expense of your own happiness?"

"Beth, I think, will never choose me. I think perhaps I was foolish to choose her over her sister, whom I have always loved as a friend. Is that not the best place to start, don't you think?"

Mr. Holbrook flinched a smile. "Yes, Vaughn. I do. And I know, because she told me so, that she does as well." Once again it appeared his emotions were very near the surface. He swallowed them back. "And you are certain she does not care for him?"

"I think he has persuaded her to try. He has certainly found an advocate in her father, and Mr. Durham, as I'm sure you know, can be relentless in his determination to see them married. Emerson knows what he's doing, I'll hand him that. It's as if he's practiced, skilled at this kind of thing. He knows how to take advantage of a situation."

Holbrook seemed suddenly agitated. He began pacing the room, flicking the facsimile with one finger nervously. Vaughn waited for him to say what he was thinking. He did not quite expect what came next.

"You've been gone a week, did you say?"

"Just shy of it now, but yes."

"There is perhaps something you should know."

"I'm listening."

"I've been to the Bowery." He threw a glance at Hamilton. "You asked me to write to you and tell you what I learned there. It was not a success."

"I'm sorry, Holbrook."

"Mr. Holbrook," Vaughn said, intervening, "speak plainly, I beg you."

"I went, Vaughn, to speak to her, to speak to her father. I found her first. I didn't know I had been dismissed until she told me. She

350

persuaded me to try to explain my side of things. I had thought that if I were successful, I might speak to him…of her, to see, you know…"

"And did he listen?" Vaughn asked, very much interested in this half-confession.

"No. And what's more, she seemed completely oblivious of the fact that Mr. Emerson's accusations on that score had any merit whatsoever."

"His accusation that you had formed an attachment to her?"

Rather than answering outright, he continued. "As I came to the Durhams' as her father's hired companion, I don't think she can see me in any other capacity. We are friends, and I am grateful for that much. It is more than I deserve."

"That's a little hard, Holbrook," Hamilton said.

"It is worth noting," Holbrook continued, unheeding, "that that friendship has provided Emerson with just the opportunity to take advantage of a situation and to make more out of it than it is. Not once, but twice now."

"What is it you are trying to tell me, Mr. Holbrook?" Vaughn asked, feeling that there was a hint of a warning in his speech.

"Emerson was there," he said. "I met him. It seems he has turned Mr. Durham so wholly against me there isn't a chance of me defending my own character. I had the dog with me—your dog, Hamilton. I let him off the leash and he ran up to the precipice. She was there, asleep. Jupiter woke her. She was…" he glanced up at the ceiling and smiled briefly, "a tousled mess. I thought it charming. I did not think what it would look like when we came down the hillside together."

"Dear heaven," Vaughn said and stood.

"You have my solemn vow I did not touch her, Vaughn. I swear to you on my very life."

"I believe you."

"Emerson, of course, made the most of it. No doubt he'll use it as leverage. If he hasn't made her an offer already, and with the threat of her character as incentive, I'll be very much surprised. Please, Vaughn, I'm not trying to get rid of you, but I desperately want you there."

"Yes, Holbrook, I see. I'll go. I'll go now."

"One other thing…."

Vaughn nodded.

"I didn't make any confession, do you hear? None of that can help her now."

"But if she—"

"She doesn't. And if she did it's too late. Without her father's approval there is no use, do you see?"

Vaughn nodded again, this time more sullenly. "I understand. I regret it, but I understand."

"Thank you, Vaughn. I'm grateful to you."

Vaughn nodded. "I'll let myself out. You have plans to make."

"Vaughn," Holbrook said, stopping him again.

Vaughn turned but it was a long time before Holbrook said anything. "Take good care of her, will you?"

"You have my word, Holbrook." And with that, and a nod of deepest respect, Mr. Vaughn left Mr. Holbrook, silently wishing him godspeed on his present mission and the strength to face head on whatever it was that was before him.

Chapter twenty-eight

A VERY TENTATIVE PEACE SETTLED over the Bowery in the days that followed Mr. Emerson's departure. It was not a peace that offered comfort or hope in brighter days to come but one, rather, that was simply devoid of disturbance. Laynie's heart was torn between saving her father from the pain of her possibly tattered reputation and causing grief to her sister and Mr. Emerson. What she herself felt was no longer worth consideration. She was beyond feeling. The emptiness that had visited itself upon her after Mr. Holbrook's dismissal did not abate but sat as a weight on her heart, it sat there, heavy and immovable, never easing, only waiting for time to give her the strength to bear it. Time or distraction. If only she could bring herself to love Mr. Emerson. It did not seem to her impossible. And yet it did seem a betrayal of her true feelings, feelings that had no rhyme or reason, to which she had given no permission to be, but simply were. If only the heart were something one could control at will.

As for Mr. Durham, despite his insistence that it was not so, it was plain he missed his friend and companion. He pottered around the house, walking aimlessly about, searching for books that were already in his library or that he had lent away to others. He had even berated Laynie for leaving out a book of household advice, hardly something that would interest himself. Why did she insist on taking things from the library without permission? Only it had never been in the library to begin with. Why did she not put things away when she had finished reading them? Only she had just put it down to find out what it was her father had wanted.

"Papa," Laynie at last suggested, having tired of watching her father's mental faculties weaken with lack of occupation and exercise, "perhaps you might just go to Town. You might meet with old friends. Perhaps, if you were to find Mr. Holbrook—"

"Bah! Don't mention his name to me, child!" he said but with more bluster than apparent wrath. He missed him. And it seemed he knew he missed him. Did he know he had been unfair, rash in his dismissal of someone he had loved and trusted and whom he had dismissed without the least opportunity of explaining himself? It was hardly a friendly way to treat someone he once professed to admire and respect. Why, an animal might have been treated with more dignity than Daniel Holbrook had been.

As to animals, Jupiter remained a fixture; he had a place before her bedroom fire. Beth did not approve, but she did not much protest, either, except to keep a wide berth of him. He was not dangerous, had shown no tendencies toward mischievousness or roguery. He was quiet most of the time, save when he needed or wanted to go out, or when he was lonely or frightened by a storm. At such times he would whimper gently, and Laynie, ever the comforter, would go to him, lie down beside him, and wait for his fears to allay and for him to rest again. It was strange of Mr. Holbrook to leave him. She wondered still why he had done it. She had read a book once, one written by their celebrated neighbor Mr. Meredith, in which a gentleman had given a dog to a woman in order to offer her some protection she might not otherwise have had. Was that Mr. Holbrook's intention? And was she ever likely to know?

She wished very much she had someone to confide in. She had Jupiter but he would give her no useful advice, except, as he did now, in his whimpering to go out. Yes, a walk in the fresh air would do them both some good. She prepared to go out but wondered still why her sister had been so distant lately. She sat in the morning room a great deal, all alone with her sewing, waiting it seemed for something though there was no guessing what. For Mr. Emerson to return, perhaps? And what then? But as for confiding in her, it just was not possible. Beth did not want her to marry Mr. Emerson despite the fact that, in the end, she might not have a choice in the matter.

Upon passing by the morning room, Laynie observed her sister sitting quietly and working on some bit of sewing. Laynie stopped to stand at the doorway, the dog at her side.

354

"Are you going out?" Beth asked her, looking up from her work.

"Yes. Jupiter needs some air, and I need some sunshine, I think. I'm feeling a little low today."

"As you have been this last fortnight," Beth said, glancing up at her from her work.

"What are you working on?" Laynie asked rather than inquiring after her meaning. She knew already what she was suggesting, but Laynie would make no confessions in that vein. What use could it possibly serve now?

"Nothing," Beth answered and casually attempted to conceal it in her lap. "Enjoy your walk," she said, veritably dismissing her.

Laynie nodded, and feeling more bereft than ever of friends, she quit the house.

* * *

The moment the door closed, Beth arose. She laid her work down—the bodice of the moss-green gown that was once her cousin's—and peeked out the window. She wished very much to reach out to her sister and yet refused to do it. Was she punishing Laynie? Perhaps in a way, and yet there were other reasons for her distance. She feared her own jealousy, but that jealousy, in recent weeks, had forged itself into something else that she did not know how to name. Was it compassion?

She had, upon first meeting him, seen Mr. Emerson as a reincarnation of Jonathan Hartright, perhaps another chance to have the sort of happiness she had once been promised and then was suddenly denied. The longer she knew Mr. Emerson the more similarities she found, but those similarities had the effect of cooling her towards him rather than drawing her on. There was something in his manner that was insincere. There was something about him that was too calculating, too manipulative and selfish —just like Jonathan, only she had been too infatuated with the beautiful and charming Mr. Hartright to see it then.

In hindsight it seemed Mr. Emerson's efforts toward herself were undertaken merely as a result of his having been denied Grace and then Laynie in quick succession. That left Beth as the only marriageable candidate. It was for herself he had come; Beth knew that. So what, then, had changed his mind upon arriving? He had said it was because they had misrepresented themselves and their relationship with Mr. Vaughn. And while it was true in many respects, he had not altered the direction of his efforts until sometime later. It wasn't Harold Vaughn's appearance at Beth's side that had swayed him but Mr. Holbrook's at Laynie's. Beth had feared, at least just at first, and after speaking with Mr. Emerson, that she had inadvertently placed her sister in peril by pushing her into the company of their father's hired companion. She had watched Mr. Holbrook carefully and in her study of him had found nothing untoward in his attentions toward her sister. Quite the reverse in fact. And while it had begun as a joke, a means of buying herself time by providing a distraction, it had developed—if her observation were correct—into something considerably more serious. She had not realized, until it was too late, what she had unwittingly encouraged by throwing them together. Laynie could deny it all she wanted, but Beth knew what she had seen the night of Mr. Emerson's arrival, and she knew what she saw now. Laynie loved Mr. Holbrook. Beth would bet her life on the fact that Mr. Emerson had seen it too. Was that, then, his motivation for changing course? Was it merely a sense of exaggerated rivalry that had persuaded Mr. Emerson to try for her sister rather than herself? She could not know, but there was one question she was forced to ask that was more disturbing than even these: Was it her habit of playing rival to her sister that had swayed her from the devoted Harold Vaughn to the all-too-charming and convincing Mr. Emerson? It was a question she feared to answer. In truth, she had answered it already. Another question yet must follow: What did she intend to do about it?

Her father poked his head in through the morning room doorway. "Has someone come?" he asked her, as he had asked a hundred times this week.

"No, Papa, Laynie's gone out to walk her dog."

"Her dog, eh? Where did she find it did you say?"

"It found her, remember, at the precipice."

"Oh yes, oh yes. Now I remember. Holbrook's was it?"

"Yes, Papa."

He did not bluster this time with the mention of that name, just stared at the ground silently and worked his mouth as if he were trying to form words. "You *will* see that she doesn't bring it in the house with her, do you hear?" he said at last.

"Yes, Papa. I'll be sure," she said, making the promise for the two-dozenth time. "I wonder why he would leave his dog?" Beth asked, and she waited for her father to hear her and to consider the question.

"Hmm," he answered. "I suppose there's no explaining some people. Perhaps he thought Laynie needed the company."

This was something of a condemnation toward herself, but she accepted it, all the more because it offered her father the opportunity of attributing some kindness to him whom it had previously been denied. "Perhaps he means to come back for him."

"Well..." he said and thought a moment, chewing once more on his words. "If he does it'll be too late, won't it?"

"Must she really marry Mr. Emerson, Papa? I don't think he will make her happy."

"Bah! What do you know, jealous girl!"

"I know she is not happy now. You will not make her, Papa, will you? You will allow her the choice?"

Mr. Durham exhaled loudly. "She will marry him, Beth. She must, don't you see? It's the only way to save her character now that people have begun to talk."

He turned away before she could answer. "No one is talking, Papa," Beth said anyway. She arose and followed him. "Do you hear me? No one has heard of it. And if they have they don't believe it. No one who knows Laynie would believe it. Papa!"

But his library door closed upon her. There was no getting through to him; she would have to appeal to a higher power. It was something she was hoping very much to avoid, but there was no putting it off longer. She put on her hat and gloves, found a light shawl, and went out.

* * *

Beth arrived at Elverton, made her request and was shown, with an unexpected degree of civility, into a bright sitting room that had once been Lady Vaughn's favorite. Upon entering the room the footman spoke, but she did not catch what it was he said. Rather than asking him to repeat it, she merely followed his direction that she enter the room and nodded her gratitude as he passed by, shutting the door behind her. It was a lovely room; it was easy to see why Lady Vaughn liked it so well. She supposed it might still be her favorite place to sit, were Lady Vaughn up to leaving her bedroom. She felt sorry for the woman and wondered what her ailment was and how acute. She sat, expecting to wait for some time to be received, and prepared to wait as long as it took.

"I don't remember inviting you to sit, Miss Durham."

Beth, surprised, stood. Lady Vaughn was seated before the window, a large book in her lap and her lorgnette in one hand.

"And why do you sit so far away? Did you come to see me or didn't you?"

"I did, ma'am. I beg your pardon, I did not know you were here."

"Well I am here. Why else would the footman have announced you?"

She didn't know and felt rather foolish for the belated realization. The footman hadn't been speaking to her at all but to Lady Vaughn.

"What is your business, Miss Durham? This isn't a social call, I take it."

Beth did not know quite how to begin and so just stood there, trying to sort out her thoughts so she could form them into words.

"Well?"

"I need your help, ma'am."

"My help." She appeared surprised by this; no doubt she ought to be. She looked through her lorgnette at Beth.

"What is the matter with you?"

"It's not me, it's my sister. Laynie has got herself into a fix."

"Yes. I had heard."

Beth's disappointment was profound. "Had you?"

"Sit, child."

She did.

"I always said your father was a fool to hire that man," Lady Vaughn said. "He picked this fellow up in London, did he, without a reference, without even stopping to think that he might be inviting a dangerous man to commune among the innocent. Your father is and will ever be a fool, Miss Durham. And now your poor sister is to suffer for it. I cannot tell you how disappointed I am to hear it."

"As disappointed as I am to know that Mr. Emerson was right and that people *are* talking. It puts my sister in an uncomfortable position, don't you see?"

"Indeed, I do. She ought to have learned by now to use more caution. I'm surprised at her but perhaps I am more surprised than I ought to be. Your father has not done his job in protecting you. But I blame myself, as well. I might have insisted. I might have saved her already had I only insisted on my way."

"But you have to believe me, Lady Vaughn, when I tell you that my sister is innocent, and now Papa is going to insist she marry Mr. Emerson."

"The gentleman for whom you have been playing rival with your sister?"

"Yes, ma'am."

"And your jealousy inspired you to come here, did it? Why should I help you? Why should not Miss Alayna marry this fellow if it means saving her character?"

"May I ask, ma'am, where you heard of my sister's embarrassment? Are there many speaking of it?"

"No one is speaking of it," she answered. "It is at an end. Now answer my question."

"No one? But you said…"

"You are very impertinent, aren't you? No one is speaking of it because I told them not to. The rumor has been put down as mere suppositious hearsay and, furthermore, should they engage in such gossip again they'll have me to answer to."

"Lady Vaughn, I am so immensely grateful to you," Beth said and felt a wave of relief wash over her even as she wondered how Lady Vaughn could be so certain.

"Well," Lady Vaughn said, softening a bit, "what is this about? And why shouldn't your sister marry this Mr. Emerson? Answer me that? Is it because you want him for yourself?"

"No, ma'am, I don't. I regret I ever did. It's my fault this has happened…all of it is my fault."

"I'm not sure I would go that far, Miss Durham," she said as Beth felt the heat of imminent tears. "Why do you take the blame upon yourself?"

Beth explained it all. She told her how they had met Mr. Emerson in Gravesend, how Beth had gone to great pains to lure him to Ashworth. How, in anticipation of his coming, she contrived to throw her sister and her father's hired companion together, despite her father's insistence that both girls were to leave him quite alone.

"Wise counsel indeed, Miss Durham. I'm rather surprised you did not follow it."

"I did not think anything would come of it."

"And what *has* come of it?"

She explained then how Mr. Emerson and her father's companion were old rivals; how, upon observing some intimacy between her sister and her father's companion, Mr. Emerson immediately began making efforts to win Laynie's admiration and to defame the other gentleman's character.

"And so you feel jilted," Lady Vaughn answered and seemed to relax a little into her chair. "That is what this is about, Miss Durham? You have been jilted before, after all. And you have certainly done your fair share of jilting. Why is this instance so particularly unjust?"

Her words were hardly the demand Beth expected, but seemed to be asked in all sincerity and with the intent of understanding. She felt encouraged by them and so spoke more boldly.

"Because Laynie does not deserve it! She was almost happy, though of course there was little point in Mr. Emerson's interference. Papa never would have approved of Mr. Holbrook's admiration of her."

"Holbrook?"

"Yes, ma'am. That is the hired companion's name."

"Not the son of Richard Holbrook?"

"I don't know his family, ma'am. I regret we know very little about him. As it turns out, Mr. Emerson knows a great deal more and has turned our father against him. He has been dismissed."

"That is possibly wise, but I am confused."

"How so, ma'am?"

"Why should you take it upon yourself to encourage an attraction between your sister and Mr. Holbrook, a man old enough to be her father?"

360

"He's not, though," Beth answered. "I don't know how old he is, but he's not anything like old enough to be our father. Mr. Holbrook is perhaps thirty. No more than that, surely."

Lady Vaughn appeared more confused yet.

"What did this Mr. Emerson say to turn your father away from his companion? He was fond of Mr. Holbrook beforehand, I take it?"

"Yes, ma'am, very much so. Mr. Emerson told my father… well…I hate to say."

"My dear, have no fear anything you say can embarrass me. If you want my help then you must be perfectly frank with me. What was said about your father's hired companion that has turned him against his former friend?"

"It is said he seduced a woman and abandoned her. Mr. Emerson is a widower, himself. His late wife and Mr. Holbrook's former lover are the same."

"And now he perceives another opportunity for rivalry."

"Yes, but as I said, it was never to be. If Mr. Holbrook cared for her, he kept it quite to himself. Papa was very clear on that subject. He was not to think of us and we were not to think of him."

"And yet you tried to encourage something between him and your sister. Did you wish to have him dismissed?"

"No, ma'am. I only… I only wanted a diversion. I—"

"You wanted time to see if you preferred this Mr. Emerson over my son. Is that it?"

A tear spilt down Beth's cheek, but she pressed on. "This is entirely my fault, Lady Vaughn. I encouraged Mr. Holbrook to think of my sister, despite my father's sanctions. I invited Mr. Emerson to come. I arranged the very circumstances that allowed for this to happen."

"And the rumors about your sister?"

"There is nothing to them, of course. You know Laynie. You know how accident-prone she is, how easily she gets herself into compromising situations. She went up to her favorite place at Hangman's Hill and there she fell asleep. Mr. Holbrook found her there and he walked her home. She insists that's all that happened and I believe her. Mr. Holbrook has always behaved the gentleman. If he has a past, I do believe it is in the past. He has behaved honorably."

"I see."

"You are certain the rumors have been ended? I don't mean to question you, ma'am, but how can you be certain?"

"It's a short walk from my kitchen to yours, you know."

"Mrs. Sullivan!"

"Your cook, yes. She told her niece, Jane, who works in my kitchen, what she saw. I've taken care of it. You needn't worry."

"I'm grateful to you."

"As you have said. So tell me, Miss Durham, precisely what it is you wish for me to do."

"I don't know. Talk to her. Talk to Papa. Make him see that she ought not to marry someone she does not love."

Lady Vaughn looked at her a long time. Beth had not thought until that moment how her words might be interpreted differently.

"You would never have forced Mr. Vaughn to marry my sister. I know you wouldn't because you didn't."

"I cannot help but think it would have been better if I had," Lady Vaughn answered with apparent regret. "But what of this Mr. Emerson? Why should she not marry him? You have not given me any reason, besides your own jealousy, to persuade me to oppose it."

"Is Laynie's disinclination to do it not enough?"

"You young people," Lady Vaughn said and shook her head. "So little knowledge of life and the world and yet so many opinions as to how to go about living in it." She hesitated a moment before going on. A sigh was the prelude to her next question. "What do you want me to do, Miss Durham? I have done enough already, if you ask me. I've rescued your sister from infamy, and I would have had her for a daughter if she would have had Harold. But she won't."

"She might now," Beth conceded, though very reluctantly, and felt the catch in her throat. "If she had an alternative to Mr. Emerson, I do think she would consider it."

"And you would be willing to give up your claims upon him?"

Beth sighed and felt the tears pool once more. "For Laynie I would," she said. "She is far more worthy of him than I can ever hope to be."

Lady Vaughn studied her carefully. She minced her mouth and seemed to be considering.

"You do not trust this Mr. Emerson," Lady Vaughn said.

"No. I don't. There's something a little too 'Jonathan Hartright' about him."

Lady Vaughn seemed to think this significant, and Beth nearly hugged her for it. "Harold doesn't trust him?"

"No."

"And you are certain your sister does not care for him?"

"I think she wants to, to please him and to please Papa. But I don't think she can."

"And how can you be certain of this, Miss Durham, if you and your sister are not in the habit of confiding in one another?"

"You know Laynie. She is always devoted. Always true and constant."

"Yes. It's why I think her such a good match for my son."

"And she is always honest. Even when she will not give words to the things she is thinking and feeling, one can always tell."

"Go on."

"I know she cannot love Mr. Emerson, because I'm quite certain—indeed, I would bet my very life on it—that she is in love with Mr. Holbrook."

Lady Vaughn sat up a little straighter.

"Perhaps she can never have him. Perhaps Papa will never forgive him. Still, it is wrong that Mr. Emerson should use her feelings for another to shame her into marrying himself. He was perhaps the first of us to see it, but he has seen it and he has used it against them both. I think if you asked me how I feel about Jonathan Hartright I would tell you I hate him for what he did, but he was never so wicked as to do something like this. Please, Lady Vaughn, will you help my sister?"

"I want time to think about it," Lady Vaughn answered, "a day or two. Can you give me that?"

It was perhaps the most Beth could hope for. It was something, at least. "Yes, ma'am. Thank you." She rose to go.

Lady Vaughn watched Miss Durham leave, thinking of all she had heard and more of what she had seen. This was a changed Beth indeed. And it was something to consider.

363

So who was this Emerson fellow? Lady Vaughn opened her copy of Debrette's Peerage to the place she had marked already and read. Any one of these entries might be Mr. Emerson's family. She had heard the name, certainly, but perhaps, after all, it was not in reference to anything honorable. She rather believed it was not. At least if he had not made his family connections known then perhaps he had something to hide. Her husband had known an Emerson, Otto Emerson, a rather crude fellow who deserved no remembering and yet would not be forgotten. Their association certainly did not provide any evidence of this young man's worthiness. In fact it was quite the reverse, supposing they were connected, and they might not be.

As regarded the notoriety, or lack thereof, of family, the same might be said of Mr. Holbrook, but then the girls weren't meant to know much of *his* background. Holbrook, however, was not so common a name as Emerson. She had known a Holbrook before. Richard Holbrook had been rather wild in his youth but had later become someone quite remarkable, earning respect and admiration among any and all with whom he associated. *She* had certainly admired and respected him, once upon a time. That was ages ago. This fellow was not his son, though. A grandson, perhaps? She turned to the entry for Richard Holbrook and read. And remembered, quite fondly.

* * *

Emerson stood in the doorway of a ramshackle cottage, the very cottage he had procured nearly four years ago. The place appeared to be in far worse condition than he remembered it; the paint that cracked and peeled, the floor littered with filth, the several pots and pails that had been placed throughout the rooms so as to catch the water as it dripped through the dilapidated roof, these evidenced humbler conditions than he could account for. How long had things been this way? How long had it been since he'd been here? He couldn't remember for certain. March, perhaps. No, February.

The money he sent should have been enough. Well, perhaps if they were very frugal. Yes, he should have been more diligent. He'd paid her just enough to keep her quietly tucked away, never enough that she would be able to save for crossing fare. Yes, he should have done better. But he could not send what he did not have.

Emerson leaned against the wall and sighed heavily. He had meant to marry her of course, but for some reason he had put it off. He was rather glad now that he'd procrastinated, though he would accept no responsibility for not keeping his word. That was his uncle's fault. It was he who had set the ridiculous terms regarding his share in the will. Perhaps he had suspected what he was up to. Perhaps there was even a chance he knew of Miss Warren and the nature of his relationship with her. The man knew everything, it seemed. Uncle Emerson might have insisted he marry her. Only he didn't; rather, he insisted he choose another under conditions more respectable, as if his uncle had ever cared for respectability! It was blatant hypocrisy, but Frederick would go along with it. What choice had he? It wasn't as though there was any real risk involved. Not really. His family, save for his uncle, were all gone. Those who had known of his entanglement with Sophie had believed him to have married her, and they equally believed that he had returned from abroad a widower. And so long as no one should learn otherwise—and why should they?—all was safe and secure as houses.

Only things had not gone quite according to plan, had they? For Sophie was not here and had not been here for some time, it seemed. Where could she have gone?

It was possible she was looking for him, though she could have no idea where to look. She would not have dared approach his uncle. It would do no good if she did. She might have gone to her own people...no, she understood very well how futile that would be. So who would she go to? Who cared for her enough to help her in her extremity, no matter how difficult, no matter how compromising?

There was only one answer to that, and the idea made him dizzy with anger. If she had gone to Holbrook...so help her!

He removed his hat and massaged the tensing muscles in his forehead. Of course she might be anywhere, really. She might be dead, for all he knew. They might be dead. He felt a pang of guilt at the thought, but really it would be better. He could hardly count on it, though. He had to know she was not looking for him, wandering about, asking questions, and raising others in the process. And supposing she could follow his trail, where would it take her?

Portsmouth? London? Gravesend? ... Surrey? There was no use lingering here. Dead or alive he had to find her and find her quickly.

But there was another matter, equally pressing. Perhaps more pressing yet. He *must* marry. Perhaps that was where he should focus his energies. Sophie would be found. He *would* find her, but he would not be inconvenienced by her any more. He would see to that, one way or another.

Chapter twenty-nine

HAROLD VAUGHN ARRIVED HOME TO find his mother sitting in her favorite old chair in her once-favorite sitting room, a book of Debrette's Peerage lying open in her lap and staring out the uncovered window at the garden beyond. He stood before her a moment, unobserved. He was almost afraid to disturb her, so engrossed was she in her own thoughts. She appeared to be troubled by something, though it did not seem she was in pain. At last he cleared his throat.

His mother turned to observe him. "You are home!" she said with apparent relief.

"Yes," he said. "I'm sorry. My business took me longer than I expected."

"And what *was* your business?" she asked him, but he was not certain he wanted to tell her.

"Are you well?" he asked her instead. "Hannah said you had dres-sed and come down, but that you had remained here these last several hours. You are better?"

"Today? Much."

"Have you eaten?"

"A little," she said. "We might dine together, you and I. Wouldn't that be nice?"

"Are you up to it?"

"Yes, if you are," she said and smiled weakly. "You look tired."

He sat.

"Are you going to tell me where you've been?"

"Kent, if you'll believe it. Cranbrook."

"Cranbrook?" she said and laughed. "Not Brookdale?"

Harry was stunned by this. How could she have known? He asked her.

"It was just a guess, I suppose. You went to see this Holbrook fellow, I take it—Mr. Durham's former companion?"

"You are extraordinarily perspicacious this evening, Mother. You puzzle me exceedingly."

"Well… Perhaps it will ease your mind to know I've had some warning of your doings. I had a visitor today."

"Oh?"

"Miss Durham came to see me."

"Did she?" he said and wondered what had brought her, but he waited patiently for his mother to explain.

"It seems there have been some rather ugly things being said about the younger Miss Durham, and the elder came to ask for my help."

"And will you help?" he asked.

"Have you heard what's been said, Harold?"

"I've heard nothing myself, but I've been forewarned that it was possible."

"It has been said that Miss Alayna has disgraced herself by keeping company with Mr. Holbrook. Why didn't you tell me the man's name before now?"

"I didn't think it would matter. The rumors aren't true, you know. I hope you will do all in your power to help her."

"As it turns out I already had, as far as that goes. It was their Mrs. Sullivan who had told Jane of it and Jane began to chatter it about here. It's at an end, though."

"For the moment."

"Have you so little faith in my ability to quash an ugly rumor?"

"No," he said, "I suppose not." He did not add that if the gossip was necessary to advancing Mr. Emerson's purpose, then he was likely not beneath spreading the gossip himself. "Was it all Miss Durham wanted?"

"No…not exactly. You know this Mr. Emerson, I take it?"

Harry nodded.

"Miss Bethany believes he means to make the most of the opportunity and insist Miss Alayna marries him."

"Is he here? Is Mr. Emerson in Ashworth?"

His mother seemed to consider the question. "I believe Miss Durham said he had been away, but… what is the significance in that? Are you planning something, Harold?" she said with a sudden look of hope.

"Perhaps," he said but feared to say more. He had been thinking long and hard about his decision. However he tried, he could not quite get over his hope that somehow Bethany would see him as the man to win her heart; but waiting for such a thing that might never happen was not worth the risk it might pose to Laynie.

"What was your business with Mr. Holbrook, Harold? Will you tell me, or is it too complicated for an old woman to understand?"

"It's not complicated at all. Something must be done to rescue Laynie from a mistake she will certainly regret. I needed his blessing in order to do it."

"His blessing? He is not her father. What need had you of his blessing?"

Harold was disinclined to answer. He felt the statement spoke for itself.

"Do you trust this Mr. Holbrook? You respect him?"

"I do."

"And you know what has been said about him?"

"We are all entitled to a few mistakes, I think, and to have the opportunity of repenting of them. He regrets his as much as I think it is possible to regret."

"And did he give you his blessing?" his mother asked him. She understood, it seemed.

He nodded.

"Do you mean to do it, then? Do you mean to ask her?"

"I think so, Mother. Do I have *your* blessing?"

"You know you do, dear boy!" She embraced him then and kissed him on the forehead. "You are a good man, Harold Vaughn. Despite your father's pathetic example you are a good man, and you are going to marry someone who will appreciate that in you."

"I think you are right, Mother," he said and arose. "I'll just go and dress for dinner now."

Lady Vaughn smiled up at her son. It encouraged him, for a moment, but the encouragement faded with the closing of the door. He went to his room and examined himself in the mirror. He was determined, it seemed, to have two women who did not want him. Beth had all but refused him. Would Laynie? He felt like a thief taking her from Holbrook as he was intending to do. But there was no use feeling guilty for it, nothing could come of Holbrook's infatuation. Mr. Durham would never allow it. Mr. Emerson would never allow it. And even if Emerson were gotten rid of, would Holbrook, the honorable man that he was, pursue it? And what would happen should Mrs. Emerson prove to be alive still? Would Holbrook return her to her husband? Unlikely. Harry supposed he was the type to offer his protection, no matter what the world might say about it. Emerson would ruin him by every and any means he could, it seemed. There were reasons such intimacies were considered sacred, though most men he knew, his father included, trifled with them as toys. These heartbreaks, each of them, could have been avoided. Holbrook, it seemed, had learned from his lesson. Was Mr. Emerson ever likely to do?

* * *

Laynie heard the bell and knew instantly who it must be. Her heart was pounding madly, the knot in her stomach made her feel sick.

As if her own anxieties were not enough, Jupiter stood, snarled and began barking ferociously at the door. She went to him and put her arms around him until he quieted. How she wished there were someone to do that for *her*.

There was a tap at her door. Laynie returned to her dressing table just in time for Beth to enter.

"He has come," she said, closing the door behind her and looking very pale. "He is waiting for you. You will remember what I said?"

Laynie nodded. How could she forget?

"You will refuse him?"

This she could not answer quite so readily.

"Laynie? Tell me you will refuse him."

Still she had no answer.

Jupiter lay back down, even while his eyes darted nervously between the two sisters and the door, through which Mr. Emerson could be heard as he was welcomed by the housekeeper.

"Do you intend to accept him?" Beth said, approaching to stand just before her sister.

The power to answer the question honestly had left her. She did not wish to accept, she simply did not see that she had any other choice.

"Laynie," Beth said and knelt at her feet, "please don't say yes. Beg for time... another week...a month!"

"He won't give me that. I'm lucky to have had these six days."

"Laynie, please."

"Why, Beth? Tell me why I should say no." And she really wanted a reason besides her own misgivings.

"Because he will not make you happy."

She suspected the same, but it was not quite enough. "You can't know that. No one can know that."

"You don't love him."

"I *can* love him, though. I know I can, given time."

"And what is preventing you from doing it now?"

Laynie shook her head. She didn't know.

"*Who* is preventing you from doing it now?" Beth asked again, altering the question somewhat this time. The alteration was not insignificant. It was no more possible a question to answer than the others had been.

"Laynie, if there is someone else..."

"There is no one else, Bethany!"

"But there might be. Why give up on hope...for him?"

"I'm done hoping. I tried that. Nothing came of it but heartbreak. And now here is the handsome and charming Mr. Emerson. He wants me, Beth. And he will have me." A tear fell and splashed on the back of her hand. Beth stood, looking down upon her in a manner Laynie could not endure. It was almost of horror. Perhaps of disgust. The tears continued to fall, but there was no one today to wipe them away. She arose and prepared herself to face Mr. Emerson. He did not like to be kept waiting.

371

"Is this because of Mr. Holbrook, Laynie?" Beth asked as Laynie reached for the door.

Laynie turned back. "Yes. Of course it is."

"I thought so," she said as though the revelation should bring her some relief, some option before now unconsidered.

"It's because of him I'm in this predicament, Beth. And it's because of my own insistence to place myself in peril at every opportunity. This is my penance. It cannot be so terrible, can it?"

It was Beth's turn not to answer. Her expression was one of mute contemplation. Almost shock. It was plainly not the answer Beth had expected. What had she hoped for? Some confession? Well it was too late for confessions now. What good would they do her now? None!

Laynie left her room before Beth could offer any further objections and stopped a moment at the top of the stairs to take a steadying breath. There was no more time for prevarication and stalling. She descended the steps as quickly as her feet would allow her. She did not wish to show any hesitation. She did not wish to feel it. Only to get this over with, to run headlong into it if she had to. At least then something would be decided.

The doorbell sounded again as she reached the foyer. She only stood there and watched. She would not answer it, it wasn't her place to answer it; a lady did not answer her own door, after all. Through the distorted glass of the window she saw a figure, very tall. Her heart skipped and thudded against her chest.

"Laynie?"

She heard Mr. Emerson's voice behind her but ignored it.

"Laynie, I'm waiting."

She looked at him. Mr. Emerson was beside her now. He glanced at the door and then touched his hand to her elbow in an effort to lead her away. She was going nowhere until she saw who it was that had come. She begged, pleaded to heaven that it was who she thought it might be, who she wished it to be—Mr. Holbrook come to rescue her. Was that what Beth had meant by the question and the subsequent look. Had she known he was coming?

At last Mrs. Fowler arrived to answer the door. She took an eternity about it. Her hand took the knob, turned it, and the door slowly creaked open.

Their guest entered, looked at her and smiled with apparent relief.

"Laynie, you are home," he observed, glancing briefly at Mr. Emerson.

"Mr. Vaughn," Laynie said in surprise. She was disappointed; she could not deny it. But she was also relieved. Very relieved indeed. Perhaps, after all, there was something he could do.

"Can I have a word with you?"

"Sorry, Mr. Vaughn, I was here first." And Mr. Emerson tried once more to lead her away.

"It will only take a moment," Vaughn said and approached her.

"Vaughn!" It was Mr. Durham this time, entering the foyer from the corridor. "Come to keep me company, have you? I'm so glad!"

"I—" Harry began and then, "Yes, of course, sir. Only I had hoped to speak with Miss Alayna for a moment, if you don't mind."

"Oh, there's plenty of time for that later. Come!"

"It is rather important, sir."

Mr. Durham looked at Harry half-suspiciously. "Not so important you can't tell me first, I trust?"

Harry seemed to consider, but in truth he had no choice. Mr. Emerson had Laynie by the arm and was leading her away while Mr. Durham was summoning Harry to follow in another direction.

Laynie watched him, noted his reluctance to turn from her; regretting, it seemed, the sight of her being led from him by Mr. Emerson. What was it he wanted? What was it he was so desperate to say to her?

The question, at least for now, was not to be answered. The door was shut between them.

"Now," Mr. Emerson said, a little less solicitously than he had spoken to her a moment ago when all could see and hear them. "You know why I've come. I've made you an offer, and a very generous one. I want your answer."

She heard him, but her mind was still on the door and on Harry who, by now, was no doubt locked away in her father's study. If he had come to rescue her would she have let him? If he had come to offer himself, would she have said yes?

"No."

Mr. Emerson's jaw tensed. "Is that no, you will not marry me, or no, you do not have your answer?"

"Look at you," she said to him. "You beseech me so imperiously. You demand an answer of me. I asked you for time—not to think on my own, alone, but to spend time with you, to learn of you and to find out, if I can, if you can make me happy. Do I look happy now, Mr. Emerson?"

He rubbed at his shaven chin, looked to the ground and thought. At last he looked up at her. "You are right, Miss Durham. I'm a beast and I beg your forgiveness."

"I'll forgive you when you have earned it."

"Fair enough," he said and smiled. He approached her.

She took a step back from him but she knew there was little use. He came to stand very near her but did not touch her.

"These last few days have not been pleasant," he said, standing at her shoulder as she, half turned from him, looked out the window. "I had to take care of some final business. I'm afraid I've been so caught up in my own losses I forgot what you must be enduring. Have you been very alone, Laynie?"

"I have," she said. "At least I have felt it."

"You have your sister."

"Do I?" she said and looked at him briefly. "Have you not thought that your capriciousness toward her might prove an obstacle between us?"

"Not capriciousness. Indecision, perhaps, just at first. You can't accuse me of indecision now."

"All the more reason for Beth to despise me. She'll hardly speak to me, and when she does..." But she thought she had best not say too much.

"When she does?"

"Suffice it to say it is not love she bears me at the moment, Mr. Emerson."

He took a step nearer her so that she could feel his breath on her. "And whom do you love, Laynie? Not me, I think."

Her answer was offered quietly. "You have not given me much opportunity to do it yet."

"Come, come. Admit it. Holbrook has worked himself into you. Why do you insist on loving someone who could never love you in return?"

She looked at him but knew not what to say, or at least she thought better of saying it.

"He isn't that kind," Emerson continued. "He doesn't get close to people. He takes his pleasures, certainly, but he doesn't love. I don't think he knows how. You don't think it was love for you that persuaded him to lure you to the hilltop?"

"He didn't lure me anywhere, Mr. Emerson. He found me there."

"By chance, I suppose?"

"Of course. How else?"

"Laynie, you are so very naïve. This business…it can only bring misery. He wants you. Of course he does. But not in any respectable way. I want to marry you, Laynie. I think you could even be happy with me if you would only bring yourself to give him up. If you would only trust me enough to let me show you how to do it."

"Show me?"

He smiled and bent towards her, but she was not going to let him take any liberties. She moved away from him.

"Do you see?" he said, plainly injured. "I have offered you everything. I've offered you my home, a secure future, my protection. Despite my uncle's terms, which are quite firmly set I assure you, I have taken the risk of bearing your tarnished character; I have proposed to rescue you, and for that you shun me. Do I deserve this, Laynie? Tell me!"

"No. I suppose not," she said, relenting. She always relented with him. Why did she relent?

"If only you did not love Mr. Holbrook."

"I don't love Mr. Holbrook!" she insisted and felt her heart break a little more.

"Say it again," he said and came to stand every bit as closely as before.

It was almost a whisper, but she said it. "I don't love Mr. Holbrook."

"Say you love me. Say you will at least try to do it. Tell me you will try to return the regard I feel for you."

"Do you feel it though?" she asked him and really wanted to know. "You have said so, but I don't believe you do. You have not treated me as anything more than a prized acquisition."

He turned her to look at him and held her there, a hand on each arm. "Alayna Durham, I am bewitched by you, mesmerized, bewildered, constantly surprised and always and utterly fascinated. I adore you, my dear, sweet, naïve creature. Please," he said and pulled her toward him so that she was enfolded in his arms, secure against his chest. It was warm there, and, for the moment, it felt very safe. "I beg you. Love me. Change me. Teach me how to love you as you want to be loved. As you deserve to be loved."

He only held her there as if she were some treasure highly prized by him. His request required no answer, or perhaps it was merely answered by the relenting of her objections. Perhaps, after all, he did love her. And, just perhaps, it was her resistance to him, her pointless and dogmatic admiration for someone else, that prevented her from feeling it.

"Marry me?" he whispered.

She hesitated only a moment. There was no use putting the inevitable off longer. He would have his way. She nodded her answer against his shoulder.

"Oh, my darling, you make me so happy."

She tried not to cry. She held it in as bravely as she could, but it was no use. Her despair escaped in a series of wracking sobs, first one and then another, followed by many more. She waited for him to be angry, to push her from him and rebuke her for her stupidity. But he did not. He only held her closer.

"Hush, hush," he said. "It will be all right. I promise, you *will* be happy."

She was grateful for the words. More grateful still for his patience. Yes, just perhaps, she would be happy in time.

When she quieted he held her a little apart from him and examined her tear-stained face. "It isn't much of a compliment, is it?" he asked her gently.

She laughed. "I'm sorry, Mr. Emerson."

"Frederick."

She smiled through her tears. "I am sorry, Frederick. I have been a little overwrought lately. That is our way as women, I'm afraid. Perhaps you know."

"Yes," he said. "There are no surprises there."

He took her hand and kissed the back of it as he held it in his. "Come," he said, "let's make the announcement," and he began leading her from the room.

"No," she said and stopped.

"Laynie?" It was a question, but a warning too.

She smiled. Or tried. "Can't we keep it just to ourselves for now? A happy secret between us?"

He flinched a smile and spoke with an effort at patience. "What is the point in an engagement if no one knows?"

"I just… I want it to be between you and me. Just for now."

"You want more time…to be sure." He seemed irritated with this thought.

"I want time with you, Frederick, to know you as I ought to do."

"You will have all the time in the world."

"Yes, I know, but…"

"You don't mean to jilt me, I hope." His hand, which had been on her arm, slid to her shoulder, and then rested on the back of her neck.

"No. Of course not. I wasn't thinking that… It's just…"

She did not like his touching her so familiarly. She stepped away from him and crossed to the window. "Will it be a long engagement?" she asked him.

"That, I'm afraid, will be up to my uncle. I can't imagine it will be long. A month, possibly two."

Why did she keep forgetting about this mysterious uncle? Did she not believe he existed? It occurred to her he offered a possibility before now un-thought of. Did it give her hope or dread to think he might not approve of her? Considering the 'rumors' that were supposedly about, it was just possible he mightn't. "I haven't even met him," she said. "Perhaps he ought to see me before we make any formal announcement."

She turned to look at him. He was watching her in a manner that was not entirely comforting. It was as if he did not see her but was thinking of something else far away. "Mr. Emerson? Frederick?"

He seemed to awake and smiled. "Yes. Perhaps you are right," he said. "But you will need to meet him as soon as may be. He is not well, remember."

"Yes, all right," she said. "Can he travel?"

"Oh, no, my dear. We are going to London, you and I."

"Not together. Not alone."

"Why not? We are engaged to be married, after all."

"Still."

"And who would you propose to serve as chaperone? Not your sister, I think."

"Papa, then?"

"Do you propose to make a family party out of it?"

"Yes, why not?"

Again she waited for him to lose patience; he laughed instead. "Yes, all right. Why not?" He held out his hand to her. "Come, let's tell your father. I know he's as anxious to hear the news as I am to tell it."

She was reluctant even to agree to this, though of course there was no escaping it. Telling her father was as good as telling the world, or at least their little corner of it. But no, there was no avoiding it. She allowed herself to be led from the room but then stopped in the foyer. She remembered that Harry was here and that he wished to speak to her. "Perhaps *you* should go," she said. "Tell him, won't you? I'll wait for you here."

"Oh no," he said. "Now I have you there's likely to be a line of gentlemen lamenting what they've missed. I'm going to keep you close, if you don't mind."

It was a compliment, she felt it. But she felt something else as well: a wave of misgiving. It was a promise. Perhaps it was a warning, too.

* * *

Harry's half-hour interview with Mr. Durham had left him feeling dismayed at the state of affairs in the Durham household. Idleness and boredom were dimming Mr. Durham's senses considerably. His conversation was not so focused as usual. He tended rather to ramble off onto vaguely related tangents, jumping from one subject to another as if they were all connected by some invisible thread of logic that Vaughn took great pains, and with varying degrees of success, to follow. One moment he was full of joy at the prospect of Mr. Emerson's attachment to Laynie, and the next moment he was speaking of his disappointment in the afternoon's weather, as if the wedding he were planning in his mind was suddenly to be postponed because of today's unexpected downpour. Did he see something in his daughter's future with that man that gave him some unexplained reason for misgiving? Harry hoped so, and was just on the verge of offering his own opinion on the matter—and his well-considered solution—when Mr. Durham suddenly took an unexpected turn in the conversation.

"He's quite a fellow that Emerson, wouldn't you say, Holbrook?" Mr. Durham said to him.

Harry, a little shocked by the address, sat up and thought to correct Mr. Durham, but he was not given the chance.

"We are lucky to have found him, I think," Mr. Durham went on. "Laynie is quite fortunate to have won the admiration of such a man, despite her foolishness. You must agree this is a good thing for my Laynie."

But he didn't agree. At least Harold Vaughn did not agree, and he knew of a certainty that Holbrook never could. Did he dare speak for him? Yes, it seemed, he did. "No, I don't agree," Harry said. "Mr. Emerson is manipulative and deceiving and not to be trusted. You have given your daughter to him—thrown her away—with hardly a mo-ment's thought."

Mr. Durham stammered. "Vaughn?" he said and scratched his head. He narrowed his gaze as if uncertain who it was he was even looking at. "I hope this isn't because you have begun to entertain some fancy for her, yourself."

Vaughn was uncertain how to answer this. He had a plan of his own certainly, but it did not appear it would be very well received just at present. Still, it was what he had come for. He prepared himself for the confession.

"Emerson warned me it might be the case, Holbrook, but I didn't want to believe him. Is it true? Is it true you have formed an attach-ment to my daughter?"

The change in address changed the question entirely. He was no longer uncertain what to say. The words were there before he'd even thought how to prepare them. "It's true, sir. I love her. She doesn't know, and without your consent I would never dream of telling her. But it is true. She is worthy of far better than Emerson. I have no hope of her for myself, but you are mistaken in him, sir, and if ever I get the chance I mean to prove it."

"Do you indeed!" Mr. Durham said and arose.

Vaughn feared he had just sealed Mr. Holbrook's doom and furthermore they both would be made to regret it, but Mr. Durham just stood looking at him in astounded silence. In time he turned back to the window and stared out into the garden, saying nothing for minute after minute. At last he was interrupted by a knocking at the door.

"Come in," he said.

The door opened and Mr. Emerson entered, with Laynie's hand in his.

"Mr. Emerson! Laynie, my darling! Come in, come in," he said. "Does this mean what I think it means?"

"Indeed it does, sir," Mr. Emerson said. "Laynie has promised to marry me."

Laynie glanced at Harry who had arisen upon her entrance. The look she gave him was one of shame, hardly of joy or pleasure or pride or any of the other thousands of emotions he had imagined himself feeling were he ever privileged enough to have someone say yes to his proposal of marriage. Laynie was not happy. Perhaps she was trying to be happy. Perhaps she had even convinced herself she *was* happy. But he knew her too well to be deceived.

With Emerson's entrance, both Vaughn and Holbrook, whether they were one man or two, seemed to have been forgotten. Harry had accomplished his task, though it had turned out to be quite a different one than that which he had originally planned. "I'll just leave you to discuss the happy plans," he said and arose. "Congratulations to you both." But he did not look at them as he said it, merely bowed blindly and quit the room.

"Mr. Vaughn?" He thought he heard his name spoken quietly as he passed through the doorway, but he would not turn back. He couldn't.

Having reached the foyer, he took up his hat and slung his coat over one arm. He was too angry to wear it. It was cool out, but he needed to be cooled. He stopped upon hearing his name again; it was not Laynie this time. He turned to find Beth standing within the drawing room doorway, looking humbled and pale.

"Mother said you had been to pay a call," he said to her dryly. "It was kind of you."

"I wanted her help."

"So she said."

"Did she?" she asked and appeared a little uncertain.

"Yes. With the rumors. They are taken care of, I think."

"Oh, yes," she said more confidently. "Fortunately they had not gone far."

"Mother would do anything for Laynie, I think."

"Would she?"

"Do you doubt her?"

"No. It's just…"

"Go on, Miss Durham."

"It wasn't the only thing I asked her help with."

"Oh?" he said and waiting for her to explain.

"I think Mr. Emerson is a bad man, Mr. Vaughn."

Harry did not know quite what to say. He would like to assure her of the fact but he did not know the facts for himself. His, too, were merely suppositions. Were her doubts any different? "Why do you say that, Miss Durham?"

"It's just a hunch."

"Yes," he said, "I feel the same."

"Do you?" she asked him and took a step toward him. They were standing on opposite sides of the foyer table, a large bowl of rose blossoms sat in the middle of it. The petals were tinged with brown.

"She can't marry him," Beth insisted.

"I agree."

"She doesn't love him."

"I know."

"How do you know, Mr. Vaughn?" she said with a look of both hope and fear in her pale-blue and glistening eyes.

381

Vaughn stood there for only a moment more. At last he moved to the other side of the table, took Beth by the elbow and led her into the drawing room. He closed the door. Beth was looking at him wide-eyed and alarmed.

"You need to know that I came here tonight with the intention of asking your sister to marry me."

"Did you? I'm so glad," she said and began to cry.

"You don't look very happy."

"I don't want you to marry her. Of course I don't, but I am very happy you would do it."

"I was too late."

"I know."

"Beth," he said and took her hands in his. "I still have hope. For you, I mean. Tell me I shouldn't."

"I can't. I want you to have hope."

He was not certain that meant he had reason to hope or she simply did not want for him to give up yet. "Does that mean—?"

But his question was interrupted by the opening of the door. It separated them, pushing Harry behind as it swung open. He stepped around it to find Mr. Durham entering with Laynie tucked within one arm and Mr. Emerson following behind. Pleased with his work, he smiled broadly, his pleasure at his accomplishment broadcast for all to see. Laynie appeared more conquered than happy. Her joy was so thin you could see the despair behind her eyes.

"What do you think, Beth, Mr. Vaughn?" Mr. Durham said by way of introduction to the unhappy news. "Laynie has agreed to marry Mr. Emerson! Let's have a toast!"

Mr. Durham approached the drinks table, poured a drink for himself, and before he had quite finished, wandered off to look out the window into the darkening garden. Laynie watched him worriedly but did not follow. Emerson did not appear inclined to let her go. She turned back to exchange an awkward look with her sister, and then with Harry. Nothing was said. No congratulations were offered. There was only a heavy silence and a hundred thoughts unutterable.

Emerson, at last seeing that the drinks had been abandoned, poured them himself and handed them round. Mr. Durham was eventually recalled to the present and to the company. He offered a toast: "To the happy couple," downed his glass in one gulp and sat.

Harry excused himself, but stopped in the foyer. Beth had followed him. He wished he had some words of comfort or reassurance to offer her, but he had nothing.

"Goodbye, Mr. Vaughn," she said. Her farewell sounded disturb-ingly final. "Thank you for all you have tried to do. I will ever be grateful."

Words once more failed him. He bowed his head and left the house.

Chapter thirty

M R. EMERSON MADE GOOD ON his promise never to leave Laynie's side. Over the next several days he was a constant presence at the Bowery. Mr. Durham wrote to Aunt Phillips for help with the wedding preparations. Her reply came quickly, but was hardly any comfort to Laynie's already addlepated father.

> *Dear Brother,*
>
> *I would like to congratulate you on your daughter's impending nuptials, but I cannot. Why on earth should you think I would support Alayna's marriage to a gentleman I did not approve of for my own daughter?*
>
> *As to your request for assistance, you know I would do whatsoever I might for my beloved nieces, but it is quite impossible. Grace is to be married this very week, and it's all I can do to keep up with the wedding preparations.*
>
> *I'm sorry, Brother, but you are on your own in this affair. But then you never took my advice in anything before now, so I don't see what use it would be for me to offer my assistance now.*
>
> *Your sister,*
>
> *Eloise Phillips*

Mr. Durham read the letter aloud and seemed not to have realized he had done it until, looking up, he saw the expressions of alarm on his daughters' faces. Emerson's countenance appeared to Laynie to be one filled with regret. He apologized for the difficulty his weakness had caused between the families and assured Mr. Durham that were it not for the very greatest of regard which he held for Laynie that he never would have dared to presume the course that had led him apply for her hand. And while he regretted very much the hard feelings that were held against him, and which Mr. Durham must now suffer, he had no regrets whatever about the way things had turned out. And neither would Mr. Durham, he was certain of it.

Mr. Durham could only nod, agreeing to little more than that which he could comprehend at the moment. The whole thing required a little further contemplation, and so he excused himself to go to his library. Emerson reluctantly followed after him.

A moment later, Beth arose to retire to her own room, leaving Laynie alone. What did she regret? Anything? Everything?

At the moment she felt numb. Were she to look at the situation objectively, she could not say that Mr. Emerson had given her any reason to regret her decision to accept him. He was all kindness and attentiveness, always patient, even when her moods were less than predictable and her emotions high and near the surface. They were not much alone together, and when they were he seemed content with her thoughtful silence. He would read to her or share with her little anecdotes of his childhood, and ask, in return, for some from hers. She was careful to tell him those that painted her in something of a better light than those Beth was wont to tell, and he seemed to accept her efforts to assure him of her capability to think and behave reasonably without doubt or question. So far he had proven a far better fiancé than a hopeful suitor. His habit of teasing, of embarrassing her, of making her feel ashamed he seemed to have abandoned. He was gentleness personified. This man she might learn to love, indeed— were she not haunted by the notion that it was all an act and would fall away the moment she could not escape him. His manner was too solicitous to be quite convincing, too efforted to seem natural. In fact, he frightened her now more than he had ever done before.

* * *

The family was just finishing breakfast one morning, perhaps a week after the private announcement of their engagement when Mr. Emerson arrived with happy news. She felt his entrance as an omen and turned from the door through which he had entered to look out the window. The sun, which usually lit the room so pleasantly, tried with all its might—and almost successfully—to pierce through the fog that had settled quite firmly on the ground outside; Laynie felt in harmony with it, trying to smile and be happy while a haze of gloom clouded her thoughts, and while Emerson stood ready to deliver his news.

"I do wish your dog would be quiet, Laynie," her father admonished her as he set down his paper. "Why, it almost sounds as though he's in the house! He is not, I hope?"

"No, Papa, of course not," Laynie answered and glanced in the direction where her sister ought to be but was not. Where was she this morning? "He's just in the garden," Laynie assured him. It was true, but only because she had put him there just before coming in to breakfast. It seemed he was standing just beneath the window now. He liked to keep as close to her as possible.

Mr. Emerson waited, letter in hand. Mr. Durham wished him good morning, but it was hardly heard over the sound of Jupiter's barking.

"Laynie, do something," her father admonished her.

She arose, crossed to the window, and warned Jupiter with a look and a finger to her lips. He whined, yawned, and sat.

Laynie returned to her place as Mr. Durham offered Emerson a seat. He approached Laynie, kissed her hand, and sat down at an unset place. He had eaten already, he informed them, and presented his letter. It bore the good news that his uncle was prepared to receive him and his bride-to-be at the end of the following week. A day and time were set. It seemed Laynie was the only one who thought this odd.

"You have to have an appointment to see your uncle?" she asked, setting down her tea with a loud clink.

"He is ill. Acutely ill. I told you this," Mr. Emerson said from his seat across from her and with a smile that seemed a little too patient to be sincere. "He is not always able to receive visitors."

"Not even his own family?" Laynie pressed.

Mr. Emerson's jaw flinched. "In order to approve of you he must be lucid. Be reasonable, Laynie."

But she didn't feel she was being unreasonable. "He can predict his own lucidity to such a degree that he can make appointments by it?"

He gave her a dismissive look that was plainly annoyed and turned to her father who was now looking over the letter for himself.

"This is excellent news, indeed!" Mr. Durham said. "Once his approval has been granted, there is nothing to stand in the way of your marriage. We will have everything underway in no time, I think. What do you say to a spring wedding, Laynie? I know it's soon, but I see no reason to drag things out. I know Mr. Emerson would rather not wait for his bride."

Laynie felt her face grow crimson. "So soon, Papa?"

"That's not so soon. It's not indecently soon."

"It's entirely possible," Mr. Emerson intervened, "that my uncle will demand an engagement that is somewhat shorter. His health, and all, you know..."

The blood in Laynie's face went cold.

"And who is to help me prepare? If my aunt refuses to help, am I to do it on my own?"

"It needn't be a complicated affair, my dear," Mr. Emerson said. "You are making far too much out of it. A quiet, simple, London wedding. There is little to plan."

She only looked at him. He had been married before, so perhaps he knew, but for her there were a million questions to ask, a hundred thousand details to attend to, most of which she could do no more than imagine. There were invitations, and clothes, and breakfasts to plan. This was no hasty elopement. He had said himself that respectability was of the utmost importance. No, she would require help. But from whom?

For the moment, however, all she could think of was the uncle. If he did not approve... What would it cost her? Embarrassment? Shame? More than she had been dealt already? She could not deny it. She wanted very much for Uncle Emerson to disapprove of her. Was it possible. Mightn't he? She asked the question, or at least began to.

"If your uncle does not approve...?"

"If he does not approve of you," Mr. Emerson said, "it's because you have given him something to disapprove of. He knows nothing, as yet, of your embarrassment with Holbrook. Do you intend to provide him with some other proof of your unsuitability?"

Why would he ask such a question? Did he suspect she had begun to consider just such a thing? Perhaps he did, for his next words were offered with the suggestion of a warning.

"I should think you would want to avoid that—at all costs. Don't you?"

"Yes, of course," she answered very quietly and determined herself to listen and to object no more. The uncle's letter required answering. Stationery was sent for, the letter was written, all while Laynie watched as her fate was sealed in the securing of an envelope. Was there no going back now?

"I'll post it myself," Mr. Emerson said and arose to leave. "There's no sense in wasting time, is there?"

"No, no. None at all," Mr. Durham said and stood. He watched as Mr. Emerson lingered by the doorway. He scratched his head and looked from one to the other of them as though he didn't know he was meant to excuse himself so that Laynie and her fiancé might have a moment to themselves—as though he had something to say. Laynie prayed he had formed some sort of objection to Emerson's plans—at least to the haste of them, or the total want of organization or assistance, even if it were only for Laynie's sake. Her father was simply not thinking clearly these days. But there were moments of clarity. Was he on the verge of one now?

"Will you walk me to the door, Laynie my darling?" Emerson said, cutting off the thought she had hoped very much her father was forming. Perhaps she had been mistaken, after all.

She hesitated to answer, but at last acquiesced. "Very well," she said and arose to follow Mr. Emerson out. In the foyer she stopped upon hearing the sound of hooves and wheels in the drive.

"Who can that be?" Emerson asked and placed the envelope in his pocket, as if he felt some need to protect it, guard it some place out of sight.

Laynie moved to the morning room and looked out the window. The carriage was one from Elverton.

"It's Lady Vaughn," Laynie said upon realizing who it was. Mr. Emerson had just joined her there; her father stood just within the doorway looking not a little perplexed.

Laynie took a seat and waited, nervously straightening her skirts as she did and wondering what this unexpected visit might mean.

The door was answered before it could be rung. Lady Vaughn was announced and entered, as all stood. She looked unusually well, strong, even robust, but she was not alone; Beth was with her. Had they come from Elverton together?

"Lady Vaughn, you are very welcome," said Mr. Durham. "Please make yourself comfortable."

Lady Vaughn looked around the room. She chose the sofa, where Laynie had been sitting until her entrance. Laynie resumed her place beside her as everyone else returned to their own seats in turn.

"I have come to offer my congratulations for the happy news," Lady Vaughn announced, "and to offer my assistance."

"Assistance?" Laynie asked.

Mr. Durham sat forward in his chair. "My lady, that is very generous of you, but it's hardly necessary."

"Of course it's necessary," Lady Vaughn insisted. "Did you think your daughter must be left to provide for her own needs in the matter of her marriage? How is she to know what she requires?"

"Well, I..." But Mr. Durham had no answer. He sat back in his chair and rubbed at his temple.

"There is no mother here to guide your daughter," Lady Vaughn continued. "She requires a hand, and a feminine one. I volunteer mine."

"I have a sister," Mr. Durham said as though he had only remembered the fact, as though he had forgotten entirely that her assistance had been refused.

"Is this the same sister with whom your daughters recently stayed, and where they were returned home early having suffered some embarrassment under her care?" Lady Vaughn inquired, nearly de-manded. "Is this the same sister whose own daughter is to be very hastily married in a quiet ceremony in her London home?"

Mr. Durham sat up in his chair. "I hope you are not suggesting, Lady Vaughn, that my niece has anything to be ashamed of in her marriage."

Lady Vaughn did not answer. Laynie was desperate for an answer and so turned to look at her sister, who was standing at the window. Beth would not so much as look at her.

"Forgive me for saying so, Mr. Durham," Lady Vaughn continued, "but you have not taken the care with your daughters you ought to have done. It is not your fault. I do not blame you, for you

389

are a man and cannot truly know of what your daughters stand in need. I have thought of them in many ways as my own, you know. I have watched with great interest as they have grown from young girls into rather promising young women, and, as you know, I have presumed to form my own plans for them—for Miss Alayna in particular. While I confess to being disappointed in those plans," she said, hedging Mr. Durham's objections which were nothing more than Mr. Emerson's after all, "I know better than to insist upon them where the happiness of two people is in jeopardy. I am not here to interfere but to offer my assistance, which I will insist you accept. I feel it my duty to make sure that everything that can be done to provide for Miss Alayna's comfort and happiness will be done. All must be undertaken with the strictest attention to propriety in every and all details. She must be presented to society by those who will and can vouch unflinchingly for her name and reputation and who have the means and power to see that her happiness is provided for in every possible way."

"Lady Vaughn," Laynie said, a little overwhelmed, "you are really too generous."

"Not at all, my dear. It isn't generosity. I loved and admired your mother every bit as much as I love and admire her daughters."

Laynie caught the plural and looked to Beth who looked to Lady Vaughn with a grateful smile before returning her gaze out of doors.

Lady Vaughn, with a finger on Laynie's chin, directed her attention back to herself. "I mean to help you, my dear, and to provide for you in every way that I can. Do you know what you need?"

"No," Laynie answered quite honestly.

"I didn't think so," she said and cast a disapproving look upon Mr. Durham. She hardly acknowledged Mr. Emerson at all. Laynie realized, belatedly, that he had never been introduced to her.

"Lady Vaughn, forgive me."

"For what, my dear child?"

"You have not met my—"

"There will be plenty of time for that, my dear," she said and arose, and still she did not so much as look at Mr. Emerson. She turned to Mr. Durham. "I apologize if I seem to you interfering," she said.

"No, ma'am. That is—"

"Alayna will need clothes, proper clothes. Beth will take her measurements and send them to me. This sense of haste is most vexing, though I do understand, I suppose, the necessity of it. As for the engagement party, it will be held in my London home, where the rooms are big enough to provide for the comfort of all those I intend to invite. Alayna will stay with me, as my guest. I trust you can find your own accommodations while you are in town. Mr. Emerson, you have an uncle, I believe…"

"Yes, of course," he answered, but did not appear to be pleased by these arrangements. No doubt he did not like the idea of his bride-to-be staying in the home of a man who she once had been expected to marry, nor with his mother who quite plainly didn't approve of him. He didn't say so, of course, but Laynie could see it in the stiff smile and the look of affected gratitude. Behind it all was a shadow of fear, a man threatened by the idea that the woman he meant to marry might not always be under his thumb. That, in fact, he might lose her yet. Had Lady Vaughn some ulterior motive behind her apparent generosity? Laynie rather hoped so.

"I expect," Lady Vaughn continued, "that since her own daughter's marriage is so shortly to take place in London, you might stay with her, even if she will not agree to help us in Alayna's preparations. Certainly she can provide accommodation to you."

"I expect she can, ma'am, and will, but the thought of leaving Laynie when…"

"But that has been your entire mission from the time she was of age, has it not, to see her married and on her own? The separation will be good practice for you, and she will not be far. I understand your objections, but I am not well, as you know, and so Alayna must be close at hand if I am to provide for her trousseau and all that she will require. Certainly you can be reasonable enough to see that."

"Yes, certainly, Lady Vaughn," Mr. Durham conceded. "Of course you are right." He examined his daughter. "My girl," he said as his eyes filled. "My little girl is grown up."

"Papa, don't," Laynie said and knew if he cried she must too.

Lady Vaughn walked to the doorway and stopped. "Miss Alayna, you will walk me to my carriage."

"Yes, ma'am," she said and did as she was bid, anxious to know what had inspired this generosity and grateful to Lady Vaughn for bestowing it upon her, who was not worthy of the distinction.

Lady Vaughn said nothing until she was seated safely inside the carriage. "I won't lie to you, Miss Durham. I'm disappointed."

"In me?"

"I'm disappointed that you could not bring yourself to love Harry."

Laynie nodded in understanding.

"I'm more disappointed he did not love you enough to decide upon making his offer to you when it would have made a difference. Tell me, child, would you have accepted him had he found the opportunity to ask you?"

"I don't know, ma'am. I care for him. I trust him. I respect and honor him. But he loves someone else. I have injured my sister accepting Mr. Emerson. It was only for knowing I would injure her more had I accepted Mr. Vaughn that I had determined myself to refuse him. I had an inkling of his intention last night. I can't say I would not have been tempted."

"Tell me truly, Alayna, do you love this man, this Mr. Emerson?"

She hesitated only a moment and then shook her head.

"Is there someone else, then?"

This she was not prepared to answer.

"I want the truth. You needn't tell me who he is, only if there is someone of whom you have grown fond."

Reluctantly, Laynie nodded.

"Does he know?"

"No."

"Would it make a difference if he did?"

"No. It's quite impossible."

"Best to give it up then, yes, my dear?"

Laynie forced a smile and nodded.

Lady Vaughn placed a hand beneath her chin and looked at her a moment. At last she patted her cheek gently and smiled. "You are a good girl, my dear. You deserve to be happy. Let's see what we can do to make you so, yes?"

Laynie nodded again, grateful for Lady Vaughn's kindness and wondering what it was she could do to change Laynie's heart and mind. She would be grateful for anything, no matter how trivial, that might persuade her to overcome her present misgivings and doubts.

Laynie moved out of the way as the footmen raised the steps and closed the door. Then, as the carriage began to move forward, she watched it go. Its passing revealed the house and Mr. Emerson standing at the door watching her.

"What did she have to say?" he asked her, but she had answered enough questions for today. She turned on her heel and walked down the drive. He did not follow, and still she did not stop until she had reached the path that led to the precipice. Was there any point going up? No, none at all; but she needed some time to herself, some time without Mr. Emerson, without the silent and condemning presence of her sister. Some time without walls and with open sky—and all the world—before her. It might very well be the last time, after all.

* * *

Mr. Emerson, irritated and a little unnerved by the sudden visitor and her uncompromising demands, stood at the door and watched as Laynie very nearly ran from him. It seemed as a moment of prescience and he resented it. He resented her, in a way. Yes, he could love her. Perhaps he did. But it did not prevent him from resenting her at times. She was holding back from him and he knew why. He had experienced the same in Sophie and for the same reason as well. Damn that Daniel Holbrook!

He was aware of a growling and looked from Laynie into the immediate vicinity of the front garden as the dog, with the half-opened gate between them, snarled and lunged. Was he in danger? Only if the dog observed that the gate was not latched and that there was an opening just wide enough for him to push through. Emerson took a step back. The dog looked in the direction Laynie had gone and ran off in pursuit of her. No doubt she loved that dog more than she would ever love him. Was it because it belonged to Holbrook, too? "I'll shoot the damn thing the first chance I get."

"Why would you do such a thing?" Beth said from behind him.

He turned with a start.

"Why would you want to injure something that gave Laynie so much happiness? Is that love, Mr. Emerson? It doesn't seem like it to me."

"Did you let him out?" he asked her.

"He wanted Laynie."

He wondered at the significance of her answer, just as he had wondered at the significance of her question. "You know very well he might kill me given the chance."

"Oh, dear. What a pity that would be," she said and turned from him.

He was half tempted to bring her back, to take her by the arm and make her apologize for that. He knew better than to follow the impulse. He had followed too many before. It was why he was in this pre-dicament. No, he would exhibit self-control, as much of it as required, until he was safely married. And then... Well, that was be-tween himself and...well...no one.

"I have come to offer my assistance," Lady Vaughn announced.

Chapter thirty-one

IT WAS AS A FAMILY that the Durhams travelled to London, just Laynie and Beth and their father alone. And Jupiter, of course, who would not and could not be left behind; Laynie would not be separated from him. Large as he was he required a ticket, which irritated her father very much, but he otherwise did not object. It was Laynie, after all, who was going to have to explain her companion to her aunt and Lady Vaughn.

Laynie was somewhat less anxious about her stay with Lady Vaughn than she was her visit with her aunt. Despite her aunt's apparent displeasure regarding her marriage, Aunt Phillips had agreed to receive them, had seemed glad for the opportunity to do it and had invited them to dine their first evening in town.

As predicted, Aunt Phillips did not welcome the dog, but she reluctantly assigned him a corner of the back garden where it was very wet and a little cold and where he barked incessantly. As everyone gathered to dine, Laynie realized how very small was the party. Just her aunt and uncle. She could not have expected Grace, of course, but Ned, too, was absent. Even Mr. Emerson had declined to come. It seemed he was obligated to spend the evening with his uncle.

"Is Ned not at home?" Beth was first to ask.

"Oh, no, dear," Aunt Phillips answered. "He's at University."

"He did not come for Grace's wedding?" Laynie asked, not a little puzzled.

"Well…," Aunt Phillips said and fussed with her napkin as it lay neatly folded on her plate. "As he's doing so well this term and we thought it best not to interrupt his studies. Will you be very disappointed if he does not make it to your engagement party?"

Of course she wouldn't, but neither could she say she would be sorry for his absence. "If he can get away, I'm certain we'll all be happy to receive him."

"And how is Grace? She is married now, as she always wished to be."

"Ah, here is the soup," Aunt Phillips said as it was brought round to each place. Had she expected something else as a first course or was she simply glad of any diversion?

"It all seemed to happen so quickly," Laynie pressed. "Why, I have only just heard the news, and now it's all over and done with. I wish I had been able to wish her well."

"Oh," her aunt replied offhandedly, "it was a quiet affair. Grace has never been one for grand celebrations and fanfare." Which Laynie knew to be untrue. Her cousin was as eager for attention and praise as any Laynie knew, Beth included.

"And who is the gentleman? Is it anyone we know?"

"As chance would have it," her uncle said and coughed, having swallowed his soup too quickly. He wiped his mouth and cleared his throat. "It was a gentleman she met while you were staying with us. I don't suppose you remember the Rutherford brothers? Very handsome? Dark hair? They might be mistaken for twins they look so much alike."

Laynie did remember them, actually.

"She was simply determined to be married, it seems, and to set up house for herself. She always did have a mind of her own."

"I hope she will be very happy," Laynie said. "I'm sorry we won't see her."

"Yes, well," her aunt said with a faint air of regret. "We are very proud of her. No doubt she will be very happy, as she deserves to be."

"Of course she will," Laynie said in an attempt to reassure her aunt.

There was a long silence, and Laynie looked to her father. He was staring blankly at the pepper shaker, while Uncle Phillips attempted to interest him in his latest investment ventures. Despite the lack of attentive audience, her uncle persisted. Perhaps his own audience was sufficient.

Laynie sought for some topic to introduce now the last had been exhausted. But had it? Her mind was spinning with the questions she wished, and yet did not dare, to ask.

"Forgive me if I'm confused," said Beth, beating Laynie to it, "but it was my understanding, Aunt, that Grace had to wait until she was one and twenty to marry. Her new husband must have some money if she was willing to forfeit her own inheritance."

"Oh, well… yes," her aunt answered though rather hesitantly. "That is he will, in time. My dear Grace has been somewhat spoiled, I think. I hate to admit it, but it is true, even now, that when she has set her heart on having something she will do anything and everything to get it. She wished to be married, to have a home of her own. And now she has married the elder Mr. Rutherford and will have her heart's desire. He is a good man, I dare say, and will make Grace very happy if only she will be a little patient with him. I do hope she does not learn to regret her haste." Aunt Phillips looked at her plate very thoughtfully and with some apparent regret, but then she suddenly seemed to awaken to Laynie's present circumstances. "Not that your haste should suggest you should ever have cause to regret, dear. Oh, no. You are a woman plainly in love and you deserve all the happiness promised you."

"Do I?" Laynie asked.

Her aunt reached across the table and offered her hand, which Laynie took. Her uncle, observing the gesture, added his own congratulations. Her father looked up from his plate and smiled, though it did not reach his eyes. Beth chased a pea with her fork and then, giving up, laid the fork down on her plate.

"Are you not pleased to see your sister happily married?" Aunt Phillips asked of Beth.

"You are not," she said, giving her aunt a determined look. "Why should I be? Your objections to Mr. Emerson weren't owing to Grace's youth alone. It was for his being married before."

"Well of course he must remarry," Aunt Phillips said. "It was merely his apparent rush to do it that gave me pause for concern."

"And, as it turned out, Grace was in a hurry of her own, so I suppose you'll say, after all, that it does not matter."

Aunt Phillips took a sip of wine and laid the glass down very carefully on the table. "To own the truth, I fear Grace's haste had something to do with her heartbreak. It has occurred to me that, just perhaps, had I realized his haste was only for the threat of losing his inheritance, I might have been a little more generous towards him. Towards them."

"You regret Grace did not marry him, then?"

"I did not say that. I would not say that."

"You are glad to be free of him, then. Will you tell us why?"

Aunt Phillips cleared her throat a little, but did not answer.

"Don't mistake my meaning, Aunt. I, too, am of the opinion that he might be in a better position to find a wife that would truly make him happy if there was a fortune rushing him along."

"Oh, Beth," Laynie objected. "Must we speak of this now? When it's all but done?"

"But it's not done, Laynie," Beth insisted. "Not nearly." She arose.

"Now, now, Beth," Aunt Phillips interjected. "He might have an inheritance to secure, but that does not exclude the possibility of his falling very much in love."

"A man once married must marry again," Uncle Phillips assured them all. This was rather a reversal of his former stance on the matter, it seemed. But then they had never heard his own opinion, only that it matched his wife's. Or so his wife had claimed.

"Must he?" Beth asked. "And why is that?"

Mr. Durham's eyes shifted momentarily from his plate to Laynie, then to Beth and back to Laynie again.

Uncle Phillips suppressed a laugh. "My dear, such questions. Suffice it to say a once-married man must be lonelier upon the loss of a wife. He must remarry or..."

"Fill the void in other ways?" Beth offered.

"Well...er...yes, I suppose that's one way to put it."

"So Mr. Emerson must marry, and Grace must wait to marry, only she hasn't. And now Laynie is to marry and we're all wishing her congratulations, when three months ago Grace's engagement to the same man was roundly objected to and now she is married anyway, having thrown away her fortune, and there's nothing at all in that to cause anyone a moment's concern because Grace must marry or perish, it seems, and Mr. Emerson must love Laynie and make her eternally happy even while she sits at the table with tears pooling in her eyes and we pretend they are tears of overwhelming joy."

"Beth!" Laynie said in shock and near-horror at her sister's unchecked impertinence.

"I'm sorry if I find it all a bit too much to believe," she said and turned from the table. "Excuse me, won't you. I have a headache. Which room is mine?"

There was silence for a long time. At last Aunt Phillips rang the bell and a maid entered. "Show Miss Durham to her room, the blue one, you know…"

"Goodnight, Aunt, Papa. Goodnight, Laynie," she said and offered an apologetic and half-pleading look.

No one answered her, and so she left the room, following the maid. The door closed upon the stunned silence, preserving it, it seemed, as it did the heat of the room that pulsed from the brightly burning fireplace.

At last Aunt Phillips sniffed and lifted her chin. "She is suggesting we have been inconsistent, I think. Perhaps we have been. I don't know. One does one's best, but children will have their way. "Perhaps we were too hard on Grace. Perhaps our expectations for her were too great. She is a young woman simply determined to be in love. She won't inherit; she has been denied that, and of her own choosing, and still I think it for the best."

"Yes, certainly it is," her husband concurred. "And all is not lost. Her children will inherit eventually, and all will be well."

All was silent for a long and awkward moment.

"Well" Laynie said at last, determined to be happy for someone, if not for herself, "I wish Grace every joy. And what's more, I'm certain she will have it."

"Well said," Uncle Phillips exclaimed and raised his glass.

Aunt Phillips gave her a grateful if somewhat tearful smile and took a sip from her own glass.

* * *

Lady Vaughn's carriage arrived shortly after the men had joined them in the drawing room. Her father wished her good night as he gave her a warm and teary-eyed hug, and then she left the house, accompanied by one of Lady Vaughn's servants, who saw her—and her dog—safely from one house to the other and delivered the pair of them into the entrance hall where Harry met them.

"You brought Jupiter," Harry said and greeted him before greeting her.

"Will it be a problem?"

"No, not at all. Do you mind keeping him with you?"

"I was rather counting on it, actually."

"Excellent! How was your trip?"

"It was quiet. Papa chattered a little about this and that, but Beth… She'll hardly talk to me these days, Harry. I wish I knew how to make peace with her."

"You will. In time," he said. He nodded to a footman to take her bags, but it was he himself who showed her to her room. "Follow me, will you? I know you're tired, but I want a minute to speak with you."

"Yes, of course." With Jupiter beside her, she followed Harry up the gleaming mahogany staircase and along corridors decorated in richly-colored and heavily-patterned papers that covered walls hung with paintings of ancestry, landscapes, and men and women from Biblical history with woeful, tear-stained faces.

"Mother asked me to offer her excuses," Harry said to her, stopping so she could catch up to him. "She retires early these days but she hopes to spend some time with you tomorrow."

She looked from a painting of Mary at the tomb—a Bouguereau, she thought—to him. "I was hoping she was better. Is she not?"

"Not as well as she'd like you to think."

"I'm sorry for that," she said and truly felt it. "And here she's gone to all this trouble for me."

"It gives her pleasure. Or will, I think, if it's a success."

"The party, do you mean?"

He glanced at her and then at the painting before them and smiled but did not answer.

"Harry, I want to say I'm sorry."

"Whatever for?"

"You know what for, I think. Your mother told me why you came that night. It was only for Beth I would have refused you, you know. If you were to ask her now, I think—"

"I won't. It's not to be considered. Not until I'm certain of you."

"Harry, you can't mean to offer to me even now. I meant what I said, you know."

"You won't consider it, not even as a diversion? We don't have to go through with it, you know?"

"Not even as a diversion, Harry. I love you too much for that. And my sister, too. You know me well enough to know I would never rob another of the happiness due them simply to ensure my own. I have given him my word, Harry, and barring some implacable obstacle, I mean to keep it."

He gave her a vaguely hopeful look. "Does that mean you are looking for one?"

"I'm not going to answer that."

Jupiter whined softly.

Laynie stroked his back and returned her attention to the painting, where she saw and actually felt the longing of the Holy Women for the man who was not there.

"Very well," he said and led her on once more toward the room she would be staying in. "If you insist on offering yourself up as sacrifice I suppose there is not much more I can say. But you should know it does not make your friends happy to watch it, and if they can do anything about it..."

"I'm sorry, Harry."

"Save your apologies for when they are truly required."

She looked up at him once more. Was he actually angry with her?

He met her gaze for a moment, and she flashed him a silent question.

"You always do sabotage your own happiness," he said, answering it. "You think it's to save others, but it isn't."

"Then what is it?"

"Willful, blatant, and obdurate self-denial." He offered a half smile. "Stop it, will you, it's irritating."

They had arrived at her door. He opened it for her and waited for her to enter. It was Jupiter who entered first. He stopped to sniff the air. Deciding it was safe, he jumped up on the bed where he made himself comfortable.

Laynie crossed the threshold and turned to look helplessly at Harry. She knew she was disappointing him, and his mother, too, but there was nothing for it.

"Good night," he said to her with another doleful smile.

"Good night," she returned.

He kissed her on the cheek—a brotherly show of true affection—and shut the door.

Laynie joined Jupiter on the bed and sat to look about the room. It was perfectly appointed. Harry and his mother had not stayed much in London since his father had left them, but it was a beautiful house and all had been arranged to provide for her comfort and convenience. Even the water in the washstand basin was still warm. If only she could stay here forever. If she refused to leave would Mr. Emerson demand her return to him? Could she refuse him now? But that was impossible. The very idea was a betrayal of the commitment she had made—and which she intended to follow through with. Did she hope for an obstacle? Yes, of course. Did she believe one would present itself? No. She had meant what she had said to Beth before. She had hoped. She had loved and longed and lost, and there was nothing left to want for. Only to have a little happiness. Mr. Emerson could give her that, surely.

Couldn't he?

With this question lingering over her, she prepared for bed and did not sleep.

* * *

Harry was up and waiting in the breakfast room when Laynie went down the following morning. She had dressed in the dove gray, as she felt it the most likely to offer the impression she most wished to convey: proper, modest, unassuming, and yet dignified and ladylike.

"You look well this morning," Harry said and stood.

She suspected he was lying. "Why? What's wrong with me?"

"Nothing," he said and laughed. "Did you sleep?"

"No. Did you?"

"A little. There is something reassuring about your being here. Not in London, I mean, but in this house."

"That's kind of you."

"Have you thought about staying?"

She looked up at him from her plate as she was filling it at the buffet. She was not going to confess she had. "Are you to inherit this house, too, Harry?"

He gave her a questioning look.

"Is it still uncertain? Have you heard from your brother?"

She sat. He joined her, though he placed himself at the head of the table. He looked as though he belonged there. "Can you keep a secret?" he said.

"I think so."

"My inheritance was never in question. I never actually told you that it was, remember."

Laynie looked at him narrowly. Hadn't he?

"I only told you I'd told your sister that. And I had. But I lied."

"Harry!"

"You won't tell her?"

"No. Of course I won't, but all the worrying she's done for you."

"For me and not for herself?"

"Do you mean to confess?"

"I ought to have done it already. It seems the time for that has passed. I never wanted it to be a lure, you know. The money, I mean. I wanted her to want me, not what I might give her."

"Yes, I understand."

"Do you?"

"Yes."

He was silent for a moment. He took a sip of his coffee and nodded for her to eat. She took a bite, chewed and then swallowed.

She thought back about the story regarding Harry's inheritance and the precarious nature of it. She did remember him telling her what he had told her sister. She remembered asking him if it was true and that he had never properly answered her. But he was not the only one who had suggested such a thing was possible. "Your mother, Harry, was she privy to your deception?"

"Oh, yes. It was not her idea, mind. It was mine, but she liked the idea of proving Beth."

"And did it work? Do you think it might?"

404

"It's irrelevant now," he said with a sort of stolid resolve that almost broke her heart.

"I told you already I'm not going to let you sacrifice your own happiness for me, so don't think it. I don't need your help, you know. I'm perfectly at peace with my decision."

"You're not going to sit there and lie to me, Laynie," he said scoldingly. "Not in my own house."

She folded her napkin and put it down on the table.

"You're not done."

"I haven't much appetite, I'm afraid."

He looked at her but said nothing. His concern for her was quite apparent, and she was grateful. She loved him. She did. And while she might be happier with him than she presently was with Mr. Emerson, it simply wasn't a possibility. If her sister were to choose another... perhaps...but she would have to do it very soon. Could she ever bring herself to love Harry as she had loved someone else? She didn't see how it was possible. Could she love Mr. Emerson at all? Yes, certainly. At least she hoped she could. And it was hope that kept her moving forward. She must love someone and learn to do it quickly, or suffocate from the effort of trying not to love another.

"I can come with you, if you like, to see old Mr. Emerson."

She was tempted, but... "No. I think not."

"You're sure?"

She nodded once more.

"Is there anything I can do for you while you're here, Laynie?"

"You can keep an eye on Jupiter. He's likely to be unhappy up there alone."

"Do you sleep with him?"

"I've never slept in a room all alone before. Do you mind?"

"Your sleeping with your dog? Why should I? I can't imagine he leaves much room for you, though."

"No, Harry," she said and laughed. "Do you mind watching him?"

"No," he said and smiled. "Of course not."

There was so much she wished to ask him as he sat there watching her trying to eat but unable to do it, trying to be brave and not quite succeeding in that either. There seemed some greater purpose to

405

her being here, some greater purpose in Harry's atten-tiveness. What was it? Had he some plan to rescue her even now? And did he really think he could do it? She was very nearly tempted to ask, but the time for that had passed. Her cab had come.

Harry followed her into the foyer, where he helped her on with her things. They bid a silent farewell and she was helped into the cab by a footman. Or perhaps it wasn't a cab. Perhaps this belonged to Mr. Emerson's uncle. It was shabby and mean, but then anything might seem shabby and mean after spending a night in the Vaughn's London home. She recalled their breakfast conversation and for half a moment wondered if his confession regarding his fortune, which was never to be a lure for her sister, was in any way a lure for her. She had never cared for such things before, and yet…

No. There was no use thinking about it.

She turned to the window and watched the passing city. The carriage seemed to drive for miles through the crowded streets before arriving at the door of a rather weather-beaten townhouse. It was well-kept inside, though a little out of date, and filled with furnishings that once must have cost a great deal, though they were now somewhat scratched and worn and faded. She was shown into a sitting room that had been turned into a sort of makeshift study and there she waited for some time, quite alone and shivering. The fire had newly been lit and had not yet heated the room. At long last the door opened and an austere-looking gentleman entered, accompanied by Frederick Emerson.

"Ah, good, you've come," Emerson said to her and offered no-thing warmer in greeting.

"Did you think I wouldn't?" she asked with an attempt to draw something a little more congenial from him.

"You stayed with Vaughn last night. I didn't know what you might do."

It was ungenerous, but she did not say so. It was also a rather risky thing to say in front of his uncle, whose first and most pressing concern, or so she had been led to believe, was that there should be no air of scandal or untowardness in Mr. Emerson's relations with her, or in her own private dealings. Why, then, would he say such a thing?

Frederick bid her to sit and so she did. He approached the desk and she waited for the introduction.

"You have all the paperwork, Mr. Grieves?"

Was this not the uncle, then? A lawyer, perhaps?

"Yes. Oh, yes," the gentleman said. "Just read everything over and sign here."

"What are you signing?" Laynie asked him.

"My life away, I suppose," Emerson answered her. And then, as if he did see a point in explaining himself, after all: "I'm simply attesting that there are no other claims upon me and that I am abiding by the terms of the will in every whit."

"Why should there be other claims upon you?" she asked and felt a chill run through her unrelated to the coldness of the room.

"There shouldn't," he said. "And there aren't." He signed his name and turned to her. "Do you doubt me?"

"No, of course not."

The lawyer checked the signature, looked over the papers to make sure all was accounted for, and then lowered them just enough to look Laynie over. "Stand, will you, Miss…?"

"Durham," she answered. Did he not even know her name?

He looked her over a little longer and then looked to Mr. Emerson. "And she will submit to a doctor's examination?"

"Examination? Whatever for?" she objected.

"It's a simple formality," the lawyer assured her. It was not assurance at all.

"To see if you are fit, of course," was Mr. Emerson's answer.

"Frederick?" It was a plea. She was appalled. She felt like a mare that was being inspected for suitability before a price was agreed upon. Not like a woman. Not like a bride at all. This was humiliating!

"It's important you are what you claim to be."

"What *I* claim?"

"They are your claims too, Mr. Emerson," said the lawyer. "Let's not forget you are vouching for her character. And there must be issue from the marriage. Better to know outright than to be disappointed later, wouldn't you say?"

She sat.

"She will submit?" the lawyer asked again.

407

"No!" she said.

Emerson looked at her very pointedly. "Yes," he said. "She will."

Laynie was on her feet and moving toward the door. Emerson caught her by the arm but did not pull her back. He walked with her as far as the foyer and stopped her before the staircase.

"We're not quite done yet, my dear," he said and looked up toward the second floor. "Ready?"

"I don't know," she said. "I want to go home."

"By 'home' I hope you don't mean Vaughn's."

"I mean I want to leave here. If that interview was any indication of the standard of respectability required, I should think nearly anyone would suit. I want to go."

For the briefest moment it appeared he was about to lose his temper. He clenched his jaw and swallowed his anger. "It's not time to go quite yet, I'm afraid. In fact I insist. Shall we?" he asked and held her arm firmly enough to let her know he meant, one way or another, to see this through.

She nodded.

"Good girl," he said and led her up the stairs.

Before the door on the second floor, the nearest to the landing, Mr. Emerson stopped and knocked. A feeble mumbling was heard from within and Frederick opened the door.

"Are you awake, Uncle? I have brought someone for you to meet."

"Hmmm?" said the figure from the bed. He squinted with rheumy eyes. His hair was a shock of white all about his head and very thin. His mouth was open, his breathing labored.

"This is Miss Durham. Miss Durham, my uncle, Otto Emerson. Miss Durham is to be my bride, Uncle," he said very loudly. "She's come to meet you."

"Hmmm!" the uncle said again and tried to open one eye a little wider in order to look at her. He mumbled something that she could not hear. Mr. Emerson stooped to listen and asked his uncle to repeat himself.

He mumbled again.

"No, of course there's nothing wrong with her. What sort of question is that?"

More mumbling.

"Yes, well," Emerson said and looked over his shoulder at her, "I certainly thought so."

"Thought what?"

"That you're very fair, Miss Durham. Don't act surprised. It isn't news to you, after all."

His uncle, with one hand, pushed his nephew aside and looked at her more carefully. He mumbled once more. Mr. Emerson turned to look at her, then looked back at his uncle. He smiled broadly and moved toward the door. She started to follow.

"No, my dear, I'm afraid Uncle Otto wants a word with you in private. Take care," he said more confidentially, "he looks quite harmless, but he still requires watching."

"What does that mean?"

He smiled again, more stiffly, and then slipped out the door.

Laynie turned to Uncle Emerson. He beckoned her near him and gestured for her to take a seat. Once more he began mumbling, but she could not hear him. At last, with her third apology and the humble request he repeat himself, he handed her an ear horn. His question, when at last she heard it, was something to the effect of, "So you think you want to marry my nephew, do you?"

"I think he wants to marry me, sir," was her answer.

"But not you him, eh? I don't buy that. Not when there's a fortune involved." He smacked his mouth in an effort to wet his tongue enough to continue speaking. "You are opposed to a fortune, are you?"

She could not help but consider the state of the house, the state of the man who lay before her. Is this what his money did for him? There could not be much of it if it were so. She turned her attention back to him. She did not know how to answer.

"Why are you marrying my nephew if it isn't the money you want? You think you love him, do you?"

She felt it best to answer honestly. Perhaps honesty would help her here, to find an escape, to find an unlikely ally in his already suspicious uncle. "I think I hope to do so, in time."

"Hope? Ha!" He laughed and appeared to be taking quite a lot of pleasure in the interview and in her company. He was looking her over a little hungrily, his eyes dancing over her face and what he could see of her figure. "You seem a respectable young woman," he observed at last.

"I think I am, sir. I hope I am."

"You don't know?"

"I am, sir, truly."

"You were informed of the examination?"

"Yes."

"And you will submit?"

She thought for a moment. Would she? Could she? "No. I won't. If you don't believe in me, if he won't vouch for me, then I see no reason to humiliate myself further."

To her surprise, Uncle Emerson laughed. "Of course you don't. What respectable woman would?"

She did not understand. "If it's merely a test, sir, then what does it prove?"

"It's that look of utter mortification I was looking for. That's proof enough for me. Besides, he's one to spoil his own prizes. So long as he marries you before there's anything to talk about, what do I care?"

"Sir?"

"I want it all done above board, you see? Or at the very least for it to look that way. You look it. That's enough for me. But he won't get anything from me until the thing is done, do you see? There's no backing out of it. He must see it through and abide by his commitments. You must marry. There must be issue. It may consequently be a year or more before you see the money. Can you live quite humbly?"

"Yes. I think so. But—"

"What is it, child? Speak up and speak out if you must. I have no patience for temerity. It won't do, do you see?"

"Why do you insist he sees it through? Is there any threat of his not doing so?"

He graced her with a look that suggested he knew of some mischief he did not otherwise dare to confess to. Was it his cynicism in the ways of all men as related to matters of the heart and flesh? Or did he know something particular about his nephew's personal dealings?

"Please, sir," she said. "If it's so important to you that this marriage appears respectable, you ought to know that it is equally important to me that it is what it seems."

"You are Protestant, I take it?"

"Yes. Why?"

"You might consider changing religions if you want a marriage in this world that is respectable, a husband as equally pure and without blemish as his bride. Marry Christ rather than a man, and perhaps then you'll be satisfied."

She sat back and away from him. She did not wish to hear any more. "I asked you a question," he said to her, "and you did not answer it."

She could hear him now without the horn. Perhaps she had never needed it. "I asked you if you loved him. Do you? Don't tell me you hope to do. Do you or don't you?"

"No. Not at present."

"Good," he said and smiled, revealing a dark gap between his crooked teeth. "I like that."

"Why? How is that in any way something that should please you?"

"He deserves someone he has to fight for. It will keep him occupied for a while longer than it might otherwise. He deserves a little difficulty. He's certainly caused enough of it."

"Do you mean for him to marry me, sir, as some sort of punishment?" The idea appalled her and she was desperate for him to deny it.

"Go," he said. "I'm tired. You needn't see the physician. There's no point. You'll do, but go."

She hesitated only a moment more, then arose and fled from the room. She nearly ran down the stairs, descending as quickly as she could. She took her things from the hall tree and was nearly out the door before Mr. Emerson saw her.

"Where are you going, my dear?" he asked her.

"Home. To Lady Vaughn, I mean. I'm going now. You can't stop me."

"Wait just one moment." He approached her but she shied from him. "Did he like you? Did he approve?"

"I don't know if he liked me or not. I think he cannot like *you* very much whatever it is he means to do for you. He approves, though."

"Good girl. Now come. Mr. Grieves wants us to agree to a date. Uncle thinks the 31st. All Hallows." Emerson smiled a little wickedly and flicked his eyebrows.

"That's hardly three weeks away. So soon?"

Mr. Emerson did not answer, but Mr. Grieves, having heard his name, appeared in the doorway.

Before she answered, however, she had something to say first. "Your uncle asked if I loved you," she began, "or rather if it was the money I was after. You know it isn't the latter, and I think you know it isn't for the former I agreed. I told him the truth, your uncle. I think I thought he would take pity on me."

Mr. Emerson exhaled a laugh and shook his head at her foolishness.

"He was actually quite pleased to know it, as if the idea that you and I might be miserable together was all he ever hoped for."

A shadow fell over his face as his features grew firm and hard with malice.

However unwisely, she continued anyway. "You know, I actually believe it was because I do not love you that he approved. I don't love you, Mr. Emerson, and I don't think you love me. I don't think you can."

Mr. Emerson, with firm and heavy steps, approached her once more. She tried to evade him but there was nowhere to go. He grabbed her roughly by the arm and jerked her toward him. "You don't mean that, my darling, do you?" he asked but had no intention of letting her answer. "I think you are overwrought. Perhaps you should go home and rest before you say something you really regret."

There was no mistaking the warning this time. "Yes, perhaps I should," she said, reluctant to acquiesce but willing to agree to anything if it meant getting away.

"Let me walk you out."

He did not give her a choice, but, his hand still holding to her arm so tightly she felt the bruises forming, he escorted her down the steps and to the carriage. Within the open door of the carriage he stopped her and kissed her very hard, pushing himself against her in a most indecent fashion. The force of his passion—she could not call it affection—left her lower lip swelling and the taste of blood in her mouth.

"You are mine now, Alayna Durham, and I mean for you to remember it."

She tried to get away from him but couldn't.

"If you go back on your word," he hissed, "I will sue for breach of contract, and you can be sure I will take your father for everything he has. Even that, I doubt, will make up for what I will lose if you jilt me now. Do you understand?"

"Yes," she said and was at last allowed to step into the carriage.

He released her arm and she could feel the blood begin to flow into it again. She did not rub it, though she wanted to very much. She tried not to cry, tried not to show him how afraid of him she was.

He began to close the door but stopped again. "One other thing," he said, smiling stiffly. "I hope you won't try to meet *him* while you're in town."

She looked at him with a rebuttal.

"Don't pretend you don't know who I'm talking about," he said, cutting her off before she could make her predictable objection. "If I find that there has been a single word, written or spoken however indirectly, between you, I won't leave either of you with a single shred of self-respect. I'll reveal all his misdeeds and just how ready you were, and no doubt still are, to encourage him to repeat them. I will ruin you both and faster than you can think to form an objection. You won't make a fool of me and neither will he. Not ever again. Do you understand me?" He didn't wait for her answer but slammed the door shut and walked away.

In a numb daze, Laynie endured the ride back to the Vaughn's home. She entered and somehow managed to maintain her composure until she had reached her room. Once there, she closed and locked the door and threw herself onto the bed, burying her face in a pillow where she released what emotion was left in her and then lay there numb, spent, and undisturbed for the greater part of the day.

Chapter thirty-two

STANDING NEAR A FAMILIAR STAIRWELL, Harold Vaughn held his hand up to the door, hesitated a moment, then knocked. He waited, while Jupiter sniffed at the door jam and the space beneath the door itself. He whimpered and then scratched at the door frame.

To his relief, and Jupiter's as well, Daniel Holbrook answered the door.

"Vaughn!" he said in surprise. He scowled a curious look at the dog and ruffled the fur on his head. "Hello there, old friend." He looked up again at Vaughn. "What brings you into Town? Nothing is wrong, I hope?"

"May I come in?" was Vaughn's reply.

"Yes, of course. By all means," Holbrook said and held the door open for him.

Vaughn entered and waited for Holbrook to secure the door again. He was slow about it, as if steeling himself for the news he must have been expecting.

Jupiter thought the sofa looked particularly comfortable and climbed onto it, taking up the whole.

Holbrook approached the dog, rubbed at his ears once more, and turned to look at Vaughn.

"How are you, Vaughn?"

"I've been better. You? How was your journey to the continent? Did you find who you were looking for?"

"Sophie?"

"Is that her name, then?" he asked with a little more sensitivity. It was plain Mr. Holbrook was a man under a great deal of strain.

"Yes. Sophie Warren is the owner of the initials and the portrait you saw."

"And did you find her?"

"No," he said. "No, we didn't find her. We found where she was last living. It was empty and pitifully kept, but there was no telling how long ago she was there. Not by the looks of the place, at any rate."

"So nothing, then, to tell you when and how she died, or if, perhaps, she is—?"

"What brings you here, Vaughn?"

"No doubt you can guess."

"Miss Durham? Laynie?"

"She's here in Town. The whole family is. Mine as well."

"That explains your having Jupiter, then. What brings them?"

"She's engaged to be married, Holbrook."

Holbrook seemed not to have heard him at first. The news inspired no reaction whatever. Perhaps a whole minute passed before he at last nodded and sat. He gestured for Vaughn to sit as well. And so he did.

"It won't be a long engagement," Vaughn continued. "I believe the terms of his uncle's will demand he is married very soon."

Holbrook glanced at him, nodded, and looked away again.

"Have you any reason to believe something ought to be done to interfere?"

Again it took Holbrook a long time to answer. Perhaps he was considering all the reasons he himself might object and dismissing them one by one. Without some reason outside his own sentiment, there was nothing Vaughn could really do. There was little anyone could do, particularly with her father so anxious for it and Laynie feeling obligated to comply. Why did she feel obligated? Perhaps that was the better question. And was there anything anyone could do to change her mind? Could Holbrook?

"Perhaps if you spoke with her," Vaughn suggested.

"Impossible."

"Why?"

"How am I to meet her, Vaughn? Do you propose arranging something?"

Vaughn perceived a look that was, behind the air of ridicule, vaguely hopeful. He handed Holbrook the square of paper on which had been written an invitation to an evening of dancing and music.

He held it in his hand and examined it, weighing it as if it were a burden he was not sure he wanted to take upon himself. "She'll be there?"

"Yes. It's for her; it's an engagement party of sorts, though it doesn't say that…just in case, you know."

Holbrook handed it back. "Then no," he answered quite firmly.

Vaughn would not accept it. "I want you to come. I'm inviting you personally. It's at my house. You'll be quite welcome."

Holbrook graced him once again with a doubtful look.

"I do understand it won't be comfortable for you, but is this really a time to be selfish?"

"I rather think my going would be selfish, Vaughn. Do you not see?"

"You might have something to say to persuade her to reconsider."

"I don't like Emerson. I despise him, actually, but I have no evidence that would prove he's done anything criminal. If she has feelings for him, if she thinks he can make her happy…"

"She doesn't."

Holbrook looked at him narrowly. "How do you know that?"

"I've known her since she was a child. She cannot lie to me. I know she cares for someone else."

"She's admitted it?"

Vaughn hesitated. "No, of course not. Will you come?"

"My speaking to her can serve no purpose."

"Of course it can. If you care for her, and if she—"

"Vaughn. It's impossible. Her father—"

"He can be persuaded. I'm certain of it."

"I'm not. And even if he could be, there are other reasons."

"I don't want to hear any pointless declarations about why you are unworthy of her. Even if it could matter now, now when she needs you most, I wouldn't believe—"

"I don't believe Sophie is dead."

This stopped Vaughn short. He had suspected it but had rather counted on the idea that their finding nothing would mean that there was nothing to be found.

416

"Perhaps it's just wishful thinking, Vaughn. Perhaps it's simply a nagging desire, one I've never quite thrown off, that one day there would be a way to undo what I have done—to make it up to her. To make it right."

"If she can be found, that would save Laynie, wouldn't it?" It was not ideal, but it was something.

"It might. If he married her, then of course he cannot marry again. I'm rather inclined to think he did not, though."

"And if he didn't..." Vaughn asked, sitting up a little straighter.

"Then he *is* free to marry again. But she must be made to know what kind of man she is marrying. If he's abandoned this woman..."

"Such can only be proved if she is alive."

"Then find out! Why are you here if there is Miss Warren to be found?"

"Hamilton is following the trail. I had to return to Brookdale. I've hired men, after all, and they must be paid. They must be given direction. And the work must commence, as quickly as may be, I think. She will need somewhere to go. Somewhere safe. I only came here to collect what I need before I go again."

"And when you find her?"

Holbrook only looked up at him from his place.

"You didn't abandon her, you know. That was Emerson's doing."

"I don't know it, Vaughn. If I hadn't gone... Perhaps if I had been more forceful when I had returned..."

"But she chose him."

"The way Laynie is choosing him now?"

"And you will just stand by and allow that to happen? Again?"

Holbrook was out of his seat and pacing the room.

"He will marry her, and soon. He can't hope to inherit without her now. It doesn't mean he can make her happy, though. I'm not certain he is very determined to try."

Holbrook was looking at him now. "Can you imagine it, Vaughn? Can you imagine having a woman like that and not doing everything in your power to make certain she was happy and well provided for in every possible way?"

"No. And neither can you. So what will you do about it?"

"What *can* I do!"

"You say you must provide a safe place for Miss Warren—if she is found. What of Laynie? What safe place has she?"

"Besides her father and her sister, do you mean?"

Harry nodded.

"There is you, isn't there?"

"Yes, but she doesn't love me, Holbrook."

"But you would treat her well. You would care for her, provide for her. And she would learn to do it, to appreciate you. And you love her, too."

Harry didn't answer. It was true, certainly, but no matter how he tried, it wasn't she he would choose had he his choice.

"You prefer her sister still, do you?" Holbrook asked, deducing the truth from Vaughn's sober silence.

"You could tell her—Laynie, I mean—what you know. You could tell her your history, let her weigh it against his character and yours."

"And turn her against me as completely as her father has been turned? I'm surprised you can suggest such a thing."

"I can suggest it because I know her well enough to trust that that won't happen. And if it will convince her to throw off Emerson, how much, in the end, can it matter?"

Holbrook did not answer right away, only gave him a dismissive look. But he was considering. Vaughn could see it.

"I think if she saw you it would help her," he pressed. "Perhaps that's all it would take, for her to see you and to remember."

"Remember what, exactly?"

"The difference between your regard for her and his."

"Do you have any idea what you are asking of me, Vaughn?"

"I do, actually, Holbrook. I'm sacrificing something here, too, you know. It's a worthy sacrifice, though. I don't think you and I would disagree there. And how do you know if you do not come, if you do not at least try, that you will not have cause to blame yourself for the ruin of two women rather than just the one?"

Holbrook gave him a dead stare. For a moment it seemed he had some reply to make, and one that would be as unpleasant in its receiving as it was in its delivery. He said nothing though, and at last he swallowed hard and looked away.

"You'll come?"

"I'll consider it," Holbrook answered. "That's all I can promise."

* * *

A tap upon her door woke Laynie from a fitful slumber. It took her a moment to orient herself to her surroundings and to allow her head to steady itself after sitting up so quickly. She slipped off the bed and opened the door to find Beth on the other side of it. She didn't know quite what to say or how to greet her, but Beth did not wait for any greeting, only pushed past her, a parcel in her hand, which she set upon the bed.

"How was your meeting with Mr. Emerson's uncle?" Beth asked, turning toward her.

"It was awful."

"Did he not approve of you?"

"Oh, yes. He approved."

"Then what is the trouble?"

But Laynie did not wish to tell her. She had forgotten about it in her napping and she did not wish to remember now. Not yet. "What did you bring me?"

"A surprise," Beth said. "It's nothing special, it was merely something to occupy my time. As it turns out, you require it."

"Require it?"

"The party is tomorrow night. Have any of your new things been delivered?"

"No, they aren't finished yet. Lady Vaughn said we might find something ready-to-wear, but there will still be alterations. With all there is to do, there isn't time."

"I was afraid of that," Beth said. "Aunt might have liked to take you shopping. But yes, I think it's too late. And since there is no chance now to have something especially made for you, then I suppose it's a good thing I did it already."

"Already?"

Beth untied the string, removed the paper, and opened the lid. From within she drew out a gown of moss-green satin with a wine-colored overlay. "Try it on," she said. "I know green isn't your color, but it's really more red now than anything."

419

Laynie looked at it in both pleasure and surprise. "It's lovely, Beth! When did you do this?"

"Over the last several weeks, I suppose, while you have been occupied with Mr. Emerson. I had to find something to do, you know."

"Yes, but why this? Why for me? I thought you—"

"Laynie," she said and took her sister by the arms. "I was jealous, I admit it, but I have never been angry with you. Not over Mr. Emerson. He isn't worth it. You are my sister, my best friend. How can I do anything but love you?"

Laynie, with the gown in her hands, fell into her sister's arms.

"Will you try it on?" Beth said at last. "I want to be sure it fits."

Laynie nodded and laid the dress aside so that she could remove what she was wearing. Beth helped her, but stopped to stare at her sister once she was reduced to only her underthings.

"What is that?" she asked, pointing to Laynie's arm.

Laynie turned so that she could see the back of her arms in the reflection of the mirror. There was a bright mark across it in the shape of four fingers.

"Did he do that?" Beth asked.

"It's nothing," Laynie said and took the dress from her sister's hands. "I bruise very easily, that's all."

"Oh, Laynie," Beth said, her brow furrowing heavily and with tears in her eyes. "Why are you doing this? Why must you go through with it? If he is unkind to you now…"

"Beth, I'm not going to have this conversation with you. I'm going to marry him. I have to, don't you see?"

"No. No, I don't see. I fear he is a bad man, Laynie. I have long felt that he could not be trusted. And this is proof."

"It is not proof. It was merely my own clumsiness. I nearly slipped down the steps coming away from his uncle's house and he caught me. That is all. I swear it." Yes, it was a lie. Better to lie and allay Beth's fears than to confess to having shared Beth's uncertainties. To say them aloud would make them real, and it was too late to do anything about them now. If she did not marry him there would be consequences, and ones she did not believe she was prepared to pay.

"Can I just try the dress on and we can talk about this later?"

Beth, plainly emotional, nodded. "Yes. Yes, of course," and she helped her sister on with the dress. Having secured the last button, Beth smoothed the fabric over her shoulders. A small cuff of organdie only barely covered them, leaving the bruise bare for all to see. Beth's hand lingered there, her fingers tracing the outline of it.

Laynie turned to avoid her but also to show her the dress. It really was very beautiful. Beth looked at it and smiled a little.

"Why did you make it, Beth?" Laynie asked.

"I don't know. I guess I thought you might want it. You don't have many nice things, you know. I usually get the nice things and you get what is left. You deserve something nice for once."

"I don't know how to thank you."

"Thank me by being happy," she said.

"I will try."

But Beth merely sniffed away her tears as she examined the dress very closely, checking the fit and smoothing it to lay just right against her. "There is something not quite right about it, I think," she said, looking very seriously at Laynie's reflection.

"I think it's perfect, Beth. Really, I do."

Beth, turning Laynie towards her, seemed to consider a little further. At last she raised her hand and took hold of the fill she had sewn into the neckline so that the bust was not too revealing. She tugged on it once, then twice, and the piece came away.

"Beth!" Laynie said in shock. "What are you thinking?"

"I'm thinking it's just a little too modest. Even for you. There," she said and turned Laynie to face the mirror once more. "The color was not a precise match anyway."

Laynie observed the neckline that was now uncomfortably low. "Beth, it's so…."

"It's perfect. You're simply going to have to accept the fact that you have an admirable figure and that there are men, a room full of them tomorrow night, who will be more than happy to admire it."

"But what is the point of that? It's an engagement party. I'm to be married."

"Perhaps that *is* the point, Laynie."

Laynie looked at her sister long and hard. There was a look on Beth's face that was oddly similar to that she had seen on Harry's but yesterday. "Have you and Harry formed some plan to overthrow Mr. Emerson, Beth?"

"A plan?" she said with convincing nonchalance. "I've not heard of a plan—not as such, at any rate." Beth once again flashed that vaguely mischievous look in Laynie's direction. It disappeared nearly the moment it had formed. "All I know is that Lady Vaughn assumed responsibility for the party so that Harry could invite whomever he wished without Papa's sanctions...or Mr. Emerson's either, for that matter."

"Sanctions? Who would come that they would not—Oh, no. You don't mean to suggest that Mr. Holbrook has been invited?"

"Why should that idea strike such terror into you? He and Mr. Vaughn are friends, and ones who don't see each other often. Papa clearly misses him, despite Mr. Emerson's meddling. Why shouldn't he come and enjoy the company? Why shouldn't he come and wish you every happiness?"

Laynie sat down on the bed.

"What is it, Laynie?"

She stared at her hands and willed herself not to cry.

"If you don't want him here, I'm sure it's not too late. I can tell Harry this very day to revoke his invitation. I'm sure it would be no trouble. Why Harry would do anything for—"

"Stop!" Laynie said as Beth turned the knob of the door as if to go and find him this minute. "Don't. You have to stop this. I think you are bent on tormenting me. You come here bearing gifts and teary-eyed smiles, you taunt me with old friends and awkward encounters, you dress me up in a gown you made by hand and then spoil it a moment later. I don't understand what it is you are trying to do. And I don't know what it is you want me to do. It seems everything causes someone pain and inconvenience."

Beth smiled slightly. It was not the response Laynie had expected. "Why should encountering Mr. Holbrook be either painful or inconvenient, Laynie?"

"I didn't mean just for myself, of course. I meant for Mr. Emerson."

422

"No you didn't. You care for him. He is a thousand times better a man than Mr. Emerson can ever hope to be. So why won't you try for him?"

"Because, Beth, it isn't like that. And even if I did want to…"

"Go on."

"There is no use. Don't you see? Mr. Emerson…he won't allow it, even if Papa would. It isn't possible. It is better that I marry Mr. Emerson."

"Better for Mr. Holbrook, do you mean? Is that why you are agreeing to this?" Beth said as if she had just come to some significant realization. "To protect him?"

"No, Beth. No. You have it all wrong." She took a great shuddering breath and stood up. "I won't talk about it anymore. Shall we show Lady Vaughn the dress? I think she would like to see it and to cast her approval."

"I inquired after her when I came. She's not well today and is resting. I think she is saving her reserves for tomorrow. Let me help you off with it."

Laynie turned back toward the mirror and watched her sister as Beth unfastened the buttons, one by one, glancing occasionally into the mirror. Laynie would not cry in front of her sister, but the idea that Beth was waiting for her to do it, as if it were some sort of proof, made it all the harder not to do it.

"I'm sorry, Laynie, if I've hurt you. I hope you know I only want to see you happy. You deserve so much more than he can ever give you."

Laynie thought of his uncle's shabby house and wondered again at the inheritance that he seemed to think was significant. Unless his uncle was a miser of the meanest proportions, it could not be much. "How do you know that? How *can* you know that?"

"I don't, I suppose. I only see that you are not happy now. Now, Laynie, when a bride is usually happiest of all. If this is love, what happens when it wears off?"

Laynie, holding the now unbuttoned gown against her, turned to her sister. "Goodnight, Beth."

"Laynie?"

"I want to rest. I need some time to think. Or rather not to think. Do you mind?"

"No," she said but with some hesitation. "I suppose not. I'm nearby—a matter of ten minutes in good traffic—if you need me." Beth kissed her and then was gone.

* * *

Beth did not like to leave her sister this way. She felt she hardly knew her now. She felt that someone had come and changed her, had made her into something else. Something complicit and fearful. If only someone would rescue her. If someone could tell her what a monster that Mr. Emerson was. But who had the proof of that? Had Mr. Holbrook? She had seen Grace, had formed her suspicions, suspicions that had been bolstered by her aunt and uncle's hintings and half-spoken confessions. But she knew nothing for certain.

The door was opened for her by a footman, but Harry stood on the other side of it, just returning home with his brow furrowed deeply and Laynie's dog at his side.

She started, though she didn't know why she should. There was something rather quiet and menacing about the dog, though he had never shown any sign of violence toward anyone but Mr. Emerson. It should have earned him her trust. She was not certain yet that it had.

"Miss Durham," Harry said, greeting her. "Are you just leaving?"

"Yes. I'm not wanted, it seems. Laynie is quite undone. I don't know why she insists on going through with this if she is so very miserable."

"Emerson, I suppose, has made some vile threats against her."

"I think you are right," Beth said and sighed. "And it isn't her character alone."

"What do you mean?"

"She says it was an accident, that she fell and he caught her, but there is a bruise the shape and size of a man's hand on her arm."

"Good heaven!"

"As far as her character is concerned, is that not why your mother took charge of the party? Was it not to vouch for her?"

"That is certainly part of it."

"Laynie has always been so independent. She's never cared much for society's approval."

"Perhaps there is more to it, then. Perhaps she fears for the damage it may do to someone else."

"Mr. Holbrook?" Beth asked. "Yes, Mr. Vaughn, I do believe you are right. But does he care for such things, truly?"

"I don't know that he does. But that may not prevent her from caring in his behalf."

"Whatever the reason for her determination to go through with it, she *is* afraid of him. I wish there was something you could do, Harry."

"As do I, but she won't even consider it as a deception. If she won't let me help her, then it's out of my hands."

"She told me," Beth said tentatively, "that she knew it would make me unhappy if she agreed, and that she could not live with that."

Harry looked at her a moment. "And would it?"

"I would be relieved to see her happily situated. I know you would treat her well. I'm sure I would get used to it in time. But yes. I would be unhappy."

Harry took Beth's hand. "You know I would do anything for either of you, my best and dearest friends."

"Yes, of course," Beth said and tried not to cry.

"And yet…the idea of meeting together, as brother and sister, it would be unbearable. It *is* unbearable."

Beth gave him her other hand.

"It is not much, I know," he said. "Were circumstances altered I would ask you differently, but think, would you, if Laynie will not allow me to rescue her, would you consider me? Would you marry me, Bethany?"

Beth had no answer. The swelling of her heart prevented speech. She threw herself into his arms and wept.

The sound of a clearing throat and the angry tap of a walking stick on the marble stairs arrested her attention. She separated herself from Harry and stood back from him to find Lady Vaughn standing in the hall watching them.

"Bethany Durham."

"Yes, ma'am," Beth said and tried to keep her knees from trembling. She sniffed back the tears that had begun to form.

"Come here."

Beth obeyed and approached to stand just before Harry's mother as she cast a disapproving look upon her. The look, in time, softened if only slightly. She glanced at Harry.

"Is this what you want, Harold, truly?"

"Yes," he said.

"And you give up on Alayna, do you, in her time of greatest need?"

"She won't have me. There must be something else we can do. If Holbrook should find something out about Emerson…"

"Before tomorrow? Is that likely?"

"Find something out?" Beth said, surprised.

"There is the chance," Harry said, "that Mr. Emerson is not in a position to marry. It's all up to Holbrook to find out."

"Is that why he's coming?"

"No. Not entirely. I… He is in love with her. I know it. He has all but confessed it. And she, I think, with him."

"Yes," said Lady Vaughn and Beth together. They looked at each other and then back to Harry.

"If anyone can convince her, he can." He paused for a moment. "And I believe he will."

Lady Vaughn descended the last step and took Beth by the hand. Beth looked at her, a little afraid, but growing in hope every moment.

"And if he can," Harry went on, "I want your blessing, mother. I want to marry Miss Bethany Durham."

Lady Vaughn, with Beth's hand still in hers, approached her son. She took his hand, too, and placed them together so that the three of them were hand-clasped.

"Very well," she said. "So long as Laynie is rescued before the announcement of her engagement tomorrow night you shall have it."

She turned back to the stairs and began to climb them again. Beth was just about to thank her when the woman turned. "It is, after all, an engagement party. We would not want to disappoint our guests."

Certainly not," Harry said and watched his mother retreat, as Bethany watched him. The moment she was out of sight, Harry drew her to him and kissed her as only a man too long in love with one woman knows how.

Chapter thirty-three

ONE MORE DAY IN LONDON meant another day of Daniel wearing down the floorboards in his flat. He was growing tired of shabby living. He was growing tired of solitude. More than that, he was growing tired of this constant and anxious waiting for any news of Sophie's whereabouts. If it had not been for the demands of Brookdale and for Charlie's insistence, Daniel never would have left the search. Was he abandoning Sophie once more? Or rather, in his absence, was he abandoning someone else? It was this last thought that had him fixed in London now. If he could see her once more, he could recommit himself to the task at hand. Unlike Sophie, Laynie was surrounded by people who would love and protect her. Sophie had no one. If she still lived, she had Daniel alone. This time he would be there for her.

If only he knew where she was—or *if* she was. The chances of her being alive still were not good, he knew. If Emerson claimed her dead, was she really likely to be otherwise? Not if her living conditions under his care were any indication. But living or dead, she was not in France. Where, then, was she?

They had asked about, he and Hamilton, showing her photograph in the village where she was last known to live, inquiring at nearby inns and train stations, at coach stops and post offices, anywhere and everywhere they could think of where she might have passed through on her way to somewhere else. But where was she going and why? Well, presumably, she was looking for Emerson. Who else was there, after all?

Putting their heads together they had determined to follow that trail, enquiring in Portsmouth and even Gravesend, where he was known and she was not. An inn there remembered him well, for he had not paid his bill. It had been paid at last, but there was no need to ask how or when. Vaughn had paid it. It was how they had known to begin this possibly fruitless search. But there must be some clue of her to be found somewhere, and God help them they would find it. Alive or dead, she had not simply vanished.

And then Daniel had been forced to return, while Hamilton searched on. He was growing mad with waiting.

He checked his watch. If he was going to go to this party, he would have to start getting ready. Was there any amount of preparation that could make him ready to face Laynie and Mr. Emerson together? No. None. So would he go? He growled aloud and pounded his fist on the mantelpiece. Was he really capable of being this close to her and not seeing her?

If only he had some word from Hamilton. Any clue he could take with him to prove Emerson was the scoundrel he believed him to be. But even if that clue should be Sophie herself, was he likely to use it, and in so doing reveal Sophie's sordid history, as well as his own? There was no point answering the question. There was no clue, nothing to tell him what had become of dear Sophie Warren, nothing to aid him in his desperate desire to divide Laynie from Emerson or he from her.

Yes, he would go to this party, but what he would do when he got there or how long he would make himself stay—assuming he would even be welcome—it was impossible to say.

* * *

The face that stared back in the reflection of the dressing table mirror was a stranger to Laynie. Hannah had come to help her dress, had arranged her hair and had done it with such precision and skill that Laynie was now nearly unrecognizable, at least to herself. Her hair had been arranged at the top of her head in a carefully organized pile of seemingly random ringlets and intertwining tresses, leaving a long, thick twist of hair to drape delicately along her neck over one shoulder. She had seen such styles in modern magazines and in fashion plates in dress shops, and though her hair was certainly long and thick enough to accomplish it, it was never something she would have tried on her own. It was too sophisticated and yet, at the same time, too carefree to seem quite proper for someone of her humble means. She ordinarily wore her hair in simple plaits and chignons or, when she was particularly lazy, merely loosely pinned in whatever manner it would securely stay. She supposed this was a little the same in theory, but in execution it had taken Hannah over an hour to secure it and to arrange it so that it looked quite expertly done. The rest of her toilet was accomplished with a little powder to lighten and even out her complexion and with the smallest touch of rosebud salve to her lips, which brought out the natural color and would, or so she hoped, dissuade her from biting them in her anxiety tonight. She must put on a face of implacable equanimity. Nothing less would do.

Hannah, finished, drew her to the full-length mirror so that Laynie could see the entirety of her transformation. She was not displeased. She looked very well, in fact, only very different. She looked older. Wiser? Perhaps. Prepared to face what lay before her? Not in the least.

Beth really had worked wonders with this dress. Moss green was not Laynie's color, but wine was. It brought out the warmth in her hair and in her skin, and the play of light with the green peeking through mirrored the brown-green of her eyes. The dress itself, the green one that Grace had given them, was one of spare design and clung rather closely to Laynie's frame. There was no heavy ornamentation, no wide circumferences nor layers upon layers of skirt to contend with, and so it rendered itself well to the overlay, which hung in diaphanous swags across the skirt, sweeping behind to create a shimmering and flowing circumference of its own. There was a fairy-like quality to it, but yet serious and daring at the same time. There had been some rather ornate pleating and beading along the very low neckline, and these had been removed to allow Beth to swag and drape the organdie overlay across the bodice as well so that the green gown fitted closely to Laynie's shoulders and the upper part of her arms, providing a more tailored foundation for the overlay, which fit loosely and draped, almost suggestively, from one shoulder to the other. Without the green beneath it, it would be quite indecent. As it was, it was tastefully provocative. Laynie was concerned with the provocative aspect, with the daring modernity of it, and was anxious for Lady Vaughn to cast her approval. For that she must wait. Lady Vaughn had spared her maid for Laynie's benefit, but she could not do without her for herself. Hannah excused herself, leaving Laynie to stare into the mirror and to wonder about the night ahead, what it would signify, who she might see and speak with, and if there was any chance at all that the evening would not simply prove to be one disappointment after another.

She remained there standing, afraid to sit for fear of crushing her dress, for a long time—minutes upon minutes—while Jupiter watched her and occasionally whimpered. He was less silent in his impatience than she was in hers. More than once she checked the mirror to make sure the bruises Mr. Emerson had left upon her arm were covered. Hannah had found for her a scarf that was a near match to the organdie, and with this draped along her back and over her arms, the bruises were quite completely hidden. She was perfectly prepared, at least in appearance. There was nothing more to do but to wait.

At long last the knock sounded on her door. It was not Lady Vaughn, however, but a maid come to fetch her. Her family had arrived. Would she care to have a few minutes with them before the guests began to arrive? Yes. Yes, of course she would.

* * *

Laynie entered the drawing room to find her father and sister waiting for her there. Aunt and Uncle Phillips had arrived with them. She was a little surprised to see them here, though of course they had been invited. Harry was present, as well, standing off to one side, an empty glass sitting on the table beside him as he ran his finger round the rim of it. He did not appear quite as comfortably in command tonight as formerly. He greeted her warmly, examined her manner of dress, offered the usual compliments, and then exchanged a long look with Beth as he released her to approach her father. Laynie would very much like to have known what that look meant.

"Laynie, my darling," Mr. Durham said and beckoned her to him.

She approached and embraced him, then stood back as he took his turn admiring her. He smiled solemnly. "You do look like your mother tonight. You certainly look like a grown woman." He kissed her on the forehead and held her to him again. "How quickly you have grown up. And now you are soon to leave me." He looked at her again. "You must like the idea of that, yes?"

"No, Papa," she said very sincerely. "I don't want to leave you. Not ever."

He nodded and left her to Bethany, as he blinked tears from his eyes that he did not wish her to see.

Beth approached and took her hand. Her aunt took her by the other, and together they stood there a moment in silence.

The sound of the door aroused Uncle Phillips who had just begun to nod. He rose to his feet but held back as Harry led the others into the entrance hall where they would receive the first of their guests and where introductions would be made.

"A word, my dear," Uncle Phillips said to her.

She stopped to hear what he had to say.

He approached her, cleared his throat, and then seemed to think a moment. "I owe you an apology, I believe."

"Whatever for?" she asked, somewhat surprised.

"Your holiday with us in Gravesend ended rather prematurely."

"Yes, and of necessity, I think. I never blamed you."

"You are a good girl for saying so, but the fault is mine. At least…it was not yours."

She did not say anything but waited for him to go on.

He cleared his throat again. "Ned has not behaved the gentleman toward you. I wish I had realized how oppressive you felt his attentions. I wish I knew he had been oppressing you with them."

"It isn't your fault, Uncle."

"Certainly it is. I ought to have raised him better. But he has behaved very ill and an apology is owed you. I'm sorry, my dear, for whatever he made you suffer, and for the embarrassment we ought to have mitigated and did not."

"You took care of the matter in the best and only way there was. It's he who should do the apologizing. It was his offense, not yours."

"Perhaps it is. But I must apologize for him. He isn't to come."

"You told him not to come?" she said, even more surprised by this and a little relieved as well.

"He was certainly invited," he said, "but he refused. He feels betrayed, you know, by his friend Emerson. He's quite heartbroken by the news. I think he really was very fond of you, my dear."

The idea of Ned's feeling betrayed was so wholly novel to her she had to consider it a moment. And yet Ned was not the only friend Emerson had betrayed, was he? She thought of the hintings and insinuations of the night before, those which she had determined, at least at the present, to ignore. They seemed suddenly rather important now.

She opened her mouth to speak, to summon the words and the courage to ask. Mr. Emerson's voice arrested her.

"Mr. Phillips," he said and entered, extending his hand, though doing it somewhat cautiously. Had he overheard the conversation? She did not think he could have.

"Ah, Emerson." Uncle Phillips' countenance changed. His manner chilled. "You have my utmost congratulations. Let's pray you deserve your good fortune." He said nothing more, but left them to each other.

"Who is fond of you?" he asked. He had been standing there longer than she had supposed. If he was jealous he hid it behind a crooked and curious smile.

"Uncle was speaking to me of Ned, that he is rather jealous of you just now."

Emerson smiled more broadly. "He doesn't mean to fight me over you does he? Old Ned is an ox in the boxing ring."

He was on his best behavior it seemed. "He won't be coming, I'm happy to say. Though I do feel a little sorry for him."

"I don't. The fellow's been spared!"

"Oh?" she said and did not quite take his meaning.

"If he were to see you tonight it might very well be the end of him. You are utterly breathtaking."

It was a compliment then. She smiled.

"I'm extraordinarily tempted to kiss you," he said, "but I'm almost afraid to, you're so perfect. Like a china doll. Will you break?"

"No," she said with a laugh. "I don't think so."

"Then perhaps it's worth the risk, after all." He leaned toward her, hesitated a moment, and then brushed his lips very gently against hers. It was so tender a gesture it sent goose bumps down her arms. "Shall we then?" he said.

She nodded and he led her out into the hall, where Lady Vaughn stood, perfectly erect in a rigid gown of plum-brown, suggesting state of near, but not quite, mourning for her absentee husband. Harry stood dutifully beside her as together they welcomed their guests. Harry saw her, smiled, and whispered something to his mother, who turned to beckon her, a look of unqualified approval on her face.

"My dear!" she said and took her hand in her own. She squeezed it briefly but said nothing more, not to her directly at any rate, but proceeded to introduce her to any and all who arrived as though she were worthy of the very highest regard.

Mr. Emerson, who appeared not to want to let Laynie out of his sight, lingered nearby. Harry, seeing him, made a faint effort to introduce him to one or two of his own acquaintances, but he quickly transferred his attention upon Mr. Durham, who was looking a little lost and confused in the growing crowd. Harry led him off to a quieter corner of the reception room beyond where he might sit more comfortably. Laynie trusted he would not leave her father alone but would provide him with someone to talk to. Uncle Phillips was no conversationalist. She scanned the room just outside which she was presently standing and observed her uncle, the first it seemed to have arrived at the refreshment table.

Laynie was introduced to a few more newcomers, but at every opportunity she looked to be certain her poor Papa was being taken care of. She could just see him behind the screen of a parlor palm, and with every minute that passed he became more and more obscured by the ever thickening crowd around him. But Harry had provided him with some company, it seemed, and she trusted his judgment enough to take some comfort in the sight of him striking up a conversation with a stranger who, no doubt, would quickly become a friend. Mr. Durham had never had trouble making friends.

With her worry for her father somewhat abated, Laynie took a moment to examine the house. She had awoken this morning to a commotion and now saw what it all was for. There were flowers every-where, in vases and bowls, festoons of them up and down the staircase and along the balcony. Every surface had been swagged and draped in some manner. Velvet, satin, lace…flowers! All this to cele-brate her engagement to a man no one but her father alone seemed much to like. And the guests! They kept coming. The introductions, con-sequently, continued to be made. How was she ever to remember anyone's name? There was one she would certainly remember...if he came. Would he?

Her attention moved to the door. She recognized no one and took some relief in that. But her relief would soon turn to anxiety, and then what? Disappointment if he did not come? Elation if he did? And then, certainly, disappointment again. She was not likely to have the chance of speaking with him after tonight.

The hall was growing crowded and Lady Vaughn, it appeared, was growing apparently fatigued. Laynie spotted Harry and sum-moned him. He saw immediately her reason for doing so.

"Let's go sit a while, shall we, Mother? We have footmen for a reason, after all. There's nothing that says your guests can't be brought to you."

"Yes, all right, Harold. Alayna," she said and held out her hand.

Laynie, it seemed, was to follow. And, anxious as she had been a few minutes ago, she did not wish to leave the door now. Yes, Lady Vaughn's guests might be brought to her, but would Harry's? If he remained, perhaps. But no, he was a man whose company was much in demand. He excused himself and left them once more, as Laynie watched him go.

And where was Beth? Laynie's attention, as she sat beside Lady Vaughn, was now divided in a multitude of directions: between her hostess and those who addressed her; Harry and the direction in which he had now disappeared; her sister, whom she could not seem to find; and the short flight of stairs that led to the front door, at the top of which Laynie had so recently been standing and where anyone newly arrived must be seen. And of course, there was yet her father to be mindful of.

"Are you looking for someone special, my dear?" Mr. Emerson said, bending low to whisper in her ear as he stood behind her chair.

"Only for Beth," she answered him.

He nodded toward the balcony, where Harry could be seen approaching her. Beth was looking very demure and humbled, and very pretty in a simple gown of pale blue. She wasn't her proud and coquettish self tonight, it seemed.

"That pleases you?" Emerson asked her with a nod in their direction.

"Yes, indeed."

Mr. Emerson's thumb skimmed the back of her neck. He fingered a curl. She was not comfortable with the familiar way he touched her, as if he meant to make a point of their attachment even before the engagement was announced.

"Excuse me, if you will, ma'am," Laynie said, placing her hand on the arm of Lady Vaughn's chair and leaning toward her to speak. "I think I'd like to go see how Papa is getting on."

"Yes, of course, my dear," she said and patted her hand. Her gaze shifted from Laynie to Mr. Emerson and narrowed. "Mr. Emerson," she said, "would you be so good as to sit with me a while?"

Mr. Emerson had no choice but to accept, and so he sat, leaving Laynie to go in search of her father alone.

Her father, twenty minutes ago, had been seated on the adjacent wall. She glanced upward once more to see if Beth and Harry were still together. They were, but Harry's attention was on the hall beyond. Laynie followed his gaze but he had a far better vantage point. She somehow knew already what he saw. She strained to see beyond the assembly room doorway, but there was no seeing around or over the crowd. She remained, only waited, standing there quite alone while the sea of strangers parted and flowed in all directions around her. She looked up again to find that Harry had gone. Beth was there still and watching her now. She smiled and held up her hand to offer a small and uncertain wave.

The strains of music wafted through the air and the crowd hushed and stilled momentarily. Then buzzed all the louder with the excite-ment of this prelude to the dancing that was soon to begin. The floor began to clear. She could see the doorway that led to the hall beyond. For a moment it was empty. And then…Harry. But not Harry alone. It was with great enthusiasm he greeted and welcomed the man who stood beside him now. Laynie had always thought him hand-some, but Mr. Holbrook this evening looked an entirely different man. He was dressed impeccably in black jacket and waistcoat and white tie. His hair was combed back, the curls and waves of it tamed. He had apparently taken great trouble in his preparations to come. It did not, however, appear as though he were much pleased to have done it. He smiled, though weakly, now and then glancing nervously about him as though he were not certain, after all, that he ought to have come at all.

"Laynie? Laynie, why do you stand there? Come here, child." It was her father. She approached him, nearly ran to him, and seated herself so near him she might have crawled into his lap like a child. She was not a child, though. Not any longer. "What is it?" he asked her.

"Nothing, Papa," she said, her heart pounding so hard against her chest she was certain he could hear it.

"Where is your fiancé?"

"Don't call him that, Papa," she whispered. "Not yet."

He was not quite alone, but his companions had carried on the conversation without him, and save for a few appreciative looks in her direction, their own dialogue went on unheeded.

"He will be that to you in another hour or so, my dear," he reminded her. He smiled, took a drink from his glass, and turned back to his companions, with whom he now appeared less enthusiastic about conversing with. That fog was descending once more upon his mind. She could see it as she alternately watched him and the door, where no one in particular appeared, nor was likely to.

* * *

"I'm so jolly glad you came," Harold Vaughn said, approaching Daniel and extending his hand. "Shall I introduce you around?"

"There's little need," Daniel said, "I won't be staying long."

Vaughn gave him a disappointed look and led him toward the assembly room, stopping just within it to make the necessary inquires—his health, the roads, had he had any trouble finding the house? No, of course not. It wasn't as if he'd walked. It was but a preface to the question Vaughn truly wished to ask but seemed afraid to utter. Daniel did not mind if he did not ask it at all and offered him one ear as Vaughn rambled his well-meaning but rather banal niceties, while Daniel took the opportunity of scanning the rooms. They were not, as he had at first supposed, quite filled with strangers. He saw faces he vaguely recognized, though he could not put names to more than a handful of them. His grandfather had once been a society man himself, but infirmity, the tragic loss of his only son, and an increasing preference for his own company had kept him, during his later years, in the country. Daniel supposed it was also to keep himself out of trouble. It had not been an entirely successful endeavor on that score. As he stood there, an obstruction to those who wished to pass out of the room or to enter into it, he received not a few strange looks. They were the looks of men and women who thought just perhaps they recognized him but then had decided against it. There were a few other looks as well—these by the fairer and younger of the company— which six or seven years ago he might have considered encouraging, but he had not come to engage in idle flirtation. He had come to see her and to warn Emerson, if he could, that his way was not quite clear.

Vaughn at last asked the question. "Is there any news? Have you heard from Hamilton?"

Daniel looked at him and looked away again without answering. Yes, he had heard from Hamilton. Was there news? Of that he was not yet certain. Yes, he supposed so, at least of a sort. He had received Hamilton's message just as he was leaving his flat. Hamilton had stumbled upon a lead. He had found someone who had known her; who had, he thought, seen her quite recently. She was nearby, he felt, but could say nothing more, not even where he presently was, only that Daniel would hear from him again very soon.

The message, though welcome, was not quite informative. He could do nothing with it but wait for what might follow, for something more than an uncertain second-hand clue that was both hope and agony of frustration. In exchange for Hamilton's news, Daniel had returned the invitation. If Hamilton needed him, he would be here. He had to come. For what purpose he had not quite decided, but yes, he must speak with her. He must at least try to persuade her not to throw herself away on the monster Frederick Emerson. If only he had some solid evidence of Emerson's villainy.

Vaughn, seeing that Daniel was not going to answer the question, suggested instead that he follow as Vaughn led them into the room and along the outskirts of the dance floor, to where a group of people were seated in conversation.

"Mother?" Vaughn said, addressing one of the women. She looked to him then to his companion.

She graced Daniel with that same look he had seen a dozen times since arriving. A look of uncertain recognition, and then... Only she did not dismiss it as the others had done. She stood, despite her son's objections—and his own—and waved Vaughn's away with a blind flick of her lorgnette. She unfolded it, held it before her eyes a moment and then lowered it. She extended her hand, not to shake as gentlemen do and as ladies sometimes do, but as someone who has just caught sight of a long-lost friend and wishes to hold tight to them a moment before they disappear once more.

"Mother, may I present Mr. Daniel Holbrook."

"Of course it is," she said to Daniel's surprise. "Who else could it be? My boy," she said, addressing Daniel, "you are the very image of...well, of a friend I once very much admired. Richard Holbrook must have been your grandfather," she said to him.

"Indeed he was, Ma'am."

"I read of his passing. I was sincerely sorry to hear of it. But I am extraordinarily pleased to meet you, who so resemble him."

Holbrook smiled and looked to the floor. He was pleased, but did not feel he deserved the distinction.

Lady Vaughn had him by the arm now, pressing herself very close to him. "You might not know this, but he had quite a reputation as a man about town in his younger days."

This surprised Daniel very much, and he said so.

"It's true. For a very brief time he was an especial favorite of my eldest sister, but my dear Papa did not approve. He was wild then and it was feared he would throw his inheritance away. I thought the world of him, myself, and had I been older..." She blushed and cleared her throat. "Of course he did finally settle down and made something truly remarkable of himself. I do admire a man capable of changing his ways. I would have taken him as a rogue, though, he was *that* charming." She laughed. "And I that foolish."

Daniel was not ignorant of her own trials in that quarter. He had heard of Sir Barrymore Vaughn's roguery. It was admirable of her to acknowledge her weakness. She had certainly suffered for it.

"I do find it puzzling, though, Mr. Holbrook," she continued as she led him along now, Harry following, "that you should hire yourself out as a reading companion. When I had heard that Mr.

439

Durham had taken on such a man I thought him daft. I've since changed my mind. If Harold is any judge, and I think he is for he loves that family perhaps more than his own—not that I blame him, you know—you have done Mr. Durham a great service. I'm afraid since you have left them he's quite come undone."

"It was not my choice to go, ma'am, believe me."

"Nevertheless, I think your influence with him significant. As it is, I believe, with certain others of the family…" She gave him a knowing look that made him just a trifle uncomfortable. "If you were to reacquaint yourself now, I don't think it would be taken amiss."

It seemed there was a suggestion hidden in her words, but before he could offer any reply he found himself standing before Mr. Durham, a crowd around him listening attentively to some story he was telling. It was rather meandering and filled with tangents, but his audience listened on patiently nonetheless.

At the first convenient pause in the story, Lady Vaughn attempted to make Mr. Durham aware of their guest. She addressed him, but he did not appear to have heard her. Daniel, in an attempt to help, cleared his throat. Another moment passed, and then: "Papa." The voice was familiar. A little too familiar. "I think there is someone who would like to speak with you."

The circle around Mr. Durham parted to allow Daniel admittance. Laynie stepped out from her father's shadow and revealed herself. She was so altered he might not have recognized her. No, it was she. He would recognize her anywhere. It was not a face to be forgotten. She glanced at him and the jolt that ran through him reminded him that he was not to be looking at her.

"Sir?" Mr. Durham said to him, recalling his attention. It took some effort to pull it away from the wine-clad woman before him. Mr. Durham's manner of addressing him seemed to have something of a demand in it, of questions: *Why have you come? How have you come? And how do you dare to approach me?*

If it was a question at all, Lady Vaughn answered it for him. "I believe you are acquainted with my friend Daniel Holbrook."

"You know Mr. Holbrook?" Mr. Durham asked, apparently puzzled.

"Oh, yes. I've known his family these past forty years or more. You ought to have told me your companion was Mr. Holbrook. I feel as though I have been robbed of good society when I might have had it. You know how lonely it can be for me at Elverton. Particularly as you will monopolize my son's time so thoroughly as you do."

"Me, ma'am?"

"You know what I mean. But look! Here are old friends. How happy we must be to meet with them again. I understand you have not seen your friend in some time."

Mr. Durham looked to Daniel and back to Lady Vaughn. "We did not part on the best of terms, ma'am. Perhaps Mr. Holbrook has told you already."

"But what is that among good friends, Mr. Durham? And trustworthy ones? We all have our disagreements now and then. Surely the misunderstanding is easily overcome."

Mr. Durham appeared to be struggling to remember what the disagreement was.

"Do you see?" Lady Vaughn said. "Easily forgotten is easily forgiven. And, after all, Mr. Durham," she said to him more confidentially, "all stories have two sides. Do they not?" This last she seemed to direct at Daniel himself. If she knew his side to the story he would be very much surprised. But then, he had all but confessed it to her son so he supposed it was not entirely impossible she had heard something of it. What surprised him more was that she seemed to think his part in the matter quite irreproachable. Well, perhaps she did not know the whole story, after all.

"I'll leave you to catch up," she said to Daniel. "Do come find me before you leave, won't you? What a pleasure it is to see you."

Her regard for him, so instant and earned by another before him, puzzled him greatly.

"Mr. Durham," he said once Lady Vaughn had left him. He found his wits rather befuddled with Laynie standing there watching him. This was not why he was here, to stare and gawp at her in that confection of a dress. He would do better to think of Sophie. Sophie and the man who had ruined her. "It is very good to see you again. I do hope you are well, sir."

441

"Very well, yes." It seemed he was thinking of what more to say. Should he reciprocate the sentiment and would that be a betrayal of his determination never to trust Daniel again? It was supposition of course, but Daniel knew himself not to be on good terms with him, and he perceived the struggle that played before him now.

"I think fondly of my time at the Bowery," Daniel added.

"I bet you do," Mr. Durham said with a hint of scorn and seemed to take exception to Daniel's words. He had not thought how he might interpret them. Perhaps he cared a little too much how it would sound to her, who was standing there, listening, watching him. How he wished to meet that gaze!

"You miss the employment, I suppose," Mr. Durham concluded.

"Papa, you are being very rude."

Mr. Durham glanced to his daughter. Daniel dared one as well. She was looking very pleadingly at her father. Her eyes met his, and she looked away again as her face reddened.

"I don't need the employment, sir. I'm not sure I ever did."

Mr. Durham looked him up and down now, in his evening clothes expertly tailored and himself as well groomed and clean cut as anyone had seen him in a decade.

"Perhaps you didn't," Mr. Durham said more considerately now. It appeared as though he were trying to remember the details of Daniel's circumstances and was having a difficult time doing it.

"What I needed," Daniel continued, "was something to do, and I found it. We had a pleasant time, I thought, you and I."

"We did, Holbrook," he said, beginning to relent. "We certainly did. But why did you go?" Mr. Durham asked. "Why did you leave us?"

The poor man had plainly diminished in senses. It saddened Daniel to see it. It worried him, too. If this should continue, and his daughters still at home… But one was soon to be married. Daniel steeled his resolve and continued.

"I had some business to attend to," he said. "My grandfather left me a house,

and—"

Daniel stopped upon observing the sudden appearance of a hand around Laynie's waist. Mr. Emerson had joined them. He was whispering something into Laynie's ear. A request to dance?

She glanced at Daniel, an apologetic, perhaps even regretful look, and nodded. If she didn't want to dance with him, why would she agree? Was his hold on her so firm as that?

He watched as Emerson led her away, his arm wrapped around her a little more tightly than was necessary, holding her to him, his hand clinging to her opposite elbow so that she could hardly move.

"Oh, Papa, I'm so happy to see old friends reunited!" It was Beth. "It's so lovely to see you again, Mr. Holbrook. How are you?"

"Well, I suppose, Miss Durham. And you?"

She offered Daniel a half-hearted smile that seemed full of significance and took his hand to join it in her father's. Mr. Durham looked at their hands together and at last shook it. He laughed and patted Daniel on the back.

"Ah, Holbrook! Just like old times."

It was good of him to forgive him, he supposed, but it was hardly like old times at all. When before had they met in a crowded ballroom with music playing and his youngest daughter on the arm of a scoundrel who might marry her and who would no doubt make her life a constant torment? Daniel was not sure how much more he could bear.

"Mr. Vaughn was supposed to dance with me, but I cannot find him. What do you think, Mr. Holbrook? Should I look for him or wait for another partner?"

It was her way, he supposed, of begging the favor of his request. He had hoped to speak further with her father, but perhaps Mr. Durham was not up to it. Would speaking with Bethany be any more fruitful? "If Vaughn would not take it amiss, I would consider it a great honor if you would consider dancing with me instead."

"Why Mr. Holbrook!" she said as if his request was the greatest of surprises to her. "It would be my very great pleasure to accept. Thank you."

He led her to the dance floor, or, rather, he offered his arm as *she* led *him*, and they joined in, late, but without upsetting the formations. He supposed Beth was just the kind to know all about clever cuttings in and reformations of squares. Or was that Laynie, after all? He

443

recalled, rather vaguely, a story of their time in Gravesend, when she had thought she had seen him and… She was before him now, and then behind him as he and Beth turned. It was rude to watch her and dance with another, but it was difficult to do otherwise. He looked to Beth.

"Have you come to wish them congratulations?" she asked him.

He did not know what to say. The only proper answer would be a lie, and he was not certain he could manage it.

"If you say yes, I'll be very disappointed in you."

"Tell me what to say, then, Miss Durham."

"Say," she answered, "that you have come to rescue her."

"I don't know that I have."

"You don't want to?"

"My own desires, whatever they may or may not be, have nothing to do with it. He made her an offer of marriage, and she has accepted it. Tell me, Miss Durham, what I am supposed to do."

Beth suddenly abandoned her flirting manner and adopted one more serious and pleading. "Speak to her, Mr. Holbrook. She will listen to you."

"And what, pray, am I to tell her?"

"You've known him longer than I have. You must have some reason to believe him unworthy. I have known him but a few months, and I can tell you what I've seen for myself. Shall I tell you?"

He looked at her a moment, a little fearful of what she might have to say but knowing he must hear it anyway. "Yes, of course," he answered.

"I have seen, Mr. Holbrook, that Mr. Emerson is a man to trifle with women's hearts. First my cousin's, then mine, and now Laynie's. And why Laynie?"

He shook his head.

"I think it had something to do with you." She looked at him and did not wait for him to answer. "I have seen a rare and remarkable friendship between my sister and yourself, a friendship that might be interpreted as something more—whether it is the case or not, I won't presume to say—but Mr. Emerson has made no secret of his disdain for you. For an inheritance he might have married anyone, myself included, I'm ashamed to say. But he chose Laynie, Mr. Holbrook, because he knew it would injure you. I can see it in your eyes. He has accomplished that aim."

"Is that all, Miss Durham?" Daniel asked her and very much wished to change the subject. While her observations, right though they were, did offer some evidence that Emerson was inconstant in his dealings with women, they provided no real evidence of his unworthiness. Neither did they disqualify his right to marry her or anyone. Daniel's own feelings for her were inconsequential now. They could not help him, and they certainly could not help her.

"There is one other thing," Beth said, though rather uncertainly. "I have seen my sister's fear and despair and uncertainty. I have seen bruises…"

His attention was full upon her now. "What?"

"On her arms. He is not kind to her, Mr. Holbrook. If he loves her, why is he not kind?"

Daniel opened his mouth to speak, but there was no answering that. He swallowed but still did not say anything. He scanned the room. Saw her. Saw Emerson, as a wave of anger and repulsion surged through him, and continued his examination of the room, particularly the space within the assembly room doorway. Where the hell was Hamilton!

"And there is one final thing, perhaps after all it is insignificant, but it does not seem so to me."

"Go on, Miss Durham," he said, uncertain how much more he could hear but knowing he had to hear it all, whatever she might have to say.

"I have seen, Mr. Holbrook, how she pales and appears suddenly lost and despairing—even while a light shines in her eyes—when there is any mention of you."

He swallowed.

"Is there no remedy?"

"Not much of one, Miss Durham, I regret to say. If I could divide her from him I would do it. If only I had some proof against him, but I have nothing of certainty. I might have it. If she will only put him off a little, I might be able to find something. But I can only divide them. I'm powerless to do more than that."

445

"Not to unite her with another?"

He exhaled in frustration and shook his head.

"And why is that, Mr. Holbrook?" she said, plainly disappointed.

The music ended, they stopped their dancing and he released her.

"Don't condemn me, Miss Durham. Circumstances are beyond me. That is all."

"You *will* speak to her?"

"If there was any way to manage it, then yes, certainly. But I don't see how." He nodded to indicate Mr. Emerson who did not seem inclined to leave Laynie's side. While Daniel was here Emerson was not likely to take his eyes from her again. As if proof were necessary, Vaughn approached the pair of them. He made a request of Laynie, no doubt begging for the pleasure of dancing with her; however it was not she who answered, but Emerson. Despite this being his house, despite the fact that it was his family who had hosted the party, Vaughn was flatly refused.

Daniel turned back to Beth, who looked at him blankly, helplessly. He offered his arm, and she took it, but it was she who once again took the lead, through the assembly room and up the stairs to the second floor.

"Where are we going, Miss Durham?"

"Mr. Vaughn would like a private word with you."

"But he was below, in the assembly room. Surely you saw him. He was—"

She didn't answer, and they walked on until they arrived before the last door at the end of the upstairs corridor. Beth turned to him. "You are my sister's friend, I believe, Mr. Holbrook."

"Yes. I hope so. I think so."

"Then be that friend. Speak to her."

"And how am I to do that, exactly?" he said with a glance over the balcony that indicated Laynie below and her too-persistent companion. "I thought you said it was Vaughn who wished to speak with me."

Beth opened the door. He hesitated a moment but at last entered. She closed the door immediately behind him, leaving him to stand alone in an exquisitely-, and comfortably-appointed study, filled with books and taxidermy and other miscellany requisite for a gentleman's study. It was rather dark in here. Too dark to read, save by the fire's light, but it was cozy and warm. He almost felt at home. Almost. He opened the lid of a humidor, extracted a cigar, smelled it and put it back. He didn't smoke. He never had. But he knew a quality cigar when he smelled one. Next to the humidor was a decanter. He unstopped it but stopped it again. He needed his wits intact. He could certainly use something to calm him, but that was not the way. His grandfather might have straightened his life out. His father never had. Yes, he had married, but…well, only out of necessity. Was that why Bethany's cousin was marrying? Daniel turned and looked to the door, anxious for it to open and afraid of it at the same time. What would he say to her? What would he confess? How much? How little? And what words would he be tempted to say, words he knew he must keep back, that were now being held in reserve for another?

He sat down before the fire and waited.

Chapter thirty-four

WITH HIS HAND ON THE small of her back and her hand in his, Laynie felt a little trapped. Mr. Emerson was not going to allow her to wander off again, it seemed, to be found with men she had been soundly warned away from, and at great peril, too. He was going to have his three dances and tell the world by so doing that Laynie was his and his alone.

"What is that fellow doing here?" he demanded of her, as though she were responsible for Mr. Holbrook's presence.

"I don't know. I think Harry invited him."

"Mr. Vaughn, I think you mean. I don't care how long you've known him, he is Mr. Vaughn to you. And Holbrook!" he added menacingly and held her all the tighter. "What the devil does he think he's doing showing his face here?"

"These aren't your people, Frederick. They are my aunt's and my uncle's, my father's and Lady Vaughn's. They can invite whom they see fit. Where are your people, as far as that goes? Have you none at all?"

"You met him. Does he look like he can dance to you? I warned you about speaking to him."

"Your uncle?"

"Holbrook!"

"I didn't speak to him. Nor he to me. He addressed my father and my father alone. I don't even think he knew I was there when he approached. When Mr. Vaughn presented him, that is."

"That's likely, isn't it? He appears in a room full of strangers, approaches the first person he recognizes and you mean to tell me it had nothing to do with you?"

448

"I can see you are going to believe what you want to believe, whatever I have to say about it."

They were quiet for a time. Laynie, spinning about the room, tried to find her sister, but couldn't. She tried, surreptitiously to find him...but couldn't. Was there no one here to save her? Or was it as she feared, that she must save herself? And at what cost?

The dance ended. Laynie wished to sit, but she knew already what Mr. Emerson had intended.

"No, you don't. We'll dance our allowed three and we'll make the announcement everyone came to hear, and we'll let them open the champagne everyone is eagerly waiting to drink."

The music began again. Laynie heard the familiar voice and turned with a welcoming smile.

"I was hoping Miss Durham might allow me the honor of a dance. If you don't mind, Emerson."

"Harry—Mr. Vaughn, I mean, I would be ha—"

"Sorry, Vaughn. I'm not finished with her yet, you see."

Vaughn's smile stiffened and faded. A knot formed at his brow and pulsed. She had never seen him angry before.

Emerson held her tightly and swung her away from him. In the blur of movement, she thought she saw Mr. Holbrook. When she looked again he was gone.

Emerson spoke very little in the course of the next dance, and it was just as well. He led her along the floor with such determined, almost threatening zeal, it was all she could do to keep up with him. She wondered if it would always be this way, he pushing her along whether she wished to follow or not, and reminding her ever and always that, as his wife and bride, she had few rights to claim for herself.

When the second dance ended, Laynie stopped to catch her breath. Her hair was coming loose, she feared, and her scarf hung a little haphazardly. She straightened it as best she could and almost wished she were not so ashamed to let others see what it was hiding.

"One more turn?" Emerson asked her, as if she had a choice.

Before she could answer there was a hand on her arm. "My dear, if you wouldn't mind..." It was Lady Vaughn, looking very serious and concerned.

"What is it?" she asked her.

"There is someone who particularly wishes to meet you. Do you mind, Mr. Emerson?"

Now it was he who had been posed a question he had no choice but to agree to.

"Not at all," he said. "If you promise to return her to me just as soon as it is convenient."

He graced Laynie with a solicitous look that appeared quite sincere, and which consequently diminished all other similar looks to mere affectation, and released her.

Laynie followed Lady Vaughn's lead as she walked slowly but determinedly from the assembly room. For an infirm woman, she could be quite forceful when she wished to be.

"Is something the matter?" Laynie asked as they made their way out of the room.

"Oh, not at all. I only thought you could use a moment to catch your breath."

"So there is no one who wishes to speak with me?"

"On the contrary! There is someone who wishes to speak with you very much."

"Who?"

But Lady Vaughn said nothing, only led Laynie up the stairs and to a room at the back of the house, where Harry stood waiting for her.

"Thank you, Mother," he said to her as Laynie was handed off.

"Now," she said, patting Laynie on the cheek. "You have a good chat, and don't worry that you will be disturbed. Harry will be here to make sure all is well and you are as safe as houses, good? Good." She looked up at her son. "Now I'm going to have a little lie-down, if it's all right."

"Yes, of course," he said to her. "It's been a great deal of excitement for one day."

"Will you be all right, ma'am?" Laynie said as Lady Vaughn turned to go.

"I will be, yes," she answered. "Only you take care of yourself right now, do you hear? We'll talk later."

"What is this about, Harry?" she said to him once they were alone.

Instead of answering, he opened the door and waited for her to enter. At last she did, but instead of following her, he closed the door.

"Harry?" she said with her hand on the knob, but it wouldn't turn.

"Miss Durham."

Laynie turned with a start. She was not alone. "Mr. Holbrook!"

There was a short space of silence. "You look well," he said and exhaled a laugh as he looked away from her. "Very well."

"It's a little much, I think. Beth made the gown."

"It's perfect." He looked again and then away, but his gaze quickly returned to her.

He himself looked very fine and gentlemanlike. He had always looked well, but this was something more, something finer and more genteel than she had ever imagined for him. And yet it seemed to suit him quite naturally. She wondered if she had ever really known him at all. "There was something you wished to speak to me about?"

"Ah, well," he said with a glance toward the door. "It seems our friends think there are a few things left unsaid between us."

"Oh?" she said and felt the pricking of hope in a heart desperately afraid to feel it.

"We part ways tonight," he said and that little spark snuffed out to leave a cold and hollow place. "Some goodbyes are more difficult to say than others."

"Impossibly difficult," she said.

He leaned against the mantle and tapped his finger on it. At last he pushed himself away from it and walked to the desk, where a decanter sat. "You are expected, I think, to make an announcement tonight." He opened the bottle and laid the stopper on the table. He drew a glass toward him and looked at her when she did not answer.

"You told me you don't drink."

He put the stopper back and pushed the decanter away from him, then turned to lean against the desk, his arms folded across his chest.

"You may if you like. It was not an objection. Merely an observation."

"Your announcement. I've come to beg you not to make it."

451

"I need a reason," she said, "something more than your disapproval."

"Is your own unhappiness not enough?"

"No, Mr. Holbrook, it isn't. If you understood just what was at stake… Not my character alone, which I suppose I could learn to bear in time, but others will be made to suffer as well."

"So you confess to being unhappy."

She wished to answer this in a thousand words. It was he who had warned her that she would know love when it came. And she knew it now, but it was nothing more than a ghost that haunted her. She wanted a man she could never have. The man who stood before her now, admonishing her to choose a happiness that was never to be hers, and to eschew a man who would destroy her and everyone she loved if she so much as flinched in an effort to extract herself from the promise she had made.

"I have not known you long, Miss Durham, but I do feel I know you well. I know you to be self-sacrificing, seeking always to please others before yourself. This is not the time for that. Do you love him? Do you trust and respect him? Or rather, is it merely that you fear him? Is fear a good reason, do you think, to tie yourself to someone irrevocably? And a man such as he, no less?"

He waited for her answer, but she was not prepared to give it.

"It is in your nature to trust, but also, I think, to know whom to trust and whom not to."

"I have trusted you."

"And have you learned to regret it?"

Yes, in a way. But not in any way that could matter now. She shook her head.

"Will you not have faith in me now?"

"I'm to take you at your word that I am not to marry him, is that it? What am I to tell my guests when I stand before them? What am I to tell *him*? That I spoke with you and you felt I had rather not? Mr. Holbrook, he is prepared to defame you quite publicly. Don't ask me to be the cause of your humiliation. I will not do it."

He exhaled loudly, turned to the desk and began fingering the glass again.

"If Mr. Emerson is really so wicked as you seem to think him, why can we not start there, with his accusations. I have trusted you, perhaps blindly, but certainly because I have wanted to do it. I need more than mere instinct just now. I need to know. I need to understand."

He turned once more and looked at her a long minute. She felt the weight of that gaze, felt the significance of it. And yet he seemed no more likely to divulge his secrets now than he had ever been. Did she not deserve some explanation? Was she not a part of those secrets herself now? If Mr. Emerson still perceived Daniel to be a threat, if he were to learn with whom she was presently speaking, alone in a private room, then those secrets would be revealed to all the world. Is that how Daniel wished for her to learn of his story?

"Very well," he said at last. "I suppose it's time you heard my side of it."

She nodded in agreement and waited for him to speak. He gestured toward the chair beside the fire, but she did not wish to sit. It seemed somehow safer, wiser she supposed, to stay just where she was.

"Some years ago," he began at last, "I found myself very much in love with a certain young woman. I was at University. She worked as a nurse for one of the professors—one of *my* professors, in fact. The fellow was something of a tyrant, in the lecture hall and at home, and she was unhappy. I thought I might rescue her. I was young. I had friends. Friends as wild and fun-loving as myself."

"Mr. Emerson?"

Daniel nodded. "I introduced them. I saw no danger. Why would I? She was in love with me, depended upon me. I saw no reason to doubt her. And I, in my impetuousness, saw no reason to wait for that which I desired from her."

"You asked her to marry you."

He hesitated to answer. "I certainly gave her every reason to believe I would do it."

"But you did not ask her? You did not say the words?"

Again he hesitated. "No," he said.

"Then how—?" But suddenly she knew. Somehow that interlude at the precipice had awoken her to the dangers that existed between men and women. She was guilty of no sin, whatever Mr. Emerson might have suggested. Daniel had not touched her. But she knew that if he had she would have been powerless to resist him. As perhaps this woman had once been.

"Do you understand?"

She nodded.

"I told you, I believe, that my parents had died when I was very young. My grandfather raised me. He was rather a stern man but well meaning. He got word of it and confronted me. I confessed. I told him my intentions, which at the time I considered rather noble. He objected. I was sent abroad. I suppose he hoped it would give me perspective, make me see that there was far more to the world than a hasty marriage to a governess of no means and little character." He paused to rub his brow. If she had no character to speak of, did he blame himself? And if Laynie was to lose hers for refusing Mr. Emerson, would he assume the blame for that as well? "I was to be gone twelve months," he continued at last. "If, when I returned, we felt the same, if she still wanted me and I her, then my grandfather would give us his blessing."

"And so you went."

"I did. I could have refused him, I suppose, but to marry her without his blessing would have meant waiting far longer. I had no money of my own, no way really to support us. He was quite generous in his terms, I see that now. He might have refused outright. We were not well matched, she and I. Much was expected of me. She was a working girl, I was... I was my grandfather's sole heir. Not a responsibility even the young take lightly, Miss Durham."

She nodded her understanding and wondered that she had ever thought she had known Daniel Holbrook at all.

"And so I obeyed. I left her with a promise I would return but with nothing further. I spent my time abroad, doing and seeing all the things my grandfather had intended I should. And then I came back, as devoted as ever and eager to prove to my grandfather that he had been wrong. No sooner had I reached dry land then I saw her. She was there at the docks waiting for the ships to come in."

"She had waited for you?"

"She was there by chance. She and Mr. Emerson were disembarking together. Eloping. In my time away he had wooed and won her, and they were to be married. That was when I left again. I never spoke to my grandfather after that. I never saw her again. And I never saw Emerson. Not until one evening in late summer in a charming and comfortable house in Surrey. I had heard of her illness. There were whispers she had died. And then there was Emerson, a widower, eager to marry again and on the hunt for a wife—proof, it seemed, that the whispers were true. There is nothing in any of this to paint him as a villain, I know, and perhaps if he had not chosen you…" He stopped, cleared his throat and looked away. "I hope you do not feel that I have misled you into believing I am more than I am, Miss Durham." He said at last.

She did not know what to say. She had made a great deal of him, indeed, but she could not say that he had encouraged her to do it. That had been her own doing.

"I suppose when you left the second time it was to live as a monk in the Himalayas," she said rather cynically.

"I think you know it was not."

"But you are repentant now?" The cynicism was there still, only this she really wanted to believe. Her idol had begun to crumble and she was desperate to see him restored.

"A man can only wander so long before he begins to lose respect for himself. I returned to find my grandfather had died, and I as sorry an example of a man as could be found. I do regret. That regret has changed me. But so has hope, Miss Durham. The opportunity to see myself in the eyes of someone who has esteemed me as greater than I am has inspired me to be what I might. You, Miss Durham, have given me that."

She was a tumult of confused thoughts and feelings. She could not bear the weight of his gaze upon her, one of gratitude, of sorrow, of disappointment, and of pleading to be forgiven. But it was not her place to forgive him. What would be the point in that if he had only come to offer his farewell, perhaps forever?

Daniel approached her and stopped to stand just before her. She would not look at him, she could only think to look at the medallion of the carpet at her feet.

"Don't marry him, Miss Durham. At least wait a bit. Consider it the last request of a dear, dear friend, and refuse him. I realize my request must bear very little weight to you now, but I beg you to consider it nonetheless."

She looked up at him. It was not true. It could not be more untrue. His request was everything, but it was still not enough. Mr. Emerson had been accused of nothing more than falling in love once—perhaps twice?—with the same woman Mr. Holbrook himself had chosen, perhaps foolishly, to admire. It was not sufficient reason to call off an engagement, and certainly not to do it so publicly.

"There is more, Miss Durham. At least I think there may be. Only time will tell, really, but certain evidences have come my way that suggest that, just perhaps, Mr. Emerson is not free to marry, and that, even if he is, the manner in which he dealt with his late wife was not one to be commended."

Laynie swallowed hard and took a step back, while Mr. Holbrook took hold of her elbow. His hand slid upward, to the spot where her scarf concealed a darkening bruise.

"You've had witness of it yourself that he is not always kind, I think."

"I don't know what you mean," she said and tried to move away from him.

His hand was on the scarf alone, and her effort to free herself only unveiled the mark that was the proof of Daniel's warning.

"It's nothing," she said. "I fell, is all, and—"

"Oh, Miss Durham, don't lie to *me*," he said and looked actually disappointed to think she might do it. His brow furrowed as his gaze dropped from her face once more to her arm. He was angry now. With her, though? His hand was at her waist. His grip was firm but not forceful. "A day or two more is all I ask of you. If there is anything to disprove him by, it is shortly to come. And if not… If I was wrong…it remains true that you do not love him. You cannot convince me you do."

"There will be a price to pay, should I refuse him now. He has made threats."

"He may try to defame you. There may even be talk for a time, but—"

"Breach of contract."

Daniel scowled. "Because of the loss of an inheritance? There is no precedence for that, not for a man suing a woman. I'd like to see him try."

"There have been other threats. He means to injure you. And he will do it, too, given the chance. I won't give him that chance. You can't ask me to."

"There is nothing more he can do to me, Laynie, save to marry you. I would gladly bear any infamy in exchange for freeing you of the monster I believe him to be."

"But you have no proof he is a monster at all," she reminded him.

The light behind his eyes went out. He looked down and released her. "No," he said. In time he looked up at her again, his look just as penetrating, just as pleading, as the firelight reflected in his eyes.

"Why is this goodbye?" she asked him. "Is it because of Mr. Emerson, or do our ways part whether or not I marry him?"

"Would it make a difference?" he said.

"Yes. Possibly." She felt perhaps that she was saying too much but he was giving her encouragement to speak, and to hope, even if it was not his intention. Wasn't it? Refusing Emerson seemed impossible. Perhaps he was an evil man, perhaps he would not be kind to her, but there was only one thing she could think of that would give her the courage to do it. If Daniel would offer himself...

He raised his hand once more and laid it gently on her waist. His thumb brushed against her ribs as his eyes danced across her face. He opened his mouth to speak. "Miss Durham, Laynie... There is one thing more you should know." He swallowed, but the words he had sum-moned were interrupted by a knock at the door. She had not had enough time. She was not ready yet. There was more to say, more, it seemed, to understand.

Daniel crossed to the door. He opened it carefully, but the moment the latch was free it flung open. Laynie expected to see Mr. Emerson on the other side of it but it was not him at all. It was a gentleman she had never seen before in her life. He was out of breath and looking hurried. He stopped, looked at her and back to Daniel again before resting his gaze, once more, upon her. Something about her seemed to make him reconsider his hurry.

457

"Miss Durham, I believe."

"Yes," she said. "How do you know—?"

"Miss Alayna Durham," Daniel said, "may I present my good friend, Mr. Charles Hamilton."

Mr. Hamilton approached her and stopped to stand before her. He said nothing, only looked at her. She began to wonder what it was he was thinking. Considering all Daniel had told her, did he think it significant that she should be closeted away with him in a private room? It seemed he did, but there was no look of judgment in his gaze.

"I'm very pleased to meet you," he said and appeared to mean it. "I've heard a great deal about you."

"Have you?" she asked, curious what could have been said.

"Oh, yes," Mr. Hamilton said very meaningfully. He turned to Daniel. "Have you told her?"

"Have you news, Hamilton? You may be just in time."

Mr. Hamilton looked once more to Laynie. The look on his face was acutely apologetic. "Yes, Holbrook. I've news. Miss Warren is found."

Laynie fell into a nearby chair. "His wife lives?"

"No," Mr. Hamilton said. "That is, yes, she lives, but they were never married."

"But she's alive?" Daniel pressed.

"You'll want to come right away."

"Yes, of course," Daniel nodded. He turned back to Laynie. "Do you understand what this means?"

Did she? She nodded nevertheless.

"He is free to marry, but he is not worthy of you. He eloped with Sophie, my Sophie, and then he abandoned her for the fortune you will give him. I think you know what you must do."

She looked up at him and blinked. "You are leaving?"

"Yes," he said. "I have to make this right, if I can."

"Holbrook?" Hamilton called from the doorway.

"Yes," Daniel said. "All right."

Laynie followed him to the door. Hamilton presented himself to her once more and bowed his head. "It was a pleasure meeting you at last, Miss Durham. I hope I may have the pleasure again."

"Is that likely, Mr. Hamilton?" she said and felt the swelling of tears.

He appeared reluctant to answer, but at last did, however dishonestly. "I cannot say. If there is ever anything I can do..."

"Hamilton, if I could just have one minute more."

"Yes, of course," he said and passed out of the room, leaving Laynie and Daniel once more alone.

Daniel stood before her. He brushed a tear from beneath her eye and took hold of her hand.

She had determined herself not to cry in front of him. It seemed it could not be helped. She sniffed and took a deep breath. "Are you safe from him now?" she asked him.

"There is no telling, I suppose. So long as you are free of him, I can bear it."

"I know you," she said and smiled weakly. "He may defame and malign you to the end of your days and you will do nothing. You will go away quietly and bear it all without complaint."

"Perhaps," he said.

"And what of her? And what is she to do now? You can't mean to make him take her back. You would not be so cruel."

"No."

"Then what is she to do now, without..." But suddenly she did realize. Her breath caught. He was saying goodbye to her, and now she understood why.

"Laynie, it is important you understand. I have always prayed for a chance to repent of what I have done."

"But you did not abandon her. *He* did. He used her and left her."

"But I let him, don't you see. And it was not the only wrong I have committed. Perhaps in some way, somewhere, I am an Emerson to someone who was foolish enough to have had faith in me."

"Don't say that. How can you say that?"

"Quite easily," he said and offered her a melancholy smile. "You once said men cannot change. I have changed, and in this way I prove it."

"Daniel!" Another tear slipped down her cheek. "I regret I ever said that."

"It is more often true than not. What kind of man would I be if I walked away now? I'm all she has, do you see?"

She nodded and looked down at their entwined hands. With her head bowed over them, he kissed her forehead.

"Goodbye, Miss Durham," he said and arose.

He opened the door and walked through it, but he did not close it behind him. He stopped to shake Harry's hand. He spoke a few confidential words, glanced once more at her, and was gone.

Laynie remained a moment in the room, alone and feeling it. Harry appeared in the doorway. "He told you?" he said at last.

"Did you know?"

"I have suspected it for some time. Don't ask me how, I won't tell you."

"More secrets."

"It can't matter now. Emerson is looking for you. He's anxious to make the announcement."

"And what am I to say, Harry? Am I to break the news to him in private, or wait until an entire crowd is watching?"

"My dear, do you not think we have made a plan for every contingency?"

"What do you mean?"

"You'll see. Do you think you can smile for him for another ten minutes?"

"I don't know that I can, actually. Where are you going?"

"Well, I need to find Beth. I need to speak with my mother, and then…it seems to me Jupiter is missing out on the fun, don't you think?"

"Harry?"

Harry winked. "Ten minutes. I won't need more than that." And then he was gone.

Laynie waited just a few minutes more and at last ventured from the room. Harry had done his job well and no one, it seemed, thought it unusual that she had been away from the party for some length of time, or that she had done it apparently alone—or not alone. As she descended the stairs, several of the guests spoke to her, greeting her with smiles and approving looks. Such attention ought to have bolstered her confidence. In truth she felt herself the cause of their imminent disappointment.

She heard Jupiter's bark, heard the clattering of his toenails on the staircase and turned. There were some gasps and looks of surprise. One or two of the guests appeared to be afraid of him. He barked again and trotted to the door, where he sniffed at the doorframe and then looked up with a disappointed expression in his observant brown eyes.

"Jupiter," she said to him. "Come," and he did. She knew who he was looking for. She understood he missed his master and understood better than she dared to express that neither of them were likely to see him again.

"He's an impressive animal," one gentleman said to her upon observing Jupiter's obedience and his apparent gentleness despite his size.

"Oh, I rather think so, Mr. Atterbury."

Mr. Emerson was suddenly at her side, and Jupiter was just as suddenly growling.

Mr. Atterbury stepped back, and the way was made for the three of them as Mr. Emerson led her toward the assembly room.

"Where have you been?"

"Only talking to Harry."

"Mr. Vaughn, I think you mean."

"If you insist, *Mr. Emerson.*"

He looked at her warningly, then observed Jupiter who was growling at him once more. He was following, still obedient, at Laynie's side, but he would not take his eyes from Mr. Emerson.

"Mr. Holbrook was here. Did he leave?"

"I suppose so. How should I know?"

"Why didn't he take his beast of a dog with him?"

"Again, Mr. Emerson, I can't answer that."

Mr. Emerson placed his hand firmly on her arm to lead her on, reminding her of the bruise that he had placed there. Reminding her, too, that another's hand had been there, much more gently, respectfully even, but a quarter of an hour ago. Resentfully she freed herself and stepped aside. Jupiter growled more loudly.

461

"I hope you don't think you're keeping that dog," he said, angry now.

"I hope you don't think—" But she stopped herself. She must wait for Harry. She had not the courage to do what she must without Harry here to defend her. If only Beth realized what she had in his admiration.

Harry was returning now down the stairs, Beth at his side, smiling widely and blushing.

"Is there something going on I should know about?" Laynie asked as they arrived before her.

"Nothing you won't find out soon enough. Come," he said, with a friendly hand on Emerson's back. "It's about time."

"Are you ready?" Emerson said, taking Laynie's hand. He smiled. It was kind but she saw through it.

"I don't know," she said quite honestly. "Are you quite certain *you* are?"

"Of course," he said and led her into the room, as Jupiter continued to growl at her side. "Only will someone put that dog away," he said, looking for a servant. They all seemed intent on ignoring him.

"I've got him, Laynie," Harry said and, taking him by the collar, placed him between himself and Beth. Beth offered him an appreciative look—not one Laynie could have expected—and joined her hand with his on the dog's collar. Jupiter, for the moment, was quiet.

As they entered, Laynie observed Lady Vaughn at the top of the balcony. She rang a little glass bell and thus summoned the attention of all below, and those, too, who had joined her on the balcony.

Mr. Emerson held her a little more closely and spoke into her ear. "Odd, don't you think, that Holbrook should quit the party so early? It's as if he hadn't known what it was for." Jupiter's absence, it seemed, made Emerson feel a little bolder.

"You imply he was disappointed. He only came because Harry invited him and because he hoped to speak with Papa."

"Not to you, though? That must disappoint you."

He was trying to provoke her now. Half an hour ago it might have worked, too. Now he was only encouraging her own vindictive spirit.

462

"Oh, he spoke to me."

Emerson turned to her with a warning look as Lady Vaughn began the preface to her announcement.

"You needn't be worried," Laynie said. "He only wished me well and every happiness. I won't be seeing him again. He only wanted to say goodbye."

Emerson looked positively vanquished. "He relinquished you that easily, did he? I shouldn't be surprised, I suppose, but..."

"I don't know why you should be surprised at all. He is going to do what it was always in his mind to do."

"And what is that?" he asked with affected interest.

"He's going to marry the woman he loves," she said and felt her heart rend in two.

Emerson was looking full upon her now, a look of confusion, even of frustration on his brow. It appeared as though he wished to ask further, but the chance had passed, Lady Vaughn had begun her announcement.

"This life we live is fraught with pain, disappointment, and heartache," she began. "But at times it's also filled with great joy. As you all know I have had my share of the former. Tonight it pleases me to share with you the latter. You have had the pleasure of meeting my honored guests, the Miss Durhams, Bethany and Alayna."

Laynie felt a nudge at her arm and looked to see her sister standing beside her, her hand in Harry's and beaming from ear to ear. Laynie cast a questioning look upon them but it was not to be answered. Bethany looked to the balcony and so Laynie returned her attention to Lady Vaughn who was still speaking, listing off the virtues and graces of these girls who, with no mother of their own, had become daughters to her. It was for them this party was given. It is of them the news is to be shared. Of them and their friends, who, though they may or may not be worth knowing, are at least desirous to be known.

"What the devil is she going on about?" Emerson asked rhetorically.

He was shushed by Laynie and Beth together.

"It gives me no end of pleasure this night to announce to you the engagement of two people very near and dear to me. My son Harold

Vaughn has had the good fortune to win the love and admiration of Miss Bethany Durham, who has, this night, agreed to marry him."

There were cheers all around and congratulations. Laynie was beside herself with astonishment.

"Bethany!" she said. "Harry?"

Bethany squeezed her hand and Harry winked, but they were too busy receiving the congratulations all around them to pay her much mind, nor to pay much mind to Jupiter who was now free from restraint. The crowd continued to gather round and Laynie was so jostled and bumped about that she soon found herself separated from Mr. Emerson, who was looking around him a little confused and bewildered.

Lady Vaughn rang her bell again and once more summoned the attention of each of her guests.

"Marriage, as the book says, is not to be entered into unadvisedly or lightly, but reverently, discreetly...soberly. Unfortunately there are times when, despite the utmost of our efforts, misfortunes befall us. One friend who has come here tonight, Mr. Frederick Emerson, has been so very unfortunate as to have suffered just such a disappointment upon losing his dear wife."

A wave of condolences spread throughout the room as Mr. Emerson, alone now, received them uncertainly.

"But in every sorrow," Lady Vaughn went on, "there is always the spark of hope, and just such a spark has ignited itself today in the joyous news that Mr. Emerson's wife, lost to him but a year ago, has today been found!"

What followed this announcement was a thrum of confusion in both word and look. The guests turned to each other. Those who had Mr. Emerson in their immediate view knew not what to say. Emerson himself was pale, straight-faced, and blinking.

Lady Vaughn raised her glass in the air and made a toast. "To the happy couple!"

"Champagne!" Harry shouted, and the congratulations commenc-ed with cheers and kind words and a determination to avoid the confusion that surrounded Mr. Emerson, who now stood quite ignored in the center of the room. Ignored, that is, by all but

Jupiter, who stood before him, his teeth bared and snarling. Emerson backed away from him and the dog advanced.

At the top of the stairs, Harry took hold of him.

"Congratulations," he said stiffly and pressed a card into Emerson's hand.

"What is this?" he said upon reading it and looking up at Harry. "Did you have something to do with this?"

"One must always pay his debts, Mr. Emerson. Sooner or later they catch up with us."

"What does that mean?" he said.

Jupiter lunged and snarled.

"So help me, Vaughn, call off that dog or I'll kill him!"

Harry summoned the footmen, who ignored Jupiter and advanced on Emerson in order to assist him in leaving the house.

"I can manage!" he said, waving them off and heading for the door, but his threatening gesture angered Jupiter, who took another lunge at him. He ran, nearly fell, down the steps to the door.

He looked up as Laynie appeared at the top of them. She had been watching from the shelter of the crowd up till now.

"Laynie, my dear. There you are!" he said with a smile. "Your dog. Will you call him off?"

"Why would I do that, Mr. Emerson?"

"Think what we have been to each other. This is a misunderstanding. I'll go and straighten it all out, and—"

"Goodbye, Mr. Emerson."

"Laynie, think what you do."

"Oh, I have," she said and gestured to the footmen to see him out.

Jupiter, too, took the cue and began barking ferociously. The door was opened and Mr. Emerson, plainly afraid, flew through it. The door shut and it was Laynie alone at the top of the stairs, the crowd of guests all around her watching.

She turned to face them with a smile. "Excuse me, won't you? I've had rather a trying night. Jupiter, come." The dog was instantly at her side. She bowed politely to her guests, most of them strangers to her before this night, and climbed the stairs to her room.

She stood back to find Lady Vaughn watching them.

Chapter thirty-five

F EW WORDS WERE SPOKEN AS Daniel travelled through late night London streets. Those streets were no less crowded for the hour. Hamilton said nothing and his sobriety did little to comfort Daniel's anxieties. He might ask him to prepare him for what he was about to face. Was she well? Was she ill? Did she even want to see him? But he feared the answers and so sat in contemplative silence, his mind racing and his thoughts jumping from one thing to another: from Sophie to whom he was anxious to see, to a sad and exquisite Laynie with whom he had just parted—perhaps forever—then from recollections of his past happiness to memories of subsequent heartbreak. Was his heart not broken now? What would it be in an hour's time? Could a heart break twice in one night?

"It'll be all right, you know," Hamilton said in an attempt to comfort him.

"Will it?"

"Maybe not right away but given time."

Daniel turned back to the window. "I hope you are right."

The carriage slowed. "We're here," Hamilton said.

The gentlemen alit and Daniel followed his friend into the house, which he entered without knocking. They had not quite got their coats off when they were met by a fair-haired young woman with very blue eyes.

"You must be Mr. Holbrook," she said and extended her hand.

Daniel took it.

"This is Anne Russell," Hamilton said to him by way of introduction. "She manages Newhaven House."

"And you help her. How is that?" Daniel asked, confused still. It had never been explained to him.

"I help find them, the women who stay. I help them to get here safely. I arrange for doctors and lawyers, for workmen when they're needed. It keeps me occupied."

"And you live here?"

"No. I'm often here. I stay nearby, when I'm not at the club or in Kent. I help to keep up the appearance of respectability. The cause is for nothing if one overlooks that."

Daniel looked at him, confused. How did his appearing to live in a Magdalene sanctuary in any way promote respectability?

"It would take a book to explain it." Charlie clasped Anne's hand affectionately and let it go again. "It isn't why you are here though, is it?"

"No," Daniel said.

"Would you like to see her?" Miss Russell asked him. "Would you like to see them?"

"Them?" Daniel asked and looked to Charlie.

"It must have occurred to you…"

But Daniel still did not understand what it was Charlie was saying. At least he did not want to.

"Come," Anne said and led him upstairs to a very comfortable bedroom that was dimly lit by the jets that burned low. It was warm in the room, but the window was open and the cool night air entered. He wondered if the draft was safe, but when he heard the coughing he understood. Cool air was easier on weak lungs than the warm, dry, suited air of a room heated by coals.

"She's ill," he observed. "Is she lucid?"

"She's sleeping, but yes."

Miss Russell turned and nodded in another direction of the room. On a cot against the opposite wall lay a small form, limbs sprawled akimbo and with a head full of blond curls. Fairer than his mother's by far. As fair as…

"This is *his* child?" Daniel said and felt the floor beneath him shudder.

"Yes," Miss Russell said. "I'll leave you."

The chair had been placed before the fire, perhaps simply to get it out of the way while the patient was being tended to. He wished to see her, to speak with her. And yet he feared to look. It had been five years. No six, now. Six years was not much. It was not much, but… A child! What was he? Three, perhaps four. Six years, it seemed, was a very long time. Gathering his courage he stood. He pulled the chair nearer the bed so he could see her, look into her face, and find the woman he had once loved so well. That he believed he loved still.

She was there. It was her. Older yes, worn, ill, tired. A remnant of her former beauty remained. It was faded, but it was there still. She was thin, too thin, and drawn. How long had she been ill? How long had she been alone and in want? And with a child, too! Emerson deserved to be hanged!

For a long while he sat, waiting for her to wake. Perhaps she would sleep through the night and he would have to return tomorrow to speak with her. There was so much he wished to know. Foremost on his mind: what might he do for her? He would do anything. He had prepared himself to do everything.

"Sophie?" he said and expected no answer. "Oh, Sophie, what has happened to you?"

Her mouth twitched into a faint outline of a smile. Her eyes fluttered open. "Daniel," she said in a voice weak from sleep, or perhaps it was from illness. "You came."

"How are you, Sophie? Are you well?"

She smiled. He knew the answer already. The evidence was before him all too plainly.

"And you dressed for the occasion, too," she said and touched his bow tie. "How handsome you look." A tear slid across the bridge of her nose as she lay on her side looking at him. "Good, kind, handsome Daniel. I should have waited for you."

"I rather wish you had. But then my life, too, is full of should haves."

"But you are happy? Mr. Hamilton says you never married."

"No. There was no one else for me but you."

She touched his face affectionately. "You've never been a good liar, Daniel. Mr. Hamilton told me about Miss Durham."

"I don't know what it is he can have told you."

"That Frederick intended to marry her. That he has been desperately hunting down a wife since the moment he received that letter from his uncle. I should have burned it when it came." She coughed again and another tear fell. "I ought to have known he would never marry me. I've always been a fool when it came to men and love."

"Don't say that."

"It's true. I chose him over you, didn't I? And this Miss Durham nearly did the same. You have stopped him, though?"

"I have given her what she needs to refuse him, I think. What happens next is up to him, really."

"And what happens to her, is that up to you?"

"No. She is well provided for. It's you that concerns me now, Sophie. My house is being prepared and—"

"No, Daniel."

Struck, he stammered, swallowed, and then: "Why not?"

"I wasn't worthy of you the first time you asked me. I'm not foolish enough to think I'm worthy of you now."

"All the more reason to accept, then."

She shook her head. "No," she mouthed and coughed some more.

Sophie rested again for a time and Daniel sat waiting and watching. Her breathing was labored, even speaking seemed a great strain. How he hated Emerson for wasting Sophie in this way. Had he succeeded in winning Laynie would this have been her in five-years' time? He had secured Vaughn's promise that Emerson would be revealed, and publicly if possible. It was only by that means that his roguery would be put to an end and that Laynie and all like her might be made safe. But Emerson had not yet fully paid for his crimes against Sophie. Not nearly. The child, too, fretted. Sophie's eyes opened.

"Adrian?"

She was so weak, so spent. She reached out to him, but he, too, was far too weak to bring himself to the mother he yearned for. Daniel arose and lifted the little boy from the bed and placed him to lie in Sophie's arms.

"Thank you," Sophie said to him and laid a grateful hand upon his arm.

She needed him. She might feel herself unworthy, but she needed him and he would remain beside her. He would overcome her object-

470

tions and marry her, and all would be as it ought to have been. He swept the hair from her brow and felt the heat of fever. Had a doctor been? Had one been sent for? He thought it best to find out and so went back down to find Miss Russell, or even Hamilton, or anyone who could fill in the details about her present condition, even about her discovery.

In a sitting room-turned-office off of the entry hall he found Hamilton and Miss Russell talking together.

"He must be mad to even consider it," he heard Miss Russell say.

"Not mad. He simply has an exaggerated sense of duty. If I know him at all, he will insist."

"But does he realize—"

Daniel announced his presence with a clearing of his throat. Miss Russell sat up straighter and made a little more room between them. Hamilton stood.

"Holbrook," he said and smiled, but the smile soon faded. "How do you find her?"

"She's fevered, as is the child. Has a doctor seen her yet?"

"He was here when they arrived," Miss Russell explained, "but he was called away. He means to return this evening. I expect him any minute."

"Daniel, my friend, it *is* as serious as it looks. You ought to prepare yourself for—"

Daniel held a hand up to stop him but said nothing. He would hear of her prognosis from a doctor and from no one else. "Where did you find her?"

"She was here in London, actually. Has been here for a month or more. Looking for him. Looking for you."

"She was looking for me?"

"Anyone who could help her, I think."

"But you found her. How?"

"She found us, really. It was a last resort, I think, but..." Hamilton shrugged.

"I don't understand."

"There are means you see, Holbrook, by which women in such trouble are led to find me, or Anne, or the house."

"Means?"

"Cryptic ads in the papers. Codified messages in the personals. Even advertisements, worded very delicately, of course…"

"Good God, Hamilton, you are neck deep in this, aren't you? But what for?"

"Oh, I think you know. Because of those like Sophie, or her child, with whom I can uniquely relate. I've been fortunate, as you know. I won't sit idle in my pile of a house and my inheritance collecting interest. I must do something."

"Very well," Daniel said and felt both impressed by Hamilton's sense of charitable philanthropy and condemned by it at once.

"This isn't your fault, you know."

"How long has she been wandering about?"

"Months, I think. From place to place, sleeping in alleyways, alcoves of closed businesses, stairwells of condemned buildings."

"And she thought to read the paper?"

"Looking for any evidence of Emerson or his friends. Those who were once his friends."

Daniel nodded and looked away.

"This isn't your doing, Holbrook. She blames herself."

"Yes, I know."

"Do you?"

"She said so."

"But do you believe it? You seem intent on taking the blame yourself. I think you both have that in common. And meanwhile Emerson is—"

Miss Russell arose and took hold of Charlie's arm. "He's here," she said and moved to the door. "The doctor has returned. Will you wait, Mr. Holbrook?"

He was going nowhere. He had no purpose but for Sophie now. He nodded.

Hamilton and Miss Russell both escorted the doctor upstairs, leaving Daniel alone with his thoughts and his anger which flared like fire in his veins. Perhaps he, too, was fevered in a way. He needed some air. Pacing the rug could serve no purpose. He would wait outside, take in some air, and return perhaps better prepared to face what lay ahead of him—whatever it may prove to be.

He exited the house and stood in the front garden, drawing in long, slow breaths of night air and releasing them.

"That was quite a performance," came a voice from behind him.

Daniel turned to find Emerson leaning against the fence, a cigarette in his hand and his eyes gleaming menacingly in the lamplight. He took a draw and exhaled.

"I beg your pardon," Daniel said, his fists clenching at his sides.

"At Vaughn's I mean, of course. Do you have any idea what you've done?"

"We're going to talk about Vaughn's party?" Daniel asked him, unbelieving. "Now? While Miss Warren lies upstairs clinging to life? Do you have no sense of shame for what you have done to her?"

"What *I've* done? That up there," he said, pointing in the direction of a second story window that might or might not have been hers, "is your doing. She never loved me."

"Not your doing? You persuaded her to trust in you, she believed you would marry her, and then, when a better opportunity comes along, you leave her? Her and your child."

"Not mine."

"Of course yours!" Daniel tried to calm himself. He must calm himself or he'd have yet another thing to add to his list of guilts this night. "She loved you," he continued, "trusted you. How do you look at yourself in the mirror?"

"You have it all backwards, Holbrook. You don't understand, do you?"

"What am I supposed to get, pray?"

"Yes, very well, I persuaded her to trust me. Perhaps she agreed to marry me because she had to. I did mean to do it. Like you, I made promises I intended to follow through with. Only…"

"Only an inheritance got in your way. Poor you, I suppose. And what of her, then? Have you any explanation as to why you felt yourself free to walk away, knowing as you did that she was utterly dependent upon you?"

"She needed me. Perhaps that much is true. But she didn't love me. She never could love anyone else. How do you do it?"

"I beg your pardon?"

"How do you persuade these women to give their hearts to you so completely, so uncompromisingly and without reservation?"

"By *women*, I hope you don't mean to include…"

Emerson shrugged and took another draw. He dropped the cigarette on the ground and crushed it with his foot. It was all Daniel could do not to take him by the collar and choke the life out of him.

"I suppose you think you'll go back now, resume your old place with the Durhams and take up where you left off," Emerson continued.

"I've said my goodbyes to them. Not that it's any of your business."

"And what now?"

"What does it matter to you? You can't possibly mean to keep dogging me about."

"It had crossed my mind. If you think I'm done with you yet—"

Daniel lunged and with one of Emerson's lapels in each fist he threw him up hard against the iron fence. The fence was topped with a series of little spears and Daniel, for just a moment, could imagine pressing Emerson's back against them until they pierced him through. Emerson's eyes flashed in fear even as he sneered menacingly—tauntingly. But Daniel was not a murderer, however tempting the idea.

Daniel released him and Emerson straightened himself, and with a look of disgusted victory, he brushed his lapels and straightened his jacket and waistcoat. But Daniel had lost his temper already and was not likely to find it soon. He cocked his arm back and let it fly, hitting Emerson square in the jaw. Emerson was flung back but steadied himself. He turned back to face Daniel with an expletive, and with fire in his eyes. They were not well matched, and when Daniel's fist flew again, it knocked Emerson to the ground, blood oozing from between his lips. He was out but not dead, and if Daniel didn't stop now he would kill him. He took a deep breath to steady himself and turned away as the door opened. Charlie and Anne stepped out onto the step.

"You'll want to take care of this mess," Daniel said without looking back. "I want him gone!"

"Where are you going?" Hamilton called after him as Daniel turned from the house. He needed time to calm himself. He needed an hour's walk, something to do besides think and brood and regret.

"I'll be back. Just make sure Emerson's gone, will you?" He approached the street, saw a gap in the traffic and crossed. He heard his name as he reached the other side.

"Holbrook!" It was Hamilton again and there was a suggestion of warning in the tone of his voice. Reluctantly Daniel turned.

Emerson was coming after him. He crossed the street at a run and was nearly struck by a horse as it drew a hansom cab. In his anger, he flung a fist at the horse's head. He was too close. The animal balked, raised itself up on its haunches and pawed at the air. Emerson was beyond himself, swearing and threatening while the cabdriver yelled and Anne screamed from the porch. The horse came down, his hooves still flailing.

Emerson was in a heap on the ground.

Daniel could not believe his eyes. Was this his fault? Had he done this? Was he a murderer, after all?

Hamilton ran toward the scene while Miss Russell stood at the curb, her hand held to her face. Daniel joined him there as Hamilton lifted Emerson's hand. He felt for a pulse as blood pooled on the street.

"Is he dead?" Daniel asked him.

Hamilton looked up at him and slowly nodded his head.

Chapter thirty-six

A THOUSAND DIFFERENT EMOTIONS WASHED over Laynie upon awaking the next morning. She was going home. She was not to marry Mr. Emerson. For both things she felt immensely relieved. Her sister and Harry were to marry. For that she felt a thrill of elation. She was never to see Daniel again. He was to marry another. She envied the woman who had won so devoted a heart as his. Her heart broke for knowing she had lost him for good. She was angry, too, at Mr. Emerson's betrayal, for his coercions and man-ipulations. She could hardly see for the rage she felt for him and the shame she felt for herself in believing in him. Above all these another emotion prevailed: Fear. Now that it was known what Mr. Emerson was guilty of, would he retaliate? Would he continue to oppress Mr. Holbrook with his accu-sation and tauntings? Would he make good on his promise to reveal Daniel's supposed misdeeds to the world?

With this question on her mind she went downstairs. Her father and sister had come for breakfast. Beth was in her own little world of apparent bliss, sitting beside Harry who sat at one end of the table, looking relaxed and once more in command of all. She wondered if Beth yet knew the truth about his inheritance and the surety of it or if he meant to save that. Perhaps it no longer mattered. Beth had learned to love him and to do it, it seemed, without reservation—fortune or no fortune. If only Laynie could find someone as steady and constant as Harry had proved to be. A heart that would be hers and hers alone forever, just as Miss Warren had Daniel's.

"What was that sigh for?" Beth asked as Laynie joined them at the table, a plate in hand and only half filled. She had not much appetite.

"Did I sigh?" she said. She had not realized it, but her emotions often found ways of revealing themselves, despite her efforts to conceal them.

"You did," Beth said. "And it sounded as though it represented something significant."

Lady Vaughn entered the room, dressed in gray and looking tired. Her entrance saved Laynie from having to answer her sister's questions. Lady Vaughn placed a piece of toast on a small plate and selected an egg, and then she took her place at the opposite end of the table from Harry.

"So," she said, "Alayna Durham will remain Alayna Durham still."

"Indeed," Laynie answered and felt, once more, a wave of relief at the thought. She felt those other emotions as well, but chose simply to focus on relief. "Perhaps I'll never marry," she said. "I'm not sure I have any interest in the pursuit of it, that's for certain. I think maybe I ought to take comfort in the idea of remaining with Papa at the Bowery."

"That's a happy thought, isn't it?" her father answered, smiling apologetically. Was he disappointed? Or did he, too, feel relief? She would like to ask him but now was not the time.

The newspaper was brought in and laid upon the table. Lady Vaughn scowled at it and slid it toward Mr. Durham, who was happy to take it up.

That sense of fear revived itself. What would be said of the party last night? And who would be mentioned, and what accusations would be laid against them?

She watched as her father examined the front page, scanned a headline or two, and opened it to look inside. A headline on the third page struck Laynie's attention, but it seemed she saw it the same moment as her father, who lifted it up to read more closely. She could no longer see it. An image of the headline loomed before her still.

A STRANGER IN THE BALLROOM
DECEPTIONS REVEALED AS SOCIETY MATRON
ANNOUNCES ENGAGEMENT

Laynie waited impatiently for her father to finish reading. He seemed to do it very slowly, scowling over it as he did. At last he folded it closed and looked up. She might have taken it, but his hand firmly rested upon it as though it was his intent, now he had finished, that the matter be forgotten entirely.

"What did it say, Papa?"

He did not seem to hear her, but in time turned to her. "Hmmm? What was that?"

"What did it say? Did it mention Mr. Emerson?"

"I don't understand it," he said and seemed really to puzzle over it. His gaze fell once more to the paper. "How does a fellow lose a wife? It's not like she can have dropped from his pocket."

But no one was inclined to answer him. It was not exactly breakfast table conversation.

"That's just it, Papa," Laynie said, at last seeing that she must be the one to explain it. "He didn't lose her. He left her."

"But she died. He told me so. He told *you* so. Why would he say she died if she had not? Was he somehow mistaken?"

"No, Papa. I don't think so."

"And he wanted to marry you, Laynie. He was determined to do it. And he had a wife already!"

"No, Papa. He only said he married her. He never did. Is he named in the article? Am I?"

"No. You are not named, thank heaven. Mr. Emerson is mentioned as a 'notable guest' whose wife was discovered to be still living in London, even while he expected to announce his engagement to another. Aside from that there is merely mention of 'the two daughters of Mr. Nathaniel Durham of Ashworth, Surrey, for whom the party was held.' Mr. Vaughn, of course, is named, and his engagement to one of the daughters, but neither of you girls are mentioned by name."

Beth appeared disappointed by this.

"Did you know you had papermen at your party, Lady Vaughn?" Mr. Durham asked her.

"Of course I did. I invited them," she said very matter-of-factly. "And that is precisely why your daughters' names have been withheld. I do know how to use my connections, you know. A formal announce-ment will be in the paper tomorrow, Bethany, if that will make you feel better, but I saw no reason to have your names mingling in the same article with…that…man."

Laynie was overcome. "I am so very grateful to you, Lady Vaughn, for the care you have taken of me. And of my sister, as well. More grateful than I can say."

"Well," she said and glanced at her over her tea, "I could not sit by and watch you sacrifice yourself to someone such as *him*, could I? You are as good as family to me now, after all."

Mr. Durham turned the paper over in disgust and went back to eating his breakfast. Laynie had wished to know if there was any mention of Daniel in it, but it seemed the time to ask had passed. Perhaps she might find some way of seeing for herself later. But for now she would simply have to satisfy herself with the knowledge that her name, at least for the present, was free from disgrace. Still, there might be something more, a hint, perhaps another article yet in which Mr. Holbrook had been named. Such things were known to happen. Aspersions and libelous claims were sometimes published under the guise of entertainment or gossip. If she could only see for herself…

"What is this?" Mr. Durham said, his eyes scanning the back of the paper now.

Laynie's heart stopped beating a moment. She remembered to breathe. "What is it, Papa?"

Lady Vaughn held out her hand. Mr. Durham, though reluctantly, gave it to her, mutely pointing at the article in question.

She unfolded her lorgnette, examined it briefly, and then handed it to a footman who was then instructed to throw it into the fire. He did.

"Papa? What is it? Will you tell me?"

He would not answer her, but seemed stunned by that which he had seen, as if he saw it before him still and was reading and re-reading the words.

"Lady Vaughn?" Laynie said, turning to her, desperate to have her question answered. "Is it about Mr. Holbrook? Has he been vindicated? Tell me he has not been further maligned."

"He is not mentioned, Alayna," Lady Vaughn said. "There is nothing at all to suggest he had any part in Mr. Emerson's foul dealings. It is at an end, it seems, and let us be glad of it!"

There seemed to be an air of sobriety about the table that Laynie felt a little discomforting. Harry, too, was quite reticent, happy in Beth's company, but quiet and withdrawn, nevertheless.

"Harry?" she said to him. "Did you read the paper this morning?"

He cleared his throat, which was to her as much as an admission.

"Is there something more about Mr. Emerson in the paper?"

Harry arose, examined the buffet table, and appeared to be avoiding the question. He did not ignore her, and so she knew eventually he would answer it.

"Harry?"

"Mother is right. It is at an end. Mr. Emerson was found dead last night, Laynie."

"What? Dead!" A wave of dread rushed through her. "How? What happened?"

"I gave him a card, given to me by Holbrook himself, which indicated the address where Emerson was to find his…wife, for lack of a better term. He arrived there, paid a visit it seemed, and upon leaving again was struck by a carriage as he was crossing the street."

"It was an accident? You are certain?"

"It was an accident, Laynie," Harry assured her. An accident or suicide. It will be up to the inquest to make that decision. There's nothing to give any indication Holbrook was even there, if that's what you're worried about."

"He would never…"

"Of course he wouldn't."

"That doesn't mean he might not be suspected."

"Then let's hope he was nowhere near there."

"He was, though. He told me he was going to see her."

"Then perhaps he had gone already before Emerson got there. He had a half hour's head start, after all."

"Harry. He wouldn't have gone and left again. He was going to marry her."

"Well, then," Harry said and cleared his throat once more. "No doubt that is what he did. But you can rest quite assured he had nothing to do with Emerson's death."

"Married?" Mr. Durham said and appeared even more stunned than before. "Married? To Mr. Emerson's wife?"

Laynie put a hand on her father's arm and did her best to relate the story without crying. "Mr. Emerson never married her, remember, Papa? Mr. Emerson told you Mr. Holbrook had deserted her, but he hadn't. He always wanted to marry her and now he has. Don't you see? Mr. Emerson was the one we ought never to have trusted. And Mr. Holbrook..."

"Yes, yes, my dear," he said and patted her hand as it rested on his arm. "Well, well. I wish him every happiness. He was a worthy fellow and I regret ever doubting him. I shall miss him very much."

"As shall I," Beth said. "He always instilled a quiet calm whenever he came to call. There was no fearing anything bad would happen while he was there. And what he has done for that woman..."

Lady Vaughn looked disgustedly at her egg. She struck it once and then put down her spoon.

"What is it?" Laynie asked her. She looked as if she were about to cry, and Laynie felt a lump form in her own throat.

"It is all so vexing!" she said. "We make such gods and monsters of men, do we not? Mr. Holbrook did not live up to expectation, and then, in the end, when it cannot matter, he has proven to be far worthier than we ever thought him. He bore his calumny with grace and gentlemanlike restraint. I've only seen the like of it once before, and from a man not unconnected to him." She grew thoughtful. She blinked and sniffed and sat up straighter. "As for that other man! Unfortunately there are too many like him. Still, there must have been some good in him at one time. He was someone's child, after all." She flinched a smile and gazed off at the space of table before her. At last she blinked again and gestured for her maid who helped her to rise. "We go home, today," she said as she stood at the head of the table. "I'll be glad to have done with London."

"Are you disappointed?" Laynie asked her. "Has not everything turned out as it ought to have done?"

"The party was a success, and for that I'm glad." She bestowed a proud look upon her son and then upon Beth. She turned her attention then to Laynie, where it rested. "You, my dear, have had a very close escape, and for that, too, I'm very relieved, though I do wish more care had been taken at the outset."

"It's my fault," Laynie said. "I've always been so careless."

"No," Beth said. "I blame myself. If I had not lured him to the Bowery, none of this ever would have happened."

Lady Vaughn, however, was adamant that it was no one's fault but his own. "We are done with that now, and I think it best not to mention his name again. But yes, Alayna, to answer your question, I *am* a little disappointed."

"May I ask why?"

Lady Vaughn smiled at her briefly and turned to her father. "Mr. Durham, I have a request to make of you."

"Yes, ma'am," he said, awaking from his own reverie and looking at her very attentively.

"If ever another gentleman such as Mr. Holbrook arrives upon your step, whether you have hired him or he has simply fallen from the sky, put away your selfish eccentricities and see that, this time, he marries your daughter."

Chapter thirty-seven

DANIEL WAITED UNTIL AFTER THE inquest—which had absolved him from all guilt and suspicion—and for the news that the Durhams had returned home, before he himself returned to Newhaven House, and to Sophie's bedside. Charlie, in the meantime, had kept him abreast of her condition, which, it appeared, was improving.

"You are better today?" he asked as he took a seat beside her.

"I'm a little stronger each day, Daniel," she answered. "I've been sick for so long. I fear it will be some time before I'm quite my old self."

"I don't need you to be your old self, you know. We are both older, changed. That doesn't mean we can't still find happiness, after all. If you'll accept me—"

"It can do no good," she said, interrupting him.

"How can you say that? Of course it can. You'll be restored."

"Daniel, you've already rescued me. Anything more would be too much."

"No."

"I had my chance. I made my choice."

"You didn't do wrong, Sophie. That devil led you astray!"

"I wish it were so simple."

Tears formed in her eyes and he returned his gaze to his hands as he held them folded in his lap.

"Do you regret? His death, I mean. Does it pain you he's gone?"

"It's such an odd combination of feelings, Daniel. I miss very much who I once believed him to be, but that man never existed and so missing him is useless. The tragedy of it, that Adrian will never know his father…" She shook her head. "But apart from that, I'm relieved. And I feel a scoundrel for it too."

"I mean to make it right, Sophie. If you'll let me. His wrongs as well as my own."

"No mortal has the power to free me of the consequences of my foolishness. Not even you."

"You're going to have to give me a better reason than that, Sophie, if you intend to throw me off. I mean to do this."

Sophie shook her head in friendly observation of his stubbornness.

"You won't tell me 'no', at least."

"If you insist, how can I?" she said with a smile. "I'm not so unselfish as that. These last years have been long ones. What I wouldn't do to be happy! And I believe you could make me so. It's what I may or may not be able to do for you that makes me hesitate."

"You've as good as said yes, Sophie," he said, and there was an honest feeling of victory that swept over him.

"All but," she said. "I have one condition."

"Which is?"

"I want you to take some time to think it over."

"I have done," he said, with a dismissive laugh. "You don't think I would make up my mind to something so momentous on an impulse?"

"I think it possible," she answered. "I want time to get better. I won't have you tying yourself to an invalid. And you need time to be sure."

"Enough time's been wasted already," he said with less patience.

"A little time," she insisted. "It's my only condition."

Daniel looked down at his folded hands. "I suppose I might go to Brookdale to make sure everything is ready for you."

"Good," she said, and closed her eyes once again. She remained this way, with her head resting upon the wing of her chair. She only opened them again when he stood to leave. "When will you go?"

"Soon, I suppose. But I can't promise I'll stay."

"I won't have you pestering me," she said with a smile.

It was his turn to be insistent. "The slightest hint from Miss Russell that you're in need or want of anything, I'll be back."

"When I send for you, Daniel. And not before then."

He gave her a glowering look in receipt of this.

"We're not even married," she said, "and we're fighting already. Now go, will you?"

He laughed and then bent to kiss her cheek. "Very well," he said, "but I won't be far." And then he turned to go before she could offer any further objections.

* * *

Weeks passed and the improvements moved forward apace. Daniel gave it his undivided attention. Well...nearly so. For there was a purpose to this mad rush of builders and carpenters, plasterers and painters. He wasn't doing this for himself, after all. Not for himself alone, at any rate. He'd faithfully directed the work which was moving forward at a fevered pace and he was feeling the exhaustion. Desperate for a break from the noise and chaos of work that could not cease until it was quite finished, Daniel sought solace in the bedroom that had once belonged to his grandfather—that which would soon be his, though not his alone. His efforts to distract himself from thought were not wholly successful. A sort of anxious foreboding had fallen upon him these last few days and he could not shake it. He knew himself to be doing the right thing. So why did he not feel quite at peace with his decision?

Looking up into the canopy of the bed as he lay down upon it, his thoughts began to wander. The stain, which still remained, and which had a moment ago seemed to him nothing but a rust colored cloud in a linen sky, began to take on a new form, shifting and changing with the gentle breeze that blew through the open windows, shaking the drapes and the rustling the bed curtains. Daniel adjusted his position in an attempt to make sense of the shifting figure. From this angle, it very nearly looked like a paper-cut silhouette, the neck, head and face of a woman. But whose? Sophie's of course. This would very soon be her house, her room, her bed—God willing.

He wanted to do this. He was determined to do it, if she would only let him. Her objections played through his head like an echo amidst the Alps. Relentless. She wasn't worthy, she had argued. Worthy of him? That was ridiculous, especially so as he felt some responsibility for having left her to Emerson's disposal. That was

485

what he had done, after all. She had declared that he was making too great a sacrifice. Under certain conditions this might be true. If he had not loved her so well before, if he had not been driven to the brink of madness by the loss of her, driven to commit his own sins in his reckless rampage, he would not have considered it now. He had very nearly given up on any hopes of finding that kind of happiness again when the dream that was Sophie Warren was suddenly resurrected. But something had happened between the loss and the reclaiming of her, impossible, perhaps injudicious to deny.

The watermark figure was different now, altered, though it was impossible to determine just what it was that made it so. A moment ago it was plainly Sophie. Now it was unmistakably Alayna Durham.

Sophie was not unworthy; he would not accept that objection. And yet there was another objection Daniel could not quite get over. She suspected that his heart belonged to another now. She knew she no longer had the right to expect his unadulterated admiration, but still she longed to be the single desire of some steady heart. Instead, she was no more than an object to be pitied. Daniel had argued, had endeavored to persuade her that this was all folly, but he had not quite convinced himself. Such was to his detriment. He would not press her, though he knew that with some extra effort he would ultimately find success. Were he surer of his own desires, he might not be here now. Were it Laynie in Sophie's position—No! He would not think of such things.

But of course this was right! He could make up for so many wrongs, both hers and Emerson's. And even some of his own. He could save her, save that child. It was hardly imaginable that he could be doing this for any reason other than the right one. Was there a wrong one? And what if she did not recover? Daniel could not think of that. It was beyond his ability to imagine. This house could not suffer much more tragedy and have any hope of becoming a home for him once again. The challenge, now that he had committed himself to his decision, was to learn to quit thinking of Miss Durham. She was too constantly in his thoughts, just as she was before his eyes now, rep-resented in a rust-colored water stain that, in a day or two, barring any interruptions, would be replaced forever with fresh white silk that bore no stains that could be misinterpreted as representing clouds or women or anything else.

This internal dialogue, incessant as it was, was as maddening—perhaps more so—as the chaos of workmen going on downstairs and upstairs and throughout the house. Perhaps he ought to return to it. He arose from the bed and reached for the doorknob just as a knock was heard upon it. He opened it and stood face to face with his house-keeper.

"A letter has just come for you, Sir. It's from London. I believe it's urgent."

Daniel received it and stared at it as the door was closed again. He studied it, half afraid to open it. There was no mistaking from whence it had come. The return address was marked quite clearly. "Newhaven House".

Chapter thirty-eight

BETH WAS MARRIED WITHOUT FANFARE, very quietly at the parish church on a crisp spring day. Mr. and Mrs. Vaughn went on their honeymoon and returned, but to live at Elverton now. Beth's visits were frequent, but not frequent enough to allay Laynie's loneliness. Lady Vaughn did her part, escorting Laynie to balls and country parties, ensuring that, whatever the reason for her circumstances, there was not a hint of gossip to be spoken of her. She met one or two gentle-men who showed some interest, but her reception of them when they came to the Bowery, and that in combination with her father's, who now was determined to keep her near him, did little to encourage them to come again. And so, in time, they ceased to do it.

She was not entirely alone. She had Jupiter, who was now an accepted fixture within the house. His complaining out of doors while Laynie sat with her father began to drive Mr. Durham to distraction, and so, at last, he gave up his objections. Where Laynie went, in or out of the house, Jupiter went too.

As the months passed, Laynie's time was increasingly taken up by her father. She did her best to keep him entertained: reading to him, sitting with him, listening to him as he grumbled on about the state of politics and how the country was soon to go to ruin as was evidenced by the inability of Parliament to keep its promises or for the London lines to keep to their train tables. Truth be told, Mr. Durham's mental faculties were diminishing and Laynie had begun to wonder how long they could last here just the two of them. His thoughts rambled. He spent hours at a time in thoughtful stupor, interrupted only when Laynie tried to leave the room or when Mr. and Mrs. Vaughn came to call. Increasingly he objected to being left to himself. Laynie rarely went to Elverton unless her father went with her, and meeting with guests with whom he was not already intimately acquainted caused him so much anxiety that it ceased to be worth the trouble. Even Jupiter was sometimes neglected. Long walks for him grew increasingly infrequent. He could exercise himself quite reliably in the back garden. Walking out with him was an unnecessary nuisance, or so her father felt. It was her only reprieve, however, and so Laynie stubbornly insisted.

"I think there is nothing for it," Lady Vaughn at last conceded. "You must come to us at Elverton."

While it was kind of Lady Vaughn to invite them, Mr. Durham required quiet and familiar surroundings. He could not endure confusion or disruption of any kind.

Neither was Lady Vaughn strong. Beth served as her nurse very often. Perhaps after all Laynie might relieve her of those duties. But could she care for her father and her sister's mother-in-law at the same time? Perhaps she had best get used to the idea. She certainly could not remain here forever as her father grew worse and as she grew more helpless to help him.

When next Lady Vaughn made the suggestion to remove to Elverton, Laynie agreed to consider it. Indeed, she saw no other solution for their present predicament. For the next week or more Laynie began to plan, to think and to scheme how it was to be accomplished. Two and half decades of memories could hardly be boxed up and put into storage. Nor did she want to do it. Might the Bowery be let? It was unimaginable. This was home. But without some kind of help, there was simply nothing for it.

Laynie lay awake one morning contemplating the fate of the Bowery and despairing over the thought of leaving it as she recalled her happy life here and those who had been a part of it—those who had come and those who had gone—when Jupiter suddenly sat upright, his ears cocked and listening for something. She had not heard the bell. It was Harry, no doubt, arriving for an early morning call. He had made himself quite a favorite with Jupiter in recent months and the dog had begun to look forward to his visits with enthusiasm. Perhaps Bethany had come with him. She would like her sister's company. Her mind seemed eager to dwell on the past today, on what might have been if only... She was, if nothing else, a foolish creature. Mr. Holbrook had come, had briefly been a part of her life, and had moved on, as he had ever been bound to do.

Rubbing the dog's head in an effort to calm him, Laynie listened for the sound of footsteps on the stairs. She could hear nothing over Jupiter's whimpering. He stood now on her bed, straddling her as if she were merely an obstacle in his way. He looked to the door then at her, sniffed her face, licked it, whimpered again and bounded from the bed to stand at the door.

"For heaven's sake, Jupiter. It's only Harry." And yet his show of exaggerated eagerness raised a vain hope within her. It was foolishness and she knew it. Mr. Holbrook was married, gone to live far away and happy with she whom he had always loved. She was not likely ever to see him again. It was Harry and Beth who had come, that was all.

Laynie, impatient to know it was so, dressed as quickly as she could before stepping out into the hallway. The moment the doorway was large enough, Jupiter slipped through it and sprinted downstairs. Laynie was more hesitant. She descended the stairs and arrived in the foyer to find it quite empty, the house very still, and Jupiter just as anxious as ever, sniffing the floors and searching each room. She followed him, through the foyer and the formal parlor to the drawing room, where he exited again. She turned back, however, upon seeing something on the mantel, something very familiar but which oughtn't to be there. It was her mother's statuette. It was perfectly restored, and yet it didn't seem quite possible. It was there, as if it had never been broken. As if it had never required mending or throwing out. She studied it a long time but didn't dare to touch it. The sheep...so oddly executed. It hardly appeared to be a sheep at all.

"There you are."

Laynie turned to find Beth standing in the doorway.

"Beth!" Laynie said and felt her nerves steady with the reassurance of her sister's arrival, while she felt a pang at the same time of disappointment. It was disappointment in herself, more than anything. Why had she entertained, even for a moment, that it might be another who had come? "I slept in. Why didn't you wake me? It was your room once, too."

490

Beth dismissed the belated invitation with a shake of her head. "I thought you could use the rest. I know Papa has been a strain on you lately."

"I've been thinking Lady Vaughn is perhaps right. It will be good to share a roof with my sister again."

The look Beth gave her in answer was not one she would have expected. Not joy, not elation, not relief. For the briefest instant, the look on her face suggested Laynie was, once again, behaving the foolish girl. It disappeared a moment later and was replaced by a cautious smile and then a nod toward the mantel.

Laynie followed her sister's gaze to the statuette. "Is this your doing?"

"Not exactly. It is a fortunate coincidence, I suppose. Are you pleased to have it replaced?"

"I was never fond of it, you know, until it was ruined."

"That's how it goes sometimes, I suppose. With things. With people."

Laynie looked to her sister. What was that supposed to mean? She was on the verge of asking when Beth interrupted her. She took a step forward but stopped again.

"I do hope you won't be angry with me, Laynie."

"Angry? Whatever for?"

Beth winced a smile. "You have been languishing."

"I thought it was Papa we were all worried about."

"Papa, yes. But you as well. Promise me you won't be angry. I have intervened. Harry calls it interfering, but I do not think he wholly disapproves. Something had to be done."

"What are you talking about, Beth?" She was beginning to feel quite anxious.

Jupiter, having finished his room-by-room search, approached Beth. Beth usually and quite unnecessarily was anxious around the dog, holding him at bay as if he might any minute become vicious and attack her. Today she knelt and stroked him. She even gave him a little hug, for which he seemed quite gratified. Perhaps he was congratulating himself for having won Beth over at last. Whatever the reason, it was certainly unexpected.

491

Beth stood again. "Now don't argue with me, Laynie, but you have a visitor."

"A visitor?"

Rather than answering, Beth looked out toward the garden, just barely discernable through the lace curtains. Laynie followed her gaze, and when she turned back again, Beth had gone. Cautiously and with trepidation, she approached the door with Jupiter at her side, drew back the curtain that covered the glass, and saw nothing. Her heart was beating wildly, though there was no reason it should. Who could it be? Only one answer came to her mind, but she dismissed it as an impossibility. Mr. Holbrook was married, happily living in some grand house in Kent with his wife, the woman he had ever and always hoped to marry, and without a thought of Laynie. Why should he think of her now, the too-naïve child of his former employer?

Though she tried to stifle it, hope was there still. She entered the dining room and prepared to leave it again via the outer doors. On quiet feet, with slow, cautious steps, she made her way into the yard and toward the formal garden. At least that was her plan, but Jupiter bounded ahead and in a dozen great leaps was at the gate, barking and pawing at it. Laynie stopped as a figure arose. She had hoped, yes, but she had not expected. She was paralyzed, frozen to the spot.

Daniel greeted his dog, opened the gate, and looked up. A smile, cautious but warm, spread across his face, touching his eyes and lighting them up. Oh, how she had missed him!

He said nothing until she was standing before him. She tried to speak but found she had no words and that her mouth was too dry to form them anyhow.

"Hello," he said.

She smiled, inwardly chiding herself. She had that word, at least. Why had she not thought of it? "Hello," she answered him.

"How have you been?"

"Well, I think. Yes, of course. I've been very well. Have you been to see Papa?"

"Yes, I visited with him a little upon my arrival. He's not as strong as I had hoped to see him."

"He has struggled since you left us. We are likely not long to remain at the Bowery."

"Is that so?" he replied, as if he had some doubt about it. A doubt that reminded her of Beth's odd manner a few minutes ago.

"How is Mrs. Holbrook?" Laynie asked him with affected equanimity. "Have you brought her with you?" How did she feel about meeting his wife? Even she could not quite say. If he was happy, if they were happy, that was all that mattered. Wasn't it?

The look he gave her now was a strange one: part surprise, part pain. "There is no Mrs. Holbrook, Miss Durham. Not yet, at any rate."

"You did not marry?"

"Mr. Vaughn did not tell you?"

She looked at him, confused, afraid to feel the hope that began to mount once more and trying to quell it. She shook her head.

"I had rather hoped he would prepare you. I see he left all the work to me. Miss Warren died, Laynie."

"Died?" she said and felt the sting of tears. How much heartbreak was one man—and so good a man—to suffer in one lifetime?

"She was very ill when we found her, I'm afraid. There was not much left in her. She died shortly after, but at least she died among friends."

Laynie knew not what to say, only blinked the tears that had gathered and stared up at poor, grieving Daniel.

"It was possibly no use anyway," he said with a doleful smile. "She had refused me. I had hoped to win her over in time, but I'm not certain now that I ever could have convinced her. At least I have the comfort of knowing she forgave me."

"Of course she did. She must have."

"That is kind of you to say, Miss Durham."

"And you have the comfort of knowing you did all you could to make things right."

"Yes."

"I'm so very sorry, Mr. Holbrook."

"There are a few things more to make right," he answered her. He hesitated a moment more, glanced at her, then looked to the ground as he continued. "She had a child...Mr. Emerson's child. A boy."

"Mr. Emerson had a son?" She could scarcely believe it. That he had abandoned a woman he had not married was horrible enough in itself, but to think he had had a child and had turned his back on him as well… And she had nearly married him! "What is to become of him now?"

"You remember my friend Mr. Hamilton?"

"Yes."

"He has found a good home for him. I had thought of keeping him myself, but without knowing, you know, that I could give him a mother who would love him…"

"Daniel." The word was a protestation, though it had nothing to do with herself. It was simply for the idea that he should have any trouble in doing it. Who would refuse such a man? Why had Miss Warren done it? Perhaps she had known there was no use.

They were both silent for a moment. The look he cast upon her was so warm a one, his gaze so intense, she felt she had to avoid it or it would consume her. She turned from him, took a few steps and turned back, though she did not look at him.

"Was it you who brought the statuette? Was that your doing?"

"As it happened, there was one just like it at Brookdale. I thought I had remembered it. It was why I took the head, to be sure. You must have thought it odd of me."

She smiled as she recalled the scene. "I was never very fond of it, you know." She stopped before repeating the words she had said to Beth. *Until it was ruined.* She feared his answer would be similar to her sister's. "It's such an odd thing. The sheep, it's almost grotesque. I am grateful to you," she said looking up at him, suddenly aware she did not sound grateful at all.

"A sheep?" He laughed.

"Yes, of course."

"It's not a sheep, Laynie. It's a dog. A wolfhound."

"A wolf—" But of course! How had she not seen it before? It seemed quite obvious to her now. And Daniel, as though she were the very girl captured in bisque, had given her a dog to match it. "Jupiter?"

"It was rather a fanciful notion, but I knew he would keep you company, keep you safe while I couldn't. At least I knew he would try."

She glanced at him half-apologetically.

Daniel took a step closer to her. He reached for her hand but seemed to reconsider and instead allowed his own to hang loosely at his side.

"If I could have done more..."

"You did all you could. In the end it was enough."

"Was it?" he asked her. "Is it?"

This she did not know how to answer.

"I was in no position then, you know, to take the charge upon myself." His hand touched hers. She grasped onto it, held it tightly. "My circumstances are quite different now, Laynie. I would like that honor, if you would grant it. Will you?"

Of course there was no mistaking what he was really asking her, and yet she feared still to be mistaken.

When I was here before...as your father's hired companion, I was forbidden from speaking my mind quite as plainly as I might have liked. Your friendship has meant the world to me. I nearly lost it, I think. I'm quite determined not to take that risk again."

"No," she said.

"Yes," she said, brimming with hope and encouraged further by the smile he shone upon her.

"And yet, were you to grant it, even now when you know all there is to know about me, I would ask for something more."

"Can you love me, Laynie? Can you love me like I love you?"

She looked at him, her eyes wide and conveying all the emotion she felt. The tears streamed but she did not care if he saw them. She could only nod. She had no voice, but he understood.

"No," he said. "No more tears." He wiped them away with his thumbs as his hands rested on each side of her face. He looked at her a moment more and drew her closer to him, close enough to kiss her. And so he did, gently, earnestly, and with a sort of restrained passion she suspected he had long been accustomed to keeping in check—and which he was not likely to restrain for much longer. Yes this, this was love! And she gave herself over to it wholeheartedly and without reservation.

There was more to consider, however, than her own wishes alone. "What about Papa? I can't leave him."

He smiled and then laughed gently. "It does seem I've gotten ahead of myself. In truth I came to resume my former occupation. Though, obviously, the terms are somewhat different now. It was the one condition of my returning that I no longer be forbidden from seeking your company. That I might, in fact, pursue it wholeheartedly, which I fully intend to do, you know. His blessing came surprisingly easily."

"You may have Lady Vaughn to thank for that. She is quite your champion."

"Well, then, don't let me forget to express my gratitude to her the first chance I get."

"I won't."

"You should know, your father had a condition of his own."

There seemed an ominous quality to his warning.

"It's his desire that things change as little as possible. My chief obligation will still be to him. At least in the daytime hours."

It was as she feared. She felt ungrateful. Daniel was here; he wanted her, and yet…was he not her father's, after all?

"If it gives you any comfort, Vaughn and I have come up with a plan that we hope will convince him to see reason. A wife is to cling to her husband once she is married. It should only follow that her husband should cling to her…not to her father. I love the man, you know I do, but he can be a little unreasonable at times."

"Indeed," she said and felt the terms very unreasonable indeed.

"Never fear," Daniel said and kissed her forehead. "We shall conquer him together, you and I."

Beth and Harry were ready and waiting to offer them congratulations upon returning to the house. Beth received her sister with an exuberant embrace and then handed her off to Harry who offered her the same, while Daniel was offered welcome to the family and a happy return to his former offices, though somewhat and quite happily altered. A sober-looking Mr. Durham was last to enter. His manner was so reluctant that Laynie began to wonder if he had reconsidered giving Daniel his blessing.

"So you are to be married," he said. "And you are to take my daughter away from me."

496

"Only long enough for a proper honeymoon, sir."

"How long will that be?"

"I thought perhaps a month."

"In Kent, I believe you said. At your home there."

Laynie's feelings were divided. Kent was not far. She had no complaint, really, about the destination. A month, however, it was a long time to be away from her father. To be with Daniel though, just she and him alone…

"Laynie should see Brookdale. It will be her home, too."

"And she'll have all her life to get used to the place. A month. No. A week should be sufficient."

"Three weeks, then," Daniel said.

Ah, so his intent was to bargain for what he wanted. She relaxed a little and watched the negotiations with a little more pleasure.

"Ten days," her father countered.

"A fortnight."

Mr. Durham minced his mouth and furrowed his brow. "Very well, then." He sat. "Have you decided when you will be married?"

"Soon, I think."

"Where?"

"Here," Daniel answered quietly. "If that meets with your approval," he said to her.

"Yes, of course."

"And then you will return," her father said, slapping his knees, "and all will be as it once was."

"Yes," Daniel said. "Sort of." There was a twinkle in his eye that gave Laynie a sense of thrill. What was it he had in mind?

Chapter thirty-nine

T HE HIRED CARRIAGE STOPPED BEFORE the Bowery gate, but neither of them moved. Their two weeks had passed by more rapidly than she could have supposed. Laynie was not unhappy to be home, only to know she was no longer to have Daniel's undivided attention.

"Are we going in?" she asked him.

"Yes," he answered but hesitated before finishing. "Though perhaps not together."

"Not together?"

"You go first, greet him, let him welcome you home. I'll follow in a few minutes, ringing at the door as I always have."

"This is ridiculous."

"Humor me," he said again.

"You have a plan?"

He smiled, kissed her and then descended, turning to hold the door and lower the step for her. He held his hand out, she took it and alit, then stood to look up at him.

He nodded his head toward the door, urging her onward. She walked as far as the gate and turned. "You are enjoying this, aren't you?"

He only smiled.

The gate hinges squeaked as she opened them, and the sound alerted Jupiter to her arrival. He began barking excitedly. Perhaps she should go and calm him first, and then she might enter as she so often did, through the dining room door from the garden.

Jupiter greeted her with unbounded exuberance, and when at last she thought she had him under her control, she led him in. She nearly ran into her father in the study corridor.

"My dear!" he said to her. He looked at her a moment, up and down. His gaze lingered on her hand, where a gold band encircled her finger, and he looked up at her again. He embraced her and held her apart from him. "Are you happy?"

"Very, Papa," she answered and kissed him.

"And where is Mr. Holbrook?"

She glanced at the clock on the mantel. "It's nearly two. I should think he would be here any minute."

The doorbell rang. Her father looked at her narrowly and then walked to the foyer as Laynie followed. Mrs. Fowler was already there, opening the door and letting Daniel in. She turned to announce him, though apparently reluctantly—what need was there to announce a member of the household?—and saw Laynie.

"My dear, you are home!"

Laynie approached and squeezed her hand but was too busy watching Daniel and her father to think of saying more.

"Mr. Durham, how are you?" Daniel said, offering his hand.

"I'm well, Holbrook. Welcome home."

"Thank you, sir," he said and nodded at Laynie. "Miss Durham," he said to her. "I hope you are well today."

Mr. Durham examined Daniel with a puzzled look, it faded as he fell prey to the scheme, and perhaps began to believe in it himself. He turned to Laynie as he waited to hear her answer.

She flushed. "Very well, thank you. It's always a pleasure to see you, Mr. Holbrook."

"Holbrook," Mr. Durham said, "if this is about our agreement…"

"I'm a man of honor, Mr. Durham. Your condition to my request was that nothing should change that mustn't. I have come to read with you. You have me for the day. Your daughter is home and she and I are on friendly terms." He glanced at her. The spark in his eye revealed just how much fun he was having with this charade. "Is that not what you wished?"

"We needn't take things to extremes."

Daniel seemed to consider this. "You mentioned, before, my accommodations."

"There is a spare bedroom off my study. It is ready for you, yes. Would you like to see it?"

"Papa?"

Mr. Durham looked a little ashamed. Daniel was trying to make a point, no doubt, but her father evidently found some changes more objectionable than others.

"Your mother and I kept separate rooms, you know. It is not unheard of. Especially in so small a house as this…"

She understood him. She felt the heat in her face and kept her protestations to herself. Certainly he must make some allowances. Certainly Daniel had a plan for that as well. Did he not?

Daniel looked over his shoulder at her as he followed her father to his study. The look in his eye this time was more apologetic than playful. A moment later she was as alone as she had ever been. Everything back to normal then she thought to herself, and she looked down at Jupiter who was looking up at her longingly.

"Home sweet home, wouldn't you say, Jupiter?"

* * *

It was many hours later when Mr. Durham at last released Daniel. Laynie had waited patiently. She had gone to her old room, the room that was hers alone. She had unpacked her things, had washed and changed her dress, and had returned to her spot beneath the beech tree where she had fallen asleep beneath the shade of the low-hanging boughs.

She awoke to Daniel's voice.

"Are you up for a walk, Miss Durham?"

Laynie blinked the sleep from her eyes and beamed up at him, happy to see him and yet not quite pleased with his formal, almost indifferent manner. She glanced toward the door to find her father watching them.

"I suppose I can manage it, Mr. Holbrook," she answered him and arose with his help, "if you will allow me to take your arm. My ankle, and all."

"By all means, Miss Durham." For all his stiff formality, his answer was emphatic and made her smile.

She slipped her hand into the crook of his arm and then turned back to wave a short farewell to her father.

* * *

Mr. Durham watched as his daughter and Holbrook walked off together, just as if they were no more than casual acquaintances. If it were not for the mischievous gleam in Daniel's eye or Laynie's bright face, Nathaniel Durham might have been worried. If any misgivings yet remained, they were dispelled by the sight of them an hour later, returning to the house smiling and windswept—extraordinarily so considering how fine and still the weather.

The rest of the day progressed much the same as it had begun, Laynie and Daniel pretending they had nothing more than mild interest in the company of the other, behaving with insufferable politeness, and yet it wasn't quite the peaceful climate Mr. Durham had hoped for. Daniel seemed to find the whole thing amusing, but it was clear by late evening, though she was trying her utmost, that Laynie's patience was wearing thin. Mr. Durham began to repent of his selfishness—a selfishness Lady Vaughn had once condemned him for and would no doubt condemn him for today if she was not too weak to do it.

They held their evening's discussion in the drawing room where Laynie could join them. She did join them with pleasure but sat apart from Daniel, as she no doubt deemed proper. Still she watched him, listened with attentive admiration to everything he said. Holbrook returned the favor. They were happy. It was all he had hoped for his daughter and far more. Perhaps he had asked too much of them. Holbrook had a home of his own, after all. If he wished to make a home for them here, perhaps he ought to consider making a few more concessions. Perhaps he would leave them to themselves tomorrow. Holbrook never had come every day, after all. And he was feeling a little more himself. Perhaps Harry might come and sit with him awhile. He was on the verge of suggesting it when Laynie arose.

"Good night, Papa," she said and came to kiss him on the cheek.

"You're not going to bed so soon?"

"I really am very tired."

She looked to Daniel, who stood. "Good night, Mr. Holbrook," she said and gave him her hand. "Perhaps, if it isn't too great an inconvenience, you might say goodnight to me before you…retire."

Laynie glanced at him, but he looked away to hide the smile. It really was quite comical to watch them, but Laynie was clearly suffering for the farce and he regretted it.

"Yes," Daniel said, "though I don't know how much longer I may be."

"No. Of course," she said dejectedly and turned from the room.

"You know, Daniel," Mr. Durham said once Laynie had gone, "I don't like to see her sulking any more than I imagine you do."

Daniel offered a doleful look in confession.

"Yes, yes. Well... I suppose you might give her half an hour to really feel your absence before you went up to her. Separate rooms...that's rather old-fashioned, I suppose, isn't it?"

Daniel's only answer was a grateful smile.

* * *

Once Laynie had reached her room, she realized how selfish her behavior was. She had no cause to be ungrateful. Daniel was only trying to make her father, and subsequently her, happy. And, clearly, aside from his distanced civility when they were in her father's presence, he did not mean to neglect her. Their afternoon's walk had provided proof of that. He was certainly attentive enough at the precipice. Perhaps a long daily walk was the solution to her father's nocturnal arrangements. It wasn't exactly decent, but it was something. And yet it made resuming the farce all the more difficult. Was she really to sleep alone? Perhaps she would be happier, after all, at Brook-dale. But that was selfishness as well. How would her father manage in his infirmity in such a large house, and one that was strange to him? And what would become then of the Bowery? Beth would inherit it, she supposed. Or it might be let.

She looked about her room and tried to imagine anyone else sleeping here. The very idea made her sad. The thought of having Daniel here was equally strange to her. It was a child's room. Perhaps Beth would redecorate it for her. It was an excuse, at any rate, to share Daniel's room.

She changed into her night shift and sat down at the dressing table. She examined her reflection in the mirror as she brushed out her hair and wondered at herself. She was no longer ashamed of her reflection. Was this the face of a married woman? She felt a child still in many ways, petulant, brooding, selfish...alone.

She heard the door creak open and she turned. Daniel poked his head in. "Is it safe?"

She nodded. Something about the room and seeing him here made her feel very strange. It felt a little wrong, as if all the former impro-prieties had been revived upon resuming occupation.

"Have you come to say goodnight?" she asked him and waited for him to do it.

He entered, closed the door and stood watching her. "Finish what you were doing."

She stared at him for a moment, her heart beating quickly. But at last she obeyed him and went back to brushing her hair. Daniel came up behind her then and placed one hand on her shoulder. With the other he swept her hair aside and kissed her neck. And then, slipping the nightdress from her shoulder, kissed her bare skin.

She supposed if he found the day's charade amusing, she might have a little fun with it now. "Mr. Holbrook," she protested, though a little breathily, "this is most indecent of you."

Daniel straightened and blinked. He stifled a smile. "My apologies, Miss Durham. It seems I've forgotten myself." He turned to examine the room. "You know," he said at last, "I do feel rather de-spicable being in here. The maiden's sacred bower."

"Does it have that effect on you, too?"

He glanced at her. "It does, rather."

Laynie blushed ever so slightly before turning once more to the mirror to tie her hair up in a ribbon.

Jupiter, who had raised his head upon Daniel's entrance, begged now to be recognized. With a moan, he stretched himself out on the rug.

"I forgot you let him sleep with you."

"Not in the bed," she corrected him. "At least not anymore. He sleeps there on the floor, where he belongs."

"That wasn't what Vaughn said."

Of course Harry had told him. She let the comment pass. She felt Daniel's gaze on her and confirmed it was so as she glanced at him in the mirror.

"Why are you blushing so deliciously crimson like that?" he asked her.

"It's the room," she said. "And it's warm in here."

"No it isn't."

She turned and looked at him. "Does Papa know you're up here?"

"Does he need to know? You're not a child any longer."

She didn't answer him.

He looked about the room once more. "Which bed is yours?" he asked.

"It's so small, Daniel," she protested.

"Is that why Jupiter's been relegated to the floor, then?"

"Perhaps," she answered.

"Very well, then," he said and began pulling Beth's bed apart and laying the blankets upon the floor before the fire. Jupiter found he had to move to avoid being smothered.

"What are you doing?" Laynie asked him.

He threw the last of the blankets onto the pile and turned to face her.

"If this is where you want me, dear woman, then this is where I'll stay."

Laynie was standing now too. "Not the floor, Daniel."

"Shall I take the other bed, then?"

"It's so far away."

He laughed as he answered her. "Then what do you suggest?"

She glanced at her bed. It wasn't so small as that, it's just that Daniel was a very large man, larger by far than Jupiter.

"The floor is good enough for me," he said and began removing his jacket and waistcoat.

Laynie lay down upon her bed and turned to allow him the privacy he did not particularly need nor want. She turned once again when he had finished and found him lying upon his makeshift bed, his eyes closed and his hands behind his head. He remained this way for several minutes, never moving, and breathing deep, measured breaths.

At last she crept out of bed and lay down at his side. Daniel turned and wrapped his free arm about her as the other rested beneath her head. He buried his face in her hair and inhaled. She shuddered and he drew her nearer. He kissed the space of skin beneath her ear and raised the gooseflesh.

"If you can't behave, Mr. Holbrook," she said, teasing him once more, "I'll have to ask you to leave."

"Well…" he said. "At least downstairs I have a bed."

"You'd rather have the bed than me?"

"I don't honestly see why I can't have both, to tell you the truth."

She didn't answer him. She was rather comfortable here, before the fire, his arms around her.

His mouth was against her ear, raising the gooseflesh once more. "Tell me to come to your bed, Laynie."

She didn't answer him. She didn't dare. Her emotions were very near the surface and threatening to reveal themselves any moment.

He waited, but as her silence dragged on he must have sensed something was the matter. He raised himself on one elbow and with a finger on her chin, turned her face toward his. Slowly, he placed a gentle kiss upon her lips. She was surprised by the heat of it, yet he was controlled, measured in his affection. It would not last, she well knew. He looked at her a moment…and kissed her again. And did not stop until the tilting of the room reminded Laynie that he should not be here.

"If my father should find you!"

"I think he'd be forgiving," Daniel said.

Though Laynie had stopped returning his kisses, he had not quite finished offering them.

"He was married once too, you know," he said, stopping only long enough to speak. "You're very existence attests to the fact that—"

"Don't say it!"

"I wouldn't dream of it, Miss Durham," he said and beamed.

She placed a hand on his cheek as she felt a tear slide into her hair. "Am I ungrateful, Daniel?"

"What has inspired this?"

"I have you. I always wanted you. And now you are here to stay, never to leave me, and it's not enough. If we can't share our lives together, night and day, what is the point of it?"

Daniel's smile broadened.

Was he teasing her as well? "Papa knows you're here, doesn't he?"

"He sent me. I told you I had a plan."

"And that was it? To behave so ridiculously civil and formal to one another that he would see his error?"

"That was it precisely."

"You really don't mind giving up your beautiful Brookdale?"

"We'll live wherever you want to live, my dear. I'll follow your lead."

"That isn't the life I was meant for, you know?"

"And I feel equally alien in it."

"You are happy here?"

"Yes," he declared and said nothing more as his eyes scanned every inch of her face. He had no need to speak a word and yet she knew she was loved. Daniel's hand raised to brush away the next tear, then slid very gently, very tenderly to her neck. He slid his fingers into her hair as he kissed her once more, tenderly, eagerly. Her face, her hair, her neck, her mouth, again and again.

"Daniel," Laynie whispered breathily.

Supporting himself on one elbow, his other hand tangled in the hair he had just unloosed, he gazed down upon her. Half-frustrated, half-amused, he answered her. "Yes, my love?"

Her mouth opened, her lips moved; perhaps he could not hear the words, though surely he understood their shape.

"My darling, you'll have to do better than that."

"Daniel," she pled quietly. Almost too quietly.

He didn't answer, only waited. He did not have to wait long. A moment more and she threw her arms around his neck and whispered the words like the wind into his ear. "Come to my bed."

And like the tide he obeyed, sweeping her up and carrying her, laying her down very gently, only to watch her for a moment more.

And then...well, some things need not be said.

The End

Also by V.R. Christensen

Of Moths and Butterflies

Imogen Everard has lived much of her life under the care of her uncle, an abusive usurer. His death may mean her freedom from him and the taint associated with the name they share. But her uncle, in his final act, does the unimaginable and leaves her with the burden of his estate and a large fortune, subjecting her to the vultures who will descend, and to the speculations of a gossip hungry society.

In order to escape the avaricious designs of her family and those who would use her, she runs away, seeking refuge in a small, out of the way village in Kent. Here, as a maid in a large country house, she gets her first taste of independence, a glimpse of that happiness she has so long yearned for.

But when she is discovered, she is returned to her family, and to the care of her aunts who assume guardianship over her. In an effort to get at her money before she should come of age, her marriage is arranged to a collector of rare and beautiful insects.

One man is about to make the acquisition of a lifetime. But can a woman captured and acquired learn to love the man who has bought her? To do so, she must find the courage to trust him. But more than that, she must find the courage to love herself.

***Hardcover edition is in two parts.

Cry of the Peacock

After the death of her father, Abbie Gray is offered a place within her wealthy landlord's family. Such an opportunity, how-ever, seems per-haps too good to be true, particularly since her own family's feelings towards Sir Nicholas and Lady Crawford have always been tinged with resen-tment. But, at last having exhaust-ed all other alter-natives, Abbie accepts the invitation, determined to make the most of this extraor-dinary opportunity.

While Abbie is being groomed ac-cording to the ideals of Society—and of the eldest son, heir to title and property—the younger brothers attempt to expose her as the mercenary they believe she must be. But when they discover that her mysterious past is disturbingly connected with their own, they are forced to ask themselves some very hard questions about the meaning of integrity and honor, and, perhaps most importantly of all, what it means to be worthy of the title "gentle-man."

Absinthe Moon

Physically superior Robert Mayhew is destined to be numbered amongst post-apocalyptic New Londinium's ruling class—if a disability, disguised by a clockwork arm, doesn't mark him for extermination first.

Emeline Newell might not be the first of her kind—utterly pure of the city's contamination. She is certainly the last. Fate steps in when the two meet. But are they destined to destroy each other, or to unite for the liberty of all those who inhabit the dying city of New Londinium?

About the Author

 **V**.R. Christensen is a native of Washington State, but currently resides in southern Virginia, where she writes about historic homes for the Friends of the Old West End website and marketing campaign based out of Danville, Virginia. She's also a yoga instructor and founder of the community outreach program HAPI (the Health and Peace Initiative) which works to coordinate yoga, meditation, and holistic healing practices to the underserved.

To find out more about her work, visit www.vrchristensen.com.

About the Illustrator

After training in Classical and Early Music, B. Lloyd studied at the Accademia di Belle Arti di Venezia, where she graduated in 2005. She has taken part in art fairs and exhibitions in Italy and Holland, including the Ootmarsum Art Fairs and Wierden Art Events.

B. Lloyd is also a writer and the founder of AuthorsAnon, a venue where both published and non-published authors of high quality fiction can share their work and gain exposure.

B. Lloyd lives and works in Venice.

For more information about B. Lloyd and her work, please visit her website at:

http://about.me/B.Lloyd

or

http://artscribe.wix.com/paintings

Or to read some of her own magnificent writings at:

http://lloyd-anon.wordpress.com/

www.ingramcontent.com/pod-product-compliance
Lightning Source LLC
Chambersburg PA
CBHW020625020726
47494CB00001B/59